THE JOLLY CORONER

A Picaresque Novel

Quentin Canterel

Acorn Independent Press

For my Family, Wife and Mariane Schaum

I would also like to give special thanks to Leila for helping to put this text to rights.

Contents

Conway's Game of Life – The Rules

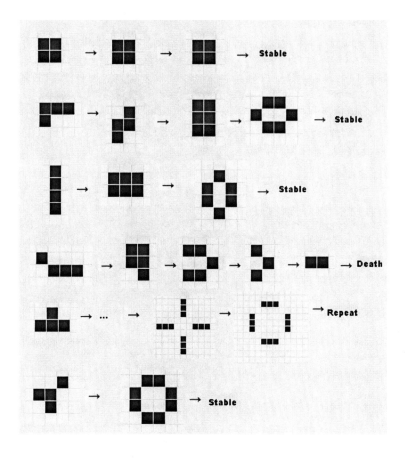

"As soon as any man says of the affairs of the State "What does it matter to me?" the State may be given up for lost."

— Rousseau

"Whereof one cannot speak, thereof one must be silent."

— Wittgenstein

"Daemoni, etiam vera dicenti, non est credendum."

— St Chrysostom

I

"For now we see through a glass darkly"

Billy was certainly in typical form: half-contemptuous, half-rapturous, laughing in his loud, hoarse manner so that his guts belched and wheezed like a mechanical bellows on the blink – these evidently oppressed by his two hundred and sixty pound frame, every bit of which wobbled in sympathetic vibration. Presently, he was enjoying a singularly good pastrami sandwich, the remains of which would probably litter his shirt collar for the remainder of the day and perhaps the foreseeable future. He had in front of him, a "tits magazine" tilted sideways, which he studied at arm's length with great concentration as he walked down the narrow, dark corridor toward his vacant apartment, whose contents almost defy description so varied were they in their unique position, form and relative state of decomposition. He hadn't even noted the small-framed Asian girl, whose sidling hadn't preserved her from the jolt into the adjacent corridor she received from his perpendicularly oscillating haunches. Normally, he would have confronted her with a crude "hello" and a glance toward her own square haunches, but today page fourteen had granted him enough satisfaction to ignore her miniscule presence. So engrossed was he in his present observations that he nearly passed his own door which rested mercifully at the end of the hall, where few ventured without pressing need. Billy hadn't ever met and had barely even seen any of the neighbors that shared his floor, but he knew quite a bit about them having searched all of their profiles on the Internet. Opening the door in frustration after a number of absent minded gropings at the greasy door handle, the familiar smells of darkness and decay entered his arching nostrils. Some may have been revolted by the climate, but he merely let off a calm sigh, thinking to himself that he really should hire a cleaner, his mind wondering back forlornly to the Asian girl who let the building's front door slam behind her. For some unknown reason, Billy had felt a certain sense of uneasiness all week. He didn't know why, but he had a pretty fatidic clarity about these things and his mind was filled with misgiving. It was nothing that a healthy dose of Grieg and a small helping of recreational diazepam couldn't cure. Lately, due to this small sense of apprehension, he had felt more distracted than usual. And it was for this reason that it was only after opening the door that he noted the yellow piece of paper taped to it that stated in large bold letters, "Pay Me," signed "The Warden". With little gusto, he removed the masking tape that held the paper in place and entered the musty gloom of his apartment, not bothering to close the door behind him.

His left hand's fleshy club wandered toward a light switch, while his right hand moved in a precise, almost graceful counterpoise to toss the magazine, which nutated midair like a dying lark before it hit the ground with a simple thud. Shambling toward a makeshift desk, he pressed the button on the blinking answering machine, which contained only two messages. One already listened to and another which caused the flesh on Billy's face to twist around the axis of his nose. It was the mysterious and (so he thought) insane foreigner who referred to himself as the recently deceased Basyli. For the last three days, this man had been leaving him a series of pleading messages in hackneyed English, each increasingly incoherent. The current one he cut short with a quick stab of his right index finger. In the blustery, brumal weather the knuckles of his hands, shown through, cold and wet to the touch like a dog's muzzle, prickly and raw as if they had been drawn through a briar. To others, his touch was normally damp, almost reptilian as his unusually cold fingers would seem to melt out of one's grasp. Some interpreted this as insecurity or perhaps a moral infirmity on Billy's part, but in fact, Billy didn't like to shake hands because of the mere fact that he profoundly disliked anyone touching his hands. After all, it was his hands, of which he was particularly fond and took a fastidious, almost vain care of, perhaps because unlike the rest of his body, they were relatively well formed.

As he began furtive preparations to relieve himself in the unlit bathroom, the phone rang and thinking it was probably "Basyli" (sometimes referred to in the official documentation as "John Doe" or on occasion more sympathetically as "B."), he hesitated to pick it up. However, when the answering machine began to sputter with the dispassionate voice of dispatcher Mark Velenet, Billy swiveled back to pick it up in his free hand as he continued to unfold his manhood with the other. "Yep, this is Billy," he groaned. He had one of those voices that made him sound like a colossal prick no matter what he said.

"Where have you been? Tried to get you on the cell. We've got another one in the wharf district", chirped the sudden, attentive young voice of Velenet.

"But I just got home…'

"Yeah, I know, but it's not far from where…"

"Yeah yeah, give me the address."

The exchange was quick and though Billy had done little to nothing all day, he hoped to enjoy a relatively tranquil Tuesday evening, given that it was statistically rare for someone to give up a violent ghost on a Tuesday. In any case, there was no avoiding it, he couldn't enjoy any of the various diversions he had planned upon coming home: watching his favorite film (Averty's *Ubu Roi*, a film from which he derived an obsessive, even compulsive enjoyment from), embellishing his self-made Wikipedia page (yes, he had contributed to the lie that is shared knowledge, professing himself to be one of the country's foremost coroners) or even perhaps fiddling with one of his many Rubik's cubes (nothing of which need be elaborated upon).

Billy, again walked down the rather drab, lowly lit corridor of his apartment building and on into the defused light of a late September evening. His building, which had been built in the Fifties was a combination of red brick, cement and plaster board and rose eight stories above the street. It was one of the few apartment buildings in this area of Hokum, which was primarily a business district, surrounded by a number of old river wharves constructed in some cases before the Civil War and in others, just afterward by opportunistic Carpetbaggers. More than a few of these where in a dilapidated state, overrun with kudzu and honey suckle. Whenever lightning hit the river, one could hear the thunderclap reverberate through their deconstructed walls, scattering the ghosts that hid within their vacant spaces, leaving some superstitious residents nervous for days afterward. If Billy were to walk right out of his apartment and turn under the bridge, he would, after a few minutes' walk, come to the vast, brown expanse of the Onondaga River. Without much difficulty, he could look across its vast, shifting surface to see the first lights being turned on in the boardwalk restaurants of Crowley. He would see, but not hear the boats knocking into one another with a hollow sound as the water became more tempestuous under the syrupy, gray air that carried the distinct smell of rain. A storm was certainly brewing. Sometimes the winter storms in this area could be very violent and many older residents still remembered the great storm of '57, where the tumid river rose up and almost subsumed Hokum within its angry torrent. It had rained frequently over the last few days, which meant the stray dogs lost their scents and wandered aimlessly and watery-eyed around the city limits in the dimming light of early evening, looking for a place to bed down before the first drops.

Hokum had a population of approximately eighteen thousand people and though appearing relatively modern in parts, it was dotted with the typical gothic horrors and irredeemable folklore of many small southern cities. Besides the Onondaga River, another natural force that threatened to subsume Hokum was the omnipresent, creeping ghost that was kudzu. During the winter, it turned white and gave a spectral appearance as it fell over entire buildings like an old Indian's, uncombed locks, resigning them (except in outline) to distant memory. National statistics report that the silent menace was currently spreading at a rate of 150,000 acres a year. Originating from China, kudzu was introduced into the Southeast in the late 19th century, predominantly for use as animal fodder, but also used to prevent soil erosion. It was for the latter reason that the plant found its way to Hokum and had since spread like a gasoline fire. Hokum was once what many would have described as a quiet, pleasant city, but it had, for at least a decade, had its privacy invaded by a crop of recent immigration, due primarily to expansion of the public mass transportation lines. For the first time in a quarter century, younger people were moving back to Hokum as a cheaper, hipper place to live, while a more unwanted presence was also beginning to be felt, that of the once roving Mexicans, who had come from the nearby alfalfa plantations to the city to find work in restaurants or as day laborers. This third and perhaps greatest menace was the one that the everyday people of Hokum feared the most.

Billy hadn't grown up in Hokum, no he had come from far away and only settled there in the bloom of his early thirties. His lax grooming practices meant that something akin in color to peach-fuzz still found providence on the nape of his sun burned neck. No one was certain from where he had come, but they were certain that it was from far away (or perhaps they had hoped so and equally, that he might return). He had become the city's coroner in his mid-thirties, not because of any great specialization in the sciences or because anyone had any respect for the wide circumference of his natural abilities. Simply, he was the only one who applied for the job. The role had been posted unsuccessfully for several weeks without a single application or even an enquiry. Then one savagely bright Tuesday morning, with no warning whatsoever, Billy stepped into the office in a khaki summer weight suit and an overly large tie and dropped his resume right on the sheriff's desk. By this time, Billy was somewhat of a local legend around the city, partially for his drinking habits and partially for what would occur due to his drinking habits. Some speculated that the only reason he applied for the job was that he had lost some late night drinking game or had engaged in a dubious dare. It was a fact that Billy was overly fond of long, drunken conversation, which usually took a philosophical bent and never varied despite the character of his audience. In fact, when he had been reluctantly named the new coroner, many thought it entirely fitting, because while most would be bored stiff by his long-winded conversations, it was unlikely that the dead would mind very much. However, this comment was slightly malicious and in fact, plainly untrue as a number of people were highly entertained by his fustian conversation and the strange turns it took. Some would describe him as completely shameless and lacking "an inner monologue", meaning his words and actions were humorous in the highest degree if one didn't mind laughing a little at another's personal foibles or misfortunes. It was very hard to take Billy seriously. In sum, Billy assumed the role of one of the city's great laughing stocks, but one with a slightly menacing, unknown quality. In fact, Billy's mood could turn vicious and a noticeably darker side would present itself, usually under the influence of cocaine or a bad hangover.

His mildly reddish hair and Italianate last name (Rubino), could perhaps go a ways into explaining his naturally quixotic nature. It was a testament to his singularly contradictory character that Billy actually had a surprising facility with numbers and could spot an extra drink or two being added to his tab even in his most inebriated of states. Nevertheless, he was overly fond of playing the devil's advocate. If you wanted to bring Billy over to your way of thinking, the best course of action would be to take an opposing view and let Billy's natural contrarian nature take hold. Though he was a master of casuistry, his debates were mordantly eristic. Playing out like a game of Chinese Whispers, they were, for his opposition, an exercise in slow attrition. Billy could often surprise one with the sinuous, discursive and even clever lines of argument he drew. However, despite his great ability to exhaust his opponents, there would be no reward for those fateful few, who having followed his arguments to the very end, would no doubt be led astray by a baffling set of conclusions. In most cases, one forgot what the original argument was about and in exasperation conceded defeat. Put simply, his victories came down to a combination of natural tenaciousness and an ability to disarm his opponents by a certain lack of common sense. It wasn't that he was banal or that he spoke utter falsehoods, on the contrary, he was blessed with the faintest glimmer of something approaching authority. On many occasions, one might nod one's head in assent of what Billy was saying (sometimes for hours on end), though at an almost predictable point, once the pall of novelty had sufficiently faded, one would realize one disagreed with almost everything that was said, unfortunately for reasons one couldn't entirely express. The problem with absurdity, what gives it its power, is that it has the silvered ring of truth, yet like anything tragic, contains the soul of its own undoing, the antinomy of its own self-facing paradox. On other occasions, one could only sit back and sip at the mirroring cup of one's fetal astonishment, marveling at the farfetched notions emanating from Billy's mouth in disbelief that anyone could believe anything he said (including oneself). It could only be the benefit of any Ivy League, Liberal Arts education and indeed, there was some informed speculation that he was numbered amongst the fouler eructations of Princeton.

In becoming Hokum's coroner, Billy didn't expect a great deal of work. Previously, no one had to fear the shadows of such a delightful city and people felt comfortable enough to leave their doors unlocked during the day. Furthermore, women wouldn't think twice about walking out at night unaccompanied. But, these behaviors were rapidly disappearing and the halcyon days of trust thy neighbor were being forgotten, especially after a recent spate of highly sensationalized murders in and around the wharf district. When Billy finally arrived at the building that housed the crime scene for which he had been called, the sky had darkened considerably and was almost the color of pitch. A group of uniformed officers stood huddled under the black eves of the crumbling motel, shielding themselves in their darkly gleaming parkas from the little rain that had begun to come down. One particularly short officer with a thatch of blondish hair was bold enough to take out and light a cigarette in the stiff wind that loitered about the lit corner of the adjacent street. The officers were initially startled out of their slouching pose by Billy's sudden emergence from the shadows. However, realizing who it was, they quickly regained their previous discomposure and saluted Billy with a knowing laugh. The tallest of the three quipped, "Sorry, Billy, for pulling you out of bed on a night like this, but I think you might know someone up there." The other officers laughed in agreement. "It's on the fifth floor, room 509. Just through the vestibule, past the lobby and up the stairs. Awe, hell, forgot you virtually live here. Anyway, the elevator is still broken. Can't imagine who would be caught dead in a place like this." The others sniggered darkly at the familiar joke.

The hotel in question was the now notorious Lido des Follies (the Hotel Theseus under previous management), which was the only establishment of its type in the area. Well known to be the haunt of prostitutes, drug dealers and general delinquents, it was also the center for the more salacious element of Hokum's growing gay population; where the spartan, concrete rooms could be rented cheaply and the cavernous halls echoed throughout the night with male groans which gave Billy the impression of a slaughterhouse for buffalo. Just down the street from "The Libido" (as it was un-affectionately called) was another unwelcome haunt, "The Southern Rustler", a notorious, but somewhat underground gay club that even included a mechanical bull. Ironically, it was this mechanical bull that prevented many of the hardcore straight types from even realizing it was a gay club despite the many obvious signs. The residents of Hokum had for a number of years tried to get the building that housed the Libido condemned, based on its sagging, moribund aspect. The establishment, they argued was completely out of character with the rest of Hokum and stood in shabby, angular defiance to all the mores and qualities that defined the city. The carpet in the lobby said it all with its crass red floral decorations, well-worn out of existence in many parts, the once lurid pattern of the arabesques was unusually complex and if one didn't have anything better to do (which one often didn't when entering this particular lobby), one could spend hours teasing out the interlocking patterns and in so doing, seek complete comprehension of its form, an entirely impossible task given that its Gordian gyrations wove into a tangled infinity, mischievously echoed in the spandrels of the hallway where crude imps peaked out of the artificial stonework with vicious smiles that immediately made one aware that one was entering an unwholesome place. The lobby was the only part of the hotel that tolerated any form of ornament whatsoever as the upstairs floors were completely made of poured concrete and resembled stalls for horses rather than rooms. The doorman at the hotel, a black midget with crossed, uneven eyes and a deformed leg, rendered almost useless, usually insisted on showing the rooms to prospective guests if anyone either attempted to reserve a room during the day or to book for more than a single night. The smell of the upstairs rooms also gave off the impression appropriate to a charnel house so rank was the fetor emanating from unknown crevices in the walls and floors. The hallways rang with deep moans of ecstasy at all hours of the day or night, many inhabitants not even bothering to close the doors. It was of no great surprise that Billy usually found his most interesting and most frequent professional engagements within these walls. He often quipped that if he could bear living here, it would be like working from home. However, even Billy had grown used to some domestic comforts and couldn't countenance living in a dive such as this anymore.

Despite several pauses and an aching desire to simply abandon his assignment, Billy finally came wheezing to the top of the winding staircase, his way lit occasionally by sputtering lamps on each floor. Doubling over for one final fit of profanity, he began walking down the narrow corridor, his patent leather shoes echoing in the palpable, dead air between the grey and white cement walls. The armpits of his normal white oxford shirt stained through with sweat. He could feel the corresponding humidity in the crotch of his weary slacks. The swirls of air generated by his passage, briefly disturbed the desiccated carcasses of mangled insects that littered both the floor and the dull plastic covers of the hallway lights. Despite his natural curiosity, he didn't pause at any of the other doors, assuming that he would visit each in due course. For obvious reasons, the rooms had been emptied on this floor and most of the doors left ajar. To see all the rooms empty at this or any other time of day was truly peculiar. At the very least, several should have been occupied by the odd pervert or black-gummed meth junkie. Occasionally, one would catch one of several resident "meth heads" sleepwalking down the hallway or trolling about in the lobby with a bag of potato chips, looking lost, their eyes and cheeks hollowed out like zombies, their ghastly, disfigured faces resembling those of wax figurines which had barely survived a fire at the museum. The police all had comical names for them such as Frances Five and Dive, Lovely Riitta or Swiss Melt and would enjoy nothing more than harassing or pocking fun at them. When he arrived at the correct door, its number labeled in brass chancery font – missing a zero – he didn't bother to knock, though the door was almost completely closed. He was able to open the door undetected as the inspector and medical examiner were conversing in low, serious tones right behind the entryway. The room was lit by a single, naked bulb that hung from the cracked ceiling, casting a dismal yellow light across a ten by twelve foot room, which stank of the same rot and decomposition as the hallway, an olio of stale urine, mildew and sulfur. As Billy put his head through the door frame, the path of the opening door struck the outside of the inspector's left elbow, causing his arms to drop from their akimbo position. The inspector and examiner quickly turned toward Billy, simultaneously parting ways like opposing sides of a great cathedral door to reveal a bulbous, seminude body laid out on a tiny, ruffled bed still dressed in a pair of 'whitey tighties' and dark argyle socks. Billy couldn't actually enter the room as it would have been impossible for all three to stand in the small space between the bed and the parallel wall, the distance between which was filled by the width of the doorframe. This led the examiner to shuffle sideways like a crab around the corners of the mattress until he managed to squeeze between the bed and the opposing wall. The lead inspector had a very conventional, inspector-like look: tall, lean and dressed in a light brown mackintosh sans fedora, whereas the medical examiner looked anything but conventional. He wore a fur Cossack hat, rounded glasses and had a permanent, weasel-like grin, from which one could only be distracted by the grossly thin mustache that mantled his fleshly lips like a grease stain. To complete the confusion, the smaller, rather plump examiner wore a cowboy string tie that was completely incongruent with his jet-black dinner suit, which he seemed to wear constantly. This man's name was simply Moncrete and he was certainly of dubious character, always on the hunt to save money by some clever trick or petty scam. Despite these failings, no one in the entire police force or medical profession would claim that he wasn't good at what he did as he was a very proficient medical examiner. Contrastingly, the lead inspector had a very inhospitable face with drawn features, whose angularity would initially shock or startle. He was of late middle age, very staid in his manners with deep furrows in his brows and a few pits in his cheeks to show his experience. His name was Frank Poundstone. Frank spoke first, almost sniffing, "'Bout time you showed up, Moncrete's got this thing all stitched up half an hour ago."

In response, Billy gave out his normal giggle, while he smiled ear to ear. "Nonsense," was his only remark.

"Boys downstairs lost a bet that said if this guy didn't look the splittin' image of you in 20 years, I'd buy them all drinks."

"Double, nonsense!"

Moncrete offered a simple statement, "It's just a case of myocardial infarction, which probably occurred fifteen to sixteen hours ago. Paperwork should as usual be a bit of a pain but..."

"We'll see about that," replied Billy cutting him short.

"Here we go again," sighed the inspector, "I hope you're not..."

"Let's see what we have here," offered Billy with a positive uplift in this voice.

"We'll have to do more tests and go through toxicology, but it looks like cardiac arrest and…ah, yes."

On these occasions, Billy would initially try to adopt a sense of what professionals call gravitas, beginning his observations with an attempt at seriousness, even industriousness, that was quickly belied by his awkward and clumsy movements. As Billy moved over the corpse with his bent upper half, he saw what was an older man's face, fixed in a spasm of horror. Billy's eyes became a premonition. Both the inspector and the medical examiner could tell a loud, raucous laugh was on its way. It had only taken Billy a few seconds to notice the shiny leather straps around the old codger's 'man-tits' and the humiliation mask that lay beside his face.

"Yep, Billy, we thought you'd get a kick out of this one," the inspector said in his slow Southern drawl.

"You bet I do, but first there is a more important point that needs to be determined."

Billy took a pad and pencil out of his coat pocket.

"What is that?"

"To determine if this man really looks like me."

"Oh, come off it, that's already been established. We need to take this guy out to the morgue."

"A round of beers is a serious bet."

He looked down at the man's rather plump nose and immediate wrote down in a hurried scrawl,

" *The imposter:*

One fat nose, hideous and not at all looking like my own."

He repeated the last sentence out loud as he wrote it down. Given his innate vanity, it is unsurprising that Billy considered his own nose more graceful and less pugnacious, especially when compared to the one stood beneath him, which he thought resembled a fat, earthy tuber that had been shriveled by freezer burn. Billy's features (or so he imagined) were surprisingly fine and one could tell that they might have colluded together in a distant, sketchy past to form something vaguely handsome.

"Even eyes, blue, a shade lighter. Perhaps, too close together." It was a rare mark of honest self-reflection that he accorded to the man a set of "even eyes", which was not only an acknowledgement of a personal defect on Billy's part (who could not help but recognize that one of his own eyes was indeed slightly larger than the other), but it was also one of the few advantages he would ascribe to the man over his own physical appearance. He continued writing and declaiming out loud,

"Clean shaven, blotchy face and hair of an inferior quality and thinning at top, combed across in opposite direction. Lips slightly pendulant, drawn in a hideous expression and no doubt thinner than my own. Double chinned."

He repeated the last phrase in an excitable manner, "Double chinned! Why that fact alone wrecks any form of resemblance between myself and this odious fat ass."

"Billy, we need to get movin' on. We don't have time for one of your…"

'I'm sorry, inspector," Billy swiveled around quickly scratching the reddish stubble of his chin with his pencil, his eyes lighting up into flame. "But, this imposter clearly looks nothing like me. Furthermore, you are wrong on another count."

"And what's that?"

"This man didn't die of cardiac arrest, but of asphyxiation by strangulation."

"How do you figure that?" snorted Moncrete feeling insulted by Billy's bold supposition.

"It's obvious, this man's a perv and the little Mexican number who was entertaining him, left the murder weapon there in the form of that plastic shopping bag and rubber fist."

"Mexican? But where…Anyway, the physical evidence doesn't corroborate that and there are no petechiae on the eyelids or…"

"Any money or identification in his wallet?"

"Nope, probably paid in cash and left wallet at home to prevent gettin' robbed or havin' his ID stolen," interjected the investigator, "but, he has got a wedding band, so it seems the boy likes to play hanky-panky on both ends."

"I've seen his type, Astroglide, amyl nitrate, humiliation masks, Belladonna's hands. These sorts get off on suffocation, slamming and BDSM. Just look at his face. Clearly suffocation, perhaps unintentional as no obvious signs of struggle."

"The only thing this boy was strugglin' with was whether to be the pitcher or the catcher," laughed the inspector.

"Indeed, but it does show suffocation," repeated Billy

"It isn't," Moncrete intoned firmly.

"It is. And the perp's fled."

"He's now after my job. And this entire story…you just came up with this in the last five minutes?" the inspector laughed.

"Yes, indeed. I see things. The whole scene plays in front of my eyes like a bad Kraut porn movie. Just call it a sixth sense I have with these types of things. Makes me feel like I should have been an investigator. No offence to you, Poundstone. Anyway, we'll still have to go to toxicology, but there is no reason we can't agree on these things in advance. OK, so you won't go with suffocation and I won't go with cardiac arrest. We could either flip a coin over it or we could compromise."

"Compromise? Compromise? What's this always with compromise?" Moncrete responded.

"In the report."

"Yes, I know. As I've said a million times, you can't compromise on a death certificate. The cause of death has to be scientifically proven and correct. This is serious stuff."

"So it's a coin flip then?"

Moncrete raised his voice in almost complete exasperation, "Of course it's not a coin flip."

"C'mon, where is the poetry in a simple case of cardiac arrest? Can you even prove what caused the cardiac arrest as you call it?"

"No, but taking his advanced age into account, the position we found the body, the fact that he is wearing a medical bracelet..."

"For diabetes," interjected Billy.

Not deterred, Moncrete continued in his forceful manner, "...all lead me to the most likely conclusion that he probably died because he was...well you know, he was...well him and the prostitute were in fact copulating subsequent to ingesting of poppers. Poundstone agrees."

"Ah, so there you have it, the man had a heart attack while copulating with an unknown person in the Lido des Follies. Doesn't that strike you as just a little bland?"

"Bland?"

"Listen Moncrete, we've been over this a hundred times, I don't want to argue over the finer points of giving the bereaved a good story. I have to sign off everything in the report and I have to deal with the family. The family doesn't want truths. They want answers. Explanations. They'll want a story. They will want to know why he was at the Lido des Follies to begin with. They will want to know who he was with and why he was with her."

"Yes, but that is not our job and even if it was..."

"Nonsense. Nonsense." Nonsense was incidentally one of Billy's favorite words as it summarized so much of his cynical *Weltanschauung*. He often used it as a condiment to pepper his conversations even when its use was unwarranted. Seeing that Moncrete was about to go into one of his long, exasperatingly pedantic monologues, Billy picked up a large black dildo, the dimensions of which seemed more fitting of a piano leg. It had been wrapped carefully in one of the plastic evidence bags left lying on the bed.

"Can I take this home with me? It's as big as a midget's forearm. How the hell...And look at this?"

Billy had finally discovered the black rubber fist that lay between the man's legs and began waving it around didactically like a professor's pointer as he spoke in an increasingly animated fashion.

"I'm not sure you wanna touch that. You don't know where it's been. Actually maybe you do," the inspector dryly intoned.

"Anyway, as I was saying, we have all this physical evidence here. All the makings of a good story and you want to leave it all out and put this man's death down to two words. I mean we have one gargantuan piece of evidence here left completely out of the picture. Someone once said about writing that when you put a gun in a room it simply has to go off. We haven't got a gun but we've got one helluva giant rubber fist. People may have their own stories, but I always write the endings and I'm damn good at endings."

"Write their endings? Edit them at best, I'd say," the inspector insinuated.

"Anyway, I have to think how we are going to liven this story up. We could really get some press out of this," Billy said with a devilish look about him. "If we can get the news stations interested, maybe we could find something that would lead to the closing down of a prostitution ring and we could all get medals. Like I've always said, I came into this profession because I hoped to find...no, I hoped to bring, people's stories back to life not to kill them."

The inspector started to become impatient.

"Look, we don't want the family thinkin' a murder occurred, then we'll have all kinds of problems and a tax payer funded investigation on our hands that I could do without. I suppose you want to play your usual game, orderin' an investigation and havin' half the police force lookin' for some imaginary femme fatale...sorry, what is the male equivalent of a femme fatale, Moncrete?"

"Hommes fatal...Hommes like pommes frites," interjected Moncrete.

"Well what if he's both like a man-woman or somethin'. Aw, hell whatever, I'm tryin' to make a point," continued Poundstone. "Anyway, you assume this hom-mes is on the run after havin' strangled this poor sop probably after a lovers' tiff, right?"

"Or blatant robbery," added Billy

"You watch too many of these television shows. Why not pursue a career in Hollywood like that guy you're always goin' on about, Campbell? If you want to think up stories about dead people and act like a crusading crime scene investigator, you're in the wrong town. Nonetheless, I'm sure it would suit that big ego of yours to have every national television network here coverin' this story with your big grinnin' mug there talkin' through the evidence. We've seen enough of that on the bleedin' local news for everybody's taste."

"But, that is how some of the best stories begin. It's not just about me, it's about the public's need to know. Who knows where it will all lead? Where one story ends another always begins, no? The press will love it. Do I need to say again that we've got a rubber fist?"

Billy offered the final phrase in an almost pleading fashion, holding the rubber fist in the air triumphantly. He seemed desperate for the others to share his enthusiasm. After all, it was certainly true: Billy suffered from a strange sort of ambition and an even stranger form of fascination. It was clear to most who had worked with him what Billy enjoyed the most about his job: to fabricate an entirely fantastical series of events that preceded the time of death and explain them in the most visual terms to an infinitely credulous press. Sure, he took liberties, but he thought it was worth it. The press and the victim's family always had a number of unanswerable questions and he was always happy to fill in the blanks. However, what people found the most incredible was his ability to maintain a straight face. It was almost as if he could give credence to these ridiculous stories and maybe he could. Ultimately, his ego led him to believe that he had a special insight into people's deaths; that their final circumstances spoke to him through some hidden voice. Though he wasn't a trained medical examiner or a police investigator, he did have a good imagination, something he felt the investigators and examiners entirely lacked. They were always weighted down by the mundane and he with his special vision could see beyond it. In fact, unless there was foul play, it was usually left to him to put all the pieces together and even if there was, it was still up to him to order the investigation. Finally, Billy had a large degree of ambition and knew with certainty that he was meant for greater things. By finding 'facts' where others hadn't, issuing lurid and sometimes sensational press releases that inevitably led to orders for a wide and varied assortment of investigations, he had managed with some success to raise his profile in the sordid eyes of the press. Ultimately, he hoped by these and other means to be considered for increased public responsibility. To his critics, he defended himself as a fastidious protector of the public's interests (quite literally), but many in the police force found him to be nothing more than an arriviste clown and detested not only his open hubris, but his frequent press conferences in which he never missed an opportunity to request an investigation into the most spurious of cases. Some even went so far as to suggest that he was an embarrassment to the public services. Though Billy did manage to get his name in the papers a great deal, it never really concluded in anything tangible and on several occasions he was told by none other than the city's mayor to arrest his desire for publicity as it was in the city's (and therefore the mayor's) best interest to reduce not increase the number of unseemly crimes that were reported. Thus, Billy was often frustrated in his efforts and on some occasions even forced to halt investigations full stop or to conveniently leave out certain bits of evidence. It was with this knowledge that Billy kept insisting. However, Poundstone rounded him off curtly,

"Look, you're the one who has to explain this all to the family. What are you gonna to tell them, that their husband or father was suffocated with a rubber fist? Because, at the moment that is all we've got."

"As I said, where one story ends another begins. You know, Poundstone, that three out of my last four girlfriends have been occupational?"

"What do you mean 'occupational'? You mean from work? As in the bodies? That's down right disgustin'."

"Obviously not, you pervert, I'm talking about significant others. You know, the city pays virtually no money for counseling for the wives and daughters of victims. Bereaved women sometimes need a shoulder to cry on. A man to fill those empty spaces."

Moncrete sniggered at this.

"Sometimes they are amazingly grateful. I have a few in the process now."

"In the process? You are one twisted fuck," sniggered the inspector.

"Some may call it a public service," retorted Billy, pointing the rubber fist directly at the inspector.

"However you want to call it, no one wants an investigation into how their loved one died next to a big, black rubber fist. No one wants that in the papers. And can you stop wavin' that thing in my face?"

"Look, inspector, as I am sure you would agree, we are both in the story telling business. But, like Moncrete says here, my stories are true, everythin' else is an invasion of dignity," the inspector responded with some firmness, looking Billy straight in the eyes.

"Why do people always talk about the dignity

"Otherwise this tale will be dead on arrival. You don't want some peevish old woman looking through police records wondering why no investigation was done and how her husband ended up in a motel room with a bunch of sex paraphernalia."

"Affairs happen all the time," the inspector rejoined in exasperation.

"You being self reveratial," laughed Moncrete, English not being his first language.

"Self-referential, I think you mean," retorted Billy.

The inspector continued, without acknowledging the other two, "Heart attack is the quickest way to end this right here without wastin' a bunch of police work. We don't want the papers all over this. In fact, I'm surprised they haven't showed up yet. We're takin' all this stuff away so it won't appear in the evidence or in the pictures. We'll give this poor guy a little break. Town like Hokum doesn't need any more bad press. We have young families here who just want to make a good start. In fact, I'd wish this whole place would be torn down so there would be no more stories."

"So you have no desire to set the atoms in motion? No spark of the creative? Can we really be sure this guy wasn't murdered after all? Can we?" gasped Billy, looking directly into Poundstone's eyes.

Poundstone was taken aback knowing he was slightly out of his depth, but quickly recovered, "No, not yet, but no use…look, me and Moncrete already went over this an hour ago. At this point, the evidence is inconclusive at best, but no one's gonna be any better off if we…"

"Do we really want to close the book here?"

"Cardiac arrest," Moncrete intoned with finality.

"I have to agree on this one," affirmed Poundstone. "Anythin' to avoid paperwork and an unsightly investigation."

"OK. OK," said Billy, slightly crestfallen. "If it must be so, to quote the final words of that peerless of composers, Edvard Grieg."

"How is it you're always quotin' people's last words? You definitely got one morbid sense about you."

Billy simply let off another raucous laugh. Moncrete made a sound like the whinnying of a horse. They both stared at him and as he didn't react or indicate that anything was awry, they just ignored it.

"I'll leave you two to it then," the inspector said as he exited the room, leaving Billy and Moncrete to themselves.

Several hours of detailed and for the most part uninteresting official work ensued and this wore on deep into the night. Billy finally managed to leave the coroner's office about half past twelve, exhausted by his dreary efforts in box ticking, filling in blank squares, conjuring formulaic text, signing his name again and again, making seemingly endless phone calls and conducting monotonous conversations in efforts to identify the yet unidentified man. He frequently lamented that the dead gave him much more trouble than the living. He would often browbeat his regular bar associates, reminding them that they should treat him well now, because when they died, they would become an administrative nightmare for him.

When Billy finally entered the sharp, gelid air of a starless night, the wind was still moving vigorously through the trees. The short bursts of serein had now abated and left in their wake a sense of freshness and renewal, delivering the few bridges and underpasses of central Hokum of their crude smells. Some said you could no longer walk under a bridge downtown without the fetor of human urine. Miles from the center, the worthless brass and wood barometer in Billy's office always read sunshine, though heavy rain and sudden squalls had been all too frequent guests over the last month. It all seemed to be building toward something, something unclear and hazy, but possessed with the unmistakable density and weight of doom.

Billy sniffed as he walked along the sidewalk that communicated with the staff parking lot via a small, manmade boscage. He profoundly hated the newish building and its disingenuous aesthetic, which was a typical modern affair composed of red brick, false quoins, and plate glass. He had long thought it should resemble some crumbling version of a Victorian madhouse and wrote a long-winded letter to the mayor to that effect. Years ago, it had been deliberately moved to the urban outskirts of the city so that the God-fearing citizens of Hokum need not have this memento mori clouding their everyday earthly activities. The entire structure was somewhat outsize given that there were only four or five employees working within its walls on a full time basis. Its sheer size perhaps gave away to some who understood these things another inkling of dark foreboding, but for now, it always felt half empty as no other municipal department wanted to share the premises. When no one was looking, Billy would occasionally piss at the roots of a group of young dogwood trees that had recently been planted in what appeared to him to be the latest superstitious attempt to hide the office's very existence. He would enjoy seeing the smoke from his hot stream permeate the air with a sly hiss of mockery. Death it seemed was something that the city of Hokum couldn't tolerate, much as many in it couldn't tolerate him. By hiding the coroner's office, Billy felt it was a personal affront to his continual attempts at greatness. The building itself was bordered on each side by anonymous industrial parks that housed amongst other things a series of steel sided warehouses, a small pottery manufacturer, numerous car part distributers, a manikin factory, a Botox clinic and a host of other anonymous red brick buildings with faded numbers on the outside (all odd as the even numbers were never built). These buildings were far older than the coroner's office and gave off a depressed, forlorn appearance, their russet-tinted windows always dark, the wide parking lots always vacant, only occupied by the odd whirlwind of dust and loose paper. For many, it was the end of earth.

As Billy peered across the street, he noted the familiar constellation of neon lights, crowned by a disembodied pair of neon lips that blinked on and off at the raunchy club down the road. A lit champagne glass moved endlessly up and down, toppling each way in predictable movements as it did. The streets were absolutely empty except for a stampede of dead leaves and discarded napkins that moved towards him alongside the adjacent sidewalk. The few chalky buildings still in view held out against the darkness as long as they could, then in an instant, they too were drawn in, erased into the milky residue of stars. Usually unaffected by the cold, Billy had to draw up his collar in order to brace himself against a sudden gust that was brewing. He had made this walk toward his wreck of an automobile countless times, usually alone and usually in the late hours of the night or the early hours of the morning. There were very few places of entertainment still open at this hour and Billy usually settled for a trip to the nearby liquor store, humanely close to the coroner's office (unsurprisingly, it seemed death and booze were amiable business partners). Just as Billy was taking out his keys in anticipation of opening the door to his long suffering Pontiac Fiero (incidentally, a car as ungainly and unfashionable as himself), he heard a quick rustling behind him in the unlit parking lot. He jumped at first and turned around to see none other than the small, hunched frame of Basyli Jach shuffling up behind him with one arm raised in the air. A hard, distinct Polish accent could be heard, "Wait, wait!"

Billy twisted his head backward and moved his arms upward in a show of some annoyance groaning, "Not you again. You somehow get my home phone number and now you even jump me at night in my office parking lot." Not deterred, Basyli kept running toward him, making impossibly small steps, repeating all the time, "Wait. Wait. Mr. Rubino, wait!" He ran all the time with his arm and finger pointing at a forty-five degree angle as if he were trying to hail a taxi, making sure he didn't touch any of the cracks in the sidewalk. He wore his typical light brown suit that looked at least a size too large and a white oxford shirt of which only the topmost button was left open. During the summer months, he would sometimes carry a faded daisy in his coat pocket or perhaps tucked between the buttons of his shirt. During the winter, it was usually the red carnation that he currently wore discretely in his coat pocket. He would be heard murmuring to himself, *Kwiat bez zapachu, jak czlowiek bez duszy.* Basyli had for the last few days, become a real thorn in Billy's side, but given the strange circumstances of his case, this behavior on Basyli's part wasn't completely unmerited. Basyli was one of Hokum's longstanding foreign immigrants though he rarely if ever spoke to anybody else. He simply didn't factor into the daily rhythms and parlance of Hokum except as a tiny point of curiosity. The strange flâneur would normally be seen wandering the streets in his slightly hunched over manner with the consequence that people never entirely saw his face and were for the most part uninterested in seeing it. In old world fashion, he always dressed in suits despite the weather. Most people he encountered assumed he was Russian, but if anyone had ever bothered to speak to him they would have quickly determined that he was Polish. Like Billy, his origins were generally mysterious but to an even higher degree. People knew he was fairly well off, but lived like a miser. Somehow it had been gathered through the very diffuse and sometimes unreliable networks of Hokum that he had been a mathematician, an expert in logic and an arcane field referred to as low-dimensional topology. Wild stories rose up around him: that he had become wealthy because his work was used in everything from encryption to epigenetic modeling and some went so far as to speculate that he worked for the NSA. More reliable sources dictated that he was a retired college professor who had translocated to Hokum after a long if not distinguished career at a small university somewhere in the Rust Belt.

The reason that Basyli had come into Billy's life was that some months ago, the mysterious Pole had uncharacteristically departed Hokum for an extended period. No one would have noticed his absence except that in the meantime a man fitting his vague description died under suspicious circumstances not far from Basyli's house. As the individual who had potentially been murdered could not be identified, it was assumed to be Basyli and a number of anonymous residents (shop keepers, bank tellers and the like) positively identified him as such, given that there were no relatives or even friends of any kind to identify him otherwise. In the ensuing investigation, due in part to sloppy police work and an otherwise deliberate attempt to avoid undue paperwork, it was somehow determined that the man was in possession of Basyli's passport which was later found at his house after the investigation had already begun. By in large, this grave mistake could have been partially due to a clerical error or perhaps it was an unfortunate side effect of Billy's constant desire to create a good story. It didn't help at all that as a result of another unfortunate coincidence, the only piece of paper found on the man's person was signed 'B. Jack', which was taken to mean Basyli Jach as the badly scrawled handwriting had turned the 'k' into an 'h'. The upshot of all of this was that it was Basyli who had been declared dead instead of the unknown B. Jack. This simple statement of fact concerning Basyli's existence (or non-existence in this case) set into motion the automatic gears of a grossly outmoded, but sometimes scarily efficient bureaucratic machine that only ground to a halt once his bank accounts were locked and his property seized. As he had no other relatives in this country or no one who knew him, Basyli presently had no means of identifying himself or even proving his existence, especially as he had never been in the practice of carrying identification (a practice he spurned due to his memories of life under a heavy handed communist regime). After numerous inquiries and a certain amount of desperate pleading, he discovered that Billy was the one perhaps responsible for sorting out this entangled mess. In fact, from Basyli's perspective, Billy was the only one in the world who could lift the proverbial curtain on the mystery and determine definitely if in his Schrodinger-like state, he was more or less a dead pussycat. It was with this in mind that he had been pursuing Billy for the last few days, desperate to have his case looked into. After all, he was told that is was Billy who had actually signed his death certificate and he was therefore, the only one who could remediate the error, if in fact an error had occurred. It wasn't every day in Hokum when a dead man showed up to the police office and professed to be alive.

In appearance, Basyli had a pair of long, sagging jowls, mirrored by his distended ears, which culminated in two very large, pendulous lobes, resembling those of Buddha. Out of the porch of each ear emerged a gratuitous shock of greyish hair. In age, he was in a nonspecific part of his early seventies and in altitude he reached a mere five foot six. He was bald at the very crown of his rectangular head and the thick laurel of grizzled hair that remained was of varying degrees of greyscale. What stood out the most in Basyli's appearance was the black streak of hair that arched his deciduous hairline from front to back. He wore a pair of oval-shaped spectacles with a silver rim. In practice, Basyli was usually reluctant to look one in the eye unless he was making a very serious point. He stood with a slight hunch and his thin lips were usually parted to reveal the tops of a greyish set of well-hidden teeth. He frequently stood with his hands in his jacket pockets or just resting outside. Whether it was a nervous tick or not, he seemed to be endlessly rummaging through his pockets for some lost item or another; usually a pack of imported Gauloises, his only luxury besides his surprisingly expensive scarves. He had a very slow and undeliberate manner of speech that started off in a mid-register monotone and continued in a slightly higher, but no less unmodulated pitch. If one were to describe his appearance in a single word, it was that of a mortician.

Before Basyli could reach the spot where Billy had been standing, Billy rudely turned and continued the short walk toward his car. Basyli came up beside him and in pleading fashion began, "Miiiissssster Rubino, Miiiiissster Rubino. As we spoke before, when you will open inquiry? I have not much money. I have no place to sleep." His discomfiture was palpable.

Billy replied nonchalantly, "As I said before, if you can give me proof of address or positive identification like a birth certificate, I would be more than happy to open an inquiry."

"But as I say before, I have no certificate or identification. They all in my house and they stop my credit card. They lock my house and I no am able to get in. They take things from my house. It is imposssssible."

These increasingly pitiful declamations rang in Billy's ears until finally tired of the Pole's perseverations, he turned around swiftly and confronted Basyli head on, exhorting him, "Look, as I told you before it is difficult, but what can I do? I don't even know who you are. What can you give me that will convince me that you are Basyli Jack?"

"Yyyaaaaach!"

"Whatever, unless you have some proof, I cannot open an inquiry. My hands are tied. I need something to go on, otherwise your case is simply hopeless."

"But Mister Rubino, what you want me do? I cannot get passport. I cannot get birth certificate. This is problem with no solution."

Billy retorted sharply, "That simply isn't my problem. There is nothing I can do at present. I'm on about four hours of sleep, my sinuses feel as if pins are being driven through them, so with all due respect, if we must continue this senseless blathering, we must continue it another time. Come by my office sometime when you have more for me. Good night."

As he spoke, Billy opened his car door and squeezed uncomfortably into his cracked leather car seat. The suspension whined under his great weight as the car sank to one side. At this point, Basyli started waving his arms around in an increasingly frantic and disjointed manner as if he was some badly built automaton.

"But you never in office. Always gone."

"Tomorrow. Tomorrow. Good night," Billy gave off, slamming his car door, leaving Basyli hopelessly shouting atop a small knoll of grass, giving the appearance that he was literally fuming as the condensation formed by his words entered the cold September air. Not bothering to watch, Billy switched on the ignition to allow the frigid car to warm up. As the loud rush of heat entered the automobile through the numerous vents, the windows quickly fogged up, atomizing the animated figure of Basyli into a gauze-like blur. As he turned on the windshield wipers, he rolled down the window and Basyli's voice, invariably the kind that stains any silence, returned to its normal volume. He had not missed a beat.

"But I have no money. I have no place to stay. You never in office. You never in home."

Billy shouted out of the window sarcastically, "You will find me, the dead always do."

As he drove off, he left Basyli standing there in the empty parking lot to watch the red taillights of his decrepit vehicle trail off into the distance. It would be a bitter, long night and the moon was nowhere to be found; more likely than not, it had been frozen in slumber under the eerie, translucent light of the Chappewock Lake.

2

"Remember me, remember me, but ah! Forget my fate."

Somewhere tucked within the small annals of the city of Hokum, misplaced within the quaint shelves of the neglected public library, if one were to look for it (and one would have to look hard for it), one would – or perhaps better said – one could find a work of a singular hand, a long forgotten name who put in writing one particularly exotic episode in Hokum's history which occurred a mere twenty-five years prior. Unfortunately for the author, the story itself outlived the memory of the person who had invested the small effort it took to write it down. In fact, the story's only appearance in print was in a now defunct publication, the bastard child of a well-intentioned, but ultimately unorganized and underfunded grass roots initiative. Over the years, the story had been told again and again in different forms, but there was only one veritably accurate version and it was the one nestled in undisturbed oblivion between two outdated books on computer and electronics repair. Due to one of those great misfortunes of history, similar in effect to the burning of the libraries of Alexandria or Baghdad, the unforeseen obliteration of the Royal Alcazar, or the destruction of the Ribiera Palace, only the first, more well-known part of the story survived in print, while the final, more intimate part of the tale was lost to all those with only a casual involvement in the story.

"The Ballad of Jean and Reg"

Or

"The Field Trip"

Part 1

The gentle musk of a desert rose filled the air as his sweaty, tired body glistened in the sultry Texan heat. Reggie was tired, dead tired and could barely stand upright as his young, tender chest heaved from running miles in the ninety-five degree heat. The .38 Colt snub-nosed revolver felt like a thousand pound weight in his left hand and he was tempted to let its dead mass drop onto the dry, red earth. It was a profound reminder of how far he had come. He could hear the police sirens in the distance, long before he could see their lights flickering in the hazy heat of the fading day. His young skin was sunburned, his black hair full of red dust, his clothes torn almost to shreds. He hoisted up his broken body for one last sniff of the fast freedom, the loose, free air that he so longed for. As the last bit of adrenaline poured through his veins, the air mixed with the faint smell of dried blood to form a delirious concoction, forcing on him, one final broken smile. It was all he could allow himself. Reggie Hortega was a long way from Hokum, a long way from the less than idyllic high school days he spent and subsequently ran away from in that lonely backwater. Thirty miles to the southeast, lay the Mexican border, a dangerous, foreboding place; an invisible divide that his father and mother once crossed under similar circumstances only two decades prior, tired, hungry, afraid, pursued by the nameless face of authority. In minutes, that same authority would be here, ready to destroy what remained of his childhood, to lock him up in a ten by ten prison cell for the remainder of his brief adolescence. True, he had committed great wrongs, but would the punishment ultimately fit the crime, the crime of never really fitting into a society as barbarous, as contradictory as our own? Reggie Hortega was no more or no less than what society made him, he was the child of the American dream, a broken dream that perhaps died there in the wilderness a thousand times each year for countless hordes of nameless nobodies. He was a bruised yellow cockspur, perishing in the unremitting dryness of a hostile and ultimately uncharted terrain.

Our story begins at Tobia Gorrio High School, where Reggie, 15 and two other friends, Manuel Varega, 15 and Inez Fernandez, 14 took Jean Hewitt, 41, a high school English teacher, hostage at gunpoint on an otherwise ordinary Friday in early May. Tobia Gorrio was like many other high schools located in the Deep South, it had a decent football team, a well-attended senior prom, a number of Bible study groups and a predominantly white student body, numbering twelve hundred in total of which less than two percent were of an ethnic background other than Caucasian.

The time was a quarter past eleven and Jean had just finished her final class for the day. She was preparing to go home to her children after the usual jog around the riverside track near the secluded teachers' parking lot. She knew she had to do grocery shopping before she returned home and had forgotten her gym clothes in the trunk of her forest green Grand Cherokee. Noticing nothing out of the ordinary, she entered the parking lot, which was little more than a gravel rectangle surrounded on three sides by tall pine trees. Just when she had bent over to open the trunk, she heard the stones shifting behind her, but she didn't think to turn around as she had already assumed that another teacher was attempting an early, pre-noon getaway. However, what came next, she could hardly expect. Suddenly, she felt something cold press behind the nape of her neck. She froze. Despite her never touching the handle, much less feeling the muzzle of a gun, she instinctively knew what it was. The voice behind her growled in a voice of barbed wire, "Shhh. Don't say a word and you won't get hurt. Don't turn around."

She had always heard of things like this happening in the movies, but she never thought it would happen to her, especially in the teachers' parking lot of Tobia Gorrio High. Nervous and trembling, she could barely muster a soft, high-pitched "OK. OK." Soon afterwards, she heard another set of feet shuffling on the gravel behind her. With her hands raised to shoulder level, she managed a weak, "If it's my purse you want, please take it."

"No. Put your hands down. This is not a robbery. Put your hands down and get in the car, quick," said the youthful, but firm voice behind her. As she began to turn around to her right, the voice said, "Don't look behind you. Get in the driver's seat." As she moved over toward the left-hand side of the car, the muzzle of the gun remained there, until she had opened the door and sat in the driver seat. Looking straight ahead and not daring to look to her left at the assailant, she asked, "Now what?" almost hyper-ventilating.

"Calm down and everything will be fine. Unlock the doors."

As she pressed the button to unlock the other car doors, she replied in a weak voice, "Listen, I have children, I don't ..."

"Shut up! Shut up, lady!"

Immediately, she heard another two people open the backseat door to her right. They were whispering loudly and slid into place behind her, one of them grabbing her hair from behind, pulling her head against the car seat. She did all she could not to scream.

"Start the car," said the voice to her left, who was still holding the gun to the side of her head. Out of the corner of her eye, she could tell he was wearing a black ski mask, T-shirt and track pants. As she fumbled through her purse for the keys to the car, she heard a voice behind her say, "Ca'mon, hurry up! Hurry up! We haven't got much time, lady!"

When she finally put the keys into the ignition and twisted the key with her wrist, the car started up with a roar.

"Don't move," the voice behind the ski mask ordered. At that instant, the masked person holding the gun ran behind the truck to the other side and opened the front door, jumping into the seat directly next to her. He shut the door with a slam and held the gun to her side, being careful to keep it below the level of the dashboard, out of view. He said in a calm, but commanding voice, "If you want to see your kids again, you do exactly what I say. Close the car door and start driving. Do exactly what I tell you to do."

"Where do you want me to drive?"

"Anywhere, just get out of here and onto the highway. And stop panicking, I promise we won't hurt you."

As he said this, he removed the black ski mask to reveal an unfamiliar face. As she would later learn, it was the slender, russet face of Reggie Hortega. In an instant, she caught a glance of his soft brown eyes, his curly black hair. Taken aback by her frightened eyes, he reminded her to look ahead and to start driving. She did everything he said, reversing out of the parking lot, driving out of the school premises and finally onto the highway. At first her driving was sporadic, she couldn't remember where anything was in the car with Reggie constantly reminding her to calm down.

Tobia Gorrio was big enough that she didn't recognize every student, but by the time they exited the school property, she had gathered that all three of the people in her car were adolescents. In fact, they were all students in the grade just below the two she normally taught, tenth and eleventh. As she would later learn, in the weeks leading up to the present incident, the three students, led by Reggie (known to his friends simply as 'Reg') had made a pact between themselves. The plan was simply to escape the daily torture of their broken homes, households in which each was subjected to varying degrees of constant physical and mental abuse. After years and years of maltreatment, like other children in their position, they had simply become numb. They were, in a sense, 'acting out'.

'The Perpetrators'

Reg, the obvious ringleader, had been in trouble with the police before, but only for minor offences and nothing at the level of abduction. He was considered a bright, but regular absentee from school. He was also described as 'morose' by many of his teachers. He never seemed interested in class and was frequently engaged in school fights, which he usually won with what one administrator described as 'ruthless effectiveness'. His father had taught him how to box when he was young and he even joined the youth team of a local boxing gym. From a young age, he was forced to defend himself from his dad's drunken rages, but he would never hit back. However, though he seldom ever participated in school activities, he was kicked off the wrestling team in seventh grade for breaking another student's ribs after the other boy referred to him by as a 'wet back'. In general, Reg never said much, but he had a calm, cool confidence about him. He was on the tall side for his age, slender but well built. He had a square jaw and soft thin lips. He had long, almost feminine eyelashes and thick eyebrows. It was plain to see he would soon become a very handsome man, though he retained a certain boyishness about him. He was still a few months off from having to shave for his first time.

His best friend, Manuel, who sat in the back seat and was the one who had grabbed Jean's hair, was of a cheerier disposition and did whatever Reg did or wanted him to do. He was the 'joker' of the group and while tall, had a slightly pudgy, but strong build. Despite his difficulties at home, it was rare not to see Manuel with a jejune smile on his face. He had been raised predominantly by his grandmother, however, when she died, his uncle had taken over the responsibility of raising him for the last three years. His uncle was a tough, hard-working man, who had little time for Manuel and saw him simply as another mouth to feed in addition to his own four children. It was hard enough to make ends meet as it was, but with Manuel it was proving unbearable. He was consistently vocal about the fact that he wanted Manuel to leave school as soon as possible and start working to pay back the money he had spent on raising him. He usually forced Manuel to work long hours after school and on the weekends in his mechanical shop. As a result, the summer holiday, only weeks away, was not something Manuel looked forward to because it only represented more grueling labor. He had to make constant excuses even to see Reg outside of school.

Inez was noticeably different from the other two, a good student, attentive, always listening to her teachers and elders. However, she lived in a foster home, where it is almost certain she suffered regular abuse.

She was taciturn and supremely introverted. She had attempted to run away from her foster parents before, but she had always come back. Her rather modest foster home contained five other children, the parents subsisting predominantly on the money they were paid by the State to take care of its wardens. She had a history of self-abuse, primarily cutting, but there were occasionally other unexplained bruises. She was a small, frail girl of five foot four. She appeared rather homely, but could have been considerably more attractive if she ever decided to smile or wear makeup instead of hiding herself in frumpy clothing. She had very large, languid eyes, long tenebrous locks and to her great embarrassment, a small amount of hair just above the corners of her lips.

'The Victim'

Jean Hewitt was an average looking woman of medium height and short peroxide blonde hair. She had struggled with her weight when she was younger, but with regular exercise and a good diet, she had kept the problem reasonably under control. She wasn't a woman who generally turned heads, but neither would she be considered ugly or atrocious. She had been married for ten years and had two small children of three and six. Her husband, Charlie Hewitt, was ten years her senior and was a devout and conscientious family man. He was also the branch manager for a large vacuum distributor and was very proud of his work and his collection of model o-gauge trains. Jean had moved to Hokum from southern Florida when she was seven and remained there most of her life except for a stint at Berry College in northern Georgia. Before she had settled down and had kids, she described herself as 'a free spirit' and wrote as much in her senior yearbook. She had been voted by her classmates as the "Most likely to appear on television or fall mysteriously out of a building".

'The Plan'

In order to execute his grand scheme, Reg had stolen a gun and a considerable quantity of ammunition from his father's shed. The three conspirators left with approximately twenty dollars in cash and a large wad of hope. As she would gradually be made aware over the next few hours, Reg had further plans. He knew exactly what he was headed for. He wanted to get to Mexico where he could disappear and never be found again. Specifically, he wanted to cross the border at Matomotos and from there, drive down the coast until they found what it was they were all looking for. Over the past weeks, Reg and Manuel spent countless hours regaling Inez with wonderful stories of Mexico that they had gleaned from their parents. Although Reg and Manuel had each been to Mexico only once when they were very young, Inez hadn't. They told her of mythical beaches with golden sands, of large white palaces and colorful parades. They filled her mind with naïve impressions of a lawless land of plenty, where they could start over and live life as adults. They told her of a life where they could all get married, find jobs and live an easy life independent of their parents. They told her of a freewheeling drive across the country, where no one would get hurt and no one would get caught. Once they got to Matomotos, they planned to release Jean and disappear into the night. As usual with these things, it all seemed so perfect, so simple.

'What Happened'

During the next forty-five minutes or so of driving that ensued, everybody in the car was palpably tense. Then, once they had arrived on the interstate highway and away from the small roads of Hokum, things relaxed slightly. Not being used to the strained intensity of the situation, Manuel asked Reg to put some music on the car radio, which Reg ignored out of prudence. Manuel then made a few failed efforts to make Jean relax, asking her what music she liked and failing to illicit a response, finally reached up to the radio himself, turning on a rap radio station to ghetto-pumping volume. At the first instance, he began to recite the words he knew by heart like an anthem:
"And then you realize that we don't care
All my homies got they gunz up in the air
Yeah, 'cuz we all 'bout puttin' wings on piggies tonight
Yeah, 'cuz we all 'bout puttin' them wrongs back right
'Dem bones, 'dem bones, let 'em roll, let 'em roll
'Dem bones, 'dem bones, be day young, be day ol'
Press pause, cuz, don't let this play on your mind
Press pause, 'cuz...in life, there's...no fast-forward, no rewind

If you see the devil tell 'im I'm well on my way
Cause where I'm goin' ain't worse than where my head first lay"

Leaving the song aside for a moment, he then said to Reg in a cheerful voice, "Look at you, holmes. Why you so tense? It's all goin' to be chill, you see.' And then again in time with the song:

"I got a shotgun and here's my baby's last lullaby,
Swing low, swing low, man, cause you's finnin' to die
Ain't no quakin', and no shakin' no mo'
'Cuz these bones don't shimmy, once they swept off the flo"

He continued the conversation without missing a beat, not acknowledging the distraction, "We gonna live like Latin Kings, for real. Let the party begin, esé. Sorry, Mrs. Hewitt, we have to take you a little bit out of your way, but we ain't gonna hurt you. Maybe you come with us to Mexico. Maybe you like the beach and hang with us a like a little chola girl."

"Mexico!" Jean shouted having never been there and not realizing that the intended destination was so far away. All of the sudden, the trip renewed a much more profound, more menacing aspect for her.

"Oh yeah, forgot to tell you that, teach. You drivin' us to Mexico where we gonna live it up like Vatos Locos. No, like like Los Reyes. Yeah. It's Nation Time and we are the royalty. This is the Minifesto: 'Cowards die many times before their death, Latin Kings never taste death'. But don't worry, we gonna let you go and shit before that if you really want," Manuel added in an increasingly excited tone, his voice jumping about in quick leaps like a boxer prancing around his adversary.

"But, that's hours and hours away, what about my kids? My family? I can't go to Mex..."

Reg interjected forcefully, "Manuel, shut the fuck up." And then in a calmer, almost conciliatory tone, "Listen, Jean...Mrs. Hewitt, that's your name right?"

Jean nodded in assent. Almost about to break into tears again, she could feel the very corners of her eyes stinging, her lips trembling.

"Listen, Jean," he continued, "Mrs. Hewitt. You do everythin' we say and you'll be back at home on Sunday night."

"Sunday!"

"Look, it all depends on how far you can drive in one day. Maybe Saturday. Who knows? You do this one thing and it will all soon be over."

Jean pressed her hand against her forehead, her brows furrowing in utter distress, "Oh, God...God. I can't believe this is happening to me. My husband is going to be so friggin' worried. Why me? Why me?"

Reg replied in a reassuring voice, "Don't worry about that Mrs. Hewitt, we'll take care of that."

Just as Jean was about to respond, she heard a sudden fit of giggling in the back seat. Almost simultaneously, an unmistakably familiar, acrid smell wafted across her nostrils. In the next instant, a disembodied forearm thrust itself between the two front seats. As Jean glanced to her right, she saw suspended between the ring and index fingers of Manuel's extended right hand a large marijuana joint. Lit at the very tip, the red border of flame was already descending in its slow, sultry way down the sides of the Zigzag paper. The image resembled a vampiress pulling a garter and stockings onto her pale, raised leg.

Reg shouted back, "Hey kid, what the fuck you doin'? You can't smoke that shit now, we still on the highway, nigga."

Manuel responded in a stilted voice like one about to sneeze, "Chill kid, no one gonna pull us over. It'll make you relax and shit."

Suddenly a large, bespectacled face emerged between the two seats with a huge, sheepish grin.

"You want some, teach? It will help you relax too. This is good shit and ain't no twigs or seeds, salt and pepper shit. My holmes says it's real G–13 shit, straight up!"

"No. No, I don't," responded Jean in a testy voice.

"Yo, man, get the fuck back in yo' seat," Reg said angrily turning around and pushing Manuel forcefully into the rear seat. "You crazy, ese? We gonna get pulled over. We ain't in Mexico yet. We ain't even close and we got three niggas and a white lady in the car smokin' dope. Open the window and put that shit out."

At that very moment, Inez could be heard giggling in the back seat as she took a deep, full drag of the joint. Manuel cracked the back window and started to remove one of the straps of the pink tank top that Inez was wearing. Inez responded by pushing his hand away, laughing, "Stop! Stop!" as Manuel began to kiss her and rub his nose against her fragile, cantaloupe-scented neck. Jean, driving at just below the speed limit, could observe all of this through her back view mirror. She could also see that they had two large military looking duffle bags with them on the rear seat. Despite everything occurring around her, Jean actually felt more relaxed. She had confidently surmised that she was not only dealing with non-professionals, but with marginally educated adolescents who ultimately (or so she thought) could be reasoned with. She had spent her entire career trying to reason with kids. In fact, it was her profession. The only thing that reminded her of the danger she was in was the hard look in Reg's eyes and the pistol he kept unfailingly trained on her. As the seconds turned into minutes and the minutes into hours, she kept thinking about her children, reminding herself that her abductors were only children themselves and that they would ultimately let her go. She kept thinking about herself at the dinner table with her family on the following day or the day after. She convinced herself that it was only a matter of counting, of addition and subtraction, of miles and minutes and ultimately, if she counted enough, forward or backward, the time between then and now would be bridged and the image she so wanted in her mind would become reality. 1, 2, 3...57 miles, 89 miles, 500 miles. It became a conjuring trick; she just had to hypnotize herself into a trance-like state, to enlist within her consciousness that magical torus of numbers that would unwind exactly where it began. It was the only thing that kept her going, this endless counting. The only other thing was to keep the straight line to Mexico that Reggie demanded.

As the hours wore on, the same pattern continued, Manuel cracking jokes and trying to add levity to the situation in between repeated, unsuccessful attempts to put his hands up Inez's skirt. For the two in the back seat, things were going well. They had gotten their first taste of true freedom. They would smoke pot occasionally and laugh, talking with wonderment about what they would do once they arrived in Mexico. Reg, on the other hand, was the polar opposite. He sat like a merciless bird of prey, keeping his fierce eyes either set on Jean or the road ahead. He held an old foldout map in his lap, which he had asked Manuel to remove from one of the green duffle bags. He rarely said a word except to give direction to Jean or to caution Manuel. Jean tried to speak to Reg on a number of occasions, but he wouldn't say a word to her, neither would he allow her to address Manuel or Inez. Despite her efforts to do so, it became quickly clear she wasn't going to be allowed into the party. Furthermore, it was also blatantly obvious that nothing would make Reg emerge from his depth of grave seriousness. Towards her, he only nodded when he wanted to answer specific questions, otherwise he simply told her to keep her mouth shut, especially if she tried to admonish him in any way. At one point, as the sun began to set over the miles and miles of endless pine trees that lined the road, Jean's phone rang without answer a couple of times only seconds after each other. Reg was adamant that she not pick it up. It was clear that he was slightly unsure of what to do.

"It's probably my husband, you know. He's going to be suspicious. I should have been home by now."

"He can wait," Reg responded curtly. As the last remains of the day faded, it began to turn dark and Jean felt as if she needed to use the bathroom at the

56

next truck stop. When she made this known to Reg, Manuel initially responded,

"Yo man, don't let her do it. She gonna run away or tell somebody what's up. We can just drop her off on the side of the road."

Reg thought this wise and allowed Jean to pull to the side of the road where she was permitted to relieve herself in the bushes while Reg retained possession of her cell phone. By this time it was completely dark. They had been driving for eight hours and Jean was beginning to show signs of fatigue. When she returned to the car from behind the tree at the bottom of the margin that sloped from the shoulder of the road, Reg grabbed her forcefully and pushed her against the car, thrusting her plastic cell phone in her face. "Call your husband now. Tell him you won't be home 'til Sunday."

"How do I tell him that? He will never believe that. He will know something is up."

"I don't know. Tell him somethin'. Tell him one of your friends' mothers died or somethin'. That you're going to stay at her place for the weekend."

"C'mon, he's not that stupid. He won't go for that."

Reg snatched the nape of her blouse, almost tearing it. He then thrust his chin into her face. "I don't know then, you figure it out. You're the teacher. Tell him somethin' he will believe otherwise...otherwise I don't want to have to hurt you."

When he finally let her go, Jean almost fell to the ground out of fear. After a short conversation, it was finally agreed that she would tell her husband that one of the teachers at the school had had a sudden miscarriage and that she had gone to the hospital to accompany her. Furthermore, given that the woman was under great emotional stress and dealing with the situation badly, she had offered to stay at her place until at least Saturday at which point she would call her husband. Once the plan was agreed, she dialed the number for her husband. As the phone rang, Reg told her, "Remember, be calm." She nodded in assent. When her husband picked up the phone, she began speaking in an anxious voice, not knowing what to say, her voice faltering, wanting to spring forth from its pent up coil. As Reg jammed the butt of the gun into her abdomen and pressed her against the car, she became more lucid. She ran her husband through the made-up story, telling him that she had already had an extra pair of clothes in her bag so that she wouldn't need to come home until Sunday if her continued support was absolutely required. She felt uncomfortable lying to him and she wasn't quite sure he had believed her story, but she assured him several times that she would call him the following day. He wasn't completely happy with the arrangement, but seemed to go along with it at present. Furthermore, the babysitter had agreed to stay until at least her husband returned home. She spoke briefly to her children, but Reg wanted her off the phone as soon as possible. Once she hung up, she had another moment of weakness, reflecting back on the disappointed voices of her children. Reg, seeing her discomfiture, immediately asked in a nervous voice,

"You think he went for it?"

"I don't know. Maybe. Yes, I think so."

For now, that was enough. After the others had relieved themselves, they immediately got back into the car. Everybody was slightly hungry and the sandwiches and potato chips they had packed and subsequently consumed were wearing off. The first thing Reg did was to force Jean to pull over into the next town as he wanted to withdraw as much money as possible before any suspicions were raised. The sky was incredibly dark and with few streetlights or any other ambient light, the stars shone brightly. The first town they came to was pitifully small and seemingly empty. They drove around the entire city center twice, not able to locate a single ATM. Giving up, they drove to another equally small town that was fortunately in possession of the needed vendor. He forced Jean to withdraw two hundred and fifty dollars of cash, not wanting any alarm bells to be raised by the bank. Reg knew instantly that they had to withdraw as much cash as possible over the next few hours as he wanted to delay the authorities figuring out that they were headed to Mexico until as late as possible. The next port of call was the gas station. When they arrived at a suitably empty one, Reg took some of the money to pay for the gas at the inside register, while Inez pumped and Manuel kept an eye on Jean. While he was gone, a Hispanic family in a green van pulled up beside their car. A little girl waved from the back seat window, catching Jean's attention. The girl made a number of funny faces at Jean, while Jean smiled, returning the favor by sticking out her tongue and blowing kisses. When Jean then tried to signal the girl through sign language to get her mother's attention, Reg suddenly jumped back in the car and grabbed her roughly, snarling between his teeth, "Never do that again or I will blow your fuckin' brains out, I swear I will." Frightened, she agreed anxiously as Reg turned viciously on Inez and Manuel,

"And what the fuck you two dumb shits doin'? You supposed to be watchin' her. Do I gotta doing everythin' myself around this place?"

Manuel protested, "Hey man, I wuz watchin' her, I swear. What the fuck is up?"

"Shhhh. Lower your voice and don't make a scene. You gotta watch her, right. At all times. She wuz tryin' to get that woman's attention over there in the van. This is real shit, man. Wake up and stop gettin' high all the time."

"Sorry kid, maybe you jus' gettin' a little loco in the head. A little crazy."

"I ain't the one goin' crazy and I ain't the one goin' to jail over your dumb ass so just listen to what the fuck I say."

"OK, holmes. Just chill out. Christ."

After that, for the next forty-five minutes, the drive in the car was completely silent. Hours before, unbeknownst to Reg, Manuel had persuaded Inez to split a marijuana laced 'space cake' from which point, she hadn't done much but stare mutely out of the car window. It was obvious that Inez was already beginning to have some misgivings and the marijuana was making her even more anxious. She started to worry, telling Manuel she was afraid and concerned that although her foster parents probably wouldn't be overly bothered about her disappearance, she couldn't be sure. This led by turns into flat out paranoia about the police, manhunts and detectives chasing them.

Finally, realizing something was up, Reg turned to Manuel as the offending culprit.

"What the fuck did you give her, man?" Reg demanded.

"Just weed, man. I promise," Manuel responded, pleadingly.

Reg told Inez to quiet down and to drink some of the tequila they had stored in the large duffle bags. After a couple of swigs, Inez passed out and slept for the next twenty minutes. The first crisis averted, the next thing they needed to do was find a suitably unpopulated motel in a suitably unpopulated town. Mexico would only be another five or six hours distant. Although there had been little traffic on the way and they had made good time, Reg had hoped they would make it far enough on the first day so that they could complete the rest of the drive to Mexico by late the following morning. He knew it was critical that they made the fifteen hour drive to the border before any possible news of their disappearance got out. As best they could, all of them had managed excuses to keep their parents unsuspicious of a single night's absence.

Without too much difficulty, they found a small motel on the very edges of a small town. It was evidently run by a Punjabi family, which had decorated the front windows with a number of religious symbols. Outside of the motel was a typical motel sign, lit in yellow with red cursive lettering, "Starlight Inn". On a small hand-painted sign below, the word "Vacancy" was written in blue, bold letters. Although Reg knew these places to be very anonymous, he did not want to risk suspicion by attempting to check into the motel himself and he certainly couldn't trust Jean to do it alone. So after going through the usual explanations of how she was to behave and what she was to say, he walked with her into the small, drab lobby that contained little else beside a wood paneled wall with a very large pane of protective glass that served as a reception desk. As she walked to the window, Jean could feel Reg's hand in the small of her back and the cold muzzle of the gun as it rested roughly against the soft material of her skirt. In the back of her head, she hoped that whoever ended up attending the desk would be made suspicious enough by the awkward scene of a nervous white woman being escorted to the desk by a fifteen-year-old Hispanic boy to call the police. The two certainly made a pair as they walked jauntily forward as if headed toward their own beheading, he with his arm extended behind her in what almost resembled a caress of affection, while she took small forced steps, much like a halting bride or a pregnant woman afraid to fall over. Her hopes for a suspicious receptionist were quickly dashed as the middle-aged Punjabi man with perfectly coiffed, jet black hair, gold spectacles and a dark moustache, addressed them sheepishly without so much as looking up from the small grey box of his portable television set. Through the plexiglass window, she heard his otherwise uninterested voice, fill with a hint of frustration as he hit the side of the television. "Double or single," was all he said in a heavy Punjabi accent. Reg replied in a confident voice, "We want a double...two double beds. Any rooms with a kitchen?"

The man replied in an almost programmed voice, the intonations on all the wrong syllables, "Yeah, we've got one in the back. It'll be more. Seventy-five dollars for the night, checkout at twelve."

With a hint of desperation, Jean tried to say something in a last ditch attempt to make the profoundly uninterested man at least look up at them, "Will the beds be big enough for two big people like us?"

To her great dismay, he replied without looking up, "Yeah, they'll be fine, mam. If not, we can bring in an extra cot."

The entire exchange occurred without the intensely focused attendant looking up so much as once from his sporadically detuned cricket match. The only time the man even moved his eyes from the TV screen was to count the money and to unhook the keys from the wooden board behind him. He then took the set of keys and shoved them through the empty lunette under the window, immediately re-immersing himself into the sports event he was so ardently watching. His only words were, "Room 47, past the parking lot, first floor on the left hand side."

In frustration, she gave out testily, "So much for service with a smile."

Without looking up, the dark man gave a large sheepish grin, flicked his eyebrows up and down, moving his head side to side, summarily returning to his program with his usual idolatry. Reg shoved the gun sharply into her back.

"OK, never mind..." she said with a defeated tone.

The couple walked back to the car as Reg shoved the gun back into the front of his pants. Afterward, the four weary travelers removed their few possessions from the truck, which consisted solely of the groceries they had purchased at the truck stop and the two green duffle bags. They walked in silence through an interior parking lot to the back of the motel, which was split into two halves and looked like a wooden version of a double layered chocolate cake, each sagging layer separated by a sickly, yellow fringe, whose color was also mirrored on the roof of the building. All of the rooms faced inward and on the second floor the wood paneled entryways were fenced in by a black, metal balustrade that in places was replaced by sections of a cyclone fence.

Having woken up and subsequently found herself in the dull shabbiness of the motel, the situation with Inez began to deteriorate further and she quickly fell to sobbing miserably. Both Manuel and Reg tried to calm her down, finally convincing her to drink some more of the tequila, which they kept drip feeding her until she began to feel sick and as result, consented to take a walk under the stars with Manuel. When the two returned, Inez was again in high spirits and even offered to cook everyone some fajitas. At the subsequent dinner, the mood between the three conspirators was high, with Reg even deigning to submit himself to the atmosphere of conviviality by telling a few humorous stories about Manuel and enjoying a copious amount of tequila, which he also offered to Jean. Although she was tired, she knew she wouldn't be able to sleep and needed a release from all the tension she had built up over the day. Tiredly, she accepted the offer and even agreed to smoke some of the marijuana after the simple dinner of fajitas, salsa and chips. Manuel and Inez were becoming progressively more affectionate with one another until they began kissing with the awkward gusto of teenagers. Sensing the discomfort on Jean's behalf, Reg suggested the two go into the adjacent room, which they did. Within five minutes, the soft moans of foreplay began to emerge from behind the closed door of the bedroom. Reg sat there uncomfortably staring and the Colt on the aluminum table, while Jean looked around the room trying to find a place to focus. A lone fly hazarded the silence, buzzing in the corner of the tiny kitchenette.

At that moment, Jean made the first of what would be her many attempts to connect with Reggie that night. The initial effort was prematurely aborted by a climax in the next room, which caused an uncomfortable smile on both their faces, the first moment of shared levity they had enjoyed the entire trip. After a brief moment of silence, she continued her bid at conversation, first trying to convince him not to go ahead with his plan; that she would promise to forget the entire thing if he merely agreed to turn around and go back in the morning. She tried to persuade him that what he was doing was crazy, that he was throwing away his future and that life in Mexico wasn't everything he thought it would be. In contrast to her previous efforts, he wasn't violent or insulting toward her. He just seemed glum and didn't say much, staring at the small fold-out dinner table, decorated with used paper plates and plastic cups. He toyed idly with the corner of a torn particolored napkin. Realizing this wasn't working, she tried a different tack and began to ask about his family and whether he had trouble at home or had experienced abuse, that she could provide him with help or access to counseling. This turned out to be exactly the wrong approach, because before she had finished her sentence, Reggie sprung out of his chair like a cornered copperhead and drove her violently against the wall, pinning her there with his hand locked around her throat. The force of the impact was so hard that both Manuel and Inez emerged from the bedroom to discover what was going on. They were wearing only their bed sheets. Reggie quickly ordered them back in the room, which they did and closed the door.

At this point, he scolded Jean with a rage in his eyes that she had never witnessed in all her life. His eyes were enflamed, leaving no trace of the sullen boy who had inhabited them just seconds before. His pupils dissolved, became even darker and vacuous like black marbles. Their dismal wattage sank into her like hot coals, burning through her skin. "Listen, you little white bitch. What the fuck you know about me? About where I live? About my family? You know nothin' and it ain't your business either, you dumb bitch. You hear me? Cuz you a teacher you think you know me? Cuz you white you think you can come fix my problems like I'm some little nigga boy? I swear I will cut your heart out if you say any shit about my family again."

At this point, Jean, for the first time since her abduction, broke down and cried. Through her warm, stinging tears, she looked up into his fierce eyes and in an instant the rage disappeared and was replaced by a genuine tenderness, a faint look of one wanting to cry, but not being able to. It was something she hadn't witnessed within the short span she had known this boy and it touched her. It was that look, she would later say, that began to melt her defenses. Perhaps it was the first time he had ever made anyone cry without a single blow. He let her go and put her gently back in one of the aluminum chairs, at which point she breathed out a soft, "Why me? Why me?" between sobs as she buried her now swollen face in her hands.

Reg looked down towards his feet and responded softly with a simple and logical assessment, "You... you were the only one we knew would be in the parking lot around that time on a Friday. Everyone else was at the student assembly and you just seemed like you wouldn't be much trouble, like a nice lady."

Jean nodded her head at this simple statement of fact and afterward took a large swig of the tequila bottle. Reg lit up another joint and offered her the first puffs, which she accepted. After she had calmed down and collected herself, they spoke for a number of hours about this and that. She told him about her family, growing up and even began talking about her experiences with drugs, music and the beach. After some of the marijuana had relaxed him, he dropped his defenses and even consented to tell her a little bit about his life, his two "prison" tattoos that had been given to him by his uncle (of which he was extremely proud). He told her about how he enjoyed the summer months hunting foxes and setting aflame stray cats in the deep forests surrounding Hokum. She didn't seem alarmed by anything. She just listened and for a brief moment they seemed to connect, passing entire minutes in silence, glancing curiously at each other's eyes that were so brimful of memory that they could only smile longingly into space. They talked until they both were on the verge of falling asleep. The night ended with Reg finally having to wake her out of an accidental slumber. He escorted her into the bedroom, where Manuel and Inez were already asleep. While Manuel and Inez occupied one of the beds, Reg offered Jean the remaining one. He would then sleep on the floor with the gun tucked under his arm. Just before lying down and feeling slightly bad about it, he insisted in handcuffing one of Jean's hands to the bedpost. He was in the end a very cautious boy.

The next morning, they woke up slightly past eight o'clock and Reg, disturbed by the lateness of the hour, wanted to start off immediately. They all felt slightly hung over and each experienced some queasiness throughout the morning. The second day of driving was quite different than the first. Reggie was more nervous, more tense. He had begun to wonder if the news channels would by now have picked up on their disappearance, particularly of Jean, given her race and position of authority. Ultimately, he wasn't convinced that the phone call to her husband had worked, neither could be sure whether the parents of his accomplices hadn't also raised the alarm. All he was certain of was that his own hadn't. Upon entering the nearby town, the first thing he did was to ask Jean to withdraw another three hundred dollars, which came close to emptying her bank account. He then asked Jean to call her husband again, which she did, but was only able to leave a message, instructing him that she would probably need to stay another night at her nonexistent friend's house and that she would call him later that evening. They drove mostly in silence, avoiding the large towns, a trick Reggie had seen in the movies. They passed Alice, Kingsville, Raymondville, Harlingen. The hours and hours of pine trees that had dominated the monotonous terrain over the previous day eventually gave way to broad, grassy vistas that ultimately gave out onto the sea, though nobody seemed to care enough to comment on the scenery.

'The Swerve'

Almost without event, they finally arrived at the brink of Matamoros in the border zone between Mexico and the United States. Once there, they had to wait in a long line of cars trying to cross into Mexico. Upon waking, Inez seemed positively frightened, almost catatonic after having fallen asleep for the last two hours with Manuel resting his head against her own in a sympathetic slumber. When they finally awoke the car had been in one of the lines for over twenty minutes. Reg notified them of where they were and the two breathed in deeply. They then sat back and held each other nervously, staring out at the cars that moved on either side of them. As they came closer and closer to the border check, everyone in the car became increasingly anxious, especially Reggie, who for the first time, resembled the boy he was. He had placed the gun under his seat and as the minutes passed, he looked younger, smaller, frailer. It was obvious that he hadn't completely thought out this part of the trip and had as a result, left himself utterly at Jean's mercy. He would now need to rely on her generous complicity to pass through border control. Everyone in the car realized this, yet no one spoke, resigned as they were to their fate as the cars crept gently forward, inch by inch. When they had come to the point where they were the third car away from being checked, Reg was almost trembling, sick with anxiety. Jean looked over at his doleful figure as it sank into the seat and for the first time on the trip she felt complete confidence. In fact, over the last few hours of driving, she had ceased to count and a number of thoughts had entered her head. At one point, she had even considered just helping them across the border and afterwards turning straight back, giving the excuse she had been abducted and subsequently let go. She had thought about a number of things, pondering them over and over again and they had left her nowhere, undecided, incomplete. Then she took one final, close look at Reg and in that instant, what had confused and darkened her mind for the last five hours became instantly clear. She then put her hand on his leg, squeezing it gently and in that way, convinced him that they would get through this one final hurdle together. She gave him a quick, reassuring smile and continued to look forward, one hand on the steering wheel, the other on his leg. It twitched with nervousness. She had no idea what she was doing and he sat there wide-eyed, opened-mouthed and shocked as she was. That was the beginning of their relationship though at the time she hadn't quite worked out exactly what kind of relationship it was. Even the vague, silly notion of Stockholm syndrome had yet to invade her as of yet uncritical brain. Though some strange suggestion of a change did peek through, successfully lighting the wick of an old memory – some dog-eared book of poetry by Lucretius she had once been forced to memorize and with it something else she felt forced to forget: wet autumn leaves pasted on a cracked windshield, the deafening ache of her unexpected entry into womanhood, then the afterward, the cold trembling through which she could manage nothing else but to scribble a passage on her hot, tearstained palm in what she thought to be indelible ink, 'to err is to be human, to swerve is to be a woman'. Now, she only wanted to comfort him like the child he ultimately was.

As the car inched forward, she began to sing a song she had often heard her father sing when he drove the family on their many trips throughout the country. She had a soft, mellifluous voice laden with a warm Southern accent that poured over him like maple syrup. She looked straight ahead with the calmest of faces, the sun irradiating her blonde hair, her sapphire eyes sparkling,

"All the boys 'round Brownsville..."

At that moment, for the first time in his life, Reggie, sitting in the passenger seat with a revolver tucked under his seat, had found love,

"Could it be..."

"Could it be..."

"...a faded rose..."

They were next. There was no turning back. She had no passport with her. Once she crossed into Mexico, it would be harder to get back. She would later say of the experience, "I don't know what it was in me, but at that moment I forgot everything: my husband, my kids. It's hard to fathom, but for that brief moment, Reggie became everything for me. He was someone almost thirty years my junior, who I didn't even know, yet he needed me and I needed him. He had something within him, something mysterious. I don't know what it was, a quiet intensity, an inner strength that was magnetic. From that point, I would have followed him to the ends of the earth."

When they finally pulled up to the customs checkpoint, the lantern jawed border guard gave them a close stare through his dark, gold-rimmed glasses.

"Hello, mam, where you headed today?"

"Just to Montonos for a couple of days," Jean replied with a gentle smile on her face.

"Yep, you and everybody else. How old are these kids here?"

"All sixteen, sir," Reggie said with complete confidence.

"Can I see some ID, mam?"

"Sure thing."

At this point, Jean went through her purse to find her ID while the border guard looked into the back seat of the truck.

"Are those two alright there? They look at little bit under the weather."

Manuel and Inez simply nodded their heads in unison and Jean replied, "Yes, they are brother and sister, they get car sick."

"How these kids related to you, mam? They look a bit old to be your kids, sweetie."

"Oh, what a charmer you are," she said handing him her ID as all four of the passengers looked at him with ridiculous, Brady Bunch type smiles. "Anyway, two in the back are mine and this little trouble-maker up here is their friend," she said ruffling Reggie's hair.

The guard handed back her ID. "Alright, mam, drive on through. You have a nice a Cinco de Mayo now."

That was it and they were through. Everyone in the car breathed a deep sigh of relief and gave out a slight cheer. Reggie looked questioningly into Jean's eyes, wondering all the time why she had done it. She simply replied in her teacher like tone, "Look, I may not agree with what you're doing, but I'll help you across the border and I turn back tomorrow. After all, I've never been to Mexico and I've always wanted to see Cinco de Mayo."

Reg was eternally grateful.

From this point, the trip took on a completely different character. Excited by their success and feeling home free, the mood rose dramatically. Everything was going exceptionally well. Even leaving Matamoros should have been difficult given their lack of any official documents or status, but they managed it with surprising ease, being waved through at crowded checkpoints with a simple flash of a driver's license, not knowing what to expect. They drove down the highway, drawn to the brisk warm air of the beaches and the charming pueblos that dotted the hillsides. South of Matamoros, the terrain turned very arid and the roads were in surprisingly good condition. Jean was unable to read Spanish and relied on the three semi-native speakers to translate everything. On the way toward a still unknown destination, they managed to exchange a fair amount of money and pick up some sunglasses for Jean. It was starting to get dark and in the couple of hours of daylight they had left they drove on down the Tamaulipas coast until they could find a small, but suitably picturesque town. Jean called her husband again and quickly spoke to her children, assuring them that she would be home the next day thinking she could always manufacture another excuse if she needed more time. Just before the light failed, they found what they were looking for and managed to sleep in a picturesque, white-washed beach town at the foot of a large hill that descended down to the coast.

The next morning, they awoke to the noise of a loud scream and a peal of laughter outside their room. It was Cinco de Mayo and a group of young children in the dusty yard bordering their room were already at work attempting to knock down a piñata with an old broomstick. The weary travelers, feeling a renewed vitality, spent the day drinking tequila, watching the colorful parades of women decked out in their vibrant dresses as they swirled like dervishes. They stopped to listen to the mariachi bands, the bright cacophony of the maracas, the sudden, surprise snap of firecrackers thrown at their feet by small giggling boys dressed in pretty charros. For them, the uninitiated, it all became a polychromatic whirl of colors and sounds. The pageants of little girls in heavy makeup, dressed up like little women, the glorious bouquets of flowers everywhere, it was everything they had dreamed about and more. Amidst the anonymous crowds of the festival, carried away by the events and wanting to satisfy her natural curiosity about everything, Jean even dared to hold Reg's hand for minutes at a time, only breaking away when she saw a white face in the crowd. At one point when she had wandered off by herself, a slim, old man dressed in a sombrero and a colorful striped serape approached her cautiously. As he came closer, she could more clearly make out the many lines of his leathery, tanned skin, his intense black eyes and his dark, greying moustache. As he brushed against her, he suddenly grasped her by the arm with two fingers of his right hand. She hadn't even seen his rough bird's claw, which emerged invisibly from the side of his dirty serape. At first she was frightened, but before she could pull herself away, he quickly whispered in her ear, "Peyote. Peyote. *Mesculine.* You like?" At first she was disoriented, not knowing why this smallish, older man had approached her. She initially shook her head, breaking free from his weak grasp as he said, "It's OK. It's OK. No problems. No problems. I show you. I show you." From his pocket, in the russet palm of his dusty hand he produced a cluster of brownish-green objects that resembled miniature, rotted tomatoes.

Jean, slightly curious said, "Oh. What do you do with that?"

He made a motion with his free hand of putting an invisible item in between his fingers and putting it twice in quick jerks toward his mouth as if he were eating. "Eat. Eat. They very good. I pick myself. Very good."

Intrigued, Jean spoke in exaggerated tones as if speaking to a child, "How much? How much dinero?" she almost had to shout to be heard amidst the loud sounds that surrounding them.

He replied, "Come with me." He drew her to a small side alley next to a shop.

He made an indication for three with his fingers and she repeated "Three? Three hundred pesos?" He nodded his head. "Is this enough for one person?" At that moment, Reg came up behind her asking her if she was alright. The older man moved away, turning his back to walk away. She said, "Wait, sir" then turning to Reg, she said, "He was trying to sell me some peyote. What's that? Is it good to eat? I don't..."

"Peyote!" Reg responded with enthusiasm, "Wicked!" At this point, Reg began speaking to the old man in Spanish, even at one point putting his hand on the man's shoulder. After a long exchange, Reg instructed her to give the man eight hundred pesos, which she did. The man then left for what seemed a very long time in which Reggie explained to her what Peyote was and she became even more intrigued. However, the man was gone for such a long period, she worried as to whether he would return at all. Reg assured her that he would and when he did, he simply handed them a large paper bag and walked on without saying a word.

After stopping at the hotel to consume the peyote, the four spent all day at the beach enjoying the hallucinations, drinking the weakish beer they had purchased from the shop. It was a wonderful day, probably the best that any of them had experienced in a long, long time, if ever. The initial feeling of nausea the peyote induced in Jean's stomach, gave way almost immediately to a sense of euphoria, even giddiness. As she would describe it later, she felt more uninhibited than usual, felt more like herself, particularly when she was young, adventurous, and most of all, free. Every color in the impressive panoply that confronted her painted her soul with a new mood, a new climate, a new music to which she gave herself away. In her mind there was a constant rhythm, a forgotten tempo about things, *tra la la, tra la la,* a waltz, yes, a waltz to which memories, in odd couplings, danced with the new things around her, a fresher set of desires which were aflutter with the pale patina of joy. Her body was the pitcher from which the past was poured and memories of the flesh, the lips, the breasts, the vagina, mixed in a drowsy concoction with images of the present. One minute Reggie was there, the next minute he wasn't, then there was the Pirate, Tom, the Viking, Corey, even the freckled brunette, Shannon, the one and only, Impaler of the Heart. All suggestions, all implied sensations. Where had they come from? Where had they gone? After that dark initiation, they were only united by the lasting sensation of touch, daisy chained by the memory of a deep arousal, raised again without grief from the mind's pitiful, trembling sail of dendrites, axons, cones and rods that make a man or a woman, that make each of them, a man, a woman, stand there, waiting for the next breeze to blow each one away, across a shuttering universe in a million fractured pieces, never to be made whole again.

Later that night, once the drugs had somewhat worn off, Jean and Reg went walking along the beach, chatting about various things, not having any specific destination in mind. At one point, Jean in her natural, offhand manner, had indelicately asked him whether or not he had ever been with a woman, half assuming that he had and thus believing the question to be innocent and rather matter of course given that she now saw him as her spiritual contemporary. However, Reg, swaddled in his still adolescent machismo, had in fact taken some offense, not to the question itself, but rather to the implication that he had not. Jean, tried her best to sooth the awkward situation, attempting by several clumsy appeals to change the subject, however she couldn't help but notice that Reg was struggling within himself with some deep humiliation – clearly he had not been with a woman. Jean feared the day had now been ruined as Reg began to create some physical distance between himself and her, walking at times ahead and other times behind, kicking the sand as he offered monosyllabic answers of wan disinterest to her now random attempts at conversation. At some point, Reg became very silent, so silent that Jean began to think something was wrong with him and he looked increasingly sullen. Suddenly, he stopped. He gave her a long, slow look and then with the full force of his muscled body, he grabbed her toward him and gave her a harsh, awkward kiss with his sun-chapped lips. It was all she had wanted. She completely surrendered herself to him, body and soul. Then that night, Jean and Reggie slept with each other for the first time between a pair of anonymous sand dunes, the waves roaring in her ears as in the romance novels she had often read. As the rockets in their red glare went off in the night sky, she could see the colorful bursts as he lay on top of her, gently throbbing. It all seemed to happen in slow motion. She purred, reaching ecstasy. At last, they were making their own movie.

Even in the immediacy of that passionate moment, the cheap symbolism of the whole affair couldn't escape her. Like many, she wrongly assumed that Cinco de Mayo was Mexico's independence day and in consequence, she then reflected on her own independence, her own freedom. For the first time in her life, she thought she had finally found someone who really needed her vitally, needed her not just as a mother or as a wife, but as a woman. Tomorrow, next week, was a long way away, she could always return to where she had come from. For once, she wanted to live in the moment, to recapture what it was to be a woman, knowing that she could fall out of the fantasy at any point back to earth. She had become what to her Mexico represented, a country of bandits, a lawless place and while she had herself turned to a form of banditry at least as interpreted by every more of the God-fearing United States, here she thought like many others, that there were only the facile laws of the heart to heed and what her heart had told her, what Reg's heart had told him, was that what they were doing was right, not wrong. There were no rules or abstract laws to obey. They were bandits. They made their own rules, obeyed their own laws. Despite her breaking a number of social conventions across race, age, gender, she would later say of the actual act of sex, "I didn't think twice about it. I didn't see him as a fifteen-year-old boy. I mean, he had to grow up much faster than anyone I knew and he had seen much more in his life than his years should have allowed. I saw a man in front of me, not a boy. He was much more of a man than any of the men I had ever had in my life and when he told me of some of the experiences he had as a kid, we could connect on so many levels because although I never experienced anything to the extent he had when he grew up, I could understand. I was taken advantage of too as a child. No one was taking any advantage of anyone here."

The day after the festival shared a similar arc with all four basking in the air of new romance. It was clear Manuel and Inez weren't completely comfortable with the new affair, but they didn't say anything and were polite. After a morning spent at the beach, they escaped the midday heat to enter a liquor store in a nearby town. Jean was now dressed more casually, wearing a pair of dark Wayfarer knockoffs and a light blue set of flip-flops. While moving through the aisles with her cart, an elderly tourist had heard Jean speaking to Reg and Manuel as they proceeded to stuff the cart full with all kinds of alcohol. The flinty tourist, an American woman who had just come off a tour bus, tapped Jean on the shoulder and fixed her with a look of cold disapproval. As she gripped the golden crucifix she wore so dearly around her neck, she admitted that she couldn't help but overhear Jean's conversation with "the two little boys" concerning which type of alcohol they wanted to buy. She then concluded in a huffy tone of voice, tilting her head to one side for effect, "But, those are just kids there. Why are you lettin' them pick out all that alcohol? That ain't right." At present, Jean herself had an armful of vodka and was in the process of pulling one more bottle from the shelf.

Not willing to be browbeaten, she turned straight to the woman and said in her most curt Southern twang, "It's for school; we're on a field trip." The woman just gasped and walked away as quickly as possible.

After another day in the town, Jean and Reg came to the conclusion that it was best to keep driving onward as Jean wasn't quite ready to go back. Although she never said it out loud, she had no intention of returning to the US in the immediate future. She thought she could string it out another few days and then return clandestinely during summer break, which was only a few weeks away. However, the farther they drove, the more unwilling she was to go back. She made a concerted effort not to think about her children fearing that it would break the illusion she had embraced so tightly. She reminded herself that they were in good hands and that she would no doubt see them soon. Over the next few days, they drove further south past the Tropic of Cancer under the vague assumption that the farther south they went, the further they were from a dark past that was no doubt extending its long fingers toward them. If they wanted to escape, they had to drive further into the light. Jean had ceased to call her husband and left her phone off, finally calling him from her cell two days later, merely telling him that she loved him and that she would return in a couple of weeks once she got things in her head sorted out. He was bewildered and for the first time in her life with him, she saw him as being completely helpless. He told her that three children had also gone missing from her school and that a number of people were looking for her. The children were wondering when she was coming home and he wanted to know more than anything how she was and where she was. She simply said, "Missouri" and hung up the phone, not knowing why she mentioned that name, a state she had no connection to and had never visited. As she looked at the gravel road before her, dotted with tumbleweed, cacti, barren earth, she now feared she could never go back, that she had somehow rendered herself temporarily, perhaps permanently unworthy of her husband or even her children. It hurt her inside, but she convinced herself that ultimately her journey would bring her back to herself and thus she could one day, she hoped, look them again in the eye without regret or shame. Though it had only been a few days, she had missed them terribly, but then a change occurred inside her and she began to think about her children, more or less as mere abstractions, the way one thought about the impoverished, gruel-eating children of Africa, the untouchables who scurried through India's waste dumps, all worthy of pity, but simply too remote, too distant to feel the warmth of their desperation. No doubt, she hated the way her mind began to work. In essence, she felt a terrible guilt, a guilt whose only basis was her not feeling quite guilty enough. She truly wondered what was happening to her and she became afraid, afraid of who she would eventually become. She never considered herself a particularly good mother, but not one who would abandon her own children even if she hadn't wanted them in the first place. Maybe they were truly better off this way. Indeed, the further she pushed onward, the further she felt she needed to push herself away. It was a rare force of nature that behaved like an inverse type of gravity, a fundamentally negative energy. Ultimately, she had to face the fact that if she wasn't worthy of their love, perhaps she wasn't worthy of anyone's. She had always felt that way and now reasoned that she could only ever begin to feel worthy of love from someone who had themselves been unloved in equal measure. Hers was indeed a bastard love, an unwanted love.

Once, when they were in a town, which had only two unnamed streets, they stayed the night in a small nunnery. The old nuns, tiny women dressed in blue, black and grey habits, were very welcoming and almost without speaking made sure their small rooms were comfortable, asking no questions and implied only a small donation was necessary of the group. After the previous days of revelry, the quiet, contemplative mood was a relief to all. It felt like a sanctuary of sorts. As they walked through the exotic desert gardens, exploring the expansive grounds, which included various types of strange cacti and a number of sun-dizzy lizards that scurried from stone to stone, Inez happened to wander down a small set of stairs that sat at the foot of an old wooden door. The well-used portal led to a hidden basement that rested surreptitiously under one of the small chapels of the little church. Pushing open the old door, she walked into a dark, musty emptiness that she instantly felt was not an emptiness at all. After a few more panicked seconds she found a drawstring that fell from the ceiling. When she did finally pull the cord, which was connected to a single sixty watt, all at once, a dull light irradiated the room and she was suddenly confronted by a crowd of skeletons surrounding her on all sides. They had been hung from the ceiling rafters and at first glance appeared quite lifelike, some wearing sombreros, others wearing brightly colored dresses. In an instant, they seemed to be crowding in on her, gathering closer and closer, penetrating through her soul out of the emptiness of their dark eye sockets. She screamed. The rest of the party, not being far away, ran to her aid and found her there amidst the skeletons, crying and terrified. Manuel instinctively came to her trembling, wiry frame, hugging her and trying to calm her but it was of little use. Jean, not understanding the significance of the skeletons, queried Reg who explained to her that they were decorations for the Dia De Muertos celebrations, which happened in November. She felt a slight shiver, but put it out of mind. Despite Manuel's many efforts to calm Inez, it was obvious that this had been the final straw. For the previous two days she had again retreated into her shell, becoming increasingly worried about the trouble she would have caused back home and the people who were no doubt searching for her, wondering if she was alive. She could no longer bear living as a fugitive and was wracked by an immense sense of guilt. It was clear she wasn't going to make it in Mexico. Over time, Manuel and her had begun to develop an increasingly deep relationship and were often seen off to the side by themselves: him hugging her, reassuring her as she cried onto his shoulder. Finally, less than twenty hours later, in a small town near Tampico, it was agreed that the two groups would part ways. Manuel and Inez would attempt to sneak back into the US, using a portion of the money they had taken from Jean, while Jean and Reg would continue on their own way. It was also around this time that Jean had finally managed to exchange her much abused, green Cherokee for a worn out '78 Lincoln Continental town car. It was jet black and in many ways resembled a hearse, except for the puce interior. The exchange was made with one ecstatic Mexican farmer whose barn they'd inhabited the previous night. It had dawned on Jean that to continue to drive around in the Cherokee was far too dangerous.

Before they had left Hokum, as a last resort, Manuel had taken the number of a Mexican relative he had a distant connection with. After a great deal of back and forth, it was agreed over the phone that the relation knew some people who could help them to return into Matamonos. With their fake IDs, it was hoped they could simply stroll back into the US accompanied by an adult, eventually returning to Hokum via Greyhound bus. The plan settled, Jean and Reggie agreed to drive Inez back to the bus station in Tampico. After a couple of sullen goodbyes and Manuel's pleading for Reg to return home with him, Jean and Reg took their leave. Once they had safely left the environs of Tampico and entered the barren desolation of a small southbound road, Jean let Reggie drive the beat-up old boneshaker. It was the first time he had ever driven a real car. Just as he had done in the video games he favored, he swerved left and right across the florid road in wide sweeps, turning the entire street into an ochre dust cloud. He was laughing out loud, seeming to have more fun than he had ever had during his short life. He pressed the accelerator and she, as was her wont, squeezed the inside of his leg. It twitched in ecstasy.

However, things quickly began to sour for the pair over the next two weeks. The money was beginning to run out and in some cases they had to resort to shoplifting which both Reg and Jean had some prior experience with. They tried to get odd jobs on farms or at resorts but these were either nonexistent or paid paltry amounts of money for what would have been hard labor. As the days went past, Jean's role became more prominent and the couple's actions bolder. Over the following six weeks, they made their first attempt to rob a convenient store at gunpoint. The process was relatively easy and the take small, but it emboldened them to try another. The first successful attempts led to similar efforts across the area as they began preying on minute out of the way towns, operating under the mantle of darkness; however, these petty robberies simply didn't bring in enough money to justify the risk, despite the fact that they assumed no one would suspect a white woman and a fifteen-year-old boy of carrying out a slew of petty robberies in rural Mexico. Furthermore, they needed gas, food and enough alcohol and peyote to keep them entertained. At the height of their daring, they even made a failed attempt to rob a small pawnshop, which represented the first time they were ever retaliated against. Jean, regardless of almost being shot was undeterred. The little girl from the South was living out her Bonnie and Clyde fantasy and the excitement only drove her onward despite Reg's protests.

Finally, once they understood that the cops were looking for them, they realized it wasn't safe anymore. It wasn't fun. They had to find some way to get back into the US, but it certainly wouldn't be easy. Police stations had picked up the story weeks ago. Furthermore, after Inez and Manuel were apprehended at the border, they were questioned extensively. The authorities knew Jean and Reg were still in Mexico and pictures were posted on local news stations, which at that time weren't quite clear themselves on the point of who had actually adducted whom. Fortunately for them, the US national news stations hadn't yet picked it up as the authorities in Hokum did their best to smother the story. After spending a night sleeping in the car in the desert chill of a town on the outskirts of Tantoyuca, Jean and Reg finally decided to turn around. The party was over. Realizing that it would be too dangerous to get back into Matanomos and across the border in the way Manuel and Inez had attempted, it was decided they needed to find someone who could take them across the border illegally. Better to suffer justice in America than potentially suffer injustice inside a Mexican prison, they reasoned. After a number of inquiries which were significantly hamstrung by the mere fact that Jean was white, American and frequently suspected of being an undercover federal agent, they finally found someone who agreed to take them on the arduous nighttime border crossing. Here they were marginally successful, managing to actually enter the United States, but not by much, as their party was soon caught by a border police helicopter as they climbed out of a river basin. A chase into the desert ensued and here we find ourselves, where we began with Reg, lost in the trackless country, carrying his faithful .38 Colt, enjoyed his last bolt of freedom.

At this point, you may fairly ask, how I came to know this story so intimately. Am I just another investigative reporter, bringing some unfortunate person's tragedy to life in the hopes of feeding the public's insatiable curiosity? Is this my attempt to gain journalistic plaudits for tackling a difficult, taboo subject within the media's gaze? No, it is because I am Jean Hewitt and this is my story; one that I have so desperately wanted to tell for so long. Universally condemned at numerous points as a pervert, a cradle robber, a thief, a rapist; all labels which fit to some degree, I have never – despite accepting the public's infamy and even their insults – been allowed to tell my side of the story, the way I wanted to tell it. So, I leave it here for you, my faceless audience and ultimately my panel of judges, I leave it here for you to judge my actions according to what your own conscience tells you. And lest you be worried, I can assure you that I am already paying a high price for any wrongs that I have committed. However, if you can spare me any benefit of the doubt, I ask but one thing, that you judge the merits of my case not based on mere physical evidence, which can certainly be found in the city's public records, but on the evidence of the heart, which I have laid here before you. Ultimately, I am not seeking redemption or even forgiveness in writing down my side of the story, neither is this a plea for understanding, nor prompted by any of the usual motivations one might have for writing a tale such as this. Though I am sure the first part of this document will go some ways in satisfying the public's morbid curiosity if some still remains, I have written the second part of this testament, which you can read here in these very same pages, exclusively for one audience in mind. It is for this one person, a person very close to me, who I will probably never meet again that I dedicate the second half of my story, which I won't even deign to call tragic. No, there is no tragedy where I am concerned, because I had a choice and everything that has happened to me has been a result of this choice. However, I dedicate the remaining part of the story, which covers my thoughts, my motives and my reasons for doing everything I have done up until the present time to this one person. For it is this very person, who has not had a choice in anything that has happened. Unfortunately, without a doubt, it is this very person who will ultimately suffer the most as a result of my actions. I can only tell you I am sorry and I know it will never be enough. Despite all that happened, Reggie (my great warrior and my dearest love) and I were never prepared for what would happen next...

3

"life←{ ↑1 ω ∨.^3 4=+/,⁻1 0 1∘.⊖⁻1 0 1∘.⌽ ⊂ ω}"

A man dressed in little more than rags, torn blue jeans and a soiled, blue workman's shirt was swinging like a trapeze artist, his hands deftly gripping the white flagpole that jutted out from atop one of the municipal offices in Hokum's historic center. The three-story building was a handsome, red brick affair with newly painted white columns, all done in the relatively modern reinterpretation of antebellum style that had become so common all over the city's center. His body and face were filthy, his hair long and wild as was his reddish beard, knotted with broken leaves and the bark of trees. From all appearances, it seemed that he was intoxicated. He was a stringy character of about five foot eight and obviously as agile as a lar gibbon. A small crowd of people had gathered below him including a couple of uniformed policemen who just stood watching as the events unfolded. The man in question had removed the American flag from the pole and had fashioned for himself a sort of cape – Captain America! In between his zany exhortations, the man was constantly shouting for Billy Rubino. Presently, he addressed the crowd in the following manner,

"And God shall wipe away all tears from their eyes; and there shall be no more death. And when they heard of the resurrection of the dead, some mocked: and others said, 'we will hear thee again of this'."

The police, who stood helplessly below, made some attempts to address the man, shouting, "Git down from there, Riley. You come on down now you o' fool." But, this only served to encourage the man. At this point, he deftly swung his body up over the sturdy pole so that after raising himself on his knees, he balanced again with his feet atop the flagpole. Climbing back over the roof's low balustrade, he addressed the now growing crowd as if he was Moses on the mount,

"Hold back ye waters! Hold back ye waters! From the ends of the earth I will shout unto thee. Lord, when my heart is overwhelmed, lead me to the mountain that is higher than I. Lead me, Lord! Lead me on, for I am your soldier. Send down your X-rays, oh Lord and show the unbelievers the tomb that inhabits their flesh. Show, us, oh Lord."

At this point, Riley trembled in his arms and legs. He began to emote as he shook and danced like a Baptist preacher. Amidst his terrible movements, some in the audience responded with sarcastic shouts of Hallelujah.

"Where's Billy? I want Billy here now," shouted Riley.

"Listen, Riley, listen. If we are gonna have to come up and git you, we are gonna have to arrest you."

At this point, Riley picked up a compound crossbow that had been hidden at his feet beneath the balustrade. He pointed this at the policemen as the crowd gasped, despite there being no arrow in the barrel. The cops responded by putting their hands out in front of their faces, "C'mon, let's be civil now. No need for that, Riley." Riley chortled with his face turned up toward the sky, putting the camouflaged crossbow up over his head and dancing around like a ninny. He then knelt down over the balustrade pointing down towards the officers like the great Urizen in one of Blake's Creation paintings.

"Lord, look at how they tremble. Oh Lord, look how they tremble. Now we are delivered from the law, that bein' dead wherein we were held and we should serve the newness of our spirits and not in the oldness of the letter. Look, I can go all day like this, you hear. But, I…I want Billy here now. I'm only gonna speak to Billy."

He then gave out a loud barbaric yawp.

"Like we said before, Billy's on his way. You just wait now. He's comin', but you still gonna have to come down here to talk to him, now."

"I want Billy to come here. I want the news to come here so everybody can see and hear what Billy done done. The Lord does object to…"

At this point, the faint ring of a cell phone was heard and though many people searched their pockets and purses, it was none other than Riley who emerged with the offending phone. He then dropped the crossbow and immediately raised the cell phone high into the air above his head, brandishing it victoriously to his now rather large audience, "You hear that? You hear that? You know who's that's a callin'? That's God a callin'." The crowd cheered, meanwhile laughing at his antics, while shouting more Hallelujahs and Praise the Lords.

As Riley picked up the flip phone and held it to his ear, he said, "Is this God or is this here Billy? What? What you say? I can't hardly hear ya. Speak up. What? No. No. Yes I'm happy with my current cell phone service. No I don't want to hear about no new plan…aw hell!"

A loud peel of laughter emerged from the crowd below and even the two hapless policemen had to laugh. This only served to anger Riley, "Consider ye of Sodom and Gomorrah.

Consider ye well and hear the word of he who held you out in his hand like a spider over the flame. Consider the ravens, consider the sparrows, for they neither sow nor reap and yet God feedeth them: how much more are ye better than all the birds?"

"Say what? What's that you say, Riley?" shouted a heckler from the crowd. "Riley, did I hear you say 'turds'? We're no better'n turds?"

The whole crowd again burst into spontaneous laughter.

"I said 'birds'. I said birds not 'turds'."

"Listen, whatever you said, God ain't gonna talk to you up there and sure as hell Billy won't neither. Why don't you be a good boy and come down here all civil. This is turnin' into a downright situation here. We gonna have to call the paddy wagon now," one of the policemen shouted.

As the exchange continued, many of the building's employees began to peek out of windows to determine what the commotion was about. In addition, the citizens below had begun to cheer Riley on, chanting his name. Riley raised his hands with each chant, encouraging them like a professional wrestler might, cupping his hand over his ear.

"Hear that, Billy? Hear that, Billy? Everybody is gonna hear what you done done. I said toil and trouble. Toil and trouble. Behold, for I will now show you a mystery; we shall not all sleep, but we shall all be changed. But, I ain't sleepin' no mo'. I ain't sleepin' no mo'." As he shouted, he walked back and forth, pummeling his fist with every word like an old-fashioned tree stump orator, pounding fire and brimstone out of his very palms. A wave of sarcastic "Amens" rose through the audience as they egged him on even further. At this point, the police were beginning to have difficulty controlling the crowd and many members of the public had taken out their cameras and phones to take pictures.

This was the scene when Billy finally arrived in his normal manner, stepping through the outskirts of the audience with his ridiculous swagger. Emerging from a street opposite the building, he had to literally push his way through the expanding throng that had gathered in a close semi-circle around the building. Unfortunately, it had only been a week since his incident with Basyli and he wasn't prepared to deal with another raving lunatic. Though Billy continued to push people aside in rude fashion, his pollution hadn't yet been detected by Riley, however, when he finally arrived at the point where the police were standing, they shouted up at him, "See, Billy's here now. He's right here. Will you come on and git down now?" The crowd then cheered, chanting Billy's name.

Riley silenced them with a wide wave of his arms and took a gigantic swig from a large, silver flask he had tied with a chain to the loop of his trousers. He was really raging now, "And so he has arrived. And so he has arrived. So since he done come, before I tell you what he done done, I'm gonna give you all some poetry that I done memorized jus' for this occasion. You all want some poetry? You want to hear some of this here poetry for the master has arrived?" The crowd shouted a universal 'yes', beginning to chant Riley's name soon afterward. Once again he silenced them by putting his finger to his lips.

"All right then. All right, here I goes. Ha! Ha! Ha! 'Hell's done broke loose and there's a fire on them yonder mountains. Snakes done turned in the grass. Satan's here a struttin' now oh, Lordy, let him pass! Satan's here a struttin' now oh Lordy, let him pass. Go down, go down Moses, set my people free.

Pop goes the weasel down through the old Red Sea. Jonah sittin' on yonder hickory branch then up jumps a whale', a man whale, I say and where's your prophet now? Where's your profit now?"

Riley gave out another barbaric yawp and the crowd shouted in their glee. Billy was hardly amused, because he had long realized that life in its infinitely affine geometry had a way of drawing distinct parallels and as far as Billy was concerned, the parallel – or negative axis – of Basyli was Riley. Indeed, over the past few weeks, Riley had become the other big thorn in Billy's side. Not long ago, the man known as Riley had been in a car accident with his wife and her three young daughters by another marriage. Driving on a wet road at night, he had run at high speed into a glorious old oak and for a time suffered partial amnesia as a result. This had the effect that after the accident, while his wife and daughters came through with only minor scrapes and bruises, he wandered the wilds surrounding Hokum living off grubs, roots, opossums and who knows what else for weeks on end. It was speculated (but never confirmed) that he had been living in the abandoned mines that dotted the Natahawa Hills. Though the police spent weeks looking for him, they could never catch him and only found traces of his passage. He was a trained survivalist and had resorted to petty thefts, such as stealing chickens or perhaps the odd tool, even matches, minor things, mostly. However, at some point over the last few weeks, he had come back into his "senses" and decided to return to his house. Unfortunately when he arrived there, he was shocked to see his wife and the three kids inhabiting his two bedroom shack, after having assumed that they had all perished in the car accident. From this one sighting, he then drew the incredible conclusion that his family members were all ghosts haunting his now accursed house. At this point, a strange scene ensued in the family's backyard with him refusing to enter the house and the wife and three children pleading to him the case that they were all in fact alive and well and could he please (if at any time it suited him) come back and work around the house because the family urgently needed the money to pay for medical bills. Not to be easily influenced by haunts, Riley sat there shouting bloody murder in his backyard and subsequently ran all the way to the city cemetery to find their graves. Not finding them in the family plot, he concocted an even stranger myth that it was due to Billy's not having signed their death certificates that they had no graves. He was convinced that out of some ill will, Billy was keeping their bodies in the morgue and therefore, being unburied, they were destined to haunt his house until they were properly interred. On many nights, both drunk and lachrymose, he shouted in his backyard that though he never amounted to much, he would promise to find a way to bury them, though they stood right there in the flesh not forty feet away (he would not let them come any closer). From all appearances, it appeared that his wife was happy enough to be done with "Ol' Riley" as she certainly did not go out of her way in trying to bring him back. She had raised her three little angels before Riley came into the picture and she would raise them afterward. She had had enough of crazy men in her life: three kids and not a man around to show for it. In reality, she was quite fed up after years of having to deal with his occasional wild fits of madness and this was only the latest, most profound example. There was some evidence that Riley had displayed a long history of mild schizophrenia, but in these parts, this just amounted to either craziness or drunkenness. In the subsequent months, many local legends surrounded Riley and he became somewhat of a Robin Hood-like figure, one that even inspired admiration. Though he lived very much on the margins of society, he would commit odd acts of kindness like leaving a loaf of bread for a homeless man or repairing the swings at the children's playground. All unseen acts, but all attributed to him, nonetheless. Furthermore, his public persona was aided by the fact that the residents of Hokum had a fairly contradictory view of authority, which meant that in some cases they respected it and in others they distrusted it profoundly. For instance, they revered the long-standing and aging sheriff, but did not like the rank and file police. They loved the city's mayor, but couldn't stand the lowly parking attendant. It mostly came down to personality, not politics. Thus, the police were naturally suspicious of Riley and in fact had it out for any character that managed to hold the people's passions. On the one hand, he was as a sort of check against a faceless, nameless authority, a lone figure striving against the excesses of injustice and tyranny; on the other, he was non-threatening, a do-gooder, someone you could laugh at and have a beer with. He became part of the city's living lore.

Pointing directly at Billy, Riley's gravelly voice rang out in all its intensity, "I wanna see my family's graves. I want their death certificates."

The crowd again cheered rapturously. Billy responded in a loud, confident voice, simultaneously quieting the crowd with his hands, "But as I told you a billion times, Riley, there's only one problem with that. They ain't dead."

The crowd gave off a loud, mocking boo over which Billy shouted, "Listen, Riley, your family is at your house where they have always been and they want to know when you're going to pay the gas bill." At this the crowd again laughed.

Riley gave back angrily, "Don't speak of the dead as if they were livin'. I done seen them ghosts too, Billy and I swear I won't go near that house. You listen here," his growling becoming increasingly angry, his eyes opened to their fullest bloom. "I want my family to go to eternal rest. Now, you give me that death certificate and set them free, you hear?" The crowd started chanting Riley's name again.

"Riley. Riley. Now how am I going to give you a death certificate for people who are living?" a small wave of boos emerged again.

"Don't say I didn't warn you, Billy. Look me in the eye and say they ain't dead. Look me in the eye. Say they ain't dead."

During the commotion, a small coterie of cops had been trying to find a way up to the roof, which was presently locked. They had gone through a number of convolutions to find the key, which ultimately could not be found. As a last resort, they broke through the door and emerged on the rooftop behind Riley. Turning on the police, Riley screamed, "Betrayers!" and ran to the opposite side of the roof. In comical fashion, the policemen chased him around the top of the building, the entire scene playing out like something in a Buster Keaton movie. At one point, Riley even jumped up on the balustrade and deftly walked along its edge as the crowd gasped and the police held back. Finally, he ran to the opposite end of the building to the crowd and disappeared over the side, leaving the police to look over the edge after him. And that was that, with nothing else to see, the crowd dispersed and Billy was left with nothing left to do. Some in the crowd put their hands on Billy's shoulders, "Don't worry, ol' Riley will gather his senses some time." Aware of his own unease after this latest in a string of strange events, Billy thought of paying a visit to the Warden, otherwise known as the "Gameskeeper". He was already aware that he owed the Warden a fairly large sum of money, but despite his not having it to hand, he knew the Warden was just the man he needed to see, for it was in fact the Warden who was responsible for keeping Billy furnished with a small, but regular supply of legal and illegal substances. In particular, diazepam, which usually helped Billy with his brief fits of anxiety or cosmic emptiness. He couldn't explain it, but at certain points, Billy felt that the universe was disjoint and that his role in it had somehow been usurped. He felt that by some strange means he had been plucked out of his existential groove, unawares. Yes, he was certain, the emptiness sank through his insides like a swallowed ice cube. A trip to the Warden would be necessary.

As Billy drove through the deserted streets of Hokum, his sense of unease only continued to grow. Contrary to what one might expect, the Warden lived in what was increasingly becoming the most popular if not the most affluent part of suburban Hokum. However, from where Billy was, the drive there would take him through a number of variegated districts. The greasy sun slithered down surfaces like a fried egg, while the windows of the now emptying buildings shown with a savage, golden color, which at times became almost blinding. In the car, he thought about Riley and the predicament that he had been put in. For weeks Riley had been making scenes around town with increasing frequency, denouncing Billy as the very Devil. Billy of course hoped that the local news stations would continue to ignore the phenomenon as the unmentionable ravings of a lunatic. Nonetheless, a deeper question still lingered in his unsettled mind. What did it all mean? It seemed that all of Hokum, at least the bit that most encroached upon him, had given itself up to a fit of temporary insanity. It was as if some noxious gas or pernicious od had escaped the deep crevasses of the Maralah Mountains and infected what was once a quiet city. Or perhaps it was the sunspots he had been hearing so much about or even the reported incidence of increasing electrical activity in the area. He had no idea what had prompted it all, he simply tried to sweep these difficulties from his mind. As he left the historic center of Hokum, he passed slowly into the more suburban areas, which lay in the northwest portion of the city. In the part of Hokum that lay to the southeast, one would find the more urban downtown areas, where the Lido des Follies and the more noisome districts lay. In their spitefulness, these areas of course bordered on the much nicer wharf district (a sort of *cordon sanitaire*) and even at times threatened to take it over. Billy indeed lived in the southwestern part of the city that was so traumatized by the Lido, which like some livid toadstool or hideous puffball spread its rancid effluvium across the region. The historic center of town, which Billy had just exited, was indeed near the geographic center of the city. The northeastern part of the city was more desolate and stretched out farther, past his office to the farmlands and alfalfa fields that lay beyond. But the wooded lanes, the nouvelle French cafes and the idiosyncratic coffee shops were all one needed to see to determine that one was entering by far the most pleasant portion of Hokum, where the more respectable citizens lived in a wilderness of subdivisions. The invasion of these subdivisions that dotted the hilly, semi-rural area was a generally welcomed event and had begun more than thirty years prior.

Hokum proper, almost an afterthought in the vertiginous country that surrounded it, rested like a discarded broach, glistening with a haughty, antiquated elegance in a river basin below a set of low lying mountains that crouched eternally beneath the autumnal mists that pervaded the region from Hunslow to Chappeqwack. In Hokum's small natural history museum (yes, surprisingly someone once felt that the city warranted a natural history museum), one would be presented with certain detailed bits of information, predominantly spoken by various animatronic devices, including a large caveman who beat the ground with a club-full of anapests as he spoke. Amongst other things, he revealed that it was almost certain, that the first significant event that ever occurred in Hokum was in the middle of the Ordovician period, when the old bones of the still unsettled Earth in an epileptic seizure, hurtled against one another until amidst the crush, the Maralah Mountains rose up out of the dark, molten fissures like a scarred set of dog's teeth: bare, rough and menacing. It took another few millennia before the Onondaga River finally snaked its way down from the now more gentle shoulders of the mountains and rested in its present coil around the broad isthmus that enclosed Hokum. There was even academic speculation that Hokum was once an island in a much larger lake and had existed as such for millions of years. Evidently, in the late Cretaceous period, Hokum had also been quite active. So active in fact that near the Bamboo Forest where the swamps took hold around the ruddy, scabby knees of the wind shattered trees, the broken jawbone of some pre-Cambrian nightmare had been discovered and was now presented behind glass next to a bootlegger's moonshine distiller at the local history museum (included in the ticketed fee, of course). This was only one of many 'finds' in the outskirts of the city. The surrounding mountains, which cast a dignified silence, were made of granite, shale and quartz. These ageless, gentle souls had for millennia, been rudely abutted by a rough and tumble series of high rolling hills, formed from red clay and soft, white limestone. Within the turns and twists of these gummy fells, there were a number of mine shafts that pervaded these elevations like rabbit warrens. Prior to the Civil War, some of the mines that were already abandoned served as hiding places for runaway slaves. After the war, it was speculated that renegades lived in them who had made off with a large quantity of confederate gold right before the surrender. Local lore held that a vast quotient of this bounty was still hidden within them. During prohibition times, the caverns had received a second life as they successfully masked the activities of illegals, this time in the form of moonshine distillers. Some sustained that bandits still lived in the caverns, which occasionally collapsed due to flooding.

Billy had just driven past this venerable museum and was in sight of the Tobia Gorrio High School when the thought occurred to him that it had been months, even years since he had actually left the borders of Hokum. Much to his dismay, the past years had kept him increasingly busy, so much so that he started to think about his job as a twenty-four seven engagement. Originally, he expected the role would be a fairly easy one and that his work hours would be relatively lax. Much to his initial contentment, it had started out that way, but gradually over the years, Hokum appeared to have become (as many said) a more "evil" place. The news stations were obsessed by the perceived phenomenon and as he looked to his right, he a saw a sign giving directions to the mass transit system that was constantly blamed as being the source of all of Hokum's ills. Though it had expanded here over a decade ago, it was only recently that the great waves of immigration had begun. First it was the blacks, followed in smaller numbers by Asians and finally by homosexuals and young professionals. However, all of these waves (mere sea swells in reflection) were ultimately overridden by the latest mass influx of Mexicans who could be seen every morning in large groups, idling around the vacant parking lots, looking for work. Billy, like many in Hokum, wouldn't have considered himself racist and from a personal perspective, he didn't care much who entered Hokum as long as they left him alone. Thus, in most regards, he had nothing against immigration in concept, however from a professional perspective he was well aware that the rising waves of Mexicans, Blacks, Homos and Junkies were giving him more than their fair share of trouble. But ultimately, none of this really bothered Billy at present, what did trouble him was a deep, inexplicable sense of foreboding, a sense that he was somehow out of joint with everything.

As he turned off the main boulevard, he noticed an Asian family standing at the corner, all covered up in winter clothing, banging a large cowbell. The eldest female, who appeared to be the mother of the three children, held up a sign that read, "One China". He couldn't hear what she was shouting through the closed car window, however, he felt that whatever it was, he was utterly disconnected from it. After all, what did it mean? What could "One China" or the "Falun Gong" possibly mean for the citizenry of Hokum? What was being asked of him? As he drove past the last of a long line of strip malls, he entered the winding road that would eventually take him past the first of many sprawling subdivisions. There between wide forested areas, he saw great tracks of red, scarred clay that resembled the momentary aftermath of child's skinned knee. Off the main road that led further into the woodland, one could see the subfusc outlines of unconnected cul-de-sacs, where the wood frames of numerous houses were starting to take shape;

another new subdivision, each bigger than the last, each with houses placed closer and closer together so that the logical conclusion would indicate their eventually becoming row houses. In the older subdivisions, the houses were noticeably smaller, in many cases made out of wood, but the yards were significantly larger. Each subdivision had its own clubhouse, communal pool and set of tennis courts. He had already forgotten what had existed there before, perhaps a small farm were one could buy pecans by the trunk full. It was a forgone conclusion that the older farms that had once populated the wooded area and had been only loosely connected by gravel roads were being torn down, the previous owners presumably retiring to some happy elsewhere. It was an all too common occurrence in this part of Hokum, to see small groups of people, huddled around each other, lost, pointing in no specific direction, saying in hushed astonishment things like, "But, what was here before" or "I seem to remember there was a…" and finally, "I can't believe how much it has all changed." To a small minority of residents, it appeared as if some darker form of Manifest Destiny had spread its shadow across the once pristine countryside; one which increasingly abided by some hidden right of eminent domain. The creeks were being dried out, the woodland gutted, the grassy fields paved over. Hokum was still a suburban paradise, but its fabric was indeed changing and its growing pains were becoming obvious. One day he thought the entire city would split at the seams in one final convulsion of madness. Even someone like himself, who was not naturally sentimental, was beginning to feel out of place, that he was becoming an unnecessary relic, that there was a spreading evil here, a type of temptation, he truly didn't understand, one that seemed to have no direction or sense of purpose. Death didn't bother him, but progress increasingly did. Maybe he was just getting older.

The banausic day-glow turned drab and grey and the low-lying clouds sped over his head as he walked from his car toward his destination. It had only taken Billy thirty-five minutes to arrive at the Warden's modest house, the very house that up until three years ago he had shared with his mother. The little brick confection was in good order from the outside and showed no sign of the turmoil that was hidden within. This fact was only partially due to the floral curtains always being drawn, the rest due to its overtly wholesome appearance. The house was fronted by a white picket fence behind which stood a small yard, which presently boasted a significant number of garden gnomes and in summer, played host to a large patch of multicolored hydrangeas and psychedelic foxgloves. It was one of many similar one-story houses on the block, which all included the same short driveway that had just enough room for a single car. In the Warden's driveway was parked an old ice cream truck which he had once used to sell ice cream and on many occasions, Dexedrine and Ritalin which he had continually taken since he was a child. In the middle of the house stood a red door, the only truly exceptional characteristic of the house. On either side of the door, there were a couple of wall trellises hung with Eden climbing roses. If one were to ask the Warden about his conscientious maintenance of the exterior, he would answer that in his line of business, appearances were everything. Although selling drugs wasn't his main profession, the Warden did have a wide variety of clients from of all walks of life. He had actually received his moniker, the Warden, from his main profession, which was primarily to operate hunting trips. He also ran a surprisingly profitable business hawking hunting paraphernalia on the Internet. Despite his glass eye, the Warden was a fairly accomplished deer hunter and a dedicated survivalist, even having a plot of land with an underground bunker. At present, he was in the process of equipping this bunker with a bespoke "supercomputer" that would send out continuous messages via satellite in the hopes of finding other friendly survivalists across the universe.

The Warden was one of those types of people who obsessed about the military and could always be found wearing some form of military-like fatigues. Though he had actually been in the military decades ago, given his weight, glass eye and general lack of coordination, it had only been as a cook. This tour of duty around the Army's oven ranges (which he had somehow mistaken for firing ranges) was modified by turns into a decorated career as a military sharpshooter. Regardless of his deficit in regards to a "real" military career being fairly common knowledge, he would admit this fact to no one and was overly fond of regaling those around him with completely fictitious stories about his career in the Special Forces. It was another thing that Billy and the Warden shared in common, the love of tall tales. Though he had lost his eye as a child due to a degenerative disease, he gave out that the loss was the result of a wound suffered in a firefight. The Warden, like Billy, was overweight but didn't have Billy's tall stature. In respect to age, he was in his mid-forties. He was always bearded and usually wore the maroon beret of the British paratroopers, who he had a great appreciation for, due partially to the fact that he traced his last name to Welsh origins and partially to the fact that he witnessed their conspicuous ability to drink while serving in the military.

For five minutes, Billy stood there on the Warden's doorstep, looking as if he were slightly uncertain about whether or not to ring the Warden's bell. As a last matter of procrastination, he decided to open the Manila envelope that he had been carrying around since he left the office. As it was work related, he wasn't exceedingly curious about its contents, but he thought he should look in case he managed to lose it during his time at the Warden's. After he had unfastened the envelope's flap, he discovered that it was a letter from the sheriff's office, confirming the receipt of his request to open an investigation into Basyli's case. Even now, he had asked himself why he had made the request in the first place. Was it out of some deep compassion for the forsaken Pole or perhaps a sense of professional duty or even stranger, a moment of self-doubt? Out of all of these potentialities, one could be certain that it wasn't the early signs of Basyli's demise, the fact that his cheeks had started to hollow out or that he had dropped ten pounds from his previously healthy frame that pushed Billy into action. It wasn't the fact that the poor man had been forced to sleep in the public library during the day or in an abandoned warehouse at night. No, he only consented to open the case because after a number of run-ins with the intransigent Pole, Basyli promised to reveal to him the greatest story he had ever heard and tempted him with an odd piece of paper. The soiled document was actually an official certificate that indicated Basyli's mandatory service in the Polish armed forces when he had been a teenager. For Billy's sake, this simple and rather commonplace document was escalated to KGB credentials. Basyli hinted at dark workings, underground maneuvers and a body double that had been planted near his own house for the sole purpose of throwing an international spy ring off his scent. It wasn't that Billy completely believed these farfetched tales, but he had become dreadfully tired of Basyli's rusty morosity, his constant entreaties, his incurable stench. Thus, in a moment of rare weakness, he gave in, knowing that the case would be hopelessly filed with many others in a dusty basement and that without his constant nurture and care, it would die like a new born pup left out in the inhospitable elements. Billy had never really seriously considered opening an inquest in to Basyli's case, one because it would have made him look bad and two, because he knew for certain that the public would have no interest in the story of a poor immigrant who had been declared dead due to a clerical error. For his own part, Basyli had approached a number of private citizens, begging shopkeepers, parking attendants, waiters, anyone who might have recognized him to make a positive claim about his identity. But, many, even those who might have helped and especially those who had incorrectly identified him in the first instance, were reluctant to do so: A) because they were never quite sure of his identity to begin with, B) because they were naturally suspicious of Russians, C) because the ones who had originally made the mistake did not want to bear the shame of changing their stories in front of the sheriff, and finally D) because the very few who had inquired had been informed that the entire process would take a significant amount of paperwork and that were they to persist, they would almost definitely be subject to an inquiry themselves, perhaps even a psychological evaluation. Furthermore, Basyli's insistent nagging had become so unbearable that even those who had considered helping him despite the many roadblocks, ultimately decided to have nothing to do with him and were on the verge of declaring him a public nuisance, throwing him out of their shops and asking him to return no more. Finally, after days living in the outdoors, Basyli's stench – which wasn't pleasant to begin with – was becoming more than most could bear.

His perfunctory curiosity satisfied, Billy shoved the papers back into the envelope and rang the doorbell, which proceeded through its normal glissando of bells. As the door opened, the Warden stood before him, wearing a pair of yellow tinted shooting glasses, a yellow T-shirt bearing the mondegreen "All alone is all we are", a camouflage baseball cap and a green fishing vest. The Warden merely raised his right hand and said, "Hao Ke-mo sah-bee." Regardless of Billy's extravagant attempts to avoid it, the Warden then shook Billy's bared hand with an overly firm grip. As he stepped into the house, he no longer noticed the ridiculous contrast between the Warden's appearance and the decorum of the two front rooms to either side of the foyer, decorated as they were with William Morris inspired wallpaper and prints of fox hunts across provincial England. After all, the front rooms hadn't changed their decoration for forty years and the entire place smelled of frankincense. The floors were nicely carpeted in a neutral tone and the white furniture was comprised of modern Hepplewhite and Sheraton reproductions. What struck one the most was the large number of porcelain statuettes, glass figurines and lace antimacassars that were to be found everywhere within the house. It was certainly an old woman's abode, one that had been carefully preserved so that when she died, time died with her. The Warden had rarely been allowed in these rooms when he was a child, nonetheless, sitting between a small Wedgwood amphora of duck egg blue and a series of red sherry glasses was a recently purchased feather duster. As in any great mausoleum, everything was kept immaculately clean and in place.

Billy always entered the Warden's abode with some trepidation, given that the man owned a large and angry pit bull (adorned with requisite chain of the junk yard dog type), which he had given the ill-advised name of 'Jesus', because primarily, he thought 'no one would ever mess with Jesus' and secondarily, he wanted to train it against some imagined infiltration of Muslims that fired his speculations. It was safe to assume that the Warden had had many awkward walks around his neighborhood with the dog, especially when he was left to shout after the aggressive alpha upon its occasionally breaking forth from its leash. Furthermore, Billy was well aware of what Jesus was capable of. The Warden never ceased to remind him of the terrible story that occurred years back when the Warden actually managed to bring a female client (a meth junkie no less), back to his home for a payment in kind transaction. When the overexcited woman leapt on top of the Warden in a transport of sexual frenzy, Jesus, thinking his beloved master was being attacked, not only tried to defend his poor owner, but managed to take a chunk out of the hapless woman's right thigh. Unfortunately, once inside the Warden's house, one never knew where or when one might confront Jesus and indeed he had had a recent run-in with the vicious marauder in a hallway when left by himself, which led to a longer than necessary Mexican standoff. It was perhaps the only time as an adult that Billy had wet his pants. Indeed, even now, as Billy could hear Jesus growling somewhere in the background he felt his knees begin to weaken. The Warden, without much application simply yelled into an unspecific part of the room, "Shut it, Jesus."

Without another word, the Warden escorted Billy downstairs and after unlocking a series of deadbolts on an iron security door into his private living space where he promptly sat back down to the video game he had paused just moments before. The downstairs space couldn't have been any more of a contrast to what was found upstairs and the only thing preserved between the two spaces was the faint scent of frankincense. Everywhere, one was immediately struck by the sheer number of books and magazines ranging on everything from computer programming to bass fishing. Furthermore, there were numbers of cardboard boxes: some opened, some not, many full of miscellaneous types of hunting paraphernalia. Cramped in the back of the room sat a large computer desk and a gaming chair with speakers built into the headrest. On the walls, instead of windows, there hung a variety of handguns of various shapes and forms interspersed with pictures of the bandoleer slung Warden engaged in diverse activities such as paintballing, fishing and hunting. Next to a small refrigerator, behind the piles of porno mags and video games, there stood one bookshelf in particular that was near collapsing under the sheer weight of the books. Waiting for the Warden to resume his game in earnest, Billy began to read a few of the titles, *Life Is a Dream*, Calderon, *The Private Memoirs and Confessions of a Justified Sinner*, Hogg, *Against the Grain*, Huysmnns, *The Man Who Was Thursday*, Chesterton, *The Secret History*, Procopius. He didn't recognize any of the names, but implied their import.

It was easy to see why the Warden was also called the Gamekeeper, mostly by those who knew him as a small time drug dealer. The name was given to him both in reference to the sheer size of his video game collection and to the diversity of drugs he kept on hand. As he sat cross-legged on the floor, his lips curled while his eyes became instantly transfixed on the large flat panel television screen before him. While taking occasional hits from his inhaler, he contorted his body from left to right as he dodged invisible bullets that seemed to emerge from the television screen. After some seconds, he spoke absentmindedly in his peppery Appalachian drawl, "Hey, wanna beer? What am I sayin'? You owe me money, dude. Did you get my note?"

"I know. I know. I saw the note. I'll get it to you. Here is fifty for the moment."

"Fifty? Dude, you owe me like...let's see twenty-seven times five plus fifty-eight plus forty-four."

"Two hundred thirty-seven," Billy gave back with lightning fast precision. "Yeah, yeah I know. I'll get it to you. Listen, I need some of the Lizzy."

"Oh, you do, do you? We'll, I got jus' the thing. One sec...oh shit, not again. I always die jus' at this part, these friggin' chink gold famers preventin' me from levelin' up." He returned the game to pause, leaving the room and after opening another long series of bolts in an unseen anteroom, he came back wearing a pair of night vision goggles on his head and approached Billy with great enthusiasm. "What time you git off your shift?"

Billy looked at his watch. "Officially, in another thirty-five minutes, unofficially, right now."

"Good, listen don't mess with the Lizzy, jus' yet. I got this new stuff I been waitin' to take that I think you'll like."

"What is it?"

"Dimethoxy-4-bromophenethylamine," he ejaculated with perfect precision.

"What? What the hell's that?"

"Look, if you really wanna know, I got all the documentation includin' the chemical diagrams. It wuz made by a lab rat buddy of mine. Met him through the shady pharmacist who used to get all the Dexedrine for me. Anyway, this is straight from the source, from the lab where they make it, dude."

"I'm not sure I can handle it. I just want something to calm me down. I'm feeling a bit anxious and…"

"Nonsense. Sure you can," the Warden said handing him a bag of a dirty white powder, which Billy stared at, dipped his finger in, then put on the tip of his tongue without much ceremony. His tongue went numb and metallic as if he had stuck it on a 9V battery.

"So what are you supposed to do with this?" he asked after tasting the substance without much affect.

"You snort it, what duya think? Give it here. Jus' watch, dude."

The Warden took back the bag, knelt down at a small glass table, which lay in the middle of the room. Brushing some papers aside, he poured a pile of the powder on the desk and deftly cut it up into a number of small, symmetric lines. As he went about his task, he began to engage Billy in a matter-of-fact conversation, "So what's been up with you? Haven't seen you in a couple of weeks now." Billy, now sitting on his knees next to the Warden, responded by relating the events, which had involved him just over an hour ago. The Warden's eyes switched on in sudden satori.

"No shit. That jus' reminded me, when I wuz last over at Big Bear a couple of days ago, I caught a sight of Riley, but couldn't get really close. Anyway, I done talked to his wife to tell her where I had seen him and she didn't seem to mind much, but she said she thinks he's plannin' somethin' big. Riley done left a note at their house when they wuz out.

He said somethin' like he wuz gonna finally rescue them. Somethin' crazy like that. Anyhow, she had no idea what that means, but she were mighty worried as it wuz the first time Riley had actually come into the house when they wuz out. I tell you that redneck is as crazy as a loon."

Finishing his statement, the Warden put a rolled dollar bill to his nose and loudly snorted two lines of the mysterious powder into each of his nostrils. He held his head up for a few seconds as if to make sure the drug would settle onto his frontal cortex in the quickest possible manner. For unknown reasons, the Warden's statements made Billy feel even more anxious and he really wished he had one of many benzodiazepams in his possession. The Warden then handed Billy the dollar bill at which point he followed suit, snorting the sordid dust up his nose.

Within the next eight to ten minutes, the drugs started to take hold. At this point, the Warden said, "I know what we're missin'," and walked over to the black stereo that sat against the wall opposite.

"We need some music. By the way, I forgot to tell you. Saw you on TV the other week. Boy, you put on a pretty good show, I tell ya…explainin' all that with the engine block hittin' her head and crushin' it like an egg. Kapow! Man that must a hurt. Think you'll catch the guy? Anyway, since we're gonna get some visuals, we need the right kinda music."

A strange event had occurred recently, one of which Billy was only too aware. Since the Warden had begun to build his online business and now spent the majority of his time surfing the Internet and Wikipedia, he had stopped reading his usual hunting magazines and instead read literary books. Furthermore, he no longer listened to his Alabama CDs, but was now a connoisseur of arcane classical composers. The rapidity of the change was certainly startling for most, who could no longer follow his conversation. It was well known to Billy after several recent conversations on the subject that the Warden had a predilection for three particular composers; in order of preference, they were Olivier Messiaen, Krzysztof Penderecki and Carlo Gesualdo, the last being a lesser known Renaissance composer. Billy, being a great fan of classical music himself, had been forced into long conversations where he had to defend his taste for Edvard Grieg ('Muzak') against assaults that his preferred music was shallow and held nothing in the way of the profundity of Stockhausen or Xenikis. The Warden had always been exceedingly proud of his ability to pick the music that best suited a particular drug experience, but whereas in the past this had always defaulted to Pink Floyd, the Doors or something of the like, recently, regardless of what anyone else might say, he usually played one of his three new favorites. For the Warden, this had the noticeable consequence of significantly decreasing his in-house business, though he didn't seem to mind. So it was that the Warden began his usual entre into soundtracking the high they were both sharing. Despite the two only being a couple of feet from each other, the Warden shouted, "You know what this stuff calls for? We need some Ge-su."

The Warden pressed the play button on his CD player and as the first, dissonant notes of the music began, Billy protested, "No, no, not now, I can't handle Gesualdo right now and as I keep telling you, William Lawes was just as ahead of his time and much more innovative and controlled in his use of counterpoint. But, I can't expect you to understand, Sir Lawes requires a highly refined palate."

This discussion had been a particular bone of contention between the two with the Warden constantly cheering the merits of Gesauldo, leaving Billy to champion the even lesser known Stuart composer. The debate was never settled and the Warden became increasingly animated,

"Naw, naw. See, that's where you're wrong, just listen to this." As the music for *Moro, lasso, al mio duolo*, built into shrill screams and eldritch howls, Billy was having trouble coping.

"No. No. No. You just like him because you're into all that satanic shit. It's like sixteenth century death metal. Listen, no one gets Gesualdo more than I do, but EVERYONE worships him now because of his bloody pathos, all those augmented fourths and the fact that hardly anyone got him back then. But, this is something I could deal without at the moment and it is not helping me at all. I'm actually feeling quite anxious."

"Aw shit, how 'bout some Spem then?"

"No Tallis."

"Dufay, 'Ave Maris Stella'? Maybe suuuum Josequin?"

"Nothing modal." The drugs were really starting to take hold and Billy began to chew the insides of his cheeks. His eyes were beginning to look dazed.

"Jesus! OK, Tomita? Genesis? Gabriel?"

"Please. Next you'll put on Jethro Tull."

"Naw man, I don't listen to that stuff no more"

"How about some Lawes for a change?"

The Warden was starting to get angry, even taking to stomping his foot and whining like a child, "But, we ain't gonna get any effects from that shit. His music's got all the personality of a Styrofoam cup. All that long slow dronin' never really resolvin' itself and those bizarre key changes."

"'Styrofoam cup'? 'Bizarre key changes'? Where did you get all that from, the Internet?"

"Yeah, well so what?"

"They are not even your own opinions."

"Well, they is now."

Billy could only shake his head in disgust. "How does a human get by with a mind like yours?"

Unperturbed, the Warden kept fingering through his ever-growing CD collection. Finding one he liked, he shot back, "I know, how about Zalenka?"

"Zalenka? Jesus. Bach with a brain but without a pulse. What have you been reading lately? Next you'll say Telemann. It's Lawes or nothing. You chose the drug. I choose the music."

"Damn you and you owe me money."

Over the next twenty minutes, as the Stewart composer's music began to waft over the room, the two sat next to each other at the foot of a couch in complete silence, staring at a faded random dot autostereogram the Warden had hanging on the opposite wall. As the drugs began to take a deeper hold, the notes began to play over Billy's mind: the trancelike slowness of it all, the false relations, the slow ascents into related minors, the prickly sixth intervals, the semi-quick descents falling in diminished fifths – the devil's interval – descending again and again to the words "Which fall upon". As the music swelled and contracted, he thought he could make out the complex patterns of the notes as their furtive, iridescent shadows wafted over the walls in stenographic brilliance. After a brief pause in the music, Billy asked the Warden to raise the volume still further. After all, he liked listening to music at extreme volumes. Suddenly, the Warden sat up, raising his voice in awe, "Look dude, I'm seein' Methuselhas."

Billy replied laconically, absorbed entirely in the music, "What's that?"

"Don't really know, but if you look real deep there into the poster it's like those shapes like you see on acid. This guy Conway created them. Little blips of television static that flutter around and flower into infinity while makin' these lovely little repeatin' patterns. Real genius that is. Anyway, when I figure out how, I'm gonna write some programs on my supercomputer I done built and then send them Methuselhas out to outer space via satellite dish to all the other survivalists out there."

"You are one gaseous cloud of utter bullshit."

"And you're a prick. Hey dude, this shit is startin' to make me feel all cold inside and your eyes are movin' all wobbly and stuff. They look like they on fire. Listen, man, you feelin' cold?"

"No, in fact, I feel slightly hot if anything. There is no ventilation down here."

"Is that so? Then why am I so friggin' cold then? You devil, you mus' be steelin' my heat. I need some blankets."

The Warden stood up then turned around to retrieve what looked like a pair of filthy blankets from the equally dirty couch upon which their backs rested. He wrapped them over himself and sat back down on the floor, crossing his legs in front of him. He was now noticeably shivering.

"I'm here freezin' and you is burnin' up. This stuff jus' ain't feelin' right. Oh, dear Lordy. I think I feel another existential crisis comin' on." The Warden gathered the blankets closer to his body and began to show signs of deep trepidation.

"An existential crisis? You? What the hell are you talking about now?"

"An existential crisis, you know like when you stare into the abyss and the abyss stares back."

Billy had become increasingly fed up with this ridiculously philosophical side of the Warden. On many occasions, he desperately wished he could go back to doing drugs with a man who wanted nothing more than to watch 'Faces of Death' or debate which ammo could best take off a deer's head with a single shot. A hint of anxiety began to creep into Billy's voice, "What are you talking about? What are you ever talking about? It's impossible for you to have an existential crisis. This is just the drugs talking."

"Naw, naw it ain't that at all. It's like an inner emptiness, a dread of the expandin' void that will one day consume us all. It's part of my online correspondence course in Existentialism, where I can earn a Masters degree in nihilism with a subspecialty in angst, moral uncertainty or human misery. It's all in my free time and I can even get a PhD. Anyway, one of my course books done tol' me how to cure a crisis in four easy steps: 1. Sit down and be calm. You probably aren't the only one in the universe having this crisis (but, maybe you are). 2. Breathe in deeply. Close your eyes and don't panic. 3. Ask yourself why you are having an existential crisis. 4… Dang nabbit, I forgot what the fourth step wuz. Anyway there is like this whole world out there I never done seen before. I been readin' these books you see and educatin' myself about all kinds a stuff they never did teach me in school."

"This is not a good thing for your head at all. Why don't you stick to the WWII books and the Credence Clearwater CDs you used to like so much? Now I come over here and all you want to do is listen to Gesualdo and debate philosophy. You were much more pleasant before when you were just a poorly educated redneck. Now you want to find your place in the universe. Next, all the meth heads will be wandering around reading Schopenhauer. I found one the other day, who died clutching a copy of Kierkegaard. I'm sure you had something to do with it. You can't get drugs anymore in this town without a philosophical equivalent of a root canal. Drugs are bad but a little knowledge is worse. Now, I'm certain I know why this entire city is going crazy."

"Well I too want to find my place in life and so I been doin' nothin' but readin' straight for the last eight months and givin' whoever I know some advice on what to read. Hey, that jus' reminded me, I've been readin' this book called *Also Sprach Sam: The Brazen Idol and The Five Ways to Overcome Your Existential Crisis*, written by David Arexus, the dude who designed the course. And to think until a few months ago, I didn't even know I had an existential crisis."

"Oh, how a little knowledge can destroy a man," lamented Billy.

"Let me just find one passage for you…"

"Please don't."

Undeterred, the Warden fished through the masses of garbage on the living room floor until he found what he was looking for and held up the badly worn paper book with a cry of victory.

"Jus' listen to this here passage, from chapter five, The Forgetting and the Forgetful. It's a conversation between the Brazen Idol and the Satyr philosopher king." As the Warden stood up with the blanket still wrapped around him, he resembled some hillbilly version of Seneca. He began to emote in a grave voice as if he was giving a public oration, obviously having some difficulties with various words.

"Behold ye, Behold ye, the terrible voice of the Brazen Idol spoke as his maw opened to scatter the winds to the four corners of the earth. At the first words, the Great Satyr dropped his aulos, his shaggy legs trembled in fear at the foot of the giant statue. The other Satyrs that stood behind him on the grassy mountainside covered their eyes and hid their faces in fear of the grave pronouncements that were to come. They stamped their hooves into the ground and gave out baleful shouts and piercing ululations so that the entire air was full of a lamentable sound. The Idol's eyes glowed an infernal red and as he spoke, the entire earth shook, 'Look ye unhappy Satyrs, who cling to the earth, beneath the bows that bend with over-ripened fruit, the thistles that catch with hurtful intent, what say you now? What have you achieved after all you have said? Fear, uncertainty and doubt? Nothing more? Analysis, self-analysis, constantly torturing yourself before a mirror as if you intend to replace the sought end with the devised means. Thus, your every act is an act of avoidance, the avoidance of torment, often by the contradictory means of tormenting others. Why this constant anxiety? Life is inherently uncertain and thus full of torment. Your own heart's uncertainty is a torment tantamount to guilt and you, poor Satyrs, would often deem the consequences of guilt to be of lesser weight that of doubt. Faith and the absolute are temporary props to rest yourselves upon until they too are blown away by the shifting sands of that which cannot be decided. Even presented with the truth, depending on the phrase, you choose to follow your hearts. In the evolution of a Satyr or the race of Satyrs, there is no star that doesn't rise then fall again. However, given you know nothing of your natures, by trying to say anything at all you're denuding the meaning from everything. It's all draining away like a puddle of rust.' Profound, ain't it?"

Billy stood up and was putting his hands to his head. "I think it's utter garbage and this is exactly why I suggest you shouldn't read books. They will ruin you and all the people foolish enough to listen to you. Seek help. These books are a bad addiction for you. In medieval times, they used to burn the authors, then they discovered it was much better to burn the books and the authors. In the final stage, they figured out that they had to burn the books, the authors and the people who read them. Where do you find these horrible things? Anyway, I need some Lizzy…where is it?" He began looking around the room, overturning boxes in a futile search for the needed pills. Unperturbed, the Warden kept speaking in his grand tone of voice, at points his eyes stared forth into blankness, almost as if he were in a trance himself,

"And jus' listen to this next passage. This one is even better, 'Can we at all conceive of the race of Satyrs as a collective conscience? If so, how would we analyze it? What would we say of its nature, its personality and how it has evolved? What is history's relationship to us as individuals? Is it something we can take or leave without regard to moral judgment? Is history merely a cycle of torment and anxiety? Of unlearning inconvenient truths and replacing them with more inconvenient ones? History raises these contradictions, building more doubt and inner turmoil, making us ever more unaware and uncertain of our true natures. Are we not the consequence of our collective history, the sum of its mistakes, yet we strip this history of meaning, rendering it harmless to ourselves? Look at the wars, the eruptions of mass hysteria, the constant building and destroying of new idols. Prey to these anxieties, how many times have we vitiated the lessons of the past only to relearn them anew? We erase them from our collective minds to make room for another set of believable truths. In this constant separation of the chaff from the grain, we can only succeed in enervating ourselves. Everything that over the centuries we've learned we subsequently forget and in this way we are always back to being anxious students staring at an impossibly empty blackboard. As we evolve and our perspectives change, we are doomed to reinterpret only the most important lessons, building up what little we know by constant accumulation so that ultimately we are left with naught but a pile of eraser dust and a few childlike scratches as the only sign that we ever lived or made any consideration at all. In face of a large, collective history, we become helplessly muddled students, struggling to find a place in a society built on torment and forgetting. It is in this society that our small, individual struggles are hopelessly lost, themselves forgotten, fragmented and worthless. The inanition of individual meaning is the mother of chaos, apathy and ultimately a heat death that we will die in a frigid sea of expanding emptiness.' You know, I just love hearin' those words over 'n over. What you think they mean?"

Billy was now furiously looking around the room and responded rapidly in an anxious, heliumed falsetto, his face sweating with effort, he began to remove the outer layers of his clothing, stripping down to only his underwear. He grabbed the Warden by the shoulders and stared into his eyes wildly, "Garbage. Pure garbage. Listen to me. Listen to me. You have to understand. You have to otherwise your life will be meaningless. Words mean something. Thoughts mean something. Music means something. We must save ourselves from the emptiness of these lies. This maddening French disease. That syphilitic Prussian wasn't wrong. There must be some redemption, something to rescue us from this eternal recurrence. There must be something that allows a man to break free from the morass that surrounds us. The triviality. There must be a way to place oneself above it all, to be a noble soul. Damn, look what you've done to me."

Billy looked down and noted that he had inadvertently wet his underwear (now the second time he had done so inside the Warden's abode). "I need some Lizzy, now!"

"Say, what yous done said about a sypha...sypha...Oh I get it, you mean Nie-chez don't you? But, the Internet said he died of brain..."

"Oh, forget it," Billy said with finality, not wanting to encourage him. "Damn it and damn you! Why can't you find anything useful in this room where even the metaphors are all mixed up in this mess? This is not helping me at all. We should have stuck to the Lizzy." In his state of distress, it was becoming increasingly clear to Billy, that at present he had a mind-body problem on his hands. Indeed, between the lobes of his fevered brain, a bubble had begun to expand, to the point his body, like some Cartesian diver, ached to feel the crack of his skull against the ceiling. As his naked feet began to rise up off the ground, the room appeared to contract at the sides until even he felt unable to breath. In his hands he gripped a cold sweat. A wave moved through his mind, until he fell once more to the floor in exhaustion, covering his head, the panic attack over.

The Warden, as if suddenly waking from a daydream, asked in a quizzical tone of voice, "My lips are numb. I feel as if I'm really gonna freeze to death. What is this?" As he looked deeply at his fingers, which were writhing within the sweep of rising chords, his voice lowered to a grave whisper, "I told you we should 'a played Gesualdo."

4

"¡Que toda la vida es sueño, y los sueños, sueños son!"

Several days later, Billy awoke in the early hours of the morning, not able to sleep. Fortunately for him, he wouldn't be on call until much later in the afternoon. It was a Sunday and Billy had woken out of a dream that disturbed him. In the dream, he had transformed himself into some sort of hot air balloon, something akin to a float at a parade. He was being pulled along by a group of indiscriminate men who were so far beneath him that they appeared to him like so many ants. He had a number of large cables attached to various parts of his body and in the breezes that bore him, he gently swayed from side to side unable to move under his own volition. The men led him onward for many days and he floated out across numerous cities, out into the desert and finally across the ocean. He tried to talk several times to the men to ask them where they were taking him, but they could not hear him. Day would turn to night and night would turn to day and they moved tirelessly ahead, heedless of his words. As he spoke, he could only watch as the tangible words emerged from his mouth. They were written in a sort of Gothic font and appeared on large scrolls of translucent air. These evanescent scrolls would twist at the ends like nautilus shells, eventually disappearing into hidden singularities. He would say words like 'tree' and a tree would materialize and the men would gather around it and pray to the skies unable to see his form. He would then say 'house' and a house would emerge out of nowhere. They would again pray to the skies. He then said 'fire' and both the tree and house would be burned as the men cowered beneath the sky begging mercy. He then said 'wind' and a great wind arose and blew the cables out of the men's hands and he, like some night slobbering Scipio, was left to soar higher and higher into invisible space. He rose past the moon and eventually reached the firmament, at which point, leaving even the stars behind it became darker and darker. He had no idea where he was going and no ability to return to the earth as he so much wanted. It was at this point that Billy awoke, his pillow soaked with sweat.

Billy hated interpreting dreams and felt no desire to interpret the one he had just experienced. He summed them all up as meaningless. Dozing off again, he had another vision of a completely different sort. He remembered a translucent vase of water, an old shaving razor with dried blood and a piece of paper held before a mirror framed in alabaster. He remembered trying to write on the paper (which resembled something more like parchment) in a clean, cursive script, but he was having great difficulty as the entire setup, propped upon a makeshift type of campaign desk, seemed to move from side to side as if from the rocking of a ship. As he tried to compose, the paper kept shifting, causing him considerable consternation. He only remembered a few words across the page in what appeared to be a different language:

"In these chapels are the images of idols, although, as I have before said, many of them are also found on the outside; the principal ones, in which the people have greatest faith and *confidence, I precipitated from their pedestals, and cast them down the steps of the temple, purifying the chapels in which they had stood, as they were all polluted with human blood, shed ill the sacrifices. In the place of these I put images of Our Lady and the saints, which excited not a little feeling, in Moctesuma ——*"

But, where had this come from? Indeed, an excerpt from the book on Cortez he was reading. Fully awake, he decided to check the time and whether it was appropriate to rise from bed. However, before his eyes could even reach the red letters of his digital clock, he'd already assumed that it would foretell some "ungodly" hour well in advance of the actual time. It was only 3:47. Billy knew that the tightness in his chest was due to what could only be a minor panic attack. Until very recently, he had never taken his random fits of anxiety seriously as they had been relatively rare up until the past few weeks. Nonetheless, the feeling in his chest was probably something that he should not have taken in stride with his usually cavalier attitude towards life. Regardles of his young age, Billy had experienced a partial stroke a few years before and since that time he was subject to all kinds of problems: moodiness, a certain degree of memory loss and sudden feelings of anxiety. Furthermore, there was evidence that his limbic brain was impacted, giving him occasional bouts of paramnesia and misattributed memories, which at times possessed Billy like visions. As for the stroke, the doctor had determined it was the result of a congenital problem, a previously minor arrhythmia in his left ventricle, which he subsequently "fixed", despite Billy being left with a deep sense that something had been taken out of him. On the whole, Billy had been very lucky and considering the seriousness of the situation, he had come off with very few side effects or impediments to his enjoyment of life except a regular regimen of beta-blockers. However, the doctor had advised him to seek a life devoid of stress and in Billy's warped mind, the job of a coroner in a small city seemed just the thing.

Billy sat awake thinking a number of things, none of which was terribly profound. Sometimes, to entertain himself, he would read the local obituaries out of mere professional curiosity. The weekend paper wouldn't arrive for another four hours, but he had one particularly important article that he had been saving next to his bed for weeks. It was the obituary of the man he had found with a rubber fist in the Lido. He had circled the article in red highlighter and put it aside, but never got around to reading it. It turned out the man's name was Charles Curtin and he was a relatively successful businessman ('Chichevache Enterprises'), property developer and father of four. Besides husbandry, he sold natural sponges the world over and in that way, sponged off the sponges. According to the obituary, he was a devoted husband and a fan of "vigorous" outdoor sports such as hunting, fishing and canoeing. Billy remembered the strange encounter with the man's wife when he told her what had occurred, simply telling her that her husband had been found in the Lido and suffered a heart attack. He had started in his usual direct tone as she leaned against the doorframe in front of him, quaffing uninterestingly out of a blue martini glass dressed only in her pink negligee. She was in her mid-fifties and had evidently dyed her air an odd blondish color, her face was pitted, but her lips unimaginably full and decorated in a garish red color. Her face was a death mask, shot through with botulism, which at least partially explained her inability to register any recognizable emotion or even reaction. Through the crack of the door, Billy saw two young Hispanic men dressed only in their underwear, holding lit sparklers in each of their hands, while he and the two officers behind him did all they could not to laugh. Once he had finished the description of what had occurred, the wife merely grinned and said that the sonofabitch deserved what he got and that once she had her lawyers on the case, she was going to take his estate for all it was worth. She even went so far as to invite him to a party she would have the following day to celebrate her divorce. Her final words to Billy were something to the effect that the only lasting memory her husband had left her with was a bad case of venereal disease. Now that he had finally had leisure to read the obituary, he was surprised to see the glowing review of the man, evidently written by his wife. Billy smiled at this and took a couple of sleeping pills. Within another half hour, after paging through a couple more tits magazines, he was asleep again with a gentle grin on his face.

When he awoke for the final time, the window shades remained dark leading him to believe that the hour was still early, however when he turned over in bed to check the time, he realized it was already past midday. The lateness of the hour didn't bother him because Billy was by habit a late riser and considering that he had just finished an entire week of late nights, the sporadic nature of his recent sleeping habits was of absolutely no consequence. In the distance, he heard the low rumble of thunder, it seemed yet another storm was at hand. Rising slowly out of bed, he entered the living room and turned on the news stations. From the blue, red and yellow masses that danced across the digitally generated satellite maps, it appeared that another hurricane was threatening the coast and would probably not hit Hokum until the early hours of the following morning. As he turned around in the low light of his living room, Billy looked forlornly at his life's detritus, a vast expanse of things that had washed up unconsciously into that forsaken shore that was his living room. If a cluttered room is the product of a cluttered mind, his mental state was indeed one of shipwreck. There before him stood the discarded drink cartons, the candy bar wrappers, the empty bottles of whisky, the piles of unopened mail, the tits magazines, CDs strewn everywhere and finally, a toppled plastic chair that had no companion. There before him, was a collection of objects that once retained some meaning for him, but now stood glaring in their utter ruination, begging him to be given some semblance of significance or order. As he felt the first tremors of anxiety, he banished them quickly, deciding at once that he would hire a cleaner. It would be the first thing he did the following day.

The walls of Billy's living room were a study in minimalism. In the adjoining room, one would find his numerous collections. Billy thought about what he should do with himself for the rest of the day. Perhaps he could kill a few hours day trading or even log into his cadre of Internet dating sites to check if any hapless women had responded to one of his rare messages. He had a thing for Asians and insisted that all the women he dated were of exacting standards: Asian, petite and generally quiet. As Billy began to prepare his breakfast of toast and cereal, he was drawn once again to the previous night's dream. Its significance was unimportant, but the mere fact that he remembered it at all was exceptional. He looked out the window of his kitchen at the dark, unmoving sky, which resembled a shard of flint ready to be struck. Given the large amount of rain that had begun to come down, it would certainly be a good day to remain within doors.

As the broken images of his subconscious mind returned again and again, floating to the surface like tethered homicides, he tried unsuccessfully to find ways to brush them aside. Not wanting to spend his day in any form of self-reflection (an exercise which he equated to morbid self-harm), he looked grimly at the almost forgotten treadmill in the corner of the room, a lab rat's toy. That was it. It had been conclusively settled. Given the poor options that immediately presented themselves, *faute de mieux*, he thought it best to brave the weather and wander down the street to his favorite bar. Despite the fact that he would be on call later that evening and despite the fact that strong storms were usually a presage for an increased workload, he would spend the day drinking. After all, it didn't seem to matter to anyone how Billy showed up for work. If fact, most people assumed that to be a coroner, one would need to be drunk most times just to cope. On one particular occasion, he had shown up to a house so inebriated that reading the address on the mailbox incorrectly, he arrived to tell an eighty-year-old widow that her husband had died of an Ecstasy overdose, not even bothering to ask her name. Although it was a feat never to be repeated, some who opened the door to him did occasionally catch the hint of alcohol on his breath. It wasn't that he was an alcoholic, but never knowing when he might be called to duty, he was occasionally the only one available to conduct the city's dirty business. In any regard, he was certain that his preferred drinking hole would not be deserted. In fact, it would be reasonably full with the usual mix of sports watchers and unrepentant degenerates. Given Billy didn't have much in common with the sports watchers, he usually found himself speaking to the unrepentant degenerates. Overall, they were a happy set of degenerates and if nothing else, provided interesting conversation, willing as they were to listen to any amount of drivel.

As he left his building, turned left down the staircase and under the bridge, he paused in the underpass to watch the rainwater gather into dark mysterious pools. At the bottom of the staircase, there were red droplets of what appeared to be dried blood, but it was not his concern given that whoever's blood it was had evidently managed to avoid the need for his services. He sat and paused only to consider whether he should bring an umbrella with him and perhaps George's obituary as some in the bar might have enjoyed reading it. No matter, he didn't relish the thought of retracing his steps. As he continued to walk past the wharf basin and down in the direction of the other wharfs, he noticed immediately that the streets of the city were virtually deserted of people. The rain came down in dark heavy drops and in the distance, the thunder grumbled. It was clear that it would rain for the remainder of the day. As he walked along one of the canals, he saw several coots hovering under a water drain that vomited water at a prodigious rate. He imagined that there would be a significant amount of flooding in the area and the news stations had hinted as much. As he walked on his lonely path toward the riverside boulevard, he saw a woman walking in his direction, wearing a large, purple hat and a matching purple raincoat, she carried a pale nosegay in one of her hands. She wore a pair of long, leather gloves and had one hand resting atop her hat, keeping it down so that he could only catch a quick, glance at the woman's ghostly face as she hastened by him. She was certainly in a hurry to go somewhere and had an expensive purple purse tucked under her arm. Across the street, a long, black limousine was waiting, its windows tinted ominously. Could it have been a Saturday funeral?

Again, it wasn't his concern anymore as his paperwork had evidently been filed well. Across the street, braving the now building wind was an intrepid jogger in nylon leggings, reflective glasses and a bright yellow, neon top. Instantly, Billy sniggered to himself darkly. What was this fool doing running in the wind and rain? Extending his life or ending it? He wished a lightning strike would come down and take the misery loving individual out of what he evidently loved the most, his misery.

After the twenty-minute walk it took to arrive at his destination, Billy was thoroughly soaked through despite wearing a large green poncho. Using his hands, he pulled back the water out of his hair and stepped across the darkened threshold. As he entered the familiar surroundings of the Red Queen, the usual mood pervaded. The bar was of indiscriminate age. Regardless of being of a reasonably large size, the interior was fairly dusky, composed almost entirely of beech wood, brass and red vinyl upholstery. The windows at the front had been partially blacked out, however whatever film they had used on the windows was beginning to wear off in numerous places. Next door, there was a Thai body massage parlor, which also had its windows blacked out. Nevertheless, despite a luminous, amaranthine light and an assortment of fake plants, no one knew for certain whether it was in operation or not. As always, the strong stench of dried beer permeated the Red Queen. From the inside, over the door lintel hung a sign that proclaimed in bold red letters, "The House of Champions". The space was lit throughout with hanging lamps that were shaded with spheres of red plastic, each the size of a human head and open at the bottom. Without any ambient light coming from the windows in front, the place was darker than usual and the air thicker so that one could only see the mere outlines of the Cimmerian figures within. One felt as if swimming through some murky, neglected aquarium. All over the walls one found the usual mélange of photographs depicting in situ sports stars, semi-nude or topless women, even the odd sports car. As expected, regardless of the weather, the bar was populated with the wonted mix of regulars who sought out an unassuming, quiet place to drink that suited them and their bearing. Unfortunately, despite the patron's best wishes and for reasons they couldn't easily imagine, the Red Queen was a bar where specimens of the female sex were seldom to be seen. On the other hand, there were to be found many similarly proportioned, beer bellied, jeans and mullet wearing men exercising themselves in various competitive pursuits such as pool, darts, foosball or occasionally playing the odd song on the jukebox, usually some blend of Ratt or Whitesnake. However, none of those other pastimes compared to the one this bar was particularly famous for. None of these other parlor games achieved the almost legendary status of 'Dead Leg', a game that attracted participants far and wide and which involved two drunken, seated competitors furiously punching each other in the legs until one finally submitted. With absolute definitiveness, after a few bouts, all competitors had rendered themselves unable to walk either due to drunkenness or extensive pain. It was one of the world's few, regularly played negative sum games where no party ultimately achieved any sort of victory over the other. But, ultimately, what most of the members of this class of discerning men came for was to sit at the bar, watch one of the numerous flat screen televisions and discuss anything from sports to politics and philosophy. Despite the run down look of many of the patrons, it was often surprising the variety and depth of conversation one could find in the Red Queen.

As soon as Billy sat at the bar, a disembodied face swum up out of the fluidified darkness into the chalky light under one of the lampshades. The only partially illuminated face belonged to that of the bartender, who was an impossibly large man of six foot seven and wore a faded grey T-shirt under another of red plaid whose sleeves were rolled up to his now invisible elbows. As he leaned forward, both of the man's hands rested powerfully on the table. Above his nicely shaped, but unsmiling lips, there hung a grey moustache. In a friendly, but confident tone, he said in a distinctly Bostonian accent, "Hey, Billy, what can I do you for?" Billy had known Ray for a number of years and had even paid an unfortunate visit to his house when his wife's brother died a few years back. Ray had come down to Hokum from New Jersey too many years ago to remember and had worked at this particular bar from before Billy knew it. Billy straight away ordered a beer and whisky. In the background, he could distinguish amongst the aural latrinalia the following snatches of conversation:

"I tol' my wife I could sleep in a ditch. Jus' leave me here and I'll find my own way home."

"Yep, boy, you wuz as drunk as ol' Cooter. You wuz hollerin' at the moon, you wuz."

"Yeah, I said, I'd sleep in a ditch, she done believed me too."

Then panning his head to the right, he caught another discussion happening just behind him between two decidedly undistinguished men. One was thin with a mouth like a deep-sea anglerfish and wore a denim suit over the back of which trailed his long gray hair that in some ways resembled Spanish moss. The other had a white, wispy beard, wore crimson glasses and possessed a toothsome smile that matched his limaceous pallor. The latter man's spoke in a loud voice and leaned against a barstool, barely able to stand. Presently, he put his finger directly into the other man's chest.

"…Yeah, the story done come to me some hows. Anyway you ever hear about those two guys who wuz out fishing over down the lake out there in Jackson. The fish wusn't bittin' none and one of them get the bright idea that they would hook up some jumper cables to a generator in the boat and try to electrocute them ol' trout so they'd jus' rise to the surface all ready to fish out with a net. Only problem wuz they wuz both in a steel bottomed boat and both of them sonofabithes dropped dead right there and then."

Inclining his head slightly to the left he intercepted yet another exchange.

"Yep, I done seen it with my own eyes, them Thai boys out there look jus' the prettiest girls you done ever seen now. Could'a almost made a fool outta me, but I ain't so particular as to turn nothin' away for a few dollars. No sir, since they done got all the right pieces in all the right places."

"We'll I for one couldn't believe he did it. That boy had an arm like a canon."

Then suddenly, out of an imperceptible distance he heard two unseen men shouting at each other and a scuffle seemed to ensue.

"Don't even mention them lyin' snakes. Them bastards. They are the Copperheads of today, sent up to put poison in the wells up there and now those very same Republicans who weren't completely opposed…"

"Are you sayin' that war in Iraq wasn't an inevitable notion by that point? It's obvious…"

"Hey, boys. What you boys gettin' all rustled up about?"

The rest was indecipherable, but soon afterward, a rousing chorus of men began half-singing, half-chanting.

"Down with the eagle and up with the cross.

We'll rally 'round the bonny flag, we'll rally once again'."

Billy shook his head and looked around him to see if there was anyone in his vicinity worth joining in conversation with. The only man close to him had passed out with his head against the bar, a trail of drool hung from his grotesque lips. After scanning the room a couple of times, it appeared that everyone was already engaged in conversations of their own. Billy was left to drink by himself and remained unmolested for two further rounds. After Billy finished his third beer, he was finally beginning to feel a buzz. As the pleasant feeling inhabited his body, his previous feelings of anxiety had long faded into remission. A wide, sheepish smile crossed his face and he began to feel an induced sense of ataraxia. At last, Billy was feeling himself again and let out a loud laugh to signal his return to normality. As his customary mood returned, he began hold court in his usual manner amongst the few barflies that remained in his vicinity. Freddie, one of his long time associations who usually wore a denim vest, round-framed glasses and a platinum ponytail patted Billy on the shoulder, "Hey, I saw you on TV the other week. That wuz a good piece you did on the murdered woman. I really liked the analogy you used, what wuz it? That the impact of the engine block slammin' into her head wuz equivalent to the blunt force impact of a sledge hammer hittin' an egg. That wuz great. You're really fixin' to open an inquest? Think you'll find the guy?" Billy, always happy to elaborate on his performances, ordered a drink for the man and entered into what would surely amount to another conversation about himself and his ambitions for the world. As he engaged in one incomprehensible line of logic after another, any worries he might have had disappeared and the general levity of those around him rose with his own. After the fifth round of drinks, the group was practically falling on the floor laughing uproariously at one of Billy's revelations, which quickly segued into another of his typical rants. Suddenly, out of nowhere, this Lord of Misrule seemed to be possessed by an invisible power that welled up within him from a distant, forgotten source.

"Yes, indeed. Man must have an intimation of purpose. A higher calling, a sense of mission that only comes with self-actualization. When I look around me, I see a number of noble spirits, whose capacity for greatness has been needlessly distracted, thwarted by the ills of this day and I list them: political correctness, calorie-counting, jogging, watery beer, low sodium diets, life coaches, SUVs...the list goes on. All these petty narcissists with their blogs, their trifling social networks thinking they are finding their own meaning in life through something so trivial as a rap lyric. All a bunch of pissant nihilists, a cabal of cultural communist!"

"You said it, Billy. Amen."

"You tell them, Billy," shouted another.

Billy continued, "Indeed, for me it comes down to the French and their petty alienation, their angst ridden paperbacks they somehow pass off as philosophy, democratizing thought to the lowest common denominator so that even a teenager can feel his acne problems are the portal into the emptiness of all meaning which he finds enough evidence for in the cynical poetry of a pop song. How can he be convinced he isn't wrong if the thinkers, the politicians, the so-called leaders who are no more than pop stars themselves are just as confused as him and kowtow to every passing fad? Why must we abide this culture of celebrity, the obsession with relativism, the constant search for a rise that has deracinated any evidence of our culture?"

"You said it, Billy. I hate them fairies. Those French are a bunch of metrosexuals."

"We need real battles to fight, real wars to win. Not with guns, but with ideas, with music, with true power. We need an occasion to rise to, but this occasion never seems to come. You Tom, you are clearly drunk, but in you lies a poet, in you, Sopwith, though drool may be falling down your shirtfront, in you, I see a philosopher. But, society has shackled us to this bar, forced these drinks into our hands so that we must sit here annihilating our spirits and for what, because they are afraid of men with dangerous ideas? They are afraid of men of ambition. They want us stupid, benumbed and slow, filling us with their trans fats, their anxiety drugs, their monster truck shows and consummate televised superficiality. In us, they breed those weeds that strangle all form of meaning, that engenders the dark bloom that is emptiness, until we become nothing more than garden variety slugs, as sickly, as vapid as all the roughage forced down our throats. I too have seen what they do once the fattening is done. I too was at the inferno in Dresden. I too was at the Sacking of Magdeburg. I too was in the Roman guard at Thessalonica. And I know, we too will be hacked apart. Anesthetized by television, that opium of the masses, we have lost the capacity to register the slightest shock or anger for what is happening to us and our society. Having been brainwashed our entire lives, we finally need to re-sully ourselves. Feel again the earth under our feet, the very soil from which we were born. Man must be re-educated. Society needs to be reformed from its splintered shards. People need a purpose. We need to take back our voice in society, our duty to be what we have always been, men of substance, a grand society of substance."

"God bless America," grunted Sopwith in his stupor as those surrounding Billy began to bang their empty glasses.

"As the great composer once said, 'Suddenly a mist fell from my eyes and I knew the way I had to take'."

Just as he was reaching his most Apollonian heights, his *Bierkeller Putsch* was prematurely ended as the door at the end of the bar opened and an unexpected presence arrived. Initially, no one noticed the visitant as it looked around itself with a benthic slowness that suited its surroundings, allowing its eyes to adjust to the sudden difference in light. Once the lonely apparition set eyes on the very person it was looking for, it dissolved itself into the corrosive darkness, making its way inconspicuously toward the bar where Billy was sitting on a high stool. No one bothered to acknowledge the strange manifestation until it was almost midway through the room, when finally, out of the corner of his eye, Billy spotted it. What was it, but the shabby eidolon of Basyli. Billy's spirit was instantly crushed as he watched the grim Pole walk up among the company of his immediate audience. By this point, it was clear that Basyli had lost so much weight that he did indeed begin to resemble a specter. Of all the people he didn't want to see, Basyli was certainly the foremost and of all the places he didn't expect to see him, it was the Red Queen. It was almost certainly the case that Basyli had never entered this particular establishment and moreover, it was just as likely that he had never even entered a sports bar before in his life. Despite their olfactory senses being impaired, Billy's audience was made aware of Basyli's presence solely by is officious *odeur*. As they turned to see the small Pole shoving his way into their midst, many of them complained, "Aw dang! What in devil's name is that?" Some even held their fingers to their noses. "What the hell? Who the heck is this guy?" Taking no notice, Basyli merely replied in a polite, but rather curt tone, "Mister Rubino?"

As the others turned away giving Basyli wide clearance, one particularly impolite barfly buzzed in a gruff tone of voice, "Mister Rubino? Where the hell you dug this one up from? You need to finish the job and put this one back in the ground. Damn if he don't stink." The other men laughed darkly, leaving Billy to entertain Basyli by himself. Prior to Basyli's opening his mouth, Billy had already decided that he wouldn't let him destroy his mood and subsequently ordered another beer.

"Mister Rubino?"

"One minute," Billy signaled.

As the beer he ordered arrived, he took one large gulp, wiping his face of the foam that had slid down his cheek and onto his chest. As he imbibed the cool liquid, he felt in much better spirits and a smile even returned to his face. Being frequently around bodies in all stages of decomposition, Basyli's scent certainly didn't disturb him unduly.

"Yes, what is it you want now?" Billy sighed.

"Mister Rubino, it has been now three weeks and there is no progress on my case. You tell me nothing. Police tell me nothing. People at your office tell me nothing. I cannot live like this much longer."

"As I said, I am monitoring the situation and have a number of very important meetings coming up regarding your case. It's all looking up. You just have to wait."

"But no one ask to talk to me. No one question me. You don't tell me about when meeting happen and I never hear anything happening."

"Didn't I tell you just last week that the district attorney himself said that there were some very interesting angles in the case and that it was lying on his desk just waiting to be opened. But, he still needs to finish a few cases that are in front of yours."

Basyli reflected for an instant and then fixed Billy with a cold stare. "I think you are lying to me. Many times I told you, I just need my papers and I can prove everything. Everything then make sense. This case take too long and I have nothing to eat in days."

Billy reached across the bar for a small bowl of complimentary peanuts.

"Take some peanuts. They are on the house. Otherwise, I can get you a bag of chips."

"I no want peanuts. I want to hear about case."

"Look, as I've told you, if you want the case to progress faster, you either have to give me more information about who you are or who the dead man is. No one, and I mean no one, will be interested in this story, not the press, not the district attorney and increasingly not me. So you have to give me something. Something more interesting than a torn up piece of paper."

"I told you. I cannot get more document. My documents taken by you and police. They are gone. My whole life, gone."

A large smile wove its way across Billy's face as he attempted to comfort the increasingly agitated man, even putting an arm on his shoulder. "This is a world of infinite possibilities. You just have to work harder. Just look at yourself. You sleep on the street. So then, what have you decided for yourself? To be...To..."

Baysli, "You are not listening."

Billy continued, "...be a bench wino."

Basyli, "But I retired. I cannot teach math. I cannot get job. *Bez pracy nie ma kołaczy.* I do things in logical way. You have no way. No logic. My life has been taken away from me and you take it. *Masz srake zamiast mózgu.*"

Billy retorted, "Well no use in getting testy. Look, what we are ultimately discussing is an issue of freewill and self-determination. You have free will, but no determination."

"I no want to talk about freewill. I want to talk about my case. *Nie wszystko się godzi...*" Basyli banged his fist violently against the bar. "You must let me talk to attorney. Give me meeting and I explain everything. No one want to listen to me."

The conversation dragged on in this fashion for a number of minutes until it entered into its usual endgame: Basyli, left helpless, with nothing else to do but to watch Billy's lips as he pontificated about this and that in many cases veering off the point, content as he was in these perorations to hear the sound of his own voice. Basyli assumed his customary pose, looking more and more miserable by the moment. Perhaps out of desperate hunger or some other unfathomable necessity, he then did something he had rarely done in the past. He took to looking straight into Billy's eyes as they danced in the dull glare of the lamp that stood above his head. In the dust suffused light, Billy's normally red hair became translucent, making it seem as if it were aflame. As Billy spoke, Basyli could no longer hear the words that were emanating from his lips and he continued to look ever deeper into his eyes, becoming almost transfixed until a cloud of darkness shadowed Billy's face and in an instant, Basyli thought he saw a terrible glint pass across Billy's eyeballs, a deep, green flash that only lasted a second. Yes, he was sure of it. He had finally seen what he had increasingly expected he would. At that moment, a look of unalloyed dread entered Basyli's face and he managed turn a shade paler than he already was. He pointed his finger directly to Billy's face and began shouting hysterically.

"Yes, I see it now. I finally see. I see it in your eyes."

"See what?" Billy asked quizzically.

"You are the Devil himself. You are not a man. You are Satan. You take people's lives and no one can see but you are the Devil."

Billy gave off a sarcastic laugh. "Don't be ridiculous. I've been called a lot of things, but…here, maybe you just need a beer to calm you down." Billy tried to calm the man by putting his hand on his shoulder.

"No, don't touch me. You are *Diabeł* and you are Lucifer. They cannot see it but I see it in your eyes. They cannot not see, but yet I will prove. You are here to destroy this city and all people. I have seen before. I will prove it. You are Devil."

At this point, Billy suddenly became more pensive. Here was another person calling him the Devil. It was the third person in two weeks. Was it just a coincidence? If he were in fact the Devil, he must have had an identity crisis because he certainly never thought of himself as evil. People, of course, were called the Devil all the time, people like Stalin, Hitler, one's boss, even the hapless meter maid or the old ogre in the upstairs apartment who would often leave plastic bags of goldfish out in the snow, allowing them to freeze into something colder and harder than hate, but what had he done to merit the moniker? Not only had he been called the Devil, but here was one saying he could prove it. Alone, the perhaps flippant comment didn't merit serious consideration, but Billy did begin to harbor some questions about his perception of reality and moreover, his understanding of morality. As much as he tried to wage war against a creeping nihilism, to be a 'noble soul' and enforce his 'negative capability', he couldn't avoid the fact that he too struggled to find meaning in much of anything. The five or so beers had made Billy pensive and he began to consider the origin and essence of evil, a topic he had never recalled addressing. He had already forgotten his recent speech and the previous shadows that had surrounded him, forced him again into a dark morass. In his helplessness, he pondered whether by his increasingly falling into a nihilistic stupor he was *de facto* embracing evil by the mere fact that he inherently lacked the conception of a credible 'good'? Or whether his recent anxiety was simply the result of his increasing angst which itself was perhaps a consequence of his profession? Due in part to his almost worthless degree in Continental philosophy, Billy had always rejected the idea that he was a bad person, that he was in any shape or form evil, simply because when he looked at the world around him, especially in his professional life, he witnessed the aftermath of several acts of evil that might have been engendered by absence and ended in absence, but they were nothing that were a part of his personal conception of absence, which was, he felt, a positive absence, the absence of doing anything at all, wrong or right. By doing what he thought was required, he deflected moral judgment and assumed the mantle of a Machiavellian or perhaps worse an existentialist, a philosophy he thought at best, half-baked at worst, contemptible. But if that were the case, he truly had caught the same sickness he had assumed was driving the world into nihilism and ultimately into madness. Billy had these and many other thoughts as he stared into his half-finished beer.

While Billy was lost in these important considerations, the barman Ray came over, inquiring as to the nature of Basyli's foudroyant outbursts, "What the hell is going on here? What is all this shouting? Who is this guy, Billy? Is he givin' you trouble?"

At this point, Basyli immediately grabbed Ray by the shirt, shrinking further away from Billy. He enjoined Ray, "He is devil. I see it in eyes."

Ray laughed. "Sure he is, but you're going to have to quiet down, you're disturbing the other customers and what is that smell? When is the last time you've taken a shower?"

"No, I no quiet down. I no take shower. You must listen. He is here to destroy city. To take everyone life."

"Is this guy for real?" Ray entreated Billy. But Billy, lost in his thoughts, ceased to acknowledge what was happening around him. He was still stuck on the fundamental question of whether or not he was in fact was the Devil. After all, was that why he was recently feeling so out of place? It seemed unlikely, but why not? Evil as a concept was alive and well and thriving in all parts of the world. Furthermore, he had just to look at himself: after all, would the Devil really be taking valium?

As Billy sat deep in thought, Basyli continued to shout at the people who were now crowding around him to see what was going on. "Look here is Devil. Look at his eyes. He signs the certificates and takes people's lives. He is the Devil. Devil. Devil."

"This guy's drunk. Hurry, get him another drink," shouted one of the patrons. The barman, who appeared like a giant when he stood next to Basyli, having had enough, walked around to the other side of the bar and began to push Basyli back away from Billy.

"Alright, that's it. You're outta here," he said in a stern voice.

As Ray continued to push Basyli towards the door, literally dragging him at times by his jacket collar until it tore, the desperate Pole continued his fulminations, all the time pointing at Billy. "Look everyone. Look him. He is the Devil. I will prove it. I will prove it, I promise." Finally, after one final, rough motion on Ray's part, Basyli was thrown unceremoniously out of the front door of the bar without Billy taking the slightest notice.

As Billy stared into his now empty glass, Ray returned to the place where Billy was sitting and said to him, "Who was that weirdo? Smelled bad enough to gag a maggot."

Billy responded absentmindedly, "Oh, it's one of my clients." As Billy began to order another beer, he felt his cellular vibrating in his pocket. When he looked at the number on the phone, it arrived as "Unknown", which for him was actually the greatest clue as to who it was on the other end. Reluctantly, he picked up the phone and heard again the expected voice of Velenet, the dispatcher.

"Hey, you know I'm not on call yet."

"I know, I know but Moncrete is away on somethin' else that's gonna take hours and we have no one else at the moment."

"Aw, shit. That ain't my problem. Just find someone else, I'm busy trying to get a buzz going here."

"I'm sorry, but there really is no one else, I've tried everythin'."

"You realize I'm over the legal limit."

"I didn't hear anythin', sir. Can you repeat?"

"Aw, hell," Billy said in exasperation. The day was truly going from bad to worse.

"I'm sorry, Billy."

"OK, what is it?" Billy responded with a defeated tone in this voice.

"'Couple of boys found a body washed up on the shore near the Hainsville highway. They said it's a dead woman. Young. Looks like another suicide off the Potowok bridge."

"But that's all the way out near Suddler's End. You couldn't get any closer to the end of our jurisdiction. I never understood why does the river have to flow that direction. Potowok is in their jurisdiction, anyway."

"But the bodies are always found in ours. We're always cleaning up their trash."

"Just our luck."

"I know, right out in the Styx. I'm sorry, Billy, but all the emergency units are engaged at this time and the storms gettin' pretty bad. Given the boys seem pretty sure she's dead, no use sendin' out emergency services with the weather bein' what it is and all and you're closer anyway. We'll get some people to assist in another hour or two."

"Shit, you mean I gotta go way out there?"

"Sorry, Billy, given the weather it's a wonder the river didn't take it down any further. But, anyways, it's not too far past your office."

"Try forty-five minutes past."

"Sorry, Billy. I tried."

"Alright, alright."

"Look, as you can see, it's a bit further west from the usual place, but the boys know where it is. You just go to the address I'm gonna give ya and they'll be there to show you where it is. They'll be waitin' for you. I told them you'd be on your way."

"They know who it is? They recognize her?"

"No idea. Never seen her before."

"Aw shit, that means I'm gonna spend the rest of the night chasin' her down."

"Sorry, Billy, what can I say?"

"Nothing, Velenet. Nothing. Just give me the address."

Billy took down the address and made his way back to his apartment garage in order to retrieve his car, but not before having a final double shot of bourbon. A cold, wet evening lay ahead so he might as well don his "Jimmy Jacket". By the time he finally started driving on the highway out of town, he was certainly over the legal limit. Despite this obvious fact, if an officer were to stop him, the hapless law enforcement representative would most certainly have turned a blind eye, realizing that Billy was on official business. Well aware of what awaited him, the fact that he was going to be working alone for at least a couple of hours amidst the inhospitable elements, meant that he brought an additional bottle of Old Crow, sipping it at intervals as he drove toward the bitter end of Hokum that lay to the southwest. The rain was falling at a definite slant and Billy's windshield wipers were having trouble coping. It took him well over an hour to finally reach his destination. When he finally arrived at the trailer home, he was more than glad to finish driving. He waited for a few minutes in front of the small house to gird himself for the hours of cold and wet he would no doubt have to endure. The trailer home was a simple, white, wooden affair at the side of the road. A single light was turned on in the anteroom. The solitary house was surrounded by miles of barren fields.

The rain was coming down even harder and was blown westward in large, visible drafts. The horizon was low and in the distance toward the north, one could barely make out the gray outlines of the Maralah Mountains. He parked his car in the gravel parking lot next to two pickup trucks and a small Winnebago trailer that had seen better days. Next to the house was another trailer upon which sat a small, pea green fishing boat. An assortment of rusted blue and orange kerosene cans lay against the vinyl siding where clumps of crabgrass grew in odd patches out of the white gravel. A small dog could be heard barking from within.

Billy knocked on the door and his ears could sense a great deal of commotion from within. After not more than ten seconds, two boys of ten and eleven answered his latest battery, the excitement quite evident in their eyes, their faces and hair stained with mud. One of the boys yelled with glee, "Mom, he's here." A small, mahogany dog that resembled a poodle was barking furiously at Billy's feet, both biting and dry humping the hem of his pants in turns. Billy tried to shake the small, hideous thing away from his leg as he certainly wasn't an animal lover. The boys were too excited by his presence to notice and it was only when the boys' mother arrived that she finally commanded, "Stop it, Precious. What has gotten into you?" As she separated the dog from his pants, she apologized to Billy and nestled the dog atop her breasts. At this point, Billy got a good look at the horrid creature and concluded that it was a hideous thing indeed. Evidently old, it had one good eye and its small teeth protruded outside the range of its gums. The dog continued to bark at Billy with even more ferocity now that it was closer to the level of his face. The woman said, "I'm sorry, I don't know what has gotten into him. I'll be right back." With that, the woman took the dog away, leaving him once again alone with the two boys.

One of the boys said to Billy in an excited tone, "Are you gonna cut up the dead body like they do on television?"

The other one answered with similar brio, "Yeah, are you?"

"No boys, not just yet, I'm just here…"

His sentence was interrupted as he heard a loud yelp in the background. The barking had finally stopped.

"I'm just here to examine the body and determine cause of death and then…"

"Well isn't you gonna cut her up and see what done caused it? I'm sure she done drownded. Killed herself on that there bridge downstream. My daddy found another one when I wuz just a little'n. I done touched her with my finger."

"You what?"

The other boy chided his brother, "Shhh. Don't tell him that. Yep, she's dead as a doornail."

At that point the mother returned to the door. She was wearing a brown open sweater and a pink, low-cut top, which revealed the freckled crest of a pair of well-appointed if not completely natural breasts. She was of middle age, but her hair was evidently dyed a deep chestnut color. She had a long face with a couple of fleshy warts near her chin. She wore a pair of jeans and held a half-smoked cigarette in one of her hands, which also bore a hideous cubic zirconia engagement ring with a rock the size and appearance of an old flashcube. She was reasonably tall, thin with her hair cut short and cropped at the sides. She wore no makeup and her lips were rather thin and pallid. She had steely blue eyes and her face was lined with the first signs of age. She began apologetically,

"I hope these boys ain't givin' you no trouble. Lord knows they give me enough. Always out playin' down the river gettin' muddy and this storm's a howlin' out there and all. You know they say it's gonna be a big one and probably knock the power out again. Good thing we got generators. You got to now days. My granddady's sister wuz on an iron lung respirator, power went out and she up an died just like that. Can you believe it? Anyway, I just got back from Mexico where I had some work done and jus' got the bandages off last week and these boys I think done jus' put all the wrinkles back on my face that I just got done gettin' rid of. Jus' look at these crow's feet comin' back. I swear these little monsters will be the death of me. Anyway, I don't know why I'm tellin' you all this as I'm sure that ain't why you're here, but I sometimes feel like I'm gonna jus' lose it. You know what I mean?"

Billy on many occasions tried to arrest her torrential flow of words, but he found it impossible to get a single word of his own in edgewise, despite making obvious gestures that he wanted to interject. Her thoughts possessed all the randomness of a Wiffle ball in flight.

"Anyway, them boys always playin' down near the river and they commin' back with all kinds of dead things. You name it: raccoons, crawfish, cats and dogs. They all wash down here in the river and these boys got somethin' morbid about them, I swear. Well, I'm sittin' here just mindin' my own business, doin' the laundry, then they come'n tell me they found a body down near the river and I'm like, 'what?' 'Whose body?' And they say 'a woman's body' and I ain't payin' no much real attention to it cause they always goin' fibbin' about somethin' they done found out down the river. You know they daddy's always bein' gone and they have gotten into all this lyin' somethin' awful. More'n I can take sometimes. So I jus' go about my business, whatchin' my TV then they goes out again in the rain after I done toll'em to stop 'cuz I gonna end up cleanin' the floor and they clothes 'cuz they ain't good for no chores. Then they bring back this little necklass here and said they done found it on her neck and then I said, well I'll be damned, pardon my French, maybe they's then tellin' the truth. But I don't know no ways and I ain't about to go down there myself so I then call my sister out in Jepsen and ask her what I should do. That fool, she tell me to don't say nothin' cause the police then will get a whiff of what's goin' on with the po' folks cause we can't afford no lawyers and they want the case all served up nice and easy, you see? Then they git the sheriff to drive down here all nice an polite until next thing ya know they will call you the suspect 'cuz that same thing happen to one of her cousins a few years back. Well then I said she is talkin' nonsense 'cuz she's sometimes not all right in the head and I mean that's crazy for anyone to think that. I mean, true to my faith, I never been mixed up in anythin' like that. You believe me don't you? I mean after all you don' think I did it, do'ya?"

"Did what?"

"Murder the poor girl?"

"Of course not, I'm just…"

"Yes, I done told her so and that's exactly what I done told her and then I hung up with her cause she wanna talk about her husband sleepin' in some ditch when he got drunk the other night at the weddin'. Then I got to thinkin' to myself maybe I should call in to the radio and ask them what I should do. You know the radio station with Gordy Gray and J.C.? They's my favorite and they answer all kinds of questions. You just don't know where they get all those answers from, but anyway they put me on automatic hold and never picked up so then I said maybe I should call the gas station cause he's gotta pick-up an can maybe take her over to the funeral parlor. Then I said to myself, I better ask the Lord first what I should do and then I sat here with my boys and prayed and prayed somethin' mighty. But right when I wuz gettin' down to it, phone rang and it wuz my sister again, tellin' me I better not speak to the police and then I jus' hung up on her right then and there. I could take no more of her hissy fits anyhow 'cuz her thoughts are all scattered and mixed up as ants on ammonia. Anyways, I finally sat down and said, there's no two ways about it. I finally broke down an called the police, I did and then I tol' em…Aw, look at me all runnin' my mouth every which ways and you standin' out in the rain and wet, gettin' yourself a cold. Why didn't you say nothin'? Why don't you come on in and I'll fixin' you up a coffee. What you say your name wus?"

"I didn't, mam, my name is Billy. Billy Rubino," the thoroughly soaked and increasingly aggravated coroner replied, stepping through the doorway.

"Hey, haven't I seen you on TV? Yes, I think so. On the news. Somethin' about a sledgehammer and an egg. That's right. I've never had anyone that's been on TV in my house. And is you from the police, the real police?"

Billy blushed, always happy to have someone recognize him. "No mam, I am the coroner mam, from the coroner's office."

"Oh, like on TV. Well, I'm almost overwhelmed. Can I get you a coffee?"

"No thanks, mam."

"Smoke, you smoke?"

"No."

"Hopin' you don't mind if I do?"

"No, mam, I don't mind."

"You favor some moonshine?"

Billy paused here. Finally, she had struck the right chord. He never normally rested on ceremony or correct police procedure, but nonetheless, the offer took him slightly by surprise.

Billy smiled a wry smile, "Really, I'm not supposed to but…"

"But what the hell, right? Weather out there is somethin' horrible and you'll be out there for a while, I suppose?"

"Yeah, maybe a little would be OK."

"I might'n have some myself. Make yourself comfortable on the couch."

As the woman went into the kitchen to retrieve the moonshine, she lit a cigarette from a pack she had tucked into one of her back pockets. At this point, Billy finally had some time to observe his surroundings. The interior of the house was accoutered modestly, but neatly. In the center of the room was a much abused vinyl settee that had numerous cracks throughout. In front of the settee was a low coffee table with a large doily upon which sat an ornate wooden box. The room was filled almost entirely with photographs of sundry relatives, especially of pictures of the two boys that had been taken at various points in their childhood. In one rather faded, Kodachrome photo, he saw what was presumably her father, standing proudly in a military uniform next to what must have been her stiffly grinning grandmother, who wore a pair of cat eye reading glasses beneath a large brown beehive. Around the room were a number of Christmas decorations despite the holiday still being several weeks off. A gas fire had been lit in the fireplace and the television was turned on to the news channel. As he looked around, he heard one of the boys who was running around the house making what appeared to be motorcycle sounds while wearing enormous ear muffs and a pair of oven mitts. As he moved to the side of the couch furthest from where the boys were playing, he sat in front of an old television, which had been turned up to an ear-bleedingly high volume. The ignored device sat in one corner of the room, muttering to itself in a newscaster's voice. Suddenly, as the serious male tones of an anonymous weather reporter switched to the more saccharine voice of an Asian newswoman, he began to take notice. "A California man has made an exact replica of his brain using stem cells he grew in a petri dish that were previously taken from his derriere. This is the culmination of a number of experiments the retired mechanic had been making over the previous months. Using materials bought off the internet, MRI scans he had requested from his doctor and knowhow he had acquired from Wikipedia, he was able to make exact copies of his organs using an old ink jet printer and software he had downloaded from a Russian website. He intends to make a complete copy of himself within the next year so that doctors will never need to find him an organ donor. When asked how he felt having an exact replica of his brain sitting before him in a jar, he reportedly said he 'was of two minds'. Amazing what mechanics can accomplish now days, don't you think, Bob?"

Panning away from the Boob Tube, Billy noticed with some small degree of alarm, in a darkish corner at the other end of the room that itself was cloaked in a vapor shroud of menthol, a scary old woman who it was obvious had long ago become part of the furniture. She sat motionless in a ragged couch with her amorphous frame (akin in shape to an old sack of walnuts) turned away from the television. She gave no further indication of her being numbered among the quick except to let out odd smirks as she would intermittently foul the air – evidently a long-standing ritual – which caused the two boys to yell in unison, "aw Grandmaw", while pinching their little freckled noses. Throughout the rest of his stay, Billy was sure that while he was speaking to what must have been her daughter-in-law, the dirty old hag would leer at him, even daring a libidinous wink. As Billy finished scanning the room, he noticed that almost everything was of various shades of mauve. It appeared, someone in the house had some form of obsession with the color. The couch, the coffee table, the picture frames, the wallpaper, even the carpet were all mauve in color. As he began to relax into the sofa, he was suddenly startled by the approach of loud footsteps. The smaller of the two boys ran up to him, holding something that resembled an old fur hat.

"Know what this is?"

He shoved the miserable object into Billy's face, while Billy, on his part, recognized from the unmistakable fetor that it was something that had in the not too distant past, contained life.

"It's a dead rabbit we found out back. When my dad gets back, we gonna stuff it an put it on the wall."

As Billy shoved the dead rabbit away from his face, the mother yelled from the next room, "Are those two mongrels still bothern' you? Leave the poor man in peace, I said or I'm gonna have Daddy give you a real wuppin'."

"No, Maw. We ain't botherin' him at all, we were just showin' him our rabbit."

"A rabbit! Where did you get a rabbit? I don't remember gettin' yous no rabbit."

The older boy, plainly ignoring his mother's exhortations, came up and stood right beside Billy's left ear. As he spoke into it, Billy could feel the small jets of saliva spattering the side of his face. "Hey listen, you like dead people right? You evern' see a ghost."

Pushing the dead animal away from his face for a second time, he said, "No, not yet. Well, actually, there is one I believe I have seen."

"Really where?"

"Well, I saw him down in the city. He's this Polish KGB agent."

"Really, Polish…aw cool. Mom, this guy has seen a ghost."

"You leave the man alone and stop talkin' all that nonsense." The woman returned with a wooden tray atop of which stood two small shot tumblers.

"This is real moonshine, it is. Oak barreled and everythin'."

She then sat next to Billy on the couch, putting the tray down carefully before them. With the hand that was holding the cigarette, she gently lifted one of the shot glasses to her mouth while handing the other to Billy. The shot glass contained an amber liquid within which there were several pieces of an unknown substance swirling about. "Bottoms up," she said, looking him straight in the eye. She downed the glass in a single swallow. He put his own down, dispensing his crass *obligatio* with similar crudeness. The fiery liquid burned the back of his throat, givin' him the distinct sensation that he was drinking turpentine. He even winced at which she grinned in practiced response. At this point, Billy noticed that one of her two front teeth was dead and almost black. "Mighty fine, if I don't say so myself. Don't mind if I have another," she said, pouring them each another tumbler full. They both repeated the ceremony after which she continued, "Now, mister…aw damn, already forgot your name. Don't know where my mind is today."

"Rubino."

"Yes, Rubino. What can I do for you?"

"Well, I need to go see the body and I was hopin' your sons..."

"Oh, yes the body. What wuz I thinkin'? You know, I jus' don't understan' it. Them people all jumpin' off that bridge and drowdin'. Don't they know it's a sin? I know I've had my share of hard days, but it jus' don't make no sense. The boys says she's young and purdy to."

"She is young. Can you say what age?"

"I don't know."

"What does she look like? Any chance you might know who she is?"

"Boys never seen her before. No idea. Maybe one of them Mexicans that work up in the fields or somethin'."

"No, she don't look like no Mexican, Mom."

"Alright, mam, well I better get down there and find out what is going on," Billy said pushing the dead animal out of his face for a third time.

"Listen, Myers, don't you see the man don't want that. Anyway, mister you just got here. There's no need for you to be runnin' down there jus' yet, she ain't goin' nowhere."

"We'll I need to determine cause of death and contact the relatives as soon as possible. It's going to take a good amount of work so I better get started."

"Alright, if you must. Anyway, I'll go get the boys to take you down there 'cuz I don't like goin' down them ol' rickety steps. Anyway, it smells bad enough down there 'n with all that mud and all even without havin' to worry about dead bodies. The idea just gives me the creeps. Not sure how these boys can stan' it, but they do got somethin' morbid about them fur sure."

"Yes, mam."

Billy stood up to leave and the mother moving quickly toward the door made sure her two boys put on all of the proper attire. It was at this point that he finally subjected the boys to closer scrutiny. Even when he had first caught sight of them, he noticed that there was definitely something strange about them but he couldn't quite put his finger on it. First off, they looked rather alien, both possessing enormous heads and relatively small bodies. The kind of kids you could see spending weekends incinerating insects with a magnifying glass. Secondly, the younger one (who he had distinguished as Myers) had incredibly chapped lips and a broken smile, missing, as he was, a couple of baby teeth, only one of which was in the process of being replaced. Their front teeth looked enormous and were stained brown due to the fluorosis that was common in the region. Thirdly, as he looked into their heavily freckled faces, they had a strange, distant look in their eyes as if there was something there that hadn't been switched on. Their hair was matted and dirty-blonde in color. At the back of their pallid, needlessly oblong necks, their dirty strands were tied into 'rattails'. The napes of their poison-ivied necks were covered in a blonde peach fuzz, while their cheeks were dotted with the scars of a recent chicken pox. Both of them had legs stained in numerous places by the reddish Mercurochrome that had been applied in great quantities to countless cuts and bruises. Myers had a pair of enormous glasses with a patch over one lens that was put there to train a lazy eye. The older one (who he had yet to identify by name) wore braces and had enormous freckles that ran up the entirety of his arms, the color and transparency of fire ants. Myers seemed to have what appeared to be a dead mouse in his pocket, while the nameless one chewed on something that resembled pine bark. As she put on their jackets, she constantly chided them for not keeping their clothes clean. The two boys wore the customary military fatigues and the nameless one, having noticed Billy's inquisitive stare, simply replied, "I'm eatin' ants." Subsequently, after the boys had been reproached by their mother for eating ants, they both put on raccoon hats and took up a pair of air rifles. As their mother admonished them one final time not to bother Billy, Myers sat there just staring at him, constantly tilting his head from side to side with a foolish grin on his face. As Billy shook his head slowly, an expression full of pity and remorse filled his face.

After looking out the window a couple of times, it was decided that the three would-be explorers should wait another five minutes. For Billy, the time couldn't have passed any slower. Once the rain had subsided slightly, Billy got up with a start, said his farewells to the children's mother (not daring to acknowledge the old windbag in the corner). However, as he was opening the front door, the decrepit old sack of bones allowed herself the pleasure of one final six gun salute which ended in a low blubbering sound that could only indicate that she had evidently fouled herself to a considerable extent. At this point, both boys and their mother cried in unison, "Aw, Grandmaw," to which the mother added in antiphon, "Why you always gotta do that when we have guests? For Lord's sake, don't you got any shame left? Well, you best listen because this is the last time. I ain't gonna change you so you gonna sit like that the rest of the day or until yo' good for nuthin' son gets back into town whenever that may be." In response, the old gorgon gave back a knowing grin of utter victory, which was the only feature Billy could make out of her silhouette, which had almost completely dissolved into the gathering darkness of a room that held within its sphere an event horizon of irredeemable ignorance.

In complete disgust, Billy left the house with the two boys, who immediately took him across the road, through a short wood into a large field of marshy grasses covered over in thick mists. The earth below their feet became increasingly wet and in places there was an inch or two of standing water. In these shallows, under the rushes, the water was pellucid and in the spring one could find a countless array of small gelatin orbs, their albumen encircling miniscule black dots, the nascent limbs of a colony of tadpoles. Now, these scattered pools lay bare, empty except the dark mud and the occasional toad frozen in hibernation. In a sudden gust, the wind would wuther, turning the surface of these living wells into burnished obsidian. Billy's feet were getting soaked through and through and he regretted leaving his galoshes in the car. As quickly as it had subsided, the rain picked up again with renewed fervor.

With some amount of difficulty, he followed after the boys for what seemed an hour, slogging through mud, sometimes up to his knees. In his legs, he began to feel a stabbing pain. He cursed the boys regularly as they hollered and danced in the rain, occasionally taking up sticks to fence one other, laughing at him whenever he fell to his knees in the slime. As they walked back toward him, they heaved great stones into the distance and as they moved away, he thought a few were aimed in his direction, though in the miasma he couldn't be sure. What he was certain of was that they were possessed of a seemingly endless energy, one that he in no way shared. Despite the cold weather, he could feel that his undershirt was damp with sweat. Furthermore, the rain began to soak through his now muddy parka. At times the mist was so thick that he had to call after them to make sure he was headed in the right direction. They would yell back, but in what seemed to be a netherworld of distant sounds, he couldn't be sure from which direction or from what distance their shouts emerged. At points he had the grave fear that he was wandering completely in the wrong direction and that by chance, he might manage to fall off some steep cliff. When he could no longer hear their voices, he became anxious, wondering how he would manage to get back to his car. He looked around him, yelling for five entire minutes with no response. He then heard the sound of slow footsteps. Was it them? The footsteps stopped. He froze. Before him he imagined he glimpsed a great shadow of a man, dressed in armor, heaving a great cutlass and running toward him with great vigor. Suddenly remembering his previous night's dream, the ridiculous thought crossed his mind that it was Cortez, himself. Though he knew the idea was preposterous, his knees began to tremble as the shadow moved closer through broken shards of light. Then, in the next instant, the mists took hold and the image disappeared. All was quiet again. Billy froze, his ears strained against the silence. He had no idea what to expect, but he instinctively knew that something was coming. Then, in an instant, out of nowhere, a big clump of mud hit him in the side of the face at which point he heard the familiar cackling of the two boys. Billy wiped his face of mud and sufficiently angry, he shouted in the direction from which the missile was hurled, "Listen you little shits, I ought to kick your little asses. Now where the hell are you?"

The boys ran towards him, their faces beaming. "Aw sorry sir, please don't be sore, we didn't mean to hit you. We're almost there." With a grunt, Billy urged them onward. As they progressed further across the marshy land, his lungs wheezed and he was forced to take numerous breaks to catch his breath. The only thing that occasionally resuscitated him was the little bottle of Old Crow. He was in constant invocation, praying to the gods that the torture would soon cease.

Billy was sure that his toes would have shriveled into prunes, his ankles, undoubtedly full of leeches. He yelled again at the boys, who he could barely see now in the pouring rain, only managing to discern the outlines of their shadowy forms. "You sure you know where we're going?"

"Yep, it's just a few hundred yards more. Don't you worry a thing," he heard their voices laughing and it sounded like the laugher of a malign universe. What had he done to deserve this? After another ten minutes, they arrived to a small cliff that overlooked a great bend in the Onondaga River, which was shrouded in a haar of mist and rain. Looking downward, one could tell that these rocks had striven mightily against the powerful forces of the river for centuries, but that in this latest stage, they had renounced any chance of victory and simply crumbled ungraciously onto the small, sandy shore below. The older of the two boys cried, "It's down there."

When they came up to the very edge of the cliff to look out over the river, they could see the brown, angry torrent that hissed below them so that a dark, yeasty foam floated atop its surface. The sky hung low, tumorous and deeply veined, its purple mass ready to burst open into a peal of fire at any point. In the driving rain that stung their faces, they descended a twisted set of dry-rot stairs down to the cluttered beach below, where the river water spun in tiny eddies. At each step, Billy prayed that the stair would support his complete weight as parts of the wooden balustrade fell apart like bits of soggy cracker under his ever tightening grip. The waves of the agitated river were crashing along the shore. From where they were standing, the river was about four hundred feet wide and it was impossible to see the opposing side. Throughout the river's tumultuous flow, one could glimpse tree trunks, loose branches and other pieces of rubbish as they floated past at great velocity; these were at times dragged to the bottom in a savage whirlpool only to re-emerge twenty feet further down river in a desperate thrust of energy as if gasping for air. Again, the rain started falling in sheets. The river thundered with a voice so loud that it drowned out the shouts of the three explorers despite they're being only feet apart from one another. Like trained dogs, the boys began to snoop around the small beach area, looking for the body. Initially, they were unable to locate it and Billy began to fear that the entire journey had been for naught or even worse, that his being drawn out there was just part of an elaborate hoax. Then as he took a last sip of his depleted Old Crow, one of the boys screamed, "I found it."

The other two ran over to where the body lay in the mud at the foot of a wall of cattails. Pushing the excited boy out of the way, Billy stood over the motionless frame to get a closer look. There below him, between his now sore legs, lay the flaccid anatomy of a beautiful, young woman. Out of reflex, he had already decomposed her into her vital statistics: tits, ass, legs. At this point in his career, he couldn't tell anymore if he did it out of male instinct or some deeply enrooted professional inclination. Either way, it didn't matter given her lack of Asian features. She was of olive complexion with long, dark hair that would have fallen to the middle of her back, were she to stand up. She wore an ankle-length, black dress that was in keeping with the serene mask of vacuity that adorned her face. Her fingernails were painted black as was her face, which had been distempered by a mass of mascara that had pooled in heavy daubs below the shallow wells of her eyes. Approximately twenty-five years of age, she resembled those ridiculous Goth kids Billy often saw around the abandoned warehouse clubs in the wharf district. As he stared down the length of her placid body, to his great surprise, it appeared to him as if her chest was moving ever so slightly. He thought it impossible and that his eyes must have deceived him. There was no way she could have survived the full mile of rapids between the Potowok Bridge and where he was standing. As he put his face closely over hers to listen for any signs of breath, he simultaneously took one of her slender wrists in hand to feel for a pulse. At that instant, the girl suddenly opened her eyes wide as if waking from a dream and coughed a great flush of water into his face. The two boys jumped back with fright as if they had seen a ghost, ready as they were to run all the way back to their mother. Billy, being as shocked as they were and unable to do anything else, simply stood stock still, staring into her chocolate eyes as she returned his astonished gaze, unable to focus for a good minute or two. She breathed heavily, then suddenly sitting up, she clasped Billy around the neck and gave him a powerful kiss, barely managing to whisper, "*Mi salvador.*" It took all the energy she had remaining. Once it was expended, her head fell back, her body collapsed under its own avoirdupois like a wilting fern upon the sand. As quickly as she had emerged, without another word, she descended again into unconsciousness.

5

"If I had wings like Noah's Dove."

Billy spent the next four days at home recovering from a cold. It had also taken him about that long to recover physically from his ordeal. His legs were still somewhat sore (an eventuality for which he had Oxycondone) and he was left with a large, mysterious bruise on his left thigh. Furthermore, he had felt the insatiable need to shower continuously, causing his skin to flake in places. He remedied this by covering himself head to toe in baby oil, the very thought of the mud and slime that had once pervaded his voluminous body made him wince. Billy had seen every manner of grossness: the bruised, the burned, the beheaded, even the muddled soup of a man who had the misfortune of being electrocuted in a bathtub during the summer months so that his deliquesced self had to be skimmed off, layer by layer. But more than any of these, he really objected to the idea of being covered in dirt and mud. Thus, he had neither thought about the two boys, the long walk through the marshes or even the mysterious woman in four entire days. He had no desire of being reminded of any of those unfortunate occurrences. Furthermore, in the interim, his mental state had improved significantly and he had encountered no relapses of his former anxiety. In fact, he had been in high spirits and even treated himself to a manicure.

Presently, he looked down at his slender fingers, admiring the polished fingernails, the perfectly shaped cuticles that shone in the soft daylight that emerged from his living room window. Fortunately, for him, he had the foresight to wear his gloves out in the marshes and thus, his hands remained unblemished, unlike other parts of his body, which were full of small cuts and scrapes. He thought to himself that they would look wonderful in the pair of Italian leather gloves he had just purchased for himself, yet another extravagance to add to his already vast collection.

Despite the adverse physical effects of the last few weeks, he could feel that the bags under his eyes had receded along with the accompanying dark circles. He was back to his old self and therefore steered clear of any major substance abuse except for the occasional dose of marijuana. Marijuana was a drug for which he had a strong distaste, enjoying cocaine significantly more, but in his commitment to avoid the Warden and his newfound existentialism, his supplies had run dry. He had always laughed at people who told him they had gone to see therapists or psychiatrists, considering them weak and self-obsessed while he could only represent the very paragon of mental hygiene. Though the recent bouts of anxiety had done little to dent his fortitude (after all, only sociopaths lack anxiety he was once told), he was happy enough to be once again without them. The *Übermensch* was back and presumably here to stay.

While Billy was at the age when most of his contemporaries had long ago settled down with kids or at the very least were engaged in long-term (if less than fulfilling) relationships, he had exhibited absolutely no interest in either. In fact, Billy viewed both institutions with a highly critical eye. He was happy to keep the disturbances and intrusions into his private life to a minimum. Although he did occasionally date Asian women, the experiences were generally short lived and ended with disastrous consequences, in particular for the other party. In a not so singular instance, he had made one of his dates (herself a gestalt of petty phobias) cry subsequent to berating her for having suggested he actually see a therapist, evidencing his less than generous opinion of therapist seekers like her. Perfectly unaware, he sat there fishing out pieces of cork that had fallen into his wine glass, while she cried into her moo shu. When Billy finally looked up, he hadn't the faintest idea why she was crying despite her having lectured him on previous occasions for his conspicuous lack of sensitivity (mentally, Billy had already written off her complaints as unworthy given his theory that like most single, cat loving women her age she probably suffered from toxoplasmosis). Billy's gauche behavior could of course seem callous to some, but really, he had little appreciation for others' feelings simply out of his complete ignorance of them. In this way, Billy might have been diagnosed with a mild case of Asperger syndrome, given he only seemed to laugh at others' misfortunes while he was more than ready to cry at the most inconsequential of personal tragedies. One particular example of his peculiar sensitivities occurred six years prior, when one of his favorite pair of gloves tore while he was pulling pine straw from his windshield wipers. Upon discovering the ripped suture, his girlfriend at the time could do nothing to console him and eventually left him a sobbing mess while she was forced to find her own way home.

As the bright rays of the midday sun slid across the far wall of his room, Billy lay on his couch drinking the absinthe he had ordered online from the Czech Republic, while paging through some his favorite breed of Japanese hardcore manga, *shokushu goukan.* Next to him on the floor was a box of Kleenex, a small crack pipe and some hand lotion. His Nakamichi speakers filled the air with one of Billy's favorite pieces by Grieg, *Solveigs Sang,* which rang with lyrics Billy could never follow, '*Gud styrke dig, hvor du I verden gaar, I verden garr, Gud glaede dig, hvis du, for hans fodskammel staar.*' By random selection this ran into the lovelorn composer's *Arietta,* but Billy only heard it between gaps of unconsciousness. Hours ago, the Warden had left yet another note attached to his front door, not realizing Billy was home at the time. The note simply said:

life begins on the other side of despair.
    - sartre

pay me.
    - the warden.

If the Warden had made his way to Sartre from Arexus, it wasn't clear where he would end up next. Best to avoid him entirely. Billy didn't bother to remove the note from the door.

About to fall asleep for his second post-prandial nap of the day, he was surprised to hear a soft knock. Who could it be at this hour? Hardly anyone ever knocked at his door despite the time of day, week or year. He concluded that it was perhaps the Warden, looking for his desired payment. He instantly dismissed the notion as unlikely, given the Warden only tended to visit his house either late at night or in the very early hours of the morning. At first, he chose to ignore the knock, but it became persistent. Whoever it was wasn't going to leave. Getting up from the couch with some effort and still wearing his boxer shorts, he walked the short distance to the door and opened it without bothering to peak through the keyhole. To his great surprise, he saw before him the very woman he had rescued just days before, dressed in a similar black dress and carrying two large suitcases, one of which bore a Pan Am sticker. Around her neck, she wore a silver dog tag chain with a razor attached at the end. She had a healthy, pleasant look to her face, but no longer wore the deep mascara under her eyes. Her skin had returned to its normal color, that of a light butterscotch. He instantly recognized the large, hazel eyes that possessed a quiet intensity about them and held within their depths a bittersweet melancholy. Billy was in disbelief. Sitting with his mouth open, the women finally laughed in canned response to break the ice and in so doing acknowledged his shock. She then asked in a quiet voice, "Can I come in?"

Not knowing what else to say, he replied with a hesitant, "Yes."

As she walked into his apartment, putting down her two vintage suitcases of sky blue, she began to look around the room which remained as it always had, full of refuse and untidiness. Billy just sat there and stared with his hand still on the greasy doorknob. Rarely was he ever at a loss for words.

It goes without saying that under normal circumstances, a man of Billy's natural accouterments would have been very happy to have a girl of her physical attractiveness standing in the center of his apartment, however Billy, only favoring Asians was left completely cold by her less than exotic charms. Billy, having finally regained his composure and not knowing what else to say, scratched his head and asked, "Ah, can I help you?"

She turned toward him and smiled again, putting the tips of her fingers together and looking down nervously at the floor as she had finally noticed his rather ridiculous boxer shorts. Nonetheless, after a brief fit of laughter kept under her breath, she managed to say in her soft, pleasant voice, "No, the question is, can I help you? You saved my life and I am here to pay you back."

Billy laughed, somewhat in relief, "OK, I see. There is no need for that. It's what I do for a living and there is certainly no need for you to pay me back for doing my job."

"And to ask another small favor," she shot back.

Afraid of what she might ask, he prompted her with some reservation in his voice, "And what is that?"

She curled her lips, anxiously standing on the tips of her toes with her hands pressed together. "Well, I have no place to stay and I sorta wondered if I could stay at your place for a couple of weeks?" She winced slightly, awaiting his response.

"Weeks?" he thought to himself. It was exactly the response he had feared. Sensing his hesitation, she extended one of her hands towards him, the fingernails all painted in black.

She continued in her cute, pleading voice, "Yes, I promise it will be only a couple of weeks and I realize you already saved my life, but I really have nowhere else to go and I need to find a job so I can get some money. I promise I won't be a bother and I can sleep on your couch or even your floor if you prefer." Billy again began cursing his fate and wondered silently to himself why all his recent cases were suddenly involving themselves into his private life by increasingly extravagant means. Certainly, one of the finer points of being a coroner was that by definition none of his clients could ever involve themselves in his life. At the very least, they should never follow him home.

Billy had always lived by himself and was thoroughly protective of his independence. He could certainly not tolerate such an outright affront on his private affairs. Billy, looking for the excuse most readily at hand, laughed uncomfortably, still holding the manga book in his left hand while is right returned to the brass door handle. "Listen, I am a busy man. In and out all the time and as you can see, I barely have room here for myself."

The girl took two steps toward him so that she stood directly under his chin as if she were about to kiss him. She said softly, making doe eyes, "Look, I can cook, clean, whatever."

"How did you get this address?"

She replied, more confidently, turning her body from side to side, "Oh, I went by your office and this man named Moncrete gave it to me. He said you might even be looking for a roommate as you often boarded people you met through work."

Billy winced, turning his head. That damned Moncrete. How could he so viciously misinterpret his words? In any case, what Billy was most upset about was the fact that people felt at complete liberty to give out both his phone number and his home address with no special consideration for his privacy. Furthermore, he now knew how Basyli had also managed to find his phone number. He would have to settle up with Moncrete later. However, just as he was about to answer the girl and invite her out of his home, his phone began to ring. As he moved away from the door to search for his cell under the mass of clutter on his couch, he dismissed himself, saying, "Hold that thought. I'll be back with you in a second." He finally located the phone after the seventh ring. On the other end of the receiver, he heard the agitated voice of Poundstone. Given that Poundstone's voice was seldom ever agitated, he realized that it was important.

"Hey, Billy we're gonna need you to come down here to Griffs' office now. Riley done finally did it."

"Done what?"

"You'll never believe it. He broke into the coroner's office and turned everythin' upside down. Made a right mess. Even dumped the bodies in the morgue all over the place, presumably lookin' for the corpses of his wife and her daughters. He done finally lost it. The place is a real mess. He spray painted the walls with all kinds a stuff like, 'Billy the Bodysnatcher' 'Billy the Devil.' Anyway, Sheriff Griffs has had enough and wants to move on him today so we're goin' up in the hills to find him. It's all hands on deck and he especially wants you there."

"Why me? What can I do?"

"He needs you to reason with Riley 'cuz he won't talk to no one else. How quick can you get over here?"

A look of resignation crossed his face: once again, things were going from bad to worse.

"I'm dealing with a bit of a situation here."

"Don't matter, Griffs wants you here, now. He's as mad as a swarm of hornets."

Billy knew there was no way out of it and had already begun to put on his slacks, nearly falling over at points as he struggled to dress himself while speaking.

"I can be at the station in twenty minutes, I'm just leaving the house now. How the hell we gonna find this guy?"

"We got a tip off from his wife who done seen him near the house a few day ago. Anyway, we're gonna bring out the bloodhouds. Couple boys said they done saw him fishin' in one of the creeks a few hours ago and one done saw a fire where Riley had been campin'."

"I see," Billy replied with even more resignation in this voice. The present conversation continued for another ten minutes until by the time Billy was ready to get off the phone, he was completely dressed, had put his coat on and even managed to find his keys. In his hurry to leave, he neglected to even further acknowledge his new arrival. On his way out with the phone still to his ear, he merely said, "I'll be back," leaving her standing there with a quizzical smile on her face. Billy walked down to the end of his hallway and out of his apartment, all the time cussing in a loud voice. Once out the front door, he walked left to the side street where his car was parked. The day was pleasant in the way that days are called 'pleasant' and towering clouds filled the sky. In the distance, he heard the sound of a Cessna as it ducked in and out of the billows. It was amongst the loneliest emanations of humankind. Billy could already tell it was going to be a long night.

When Billy pulled up to the sheriff's office, which sat throned between two other public offices just outside the center of Hokum. The sun was still high in the air and made the tips of the barren trees glow with a warm, jonquil light. In his ears, he heard the faint tintinnabulations of Grieg's Lyric Suite, 'Klokkeklang', which he likened to something half out of Mussorgsky's 'Pictures at an Exhibition' and Debussy's later, enchanted spires, emerging from the laconic depths of some ambiguous sea. If he had arrived weeks earlier, before the maple trees had lost all their leaves to the strong October winds, he would have sat there in longing, sifting the air as the red light of the afternoon shown through the multicolored leaves that imbued everything with a hallowed luster, the magnificence of a stained glass window. In the utter silence of an autumn afternoon, the smell of distant wood smoke filled his nostrils. The sensation was enough to take one's breath away, but Billy, who harbored no sentimentality, sat there unmoved. It was an unmentioned, but widely recognized phenomenon that whenever one stood on the first stair of the sheriff's office, one had the inexplicable preception that one had entered upon sacred ground, the very altar of justice, which incarnated the profound law that governed the land in its austere senility.

The sheriff's office was housed in a historical building, perhaps Hokum's most historical building if judged merely by the absolute number of noteworthy events that had occurred within its walls. The building had withstood the test of time. Stubbornly it resisted any major alteration and had existed there for well over one hundred and forty years. Previously, the building was the simultaneous location of the city's courthouse, jail and sheriff's office. It was a quaint symbol of Southern simplicity, where the judge, jury and executioner could all coexist under one roof, saving the need for much in terms of practical bureaucracy or the loathsome effort of a moment's self-reflection. Though many famous incidents in Hokum's long history had occurred there, they had been long forgotten by most. In form, it was a red, gabled building with a front facing porch and a number of pleasant historical details, such as the ornate, whitewashed woodwork. The sheriff made sure that the building was kept in suitable condition as in his mind the office was the physical incarnation of the pride of the entire county. Outside of the building stood a white, wooden sign that read "Hokum County Sheriff's Office" in gold letters. Billy was always struck by the marked contrast it represented to the coroner's office. On the small, grassy rise that acted as a footrest to the imposing holy bushes that encircled the entire building, a couple of Mexicans in dingy, brown clothing were raking up leaves into large translucent bags. Given its position on a grass plateau above the sidewalk, one immediately felt that one was entering a place of great importance. Furthermore, the sheer size of the building (aided by a trick of perspective), made one naturally assume a reverential if not entirely contrite pose as one walked up the wide flight of stairs, unconsciously, as if by habit, bowing one's head as if engaged in a silent plea for mercy.

When Billy opened the metal, forest green door to the meeting room, the briefing had already begun and Billy was forced to sidle as inconspicuously as possible into a place against the wall at the back of the room were many were already standing. The meeting was held in a relatively small room on the second floor. Its walls, made out of the large cinder blocks one often sees in libraries and other official buildings, were painted a soft, margarine yellow. The room was nondescript, being possessed of a large whiteboard, two windows, a small wooden lectern, two flags and a number of school room desk-chairs. The officers dressed in their khaki shirts and dark russet pants all sat at the desks, attentively taking notes and hanging onto Sheriff Griffs' every word. Sheriff Griffs, known affectionately as "Sarge", looked exactly as one might have expected he would. He was tall, well built and had a thick, white pair of handlebar mustaches that twisted upwards into fine points of ecru. As he was a near constant pipe smoker, the lower half of the mustaches were stained brown and yellow. Despite his six foot three frame, Griffs didn't look imposing and had a pleasant, grandfatherly look about him, having achieved the ripe old age of seventy-six. Like most in Hokum he had strong Southern drawl, but his naturally deep voice made his own accent appear more gentlemanly. When one was in his presence, one immediately felt secure and his open mannered movements and broad gestures made one feel even more comfortable. Presently, he was dressed in a yellow oxford shirt and wore a tawny cowboy hat. On the bottom half, he wore brown slacks, a sepia twist belt and a requisite pair of cowboy boots. He had evidently witnessed too many television portrayals of small county sheriffs and was all too willing to fill the cliché. He was after all a rather larger than life presence in the community. Moreover, he was a living artifact, part of the vision-myth that Hokum wanted to retain of itself. It was a given that he would be in attendance at all the county fairs and public entertainments. Many in Hokum thought he should have been more ambitious and striven for the mayorship or possibly even the govenorship, but he would wave these suggestions aside and declare with a fond sparkle in his eyes that his humble beginnings had 'no place in the Big House' and that he would be happy enough if he could leave this world with enough good deeds to 'walk in the tall cotton'. It was exactly these types of quaint idioms and the corresponding homespun wisdom that endeared him to the population. By common consensus, he was the sort of guy you wanted with you on a fishing trip or perhaps just to kick back a few while watching a local high school football game. At this point in his career, no one was actually aware of what his day-to-day duties were comprised of, but he was certainly very visible in central Hokum, waving to old ladies, kissing babies and handing out candy to the children. However, as he stood at the lectern in front of a room packed full with sheriff's officers, he had lost the casual Southern charm that he so frequently displayed in his normal day-to-day life. The mood amongst the audience was reminiscent of a mob of townspeople who had gathered together to prepare for a lynching, the eyes intent, the jaws locked, the teeth on edge.

Noticing Billy almost immediately, Griffs piped up, "Jus' the man we've been waitin' for. The man of the hour." As the entire room looked around at him, Billy apologized under his breath for being late and sat in the last vacant chair that was left at the back of the room. "Don't trouble yourself," Griffs continued. "You had no way of knowin' what wuz afoot. But, you's part of the reason we all are here through no fault of your own." The sheriff continued to pace silently from one end of the room to the next, leaving others to wonder what he was going to say next. He at first paused, looked at his hands pensively and said softly, "Sorry, I done lost my train of thought. Where wuz I?" He sat like this for a full thirty seconds and then suddenly, he erupted in an angry tone of voice, "Oh, yes. Now as I wuz sayin'…now this man's lower than a snake's belly in a wagon rut. This man has come on our turf and defiled the bodies of our town folk and I simply won't stand for it no matter how you or anyone else here in town might like this crazed fool. There simply has to be law and order here in Hokum and we ain't fixin' to back down or shake like leaves in the wind. No, we are goin' to stand up like men and do our duty. I'm as mad as a mule." At this point, Griffs pounded his fists. "It's bad enough we now have the Mexicans breakin' into people's houses every which way. We got homosexuals runnin' around in the streets playin' hanky-panky behind each other in the public stalls. Now, we have to worry about people breakin' into the morgue? What kinda place is this this becomin'? That just ain't right." The officers all nodded in agreement, one in particular giving out a confident, "Yes, sir." Sheriff Griffs continued, "Now I'm about to tell you what we gonna do about this little situation here, sure as my name is Sheriff Griffs. Ya'll want to know what I'm gonna do? Ya'll wanna hear about about what we gonna do?" The rest of the officers joined in a chorus, "Yes, sir." "Well, this is what we're gonna do. First we're gonna go up yonder in them hills and we gonna stick the dogs on him. He can run but he can't hide. We gonna chase him like a fox outta his little fox hole, we are. Then when we catch him, we're gonna bring him right back here and make him clean up that mess he done made. Then we're gonna make a public example of him and show him that vigilantism just don't work around Hokum." "Yes, sir" the cries went up again. He began to crouch down like a high school coach marshaling his team. "So listen here boys, let's get out there and go find this sonofabitch. Let's show him we not gonna sit around like a bunch of ladies and let this stuff go on. Let's show him who runs the law around here. Let's show him what the Hokum County Sheriff's Office can do when riled up." The officers had already stood up in unison, yelling "Yes, sir" after each of his exhortations. "Let's, get on then," the sheriff finally said, leading the rest of the shouting mob out of the same door that Billy had just entered through.

After the last officers had filed out of the room, leaving Poundstone and Billy to themselves, each looked at the other with a shrug of the shoulders and a knowing smile. "What a mess," Billy offered.

"Yes, indeed. What a mess," Poundstone replied.

"Speaking of messes. You'll never guess what showed up at my doorstep like a stray dog. I swear, when I get my hands around Moncrete, I'm gonna wring his little Indian neck."

"Let me guess, that little Goth girl?"

"How did you know?"

"Moncrete done tol' me she'd been snoopin' 'round the coroner's office lookin' for you when you wuz off. He told me he wuz fixin' to go by your advice and put the atoms in motion. Give you a good story you may never forget. I done laid eyes on her myself and I certainly wouldn't mind her crossin' my threshold, no sir."

"Look, I have standards and strict guidelines I abide by and this is outside any of them."

Poundstone's forehead wrinkled and his eyes narrowed into a bemused pair of slits, "So what you complainin' about? He reasoned you liked to put girls through your little process and here one is and you still complainin'."

"First, she's not grieving which means more work for me and second and most importantly, she's not Asian. Let's face it, all women love you when you're a baby, a few less of them when you're an adolescent, a very small minority when you're an adult and by the time you're old, you're pretty much universally reviled or worse yet, entirely ignored. If a woman is going to hate me at least I better like looking at her and I only like looking at Asians. Is that so hard for everybody to understand?" Billy retorted, becoming noticeably angry.

"Listen, now just calm yourself. She's damned lucky as far as I can see. It's a miracle she even survived at all bein' all dressed up like that and given how rough the water wuz. She must've grabbed on to a log or somethin' and floated on down the river some ways. If she had gone down any further, she would've definitely been done for as she would've hit them rapids. You know who she is yet, anyway?"

"No idea, I don't know what it is that we're managing to find all these unidentified people in the city now days with no relatives and no form of identification."

"It's them drugs I tell you and the mass transit system bring all the funnies in. Even at the hospital, once she woke up, she refused to give away her identity fearin' that someone would come for her. Anyway, the head nurses at the hospital done pleaded with the woman, but she wouldn't budge. Finally, after four days, which she spent mostly asleep, they had to let her go given that she hadn't suffered any critical injuries except exhaustion and a bit of hypothermia. Anyway, looks like she done mixed herself up in some drugs because one of the nurses said they found a few needle tracks down her arms."

"So, what you're saying is that I just left a heroin addict in my house?" Billy said suddenly worried.

"You mean she's still there? You just left her there?" Poundstone guffawed, a large grin crossing his face.

"Yes, what else could I do? I had to run over here and didn't have suitable time to kick her out. I've been on the phone the entire time since before I got here, tying to chase down Moncrete and then I got tied up with people at the office. I been out four days."

"Who-wee," Poundstone shouted, giving Billy a big slap on the back so that it rang like a hollow barrel. "You remember the old joke about hurricanes and women don't you? You gonna have you some fun tonight," he laughed.

"I don't think it's very funny. I don't think it's very funny at all," Billy replied in a hurt tone, the worry rising visibly into his eyes. He had surmised it immediately: there was nothing to be done. It was a fait accompli. He was trapped and would spend the rest of the night thinking about the unidentified woman rummaging through his valuables, his private effects, stealing his leather gloves, perhaps even raiding his collection of Rubik's cubes. Billy's mind instantly became a calculator, a giant Analytical Difference Engine similar in constitution to the one locked behind glass at the British Science Museum, the gears of which began to turn in unison, performing countless discrete calculations and discursive simulations. First, he ran through all the valuables in the apartment and summed up their values, then he considered the multiplier effect of the irreplaceables and the embarrassment he would no doubt experience once he had to relay to the police the specifics of some of the items that had been stolen. Finally, he thought of the woman inviting her heroin junkie friends to ravage his apartment further and he suddenly felt a shadow of his former anxiety returning.

He turned to Poundstone suddenly with fear in his eyes. "You think there is anyone we could send over to my place if I gave them the keys to my apartment?"

"Sorry, my friend. As I said, it's all hands on deck."

As Poundstone walked him out of the room, he put his arm around Billy's shoulder and tried to speak in comforting tones, "Well don't you worry none, I done spoke to the girl myself and she seems like a nice girl. And as far as those tracks go, there weren't a whole lot. Just a couple needle pricks. Anyway, I don't want her gettin' mixed up in anythin' else and she seems pleasant enough so I wuz gonna speak to one of the nurses tomorrow morning who seemed to know her and when I get some more information, I'll give you a holler."

This was little consolation to Billy as he reasoned through the numerous scenarios and the probable consequences of leaving an as of yet unidentified person in his apartment for what would probably be the remainder of the night. How could he be so stupid? He could easily imagine himself becoming the laughing stock of the entire police force when it was found out that his apartment was ransacked by a heroin addict he had left there without so much as asking after her name. In the drive to the outskirts of Hokum, he had the same thoughts playing though his mind again and again. It became a compulsion, a sort hypnotic loop that his mind couldn't break out of. For once, he damned himself for lacking true friends that he could rely on and the Warden wasn't picking up his phone. Having nothing else to do, he began to try to comfort himself, considering the potential positives, that the girl had appeared 'nice' and really in need of help, but being the inveterate pessimist that he was (though he tried hard to fight against it), he also kept returning to the fact that she had tracks running up and down her arms and a pair of suitcases, which indicated she was for all practical purposes a homeless vagrant (unbeknownst to Billy, she had actually been living in the Lido prior to his finding her). He sat wretchedly in the back of the police van as the other officers joked and laughed about what they would do once they caught Riley. He thought of calling his house to see if anyone picked up the phone, but after several failed attempts he gave it up. Unfortunately, due in large to the Basyli affair, he had turned his answering machine off in frustration and wasn't even able to leave a message.

As the police van entered the winding roads that led up toward the Maralah Mountains, Billy began to feel a strong queasiness, brought on by worry and mental fatigue. One of the officers, noticing Billy's unusual silence and the abject look on his face turned around to him and said, "Don't yous worry none. We're gonna get this guy for you." Billy could only nod his head, not wanting to say much else. The plain-faced officer, not content that he had sufficiently assuaged Billy's fears, turned to address the rest of the passengers. "Hey, look here, fellas. Billy's lookin' here like he's been rode hard and put up wet. Let's give the boy some kinda encouragement so that he's sure we're gonna catch ol' Riley. Let's all show him we're gonna get this guy off Billy's back." The rest of the officers responded by cheering and patting Billy on the shoulders, trying to convince him not to worry. After the many words of heartfelt encouragement, the officers broke out into an impromptu chorus of '*Don't It Make You Want To Go Home*', which continued in a repetitive cycle for the next ten minutes. Billy, wanting nothing more than for it all to stop, managed a forced smile. When the original officer turned back to him, he laughed, "See, I told you you had nothin' to worry about, the boys is all behind you. You're one of us. Like the Marines all say, never leave a man behind."

The van continued its winding path up one of the smaller mountains in the Maralah range. Despite the hour not being exceptionally late, the sun had already begun to set its incarnadine rays across the western side of Hokum. From their purchase on the shoulder of one of the mountain's many outcroppings, the officers were presented with a magnificent vista. For the briefest of moments, just as the road turned back on itself to wind its way across another manmade ridge, Hokum lay down before them like a promiscuous woman, reclining in all the decadent luxury of rouge eveningwear. At its outermost limits, its erubescent arms seemed to stretch forth to embrace the very ankles of the mountains as if it would rise up supine to embosom them all with the faintest kiss of dusk. For a brief instant, there was nothing that didn't shine forth with the brightest effulgence or darken again with the utmost contrast; the intersecting planes of dark and light gave a perception of limitless distance, indomitable form and ultimate perspective. As Billy looked from the very corner of the window, between the plaintive clarinet of Grieg's 'Aften pa Hoyfjellet', he saw the numerous church spires that rose in the dusky air like ensanguined barbs, the baseball stadium that curled about itself like an Abyssinian cat, the train station, its dumb block consigned to a form beyond intelligible utterance, finally, the numerous winding roads, cast before him like discarded beads at Mardi Gras, each colored with the red or white train of car lights making their lonely way home during the rush hour. Finally, in the wan distance near the nematic river, which glowed as if on fire, he tried to locate his own apartment building where he thought the dark woman would be presently occupied, ripping away the last vestiges of his personal life.

He was suddenly woken from his unpleasant reverie with a jolt. The van stopped in a small, gravel parking lot at the edge of a tall ridge overlooking a dark sea of pine trees. Looking to his left, he could see directly into the other police van, the very same that his van had been trailing for the duration of the drive and beyond it, the two police cars that were the leaders of the convoy. In the dimness of their interiors, he saw the dark silhouettes of the other officers who were already filling out of the opened side doors. Although Billy wasn't quite sure where they were or why they were even here, he could tell that they had arrived three fourths of the way up one of the smaller mountains that joined the Maralah range from the jigsaw crush of nameless hills, each of which was ridged like a rotted molar. The sun was in the midst of putting on a rapturous display of colors: the delicious aquamarines, the cool magentas, the brave yellows, the timid violets that saturated the air all mixed their wistful hues among the languid clouds that hung like torn pieces of colored tissue paper just over the horizon. As Billy turned his head away from Hokum and towards the glabrous peaks that towered above him like a huddle of mantled gods, he saw, or thought he saw an almost imperceptible movement, just over the ridge of the most distant mountains and amongst the thickets of knotted pines. Unfortunately, it was so distant that he had to squint his eyes to make out its exact form. Yes, he was sure of it now. What else could it have been but the lone silhouette of the intrepid runner, ascending toward the crest of one of the mountains? It was almost too much for him to bear and he turned his head away in disgust.

As far as Billy could tell, they had parked at some scenic viewpoint along the mountain. As the doors of the van he was riding in opened, the officers suddenly assumed a very serious demeanor. He could already hear the loud barking of the four bloodhounds that had been released from the cages of the K-9 unit van that followed them. He was the last to leave the vehicle and had some difficulty squeezing between the seats. When he finally emerged, the first thing that came to his sight was one of the officers, holding in the air an old piece of denim, allowing the now excited dogs to sniff at it. Instinctively, the other officers began to gather around the figure of Sargent Griffs who had ridden in the first car. Standing in his usual commanding pose at the upper edge of the gravel parking lot that sided the road, he began to address the officers,

"OK, boys, Riley's house is jus' down that a ways. We heard reports that he likes to come over this way nearer to the old mines so we're fixin' to go down this way in case we can catch him in between his house and the ridge leadin' up to the mines. We're then gonna go back due southward and follow the side of the ridge to his house and see if his wife done seen him recently and if she knows exactly where he might be. And if none a that works, then we'll go back up over the ridge again to the other side and see if we can't pin him on the mountain between the road and the old mines. Any questions before we start?"

"Yes," one officer raised his hand. "What if one a us sees the ol' coot? Are we supposed to shoot him on sight if we sees him?"

"Listen, fella and this goes for all 'uv ya. Now, I don't want anyone gettin' ahead of themselves. We jus' wanna try to catch him alive first and then bring him to justice. OK, is that understood?

"Yes sir," the officer returned.

"Any other questions?"

"Yes, sir," another officer raised his hand. "How we even gonna manage to get sight of this guy in the darkness all up in the woods and all?"

"Lord, I tell you, if this guy ain't one hand short of a full deck. What you think we got them dawgs for?"

The rest of the party started to laugh.

"OK, good, if there are no more questions, let's all now get together for a little prayer."

All of the officers gathered in a circle, each putting a hand in the middle of the impromptu ring so that every hand was atop another. Billy, who stood outside of the circle by himself, could barely make out the gentle voice of Sheriff Griffs as it began a familiar prayer. Right from the beginning, the entire party closed their eyes and listened in utter solemnity to his heartfelt words. After he finished a lengthy preamble prayer, which included a few colorful additions and numerous requests for family blessings, at his request, the officers intoned in a common voice the final words of the Lord's Prayer after which they said their "Amens", finally dissolving the circle in a non-homeomorphic manner in order to form a single file line, which Sheriff Griffs led down a small path that led in quick descent into the heart of the forbidding forest. The sky had now darkened considerably and it was becoming difficult for the party to see one another without the aid of flashlights. When they finally arrived after fifteen minutes' walk to a flat area large enough so that they could all stand in one loose mass, the K-9 officers let the dogs loose. As the party walked in a ragtag fashion through the surrounding woods, the flashlights which were now turned on, were moving every which way, their white beams zigzagging along the forest floor in crazy patterns, moving occasionally up the sides of the tall oak trees whose great arms wove over them into a thick canopy. The air was frigid and it was likely the temperature would drop below freezing. The group of approximately twenty-five men moved about without saying a word to one another, their feet rustling in the leaves, the forest echoing with the strident barks of bloodhounds. As Billy looked around him, he stared with utter disinterest and even contempt as the ridiculous officers turned their heads cautiously in every direction, seemingly in competition to flash each other meaningless hand gestures as if they were part of some kind of commando patrol unit. They walked in this way for what seemed like half an hour, until they arrived at a deep gorge where the sound of a small, hidden waterfall could be heard. Down on a flat landing of green moss, on the opposite side of the ridge, there stood the lopsided house where Riley's family resided.

The one-story house was of a grey and green pallor, the wood planks on its outside evidently rotted by the lichens and funguses that grew on it like a second skin. It was an old sort of creole cottage, the type that had become very rare in the area. The front patio that ran the length of the house was filled by an enormous amount of junk of all kinds: car parts, broken cathode tubes, an antique icebox, a bent out of shape swing set and even an old jukebox. The entire house sagged in the middle and gave the singular appearance that at any point it would fall in under the pressure of its own weight. It lacked any form of front yard, but ran right up to the dirt road that turned in front of it in an angry skid. Just behind the house, over the roof that bowed like a horse saddle or perhaps a brachistochrone, one was able to discern the outer corners of a moss filled yard that stood at the foot of a natural wall of granite. A single, lugubrious window was lit by a flickering light that emanated from an unseen flame. In the living, breathing darkness that surrounded the doleful abode, one could barely detect the faint trace of smoke as it wove upward in shadowy knots, dissipating only at great lengths into the night sky. In front of the house, three young girls, none of them older than eleven, stood wearing nightgowns, glaring at the disjointed troupe of officers. Each of them stood in perfect stillness, each possessing exceptionally light blonde hair that trailed to the middle of their backs. Even Billy had to admit that in the present light, as the moon shone its crepuscular rays on the girls' pallid skin, that they, dressed in their white nightgowns, which also glowed a spectral color, resembled phantasms. The remainder of the officers walked down the ridge with difficulty, so that some, including Billy, fell at each step down the steep decline of new, unsettled earth. Once the party arrived at the bottom, they crossed a small creek using an old, wooden bridge that spanned not more than four or five feet. Griffs instructed the other officers to hold back while he and his lieutenant, Tommy, spoke to the three girls who remained there, eternally still, looking imperiously at the sheriff. The sheriff in his usual warm manner bent down to address the girls, "Well how are you little princesses doin' tonight? If you three don't look cuter than a sack full of puppies. What you girls doin' out here? Ain't it well past your bed time?"

"No," the youngest daughter shot back with her arms straightjacketed at her side, her face in a deep frown.

"And what's your name, little honey pie?" the sheriff asked, rubbing her head with one hand as if he were burnishing a brass orb to which she responded by removing his hand forthwith.

"Are you here, lookin' for our daddy?" the oldest girl inquired sternly with her arms crossed in front of her chest.

"Well, yes in fact we are, little darlin'. Would you like us to find your daddy for you?"

The smallest one, who stood in the middle, nodded her head, also crossing her arms. The oldest one then declared in a stern voice, "Yes, we would and tell that ol' good fur nothin' that he needs to come an fix up the chicken coop."

The officers behind Griffs laughed in low tones.

Griffs smiled back at the officers, then turned again to address the spirited little girl, "OK, I'll try to tell him."

At that point, the youngest one, indomitable and not to be outdone, began in a suspicious tone, "Say, you a policeman? Our pappy done anythin' wrong?"

"Well, no dear, we jus' want to talk to him."

"He ain't worth a turkey's life at Thanksgiving and he's crazy as hell too: out shoutin' all hours of the night so I can't get no sleep. I don't know when he gonna finish goin' crazy. He thinks we done died and gone to heaven and he ain't even finish tellin' me the story about Tikki Tikki Tembo yet."

The officers laughed again.

"Is that right, dear? Well I'll make sure he does that as soon as you get back. Is your mom here?"

The middle girl, who stood on the left hand side said, "Yep, she's inside. Who wants to know?"

"Well, we jus' want to speak to her, little darlin'."

"You sure you're not tryin' to pull a fast one on us? Our mom says the police are crookeder than a barrel of fishhooks. If you are tryin' to pull a fast one, me 'n you is gonna mix."

"OK, dear. Look at the pants on you? Look I know bettern' to mess with you. And anyway, I ain't no policeman. I'm the sheriff."

"Ain't that the same thing?" the middle child said, putting her hands on her hips.

"Wow, if you ain't got a little sass on you, girl. Anyway, here, why don't you girls have some sweets and go on to bed?"

He handed the girls each a sweet from his pocket, which aroused instant delight in their faces. Having finally quelled the stone resolve of their little brains into submission, he patted each girl on the head and stood up to make his way toward the house. As he walked toward the steps, he took the three girls along with him, holding the two youngest by the hands. "Now, why don't you good girls show me to where your mammy is?"

Once he completed the short walk to the house and made his way up the stairs, he and the girls walked straight into the darkness that lay behind the white screen door, while Tommy, the six foot five former high school football legend, was left to trail behind them. Outside, it was complete darkness. In the spring, the scenery would have been illuminated by countless lightning bugs that would slowly orbit in random patterns so that their intermittent bulbs led one to pursue them through the shadowy corridors of the forest thicket. However, as the summer had long ago given way to autumn's chill, these roving lanterns had been replaced by tiny Pipistrelle bats, who themselves would seek a less permanent slumber in a matter of weeks. As Billy looked helplessly into the night sky, he could see them flitting this way and that, their fierce acrobatics almost imperceptible. He, like most, thought of them as no more than flying rats. At this point in time, Billy could do no more than to close his eyes, trying to pretend he was anywhere else than where he was. As he breathed in, the pungent perfumes of pines filled his nostrils, the evanescent memories of a wood fire stirred in the silence, reawakened by a gentle draft that spilled over the pine branches heavy with their dormant saps. As the nighttime air froze, the dead leaves turned over one another, dancing amidst a sudden mountain breeze, they rose up in an invisible column of air as if seeking form or even utterance, then in an instant under the susurrant murmurings of drowsy tree limbs, their playful spiral was dashed, their gentle shadows cast hither and thither. As the trees rocked and swayed as if plagued by bad dreams, deep inside their slumbering hearts the dried sap thickened, waiting in suspended animation for another spring.

All in all, Tommy and the sheriff were inside the house for what must have been fifteen minutes. When they finally emerged, he announced the present state of affairs to the gathered officers, "She didn't want to help much but she said she hadn't seen him since yesterday when he came 'round yellin' somethin' about gettin' their bodies back. Well we now know what that means. Anyway, she thinks he stays jus' over yonder across the ridge in one of them old mine shafts." The detour to the house now finished, the party began again to ascend the other side of the gorge from which they had come. This time, instead of heading northwestward toward where the vans were parked, they headed to the northeast in the direction of the jagged ridge that rose high above them. Billy, having long ago grown tired of the expedition, was not only bored and worried, but his legs had started to ache again. He cursed his profession and wondered why out of all the coroners he knew, he was the only one who ended up in these ridiculous situations. He was sure that the coroner of Jasper or Crowley, weren't out in the night trekking through the trackless wilds (one thing about the dead, they usually stayed put) while their apartments were being pilfered by heroin addicts (in this line of business, one usually only dealt with former addicts). No, they were probably tucked comfortably within their homes, enjoying a nice dinner that their wives had prepared for them, or perhaps even at a bar, enjoying the last sips of a cold beer. No, not him, for in his mind, his fundamental *Weltschmerz* led him to believe that he was more or less the most accursed man on earth. Billy wondered if there was in existence some form of celestial tribunal before which he would be called to appear, only to be prosecuted for crimes committed against himself. He really wished he'd had some diazepam.

In his present state, Billy was clearly in no mood to appreciate his surroundings, but if he were, he would have been able to admire the vastness of a clear night sky completely bereft of clouds. He would have been able to wonder at a harvest moon that finally managed to rise over the mountain ridge and shone within its cold, marble nudity a blushing fullness, rendering the flashlights almost redundant. He would have been able to imagine, but not see, this same moon's clear, unbroken reflection as it floated midway out on the Chippewok Lake. He might have even been calmed and to a certain extent reassured by the stillness of the wind, the quiet gurgling of the hidden stream, which they followed upward toward its source at the summit. The way was hard going as the climb became increasingly steep. At many points, the band of officers was forced to walk this way and that, retracing their steps to find the path of least resistance. In addition, they were forced at times to climb on all fours, sticking their fingertips into the soft under soil to keep themselves from falling. It was all the more traumatizing for Billy as he had this time neglected to bring gloves of any sort. He had to endure each clump-full of butter-like earth, each missed grasp at a jagged rock face, all borne with his own brand of self-recrimination as he felt his recent manicure being slowly ruined.

At several occasions during this part of the journey, Billy held up the entire group and it was left up to a set of unfortunate officers to help him along. He offered on numerous occasions to remain behind, but this of course was out of the question. Suddenly, at a midpoint of one of the steepest climbs, the entire party froze for what to Billy seemed an eternity. At first Billy, pressed chest-first against the side of the mountain, wasn't sure why they had interrupted his progress at exactly the most inconvenient point. However, his curiosity was soon relieved. It quickly became clear to him that for the first time, the dogs had evidently caught on to a scent and were now pointing in the direction of an even steeper climb up a small ridge. Furthermore, he discovered that one of the officers claimed to have heard something rustling in the bushes. It was at this point that the entire party was suddenly galvanized into action. The dogs were straining against their leashes as the officers struggled up the muddy side of the ridge, sliding backwards on numerous occasions. Finally, finding a suitable path, the chase began in earnest. There was a great deal of shouting and then, in the next instance a shot rang out, though given the distance and the echoes that the mountain gorges produced, the direction was unclear. It was at this point that one of the officers in the front of the pack stated the obvious, "Sounds like he's shootin' at us."

Sheriff Griffs responded, "Sounds like he's armed and dangerous. Alright, someone give me the horn. Now!" Griffs then took an electronic megaphone from one of the officers next to him,

"Listen, Riley, whether you like it or not, we're a commin' for ya. Might as well give yourself up. We don't want no trouble but if you're gonna make this difficult, we have no problems takin' you by force."

Another shot was heard in the distance.

"OK, now. We tried to be civil. If you want to turn yourself in just holler and we'll come up and git you. This doesn't have to go the wrong way."

The party stood there frozen, their ears straining against the silence. They listened for any sign of a human voice whatsoever, but none was forthcoming. Then Sheriff Griffs took the megaphone to his lips once more, "OK, have it your way then." The party continued their way up the granite ridge. As they went forward, the dogs became increasingly excited at every step. Billy, now thoroughly tired, could feel the ring of sweat that hung around his neck and down his chest. He had long understood that his body wasn't meant for such exercise and as a result was beginning to revolt against him. Rather than walk, he began to fall forward in a kind of perpetual tumble. He simply bounced from one tree to the next, hugging each, while losing his overall sense of direction, not really caring which way he went, but knowing all the time that he would be urged on some reckless course up this infernal mountain. The incessant barking of the dogs was driving him mad. At one point, the officers suddenly stopped short and Billy was relieved to be able to regain his breath. As he lurched forward, wheezing loudly, he vomited the very last remains of his lunch on the ground, cursing Riley under his breath in every way he knew how. He heard one of the officers come back down the ridge alongside Griffs and whisper loudly, "Seems like he's up this a ways, not too far from where we're standin'." The entire posse started on their relentless course again. As they progressed, they increasingly found various signs of Riley's passage: old campfires, a discarded shirt, used gunshot cartridges. Suddenly one of the officers thought they had spotted Riley and the entire group began to run in one direction up the steep hillside. When they got to the top of the latest of many ridges they came to a large, empty opening that led into an ancient mine shaft. It would take another small climb to reach the adit, but the dogs were intent as ever, ready to dart into its cool blankness. One of the K-9 officers closest to the entrance whispered down from the top of the cave's ledge to the rest of the party who were just catching up to him.

"Looks like he went in here," the officer whispered in a loud, rough voice.

"You sure 'bout that, Griffiths?" the sheriff shouted back. As he was out of breath, he spoke like he'd just been punched in the stomach.

"As sure as I gots breath in my body," the doughy-faced officer declaimed.

Griffs stood paused for a moment, evidently thinking about what to do next. While he did so, he put one of his long legs up on a low stone and leaning forward on one knee, he began drinking from his usual bottle of homemade sarsaparilla, a *vade mecum* for his daily existence. "OK, I guess we're gonna have to think 'bout what to do next."

The dogs where now whining mercilessly, their noses sniffing the air above them. A frigid wind began to blow, rustling the trees that encircled the stony area upon which they stood. They had come almost to the very top of the low mountain and there was little more above them than the sky's cobalt mantle and a few hundred yards of rugged peak. After peering up into the darkness at the roof of the cave mouth, the same K-9 officer who had spoken earlier, whispered loudly in the direction of Griffs, "I think I can hear him movin' up in there. It's got to be dangerous. These things can collapse at any point and it's been rainin' a lot."

"Yes, I know. I know," Griffs responded knowingly.

"Get up to spelunkin' in one of those and the roof comes down, they'll never find ya again."

"Yes, I know, I know. I done thunk it through."

The sheriff's brows furrowed and he bowed his head in deep thought while the officers around him waited, frozen like mute statues, not daring even to speak to one another. After what amounted to three minutes of silence, the sheriff signaled for Billy to come up alongside him. Billy did so reluctantly and the sheriff grabbed his arm and pulled him close. "What you think, boy?"

Billy answered, finally in possession of his senses again, but not of his breath, "No idea, boss. Seems like he's probably long gone."

Griffs responded dryly, "Nonsense, he's up in there and he's got nowhere to go. Like a fox trapped in his own hole. I guess we're goin' to have to go up into the mineshaft after him. Jus' you and me and Tommy here."

"Wha...wha what? But that's crazy," Billy replied, not believing what he was hearing.

"Crazy is all I'm left with."

"But..."

"Don't sound so incredulous boy. This is real police work we're doin' here. We gotta be tough. We gotta be struuuong!"

"But..."

"Listen boy, if I wanted so many 'buts' thrown in my face, I'd a become a barstool not a sheriff."

"But..."

Griffs simply raised one of his bushy eyebrows and gave him a stern look that precluded further debate. So here, on this hard cleft in the frigid middle of nowhere, is how it presently stood with Billy: already worried about the state of his apartment, exhausted and in pain after climbing the side of a small mountain, here he was, again expected to risk life and limb for a man he cared nothing for. Billy felt as if tears were stinging the very corners of his eyes. What was he to do? How could he wish himself out of the situation? Suddenly an idea crossed his mind, the briefest of aperçus. A way out, he thought. With renewed hope in his eyes and a lilt in his voice, he turned to Griffs. "Listen, I have an idea. What if I promise to tell him where the bodies are and to show him their death certificates then maybe he'll come out on his own?"

Griffs sat there pensively. finally responding after great mental effort, "Hmm, it's worth a try. Why don't you go up there yonder and just holler inside and see if you get him to talkin'. Say what yous done just said to me. That's a good head on you, boy."

Billy, happy that he had a least temporarily avoided the trip inside the cave, began to walk toward the adit. After some great effort and assisted by two officers, he was helped up the short ledge that stood under the cave entrance. Staring into the blackness he began to shout, "Hey, Riley. It's me here. It's Billy." There was no response but the distant echo of his voice and faucet-like drips that suggested the isolation of infinite space. All the officers were now staring into the void, inclining their ears in attempts to hear the faintest reply or sound of movement. Unwilling to reply, the cave mouth gave forth nothing more than a dank, musty fetor, the stale breath of a thousand-year slumber. As unpleasant as it was, Billy was undeterred. "If you can hear me, shout back." Again silence. "Listen, I'll get you those death certificates you wanted and show you where your family's bodies are. Your hear me?" Silence again. Then Griffs, who stood next to him, shook his head and signaled for Billy to come down from the ledge. After Billy descended the ledge, Griffs pulled him to the center of the gathered crowd of officers.

"Dag nab it. This jus' ain't workin'," Griffs growled in frustration. His face darkening, he threw his half-empty bottle of sarsaparilla on the ground.

"What we gonna do now, sir?" one of the officers asked.

"I don't know. I jus' need to think."

Griffs sat there in silence for another two minutes at which point he made the low moans of a cow. Amidst his lowing, the officers looked around themselves confused, then the sheriff, not heeding their astonished looks, finally continued, shaking his head, "Dang, I guess there's nothin' else to it. We gotta do what we gotta do."

"Wha…what does that mean?" Billy asked in fear, almost trembling.

As he looked up with a steely glance toward the opening of the cave, Griffs pulled out a Luger pistol from the brown leather case at his side. Without looking away, he spoke in low, conspiratorial tones to Billy,

"What we knew we always were gonna have to do. Like I said before, you, me, Tommy, Sweets and one of them there dawgs is gonna have to chase him out of that there cave." At this point, a broad rictus began to cross Griffs' face. "Aw shucks, reminds me when I wuz in 'Nam chasin' the Charlie. That wuz way back in '68." Without looking at Billy, keeping his eyes trained on the cave mouth, he replaced the cartridge of his gun, simultaneously asking Billy, "Say, you see any action, boy?"

"No sir, not really."

"Not really, what does that mean? Oh, I forgot you is one of those Ivy League types. Look at you all sweatin' like a whore in church. Ain't nothin' gonna happen to us in there. Anyhows, you's got you a sidepiece on you?"

"You mean like a gun?"

"Of course I mean like a gun, what else you think I could mean?"

"No, sir I don't."

At this point, he turned straight toward Billy and looked him directly in the eye. "What? You don't carry no sidepiece, boy? Don't nobody should be walkin' the streets without a sidepiece, boy. 'Specially in law enforcement. Tommy back there wuz in Desert Storm and he still sleeps with a Desert Eagle under his pillow."

"Well, sir, I'm not really in law enforcement, I'm just the coroner," Billy added sheepishly.

"Nonsense, that means you jus' get to the action too late. Now's your chance to git one of them live. Maybe you'll even get yourself on TV. You seem to like that a lot. Anyhows, Tommy," he called back to one of his subordinates.

The lantern jawed Tommy ran up immediately to his side, the bottom half of his mandible flexing and grinding as if he were a dog ready to fight. "Yes, sir."

"Git this boy a side arm."

"Well sir, I only have one. What am I gonna use?"

"What? Aw forget it, am I the only one 'round here who comes prepared?" At that, Griffs reached down to his previously hidden ankle holster and pulled out a Glock 26 9mm semi-automatic pistol and pushed it in the direction of Billy. He said with some agitation in his voice, "Now I'm down to two."

Billy, taking the gun reluctantly out of his hand, demurred, "Sir, I really don't think I need a handgun, I mean…"

"Nonsense, if there's anythin' I know from the military, it's to be prepared."

"You really think we need to go in there guns blazing? After all he just made a bit of a mess in the coroner's office. I'm sure we can clean…"

Griffs' eyes filled with a sudden rage. "Listen, he defiled the bodies of citizens. Those were citizens of Hokum in there and it's our duty to protect them and therefore it is our duty to go in there to bring him in so he pays the price fur his crime. And in the event that at any time durin' our pursuit of him, he chooses to act all ornery or resist us takin' him in. If, God forbid, he puts us in a situation where it comes down to us or him, you know for damn sight sure it's gonna be a bad day for him. We'll send him back to the morgue quicker than he expects. Now take it from me, you don't know if a firefight might break out and I'm a damn sight sure I'm not gonna come out on the loosin' end. I assume you know how to shoot?"

Billy, afraid to say no, answered back feebly, "Yes, sir, of course."

"At least you got that right."

At this point, Griffs turned around to the small company behind them and announced with his hands raised, "OK, listen here. No use in all of us goin' up there an causin' a commotion. This cave's liable to collapse. So here's what's gonna happen. Me, Tommy, Sweets and Billy here are goin' in by ourselves to try to corner him or fetch him out. The rest of ya'll wait here till we get back and if you catch him runnin' this way, ya'll knows what to do."

The officers behind him all nodded their consent. For the second time and with great reluctance, Billy climbed the limestone ledge that had been gradually eaten away through countless years of rain and wind. Once atop the ledge, standing at the very lip of the tawny mine, he stared once more into the blankness of the cave mouth and saw nothing but pitch black. In his left hand, he clutched the pistol, which Griffs had provided him, careful at all times to point it away from himself. Griffs came up alongside him with Tommy and the man named Sweets in tow. Sweets, who was a member of the K-9 division, held one of the bloodhounds by a leash as it snarled and barked at the empty darkness. Before they entered the cave, Griffs turned to the four men, speaking to them in hushed tones, "OK, Sweets, you go in there first with the dog and Tommy and I will sit back."

"Cave not no good for the dog's feet," interjected Sweets.

"He ain't gonna mind too much no how," Griffs continued, "Anyhow, as I wuz sayin', Tommy and I will be behind you and the dawg, then you..." he pointed in Billy's direction, "You, Billy, you hold up the rear and make sure you don't go shootin' any of us none where the sun don't shine, OK?"

The three of them quickly nodded their assent. At this point, Billy was handed a large stainless steel flashlight, which he presently turned on as did the others. Without further ceremony, Griffs grumbled beneath his voice, "Well here goes" and with that they entered the chilly breath of the mineshaft. The floor and walls of the cavern were wet and water ran down the walls into holes that seemed to disappear into nowhere. One certainly felt that they were entering the throat of some hideous, Pantagruelian creature, one with a particularly bad halitosis. Initially, they had no need to crouch as the opening to the shaft was fairly large, but after a few feet, all the men found it difficult to make their way without getting on their hands and knees. Just when they thought they could go no further, they ducked through an open hole and found themselves inside of a much larger cavern. By this point, their sleeves and pant legs were covered in mud and soaking wet. Billy resorted to blowing on his hands to keep them warm, nevertheless he was becoming increasingly upset as he noticed a tiny, red scratch on one of his forefingers that he had rubbed against a sharp rock. Being able to stand up again, they took some time to look around them. The sides of the cavern were soft and smooth, made as they were out of brown limestone that in places crumbled at the touch. Evidently, the shaft had intercepted a cave somewhere as the caverns they entered became progressively larger. However, the way was made more difficult as they now had to contend with numerous, jagged rows of sharp stalagmite and stalactite. Whereas previously, old wooden support beams could be seen at regular junctures to accompany the inchoate traces of rusted iron rails, these all gave way to the vaulted ceilings and jilted galleries of a maniac cathedral. To Billy, every new path they chose seemed identical to the one they had just left. He hoped more than anything that the dog, which led them through the increasingly anfractuous caverns had more sense than they did. By this point, Billy was significantly more confident in the dog's sanity than that of the men whose crazed enmity surrounded him. Any time the dog appeared to lose the scent, he fretted that they would be trapped hopelessly in the cave's bowels for all eternity. At times the dog circled, seemed to go back on its tracks, looked uncertain, only to suddenly move confidently in a completely opposite direction. Having been quiet the entire time since they had entered the cave, the sheriff's only addition to the proceedings was his comment that it was "colder that a witch's tit."

At one point, when they had reached a particularly tight spot, the dog barked and started moving in one direction. Soon afterward, they heard a splash of water, which prompted the dog to bark furiously, his maw beginning to fill again with the thick mucus that seemed to drip from it eternally. The entire party was startled by the dog's vociferousness and suddenly feeling that they were not alone, they moved their beams furiously around the cavern, but to no avail, nothing appeared but the slimy, gastric walls that had accompanied them for the better part of an hour. Then suddenly, one of the beams lighted on a crouched figure with his rear turned toward them. They could make out a shock of wild hair, blue denim and a pair of turbulent blue eyes. "There he is," shouted Sweets and the dog barked and drew forward as if it wanted to break its leash. At that point, they made their way as quickly as possible through the underground caverns that ran into one another. Before them, they saw another flashlight moving erratically through the darkness. It was obviously Riley on the run in front of them. At one point, he seemed less than thirty feet away, but given his natural agility and knowledge of the cave it wasn't long until he separated himself by a much larger distance. It appeared that no one had considered how they would find their way back through the labyrinth they had thoroughly immersed themselves within. Billy had a number of cuts and bruises from the ordeal and continued to worry that either the roof would collapse or that they would manage to fall down into some hopeless sinkhole. It was clear from the focused demeanor of the others that no one else seemed to give a farthing, particularly Griffs who was too busy urging everyone forward. Finally, after ten minutes in brisk pursuit, they came to another large cavern and stopped when the dog began barking up a wall. When the breathless crew drew their flashlights up along this very same wall, they saw Riley lying on the ground above them staring out of a small hole high up on one side of the cave. Without allowing the space of a second to pass, Griffs yelled up at him in an angry voice, "Alright, you stop there now. You gots nowheres else to go." They other officers duly trained their guns on him.

At this point, Riley shouted back, his own shotgun in turn trained on them, "Over my dead body."

Griffs then called to him, "Look Riley, we've been runnin' high tail over hell's half acre after you. Jus' put the gun down and nobody will get hurt."

"I ain't puttin' my gun down till ya'lls put your guns down."

Griffs, standing in front of the others, turned around and whispered to them, "Look at him up there. What a cryin' shame. If he doesn't look like ten miles of bad road." He then turned back towards Riley and shouted, "Listen, we don't want no trouble here. We just want to talk. Now what you done done wuz wrong."

"Well, what Billy done wuz wrong too."

"Well, Billy's here with us. Why don't you jus' come down and talk all that mess out with him, man to man?"

Griffs, then pushed Billy forward right into the sight of Riley's gun.

"There he is. There's the devil I'm after. I'm surprised you even came here to show yo' face."

Billy responded in the calmest voice he could muster, "Put down the shotgun, Riley."

"You come take it outta my cold dead hands. Jonah stayed in the whale's belly a whole three days so if you want to try, I got plenty a time."

"Look Riley, what is it you want from me? What can I do for you?"

"You know what I want. How many times I gotta tell you? If you don't git it by now maybe I'll speak to Griffs as he can understand. Sheriff Griffs?"

"Yeah."

"Can you tell this sonuvabitch what I want?"

He heard Griffs whisper behind his ear, "If this boy ain't as confused as a fart in a fan factory."

"Riley, listen, Billy here has agreed to give you them death certificates and show you where your family's bodies are buried."

"Listen, don't piss on my leg and tell me it's rainin'. I want to know where those bodies are now, otherwise I will shoot that devil between his eyes, I swear I will."

"No…no…no…that won't be necessary," Billy responded waving his hands furiously before him.

"Well don't have a conniption fit up there," Griffs yelled. Again he whispered in Billy's ear, "If that boy had an clue it would die of loneliness." Griffs then shouted up to Riley, "Look, we gonna give you the death certificates, right. Hear? We got them on us right now. Billy's gonna bring them up to you now, he is."

"I wanna see them."

"Alright," Griffs answered. Turning to Billy, he said in a low voice, "OK, show him the death certificates. You got them on you, right?"

"No...no...I don't."

"What? Then jus' show him any ol' piece of paper then. It don't matter nohows."

"I haven't got any."

"Haven't got any? What? Boy, you's 'bout as useful as a screen door on a submarine."

"What is goin' on down there now?"

Griffs fired back, "Well it seems that Billy's forgotten the certificates back in the van, but we gonna get them to you fur sure."

"Listen, I ain't got time for this foolishness, either you have them or you don't. "

"Riley, we're doin' the best we can."

"Then tell me where them bodies is hidden 'cuz I don't believe yous done given them a proper burial."

"OK, Billy, go ahead and tell him," Griffs yelled in an uncomfortable voice.

"What am I supposed to say?" Billy whispered loudly.

"I don't know, you're the coroner," Griffs responded in obvious frustration.

"What's all that whisperin' goin' on down there?"

"Nothing, Riley. Billy is jus' goin' to explain to you what the situation here is."

"OK, get on with it then. I ain't got all day."

"Well, you see Riley, here's the thing. Riley, you see, the bodies, well, they're still in the hospital, you see."

"What you tryin' ta say? You ain't tryin' to tell me they ain't dead again, are you?"

"Well, they aren't. That's exactly what I've been tryin' to tell you."

Riley responded with fury in his voice, "You tryn' a tell me I'm a liar, that I ain't seen their ghosts with my own two eyes?"

"No, I'm not trying to say that at all. What I've been trying to tell you is that they are in a coma, you see. They ain't dead yet, they're just in a coma."

Even Sheriff Griffs couldn't restrain himself from giving out a "Huh?" and scratching his white hairs in confusion.

"That's why you can see them because they…they are in purgatory."

"Purgatory? Purgatory, where's that?"

"It's the world between this one and the next. It's where the dead go before they are allowed into heaven. The place officially opened up shop in 1254 at the First Council of Lyon under the auspices of that pissant polemicist Pope Innocent IV who wrongfully robbed hell of an entire generation and more. I don't want to go into all the details, but you can think of it as a sort of drab departure lounge before the red-eye to heaven."

"Hmmm…we'll, that does seem to make some sense." Riley sat there pensive, obviously turning the concept over in his mind. "Say, you tryin' to pull a fast one on me cause you thinkin' we's in the devil's livin' room that I'm jus' gonna believe everythin' you say?"

"No, no we ain't," Griffs interjected finally catching the drift. "They're still in the hospital in intensive care. I done seen them with my own two eyes."

"We can take you to go see them if you want?" added Billy in hopeful tones. The two of them had ridiculous smiles on their faces and looked like used car salesmen about to close a deal.

"Hmm...Is that so? Hmm. We'll maybe I better'n check if you're tellin' the truth or not. But, for that I don't need you no hows and if you two is a lyin', you gonna pay. You hear that? You're gonna pay with yo' lives."

"We ain't lyin', Riley, I give you my word," Griffs added again.

"Yeah, and we can even take you there now if you want," Billy asked for a second time.

"Alrgiht, that settles it fur now. I'll go myself and check it out. Ain't no use in havin' ya'lls messin' 'bout my business. OK, see ya'lls."

With that final statement, Riley turned around, stood up and in the blink of an eye, disappeared again into the darkness leaving the ragged *comitatus* there to implore feebly after him. They had no immediate way to arrive where he was standing so it was impossible to engage in any form of pursuit. After fifteen minutes they finally managed to find the tunnel Riley used to access the ledge. Once the dog had again got the scent of Riley, they followed the canine down another series of tunnels for what seemed an eternity. Finally, at the point where they were just about to turn around and give up the search as hopeless, they found another tunnel that gradually led upward. They followed this a good distance until they came to a small crawl space with a hole in the ceiling where the light of the moon shone through. Evidently, there was a second entrance to the cave. The four would-be pursuers crawled out of the hole and found themselves in a completely different part of the mountain. By this point, the wind had started to blow wildly and they had to face the fact that Riley's immediate scent had been driven in every direction across the face of the mountain. There was no use to it. He had successfully managed to elude them.

Dejected and looking obviously downcast, the party walked back to the rest of the group and rejoined them at the mouth of the cave. When they initially appeared out of the darkness of the surrounding forest into the stone clearing where they originally entered the cave they were welcomed by a wilderness of raised guns. The officers, despite being radioed by Griffs only minutes before, were on edge thinking that Riley had managed to raise a local militia. Griffs quickly announced themselves and descended into their ranks to share the bad news. Amongst the entire crew, Billy appeared to be the only one who was happy, relieved as he was to find himself outside of the potential deathtrap. For Billy and everyone else in the car, the drive homeward couldn't have been any longer. The other officers even took it upon themselves to console him, promising him they would catch Riley the next time. Billy in no way cared for any of this and was only happy that he would be able to return home.

6

"...because as we know, there are known knowns"

When Billy finally arrived at his apartment that night, it was well after 2 a.m. and he was so sore and full of bruises that he had almost forgotten what potentially awaited him. All of his clothes were soaked and covered in red clay as were the deep gashes in his forearms and ankles. As he walked, his feet squished, leaving large puddles. Having lost the will to live, he was ready to confront anything. When he finally took his keys out and opened the door, he almost collapsed into the doorway. A very unfamiliar, chemical smell entered his nostrils. His pupils had yet to adjust in size to the darkness and he could see virtually nothing. When he finally managed to flip on the light switch, his stomach sank with horror as in an instant he took in the barren floors and surface areas of his living room. His first reaction was that everything had indeed been stolen as he had imagined. Then, when he looked at his couch, he was shocked to see the semi-naked figure of the girl he had left in his apartment wearing nothing but an old oxford shirt he could recognize as one of his own. She lay there, almost completely still, sleeping face down, her nude, unblemished legs stretching over the length of his grey couch. As Billy stood there aghast, the light finally filtered through her eyelids and they twitched into life like butterflies leaving their slumber woven chrysalises. Almost as if in slow motion, she stretched, yawned and eventually rose from her prostrate position. She then brought her left hand to her forehead in order to shield her eyes from the sudden light, which her dilated pupils were still busy adjusting to. When she was finally able to take in Billy's haggard form, she giggled mischievously seeing his ragged, muddy figure in the doorway, his mouth still agape in disbelief of what he saw. Billy now recognized the unfamiliar smell as the peroxide used in cleaning agents, a scent that hadn't invaded his abode for a good many years. For an uncomfortably long period of time, he hadn't managed to say anything and in the awkward silence, she ventured a soft "hello". Receiving no response, she now began to wonder whether shock was his constant expression. As his head slowly swiveled from side to side, she finally realized the cause of his discomfiture and spoke up, "Oh, yeah, sorry. I cleaned up a bit. I hope you don't mind."

"What have you done?" Billy gasped incredulously.

"I'm sorry, I cleaned up. I thought you would have liked it. I can put everything back."

Billy, not having the mental stamina to deal with the present situation merely closed the door behind him and walked like a zombie towards his bedroom. The girl, jumping off the couch, ran to his side, "Do you want me to take these clothes? You're a complete mess. I'll wash them for you."

Billy merely raised his right hand in a type of wave, went into his bedroom and closed the door. Within five minutes he had changed his clothes and fell face down into unconsciousness.

Twelve hours later, Billy arose to the sharp light of mid-afternoon. At first, he was slightly disoriented, not remembering what had occurred the previous day. He felt congested as if he were coming down with another cold. He went instinctively into the adjoining bathroom and looking into his now fogless mirror, he counted the many scrapes he had accumulated over the previous night: seventeen. Furthermore, his right leg had become so sore that he had to walk with a limp. As might a somnambulist, he entered the close confines of his rather small shower. He then turned the taps on to a scorchingly high temperature and stood under the showerhead's hot deluge for a full fifteen minutes without moving. Although the bathroom was entirely filled with steam, it was only after forty-five minutes that Billy emerged like an otherworldly Silenus through the parting clouds. When he finally removed himself from the bathroom, he immediately set to caring for his long-suffering hands and was horrified by the trauma that the previous night's unnecessary activities had wrought upon them. Finally after another forty minutes of preparation he emerged from his room into the kitchen. He was initially shocked to see his new ward standing in the corner over the stove and even had to shake his head, finally muttering, "Oh, you're still here?"

"Good morning, how are you feeling? You looked so tired last night. I prepared you breakfast. Huevos Rancheros. I hope you don't mind, but it was all I could put together from what I found in your kitchen?"

As he approached his small kitchen table, she pushed the plate gently in front of him. Given he hadn't eaten since lunch the previous day he was exceedingly famished. Billy took the plate thankfully. Without saying a word, he sat down and ate quietly. To his great surprise, the entire meal was actually quite good and incredibly satisfying. Furthermore, it was one of his favorite dishes. How had she known? She asked him tentatively, "Are they OK? Do you like them? If not, I can do something else."

Billy merely nodded, showing his satisfaction. The girl sat there watching him anxiously as he ate. She was dressed again in one of her black tops, a Screamo T-shirt with the words "PageNinetyNine", this time matched with a pair of black jeans. When he had finished the meal in less than a handful of hungry bites, she asked again, "You look hungry. I can make you some more if you want?" Billy only shook his head and looked around the kitchen, cleared as it was of the discarded beer cans and bags of refuse that had previously populated the yellow linoleum floor. Gone were the resident clouds of dust that moved effortlessly across the tessellated floors like tumbleweeds whenever any of the doors of his apartment were opened, gone were the stains of dried tomato sauce that sat like sores on his kitchen counters, gone were the bowls of semi rotten fruit that formed a still life *memento mori*. He finally asked, "Where did you put everything?"

"Oh, outside, you must not have seen it."

"No. And so you've obviously taken it upon yourself to clean my place?"

"Yes, I'm sorry, I didn't mean to intrude, but I..."

"Intrude? Intrude? This is a disaster!" He got up and walked into the living room. "How am I now going to find anything? You've cleaned it all up and now I know where nothing is."

"I'm sorry, but it was such a mess."

"No, correction. Not a mess. A mess is when you know where nothing is, but I on the other hand knew exactly where everything was."

"OK."

"Anyway, haven't you heard of a little 'delight in disorder'?"

"A what?"

"Oh, forget it. I'm going back to sleep."

Billy promptly went back to bed and slept for another four hours. He had already told the office he wasn't coming in that day and probably not for another week. When he looked at his watch again it was already past seven in the evening. He emerged from his room to find the mysterious girl still watching television.

"You're still here, I see."

"Yes."

"It's late and I need to run into the office for a few hours. You're not going to off yourself or shoot up in here are you?"

Initially taken back by the question, she then rubbed her arms and said looking down, "No. Not anymore."

"OK."

"Look Mr. Rubino, you might think nothing of me. That I'm just some little junkie you found on the street. But you saved my life and I have to repay you. I will get a job and I will leave your house, but whatever happens I still have to repay you."

"As I said…"

"No, it's important to me. I've done a lot of bad things in the past, but I didn't hurt anyone, except myself and I want to make a new start. I've never robbed. I've never cheated. I've never willingly hurt anyone. I just want to start over and you've given me that chance."

The speech was already boring Billy, but he knew there was no use in dissuading her. At this point she was in tears, "I'm sorry, Mr. Rubino, but I owe you my life. You don't know how much it means to me. And I ask you, beg you to just let me please pay you back. I don't know how yet, but I will. I promise."

Billy nodded his head. He had no idea what else to say, "OK, I better go then."

As he turned to leave the girl, he felt a bit more encouraged by her character. Intuiting the change, the girl ventured again, "Oh, sorry Mr. Rubino, is it OK if I stay here?" She was now standing on the very tips of her toes, nervously knitting her fingers together.

"Stop calling me Mr. Rubino. Call me Billy."

"Yes, Billy can I stay here? Please. It would mean a lot."

"I suppose if I said no, I probably wouldn't see the last of you, would I?"

"No, not until I pay you back," she said with a smile on her face, shaking her hands as if drying her nails. She already anticipated his surrender.

Billy mumbled with a deep sense of exhaustion in his voice. "Yes, I suppose so."

At this, she jumped up before him and gave him a powerful hug, even kissing him on the cheek. "Thank you so much, I promise I won't get in your way."

"Sure, just don't clean up anymore. And tell me, how does one actually screw up killing oneself? I only get to see the success stories."

She thought about it for a second, looking hurt and then returned a mischievous smile.

"Well, you'd never imagine how quickly one can learn to swim when one starts to drown. Call it a survival instinct."

"Is that so, well stay away from the cutlery and the power outlets because I couldn't face anymore paperwork and I wouldn't want to have to clean up your mess."

She laughed, mistaking Billy's utter seriousness with a very dry form of humor.

"You never know, I already found your stash of sleeping pills."

With the vague image of a smile, he then turned to walk out the door. As he opened the latch, the excited girl called after him with a voice of slight confusion,

"Don't you want to know what my name is?"

"No, but I'm sure you will tell me anyway."

"It's Dawn."

"Just Dawn?"

"Yes, just Dawn."

"OK, if you're true to your name, then I hope to have gone through the worst of it." He then turned and walked out the door.

"You want me to make you something before you leave?"

"No, I'll be back in a couple of hours, but help yourself and stay away from my pills as I'm saving them for a rainy day. "

After his episode on the mountain, Billy had decided to take a few days off in order to recover, however, while he slept, Sheriff Griffs had left a message for him, requesting his presence. It was agreed that Billy would drive out to the sheriff's house that night to discuss the details of his new assignment. He then recalled that Poundstone had also promised to call him in order to reveal the identity of the mysterious girl. However, Billy had since learned that the investigator had been reassigned to a new case and had probably forgotten to do so as a result. It was of lesser consequence now anyway. When he left his apartment and walked left toward the car garage he glanced a man walking in the opposite direction. He would have thought nothing of it except for the fact that when he passed the man, the hooded figure deliberately bumped into him, managing to knock Billy slightly off balance. When Billy turned around to ask what the problem was, the man just swiveled and looked at him without apology, his face shrouded in the darkness of the hood. Billy called the man an "Asshole", to which the dark figure simply spat on the ground, turned around and continued to walk in the opposite direction not taking his eyes off Billy. When Billy finally arrived at the sheriff's house, he discovered much to his surprise that the mayor of the city was already there, sharing a tall glass of brandy with Griffs. The mayor was a short, portly man who was never seen in a suit and could usually be found wearing jeans, a T-shirt and a brown corduroy jacket. He also favored ten-gallon hats and was usually in a good mood, his face crimsoned by the copious amount of alcohol he drank throughout the day. His face was bulbous and it always appeared as if one saw it through a fishbowl so that his every feature was magnified beyond proportion. The two men were in a jovial humor and it took about an hour until he finally figured out why he was even there. At one point, the mayor, who kept spilling beer on Billy's shirt as he spoke (his manner generally emphasized considerable gesticulation), interjected in with a typical anecdote of his,

"Last time I was out on the course, three weeks ago I think, I met this ol' fella, Ivy League type, who was from out in California and he says to me, 'You know, in California, we are prey to all kinds of natural disasters: mudslides, earthquakes, wildfires, floods, locusts, hurricanes, you name it, we got it. But, you guys out here in the South have by far the worst.' And I said, 'What is that?' And he turns to me and says with a perfectly straight face, 'White trash.' And we had a big ol' laugh together. I took him into the club and showed him the picture we had of ol' Tubbs. You know Tubbs, big black guy. Anyway, we got him all drunk and dressed up in this black Nazi uniform for Halloween, it was the biggest laugh you ever done seen. Anyway, we took a picture of him and put up this poster in the club with him lookin' all serious in this uniform and below it, the caption says, 'We are an equal opportunity employer'." At this point, the mayor broke into a horrendous laugh, spilling almost half his beer on Billy's shirt. Without remarking on the accident, he continued, "Anyway, I think this guy was kinda light in the loafers. The little hoser didn't find it funny one bit."

Sargent Griffs then turned around to Billy and winked at him, "Well Billy here knows all about that, don't ya? You went to one of them fancy schools up north there where you can even get a degree in studyin' trannies." At this point, the sheriff gave Billy an entirely unexpected wallop on his hindquarters that made them burn for minutes afterward. This friendly gesture was accompanied by a large smile and another knowing wink. Griffs then shook him by the shoulder,

"For the next couple of weeks, Billy here is goin' ta be my G.B.F. Ain't that right?"

"Yes, sir."

After a few more entertainments of this sort and a number of old "war stories", all topped off with two tall glasses of mint julep and another two Amber Moons (in anticipation of the following day), Billy finally discovered what he had been called for. To his horror, he learned that he had now been officially placed in charge (at least in part) of the "Riley situation". Evidently, Griffs had taken the entire affair personally and had convinced the mayor to sanction a number of irregularities. For Griffs, Riley was a vigilante who flew in the face of the law, while the mayor shared some anxiety about Riley's recent popularity amongst the people. He further worried about the consequences to his image if anyone were foolish enough to believe Riley's charges. Some had already insinuated that Riley's requests for his family's bodies were merely part of an elaborate form of public protest against all manner of ills including overseas wars, the growing crime rate in Hokum or the massive increase in police brutality that didn't sit well in some quarters. A couple of misguided people who had witnessed Riley's rooftop antics and the subsequent police reaction had even gone so far as to picket outside of the mayor's office for human rights. Thus, amongst the irregularities that Griffs and the mayor came up with were the following: a twenty-four hour police patrol around Riley's house, further patrols around the city's known cemeteries and an immediate reward for anyone who could give any information as to the whereabouts of the outlawed man. Billy's particular responsibilities (or so as they were described to him) were relatively straightforward and certainly fit into the category of irregularities. He was charged with driving Riley's family to the hospital over the next couple of weeks so that they could pretend to be in a comatose state in the instance that Riley ever decided to show up to the hospital in person. The family, despite being extravagantly suspicious of the police and authority in general, exchanged their cooperation for free meals, forgiveness of their previous hospital bills and complimentary medical exams for the little girls, which included the medicines that the family lacked. Regardless of his being off for the week, Billy was informed that he would nevertheless be required to carry out his tasks as from their perspective his time was of less consequence than that of the sheriff's officers. Billy found the entire plan utterly ridiculous but was powerless to object. Thus, it was in a profoundly grim state of mind that Billy returned home.

When he arrived at his garage and walked toward his house, he was surprised to find the same man loitering about in the darkness. When he walked up to confront the dismal presence, whose identity was still masked under both a gray hood and a lowered baseball cap, the man appeared to pull something from his pocket. Undeterred, Billy continued to approach him, trying to catch a glimpse of his face. He then asked gruffly, "Can I help you?" At which point, mysterious figure put his hand back into his pocket and walked quickly in the opposite direction without saying a word. Billy had seen hoodlums in the neighborhood before but never this close to his apartment. Given the nefarious influence of the Lido, it was only a matter of time until the purveyors of its ill airs made their way into his immediate environs. When Billy arrived again within the comforts of his apartment, Dawn had dinner prepared and waiting for him. Upon finding her dressed in yet another black outfit, his first words to her were, "So you've decided to behave yourself and not attempt anything naughty in my apartment. What you do outside I don't mind, but I must ask, why do you people always dress as if you were about to attend someone's funeral? It's morbid. Are you so death obsessed? Is the burden of life so truly painful for you or is this some ill-advised designer fashion?"

Dawn looked down at her black dress and in a second replied with equal spunk, "And this coming from a coroner. Well, if you don't like it, maybe I could try something else. Maybe a geisha outfit? Sir, your dinner weaady suuur." She bowed low, putting her hands together in prayer as a Japanese woman might. In the process of cleaning his room, she had evidently seen the scattered pictures of some of his previous 'girlfriends'. His only response to her little pantomime was a cold stare thrown aimlessly in her direction as he muttered inaudibly, "Guests are like fish you know, after a couple of days…" Not hearing what he said, Dawn apologized to him, telling him that she was only kidding and that she would adapt her wardrobe according to his fancy when he gave her the money to do so.

The next days continued in the following fashion: her doting over him and he sitting there helpless to do anything except attempt to rebuff her subtle advances with sharp insults. At points it became embarrassing. She had even written a poem for him and left it in an envelope under his bedroom door.

Billy-G.O.A.T.

Half human, half goat,
He is buzzing about the brazen field,
Disheveled, nothing escapes

His mechanical grasp.
Flowers sprout in the presence
Of his ponderous manhood.

If a maiden sang,
'Her love is like an avalanche,'
His armored jaw would tense,

His breath suffocated by the simile.
'His life will be her tapestry,' she thought
Then considered, 'Love disappears

At his touch like an itch',
Wistful, she offered with musing eye,
'If I were free to love

Whomever I wished...'
Having heard, his heart spoilt
Like cabbage in a landfill.

'Love is a sickness
Of which he has cured me,'
She sighed, undoing again her needlework.

After reading it, he was completely and utterly bewildered by the content and threw it amongst the waste of paper under his bed. He simply shook his head, not comprehending the enigmatic work at all: modern poetry was really something else that disgusted him. He assumed that this was exactly the sort of thing these devil-worshiping necro-nerds got up to. He felt almost sorry for her whenever she looked at him with those bloodhound eyes to the point where it quite sickened him. This strung-out little minx, who when combing her hair, pulled down each glistening strand to its very tip between her bare, spread legs as if to string her lyre-like form; oh, how she pined (and dreadfully so) for the pluck of that one paphian chord that had yet to be struck between the two. Couldn't she ever have enough and be done with her idle dreams of romance? Couldn't she satisfy the pangs of her heart with the steady drivel of romance novels? After all, what had she seen in him? Certainly something that most other women hadn't. It was a ridiculous state of affairs, he thought. She had merely woken like a young duckling from its birth egg and his face was by chance the first image imprinted on her fragile mind and here she was all Florence Nightingale addled, destined to follow him for eternity. It was the irony of the thing that hit him the most: of all the women he had wanted to conquer it was the one he was least interested in that was overly keen on conquering him. It wasn't that Billy had an attraction for singularly beautiful women, no, it was quite the opposite, but he was fastidious in his tastes and there was only a certain type of woman that satisfied him and it was the Asian cat-faced type, a breed far removed from what he saw in Dawn's tawdry charms. For Billy, her attentions were becoming increasingly an annoyance. At one point, she even asked what his birth sign was. When he responded, "Gemini, I think" she immediately went back to her magazine and determined that the two had compatible signs, even blaming his overt indifference toward her as representative of his fierce individuality and ambition.

Not being able to take any more of her lovelorn looks, her plaintive sighs, her incessant desire to "take care of him", ironing his shirts, straitening his collars, arriving to his rescue with a well-timed napkin whenever an errant piece of food dribbled from his lips onto the front of his now starched shirts, he decided the only course was to leave the house to get some fresh air. Using the excuse of dumping her with a number of suits and dress shirts that needed to be ironed ahead of his returning to the office (Billy as a rule never wore suits, but preferred slacks and button down shirts), he took leave of her as she gladly set to work on the mountain of shirts and outdated summer suits that probably no longer even fit him. Free of her constant attention, he slipped out of the apartment, deliberately avoiding her gaze and thus depriving her even the pleasure of asking him what he wanted for dinner. Uncertain of where to go, he immediately defaulted to the Red Queen. However, he soon reconsidered for two reasons: one, he wanted to avoid at all costs running into Basyli and two, Dawn had become acquainted with the bar through their regular conversations and he was afraid she might actually show up there to ask him what he wanted for dinner. Thus, without any specific destination in mind, he wandered the streets of the wharf district, aimlessly casting about, his mind completely unfocused.

After walking for about forty minutes, he found himself heading instinctively in the direction of the Lido. At present, he was in the liminal space between the Wharf district and the area, which was now derogatorily referred to as the Lido District. If he kept walking another five minutes in the same direction, he would eventually arrive at the mauve, neon lights of the Southern Rustler. Billy certainly wanted to avoid the Lido District at all costs. Thus, he decided to turn around and head back in the direction from whence he came. He ended up on a small side street, in width not much wider than himself. The street was cobbled, lined on each side by brown brick row houses. The uneven path went only a little ways before him until changing its mind it quickly ducked downward out of view as if pursuing an idle thought. He kept walking along the noncommittal street until he noticed a bright red door with a blue light above it to his right. He had seen this door and the blue light several times before, but had never walked inside. Given how out of place it was, there was no chance of missing it. The door itself had the look of being recently painted and was enclosed by a simple white molding. It was the kind of entryway that during the day one wouldn't have noticed, but in this faceless, anonymous street, its blue, hovering light made it stick out, succeeding to arouse one's curiosity even the more so given that there was no sign or posting to explain the blue light's mysterious pollution. He had always assumed it was a bar (or perhaps even a brothel), but was never sure given the light seemed a rather noncommittal beacon, a strange invitation.

After standing before the threshold for a minute or two, having nothing better to do, he pushed the door open and was immediately presented with a long wooden staircase that invited him upstairs into darkness. Taking the invitation, he walked up the flight of stairs to the landing were he came to another door on his right, which was open and lined with strings of hanging beads. In the space above the lintel, written in a faded, blue, carnivalee font, appeared the phrase 'Le Gala des Incomparables.' From behind a dark curtain, he could hear low music emanating from inside which sounded something like a New Orleans dirge or perhaps some tired blues lament by Billie Holiday. He walked through the plastic beads, parting the black curtains and found himself in a narrow room lit by a low, blue light that pervaded the entire space. The room was dark enough that it only permitted entry to shadows and silhouettes. The walls of the room were also painted a deep blue. At the very front (the only part of the room that was lit to any significant degree), there was a wooden bar that spanned the entire width of the space. Above the bar to his great surprise there seemed to be a small, well-lit stage hung with faded velvet curtains, again the color of blue. The carved frame that surrounded the stage curtains was ornate, filigreed in both red and gold. Behind him there were a few empty tables, each lit by a small lamp covered by a red Victorian lampshade. Incidentally, these along with larger variants were the same lamps that were to be found on the bar at the front of the room. The bar, if it were to be called such, was almost entirely deserted except for one senior citizen who perched just off center in a khaki mackintosh and another younger man, middle-aged and overweight who sat hunched over the counter, staring darkly into his drink. The second man was sitting off to one side of the bar, which ran long the same wall that enclosed the door from which he had entered. The place had a dark, glum look about it, a mood that was only relieved by the Victorian lampshades, which allowed for the atmosphere of a lady's boudoir or New Orleans style brothel. Before he turned left to walk toward the front of the room, he looked around the walls, which were lit by small footlights and were for the most part blank except for three exceptionally large paintings, one on each wall. Billy wouldn't have recognized them, but the famous reproductions included 'The Wine of Circe' by Edward Burne Jones, another was 'Duelo a Garrotazos' by Goya and the final one was 'Laocoon' by El Greco.

Billy had a strange feeling about the place, but nevertheless decided to try the bar given that he was already there and his feet had begun to hurt. He took a place at the counter in a high leather stool, the second seat to the right of the old man who was also glowering into his drink with great sadness. Immediately, an old, black midget with a large head full of white hair presented himself while polishing a glass. He didn't say a word, but his attitude indicated that he was there to take Billy's order. The petite man was dressed impeccably: wearing the three-pieced suit of an old fashioned butler, he even carried a golden pocket fob. Billy ordered a double whisky, which was brought to him forthwith. While the barman prepared the drink, he wondered how the tiny man was able to reach his height and finally, looking over the counter, he noticed that the floor beneath the small man was raised significantly higher than the one on which he stood. Billy sampled the whisky, which had an exceedingly strange, but not unpleasant taste about it. It had a deep oaken flavor, but lacked bitterness and instead had a slight languid finish to it that he couldn't immediately recognize, something ancient yet familiar, something of dark, rainy days, something perhaps of mildew. Once the old barman had completed his duty, he took out his golden watch and observed the time, after which he went to the back of the bar and rung a large brass bell with a tiny hammer. He then put on an old stovetop hat that hung on a brass peg and took up what appeared to be a large, red megaphone and a black magician's wand. After arranging himself and straightening his bow tie, he walked up one of the small pair of stairs that lined each side of the stage. Once on stage, he stepped into the clinquant glow of a small spotlight that he had previously activated by switch under the bar. He then announced through the megaphone, "Ladies and gentlemen, the one and only, Miss Gloria." Billy looked to his left as for the first time since he had entered the room the old man next to him showed signs of life: he began to clap and instantly his eyes brightened up.

The small barman then left the stage and wandered back to the bar taking the opposite staircase downward. Suddenly, from behind the curtains emerged a tall, thin, but incredibly toned black woman dressed it what appeared to be red carnival wear, feather boas, peacock fans and all. Once on the stage, she struck a pose and then stood powerfully for a full two minutes without moving. Her mere presence drew looks of awe and immediately demanded the attention of the spellbound few who inhabited the room. It seemed to all present as if she had command over the very elements of earth, as if she had the ability to make time stop at least within the confines of that small space. Her skin was dark, her legs powerful and lithe, the lines of her long calve muscles flexed atop the high, red heels. She stood there with a smile on her face, ever so gently trembling in her powerful pose. She then raised her hands to each side at thirty degree angles and waited for the audience, primarily the midget and the old man to applaud her. She again smiled with ivory teeth that cut through the darkness like the unsheathed knife of an old betrayal. Finally, some sound emerged from an invisible record player, the first seconds all crackle and pop until a strange music wafted over them, something akin to the beginning of 'Temptation'. As the sinuous music reached around her waist to embrace her, she closed her eyes and began to sway at the midriff until her whole body writhed like a column of cigarette smoke or perhaps like some desert viper. She then began to move her long limbs in slow, suggestive movements all the time keeping her eyes focused on some invisible point above her. Despite his predilection for Asians and much to his own surprise, Billy was captivated by her dark sexuality. Under the pale flame of a spotlight that followed her across the stage, her flesh began to glisten with perspiration. She then looked out into the crowd, catching each audience member's eyes in turn until she landed on Billy's. For his part, he felt mesmerized by her dark, brown eyes that never wavered for a second. He was not only drawn to her, but he was drawn in a manner that he had never been drawn before. In a way, she possessed him.

As she danced, his eyes remained locked on hers and hers, seemingly on his. Billy didn't notice it, but she had a strange look in her eyes as if she somehow recognized him. It was a look that resembled a mix of suspicion and curiosity. After a couple of dances were done, she bowed to the audience and came down the stairs to the front of the bar where she first began to exchange pleasantries with the old Caucasian who sat next to him. After a few minutes of laughter and mock rebuffs, the old man dropped a ten dollar bill into her glass at which point she came right up to Billy, sat down on the chair opposite him and put her hand near his groin. For Billy's part, there was an instant reaction. Just prior to her coming over, Billy had for the first time in years felt the strange sensation of something being caught in this throat. Now, any sensations he had were instantly confined to the nether regions of his body. He would have enjoyed teaching her to put the devil back in his hole. In a slow, deep voice, Miss Gloria whispered into his ear, "Aren't you going to buy me a drink?"

Billy responded, "Sure" and signaled the bartender over. When the barman arrived, before Billy could say anything and without taking her sultry gaze off of him, she simply put two fingers into the air at which point the barman went away, soon returning with two large glasses of unmixed bourbon. It was then that Billy finally had a chance to look at her face up close and outside of the spotlights. He quickly surmised that she was certainly an older woman, having lines around her lips and eyes, but was none the worst for it. She was probably in her mid-forties, but had very well preserved skin and a beautifully strong set of features: full red lips, perfect teeth and a set of brown, almond eyes. Her eyelids were dusted with the gold stuff of moth wings. She took her headpiece off and laid it on the table, revealing a full weave of dark hair. As her hand moved around his manhood, he felt the definite twitch of arousal, *la petit mort*. She then said,

"You had me scared to death, honey. I thought you was dead."

"Huh," Billy breathed softly, "What do you mean?"

"Don't pretend like you don't know. It wasn't that long ago. You had me runnin' out of there like nobody's business, thinkin' you had a heart attack."

"Wha...what? You must be mistaken," Billy replied as if suddenly awoken from an all too pleasant enchantment.

"Me? Listen sweetie, I ain't the one who was mistaken. You's lucky I'm still talkin' to you honey after what you done did."

In that instant, Billy realized her mistake as he thought back to his last visit to the Lido and the man he had found next to the black rubber fist. He remembered with dread that all of the officers including Poundstone were of the opinion that he resembled the dead man and so must she. After the initial shock and disappointment, an instant feeling of horror crept up his spine as the moment of recognition continued to descend over him: indeed, this was no woman before him, it was a man who was fondling his manhood. "Oh, dear Lord," he heard himself pronounce, almost involuntarily. Words he had never uttered his entire life. A long, wet gulp ensued whose finishing note sounded between them like a brick falling into an otherwise calm sea. Although Billy was on his fourth shot of whisky, he still minded and looked down at what he thought was a woman's hands and noticed their unmistakable male quality: they were large, veined and slightly muscular like those of Olive Oyl. Then he looked at her neck and while thin and somewhat epicene, it bore the unmistakable sign of an Adam's apple. Feeling instantly uncomfortable, he moved the man's hand away from his groin.

"I'm sure of it. You've got me mixed up with someone else," he replied gruffly.

"Are you kiddin' me? I could'a sworn you was dead. I even put my head on your chest and you wasn't breathin'. You have a brother or somethin' cause I don't know how you standin' here in front of me?"

"What are you talking about? What happened at the Lido?" Billy asked in false ignorance, wanting to find out the real story behind the episode.

"Of course, I'm talkin' about what happened at the Lido. And you's a dead man for sho'. Let me see your palm."

"What?"

"Let me see your palm. My mother was from Haiti and I know a thing or two about voodoo, hoodoo and all kinds a shit. I can read cards. I can read palms and I know when someone is dead when I see them. Let me see your palm."

Billy reluctantly lifted his palm and showed it to the man. Miss Gloria studied it intently and then jumped back in horror, his eyes widening in fear.

"Just as I thought. You ain't got no lifeline. You's dead for sho. Either that or you's Bacalou." Immediately, the man grabbed his purse and pulled out a small nickel-plated Derringer belt gun and pointed it at Billy. He also grabbed a small amulet that he wore around his neck that resembled a tiny, cloth bag. Billy, for his part, instinctively put up his hands.

"Listen, I don't even know who Bacalou is."

"That's the devil."

"Well, I sure ain't the devil. I am Billy Rubino, the city coroner. Just look, I'll take out my ID and show you." After Miss Gloria gave him a brief nod of affirmation, he pulled out his wallet then subsequently his work ID and showed it to the man. Miss Gloria grabbed it from his hand suspiciously. Gradually lowering the gun through a slow détente, he put it back in his purse and sat down more calmly. Suspicion nonetheless hung in his eyes.

"What is you doin' here then? You lookin' to arrest me, 'cuz I didn't kill that cracker. That cracker jus' up and died, right there."

Billy, surprised by the sudden male quality of the voice was equally surprised that no one had seemed to pay the slightest attention to what had just occurred. He nonetheless answered in a world-wearied voice, "No, I'm not here to arrest you. I just came here to get a quiet drink."

"How come I never seen you before and you look just like that cracker too?"

"Well, I was on my way home and thought I'd stop in because I had no place else to go."

The man looked at him sternly and there was a minute of silence between the two. Then, suddenly, Miss Gloria burst out into a healthy fit of laughter.

"You had me scared for a minute. You're the splittin' image of that man, I swear. I was like, how the hell he come in here after he been dead and gone all this time? Daaayymmnn!"

Billy didn't like the idea that he was continually mistaken for this deceased man but decided to let it pass. "Yeah, I worked the case and had to tell his wife and all what happened. We found some pretty interesting items in that room. How did you meet this guy anyway?"

Leaning towards him, Miss Gloria began to speak in low, conspiratorial tones. "Well you know, Miss Gloria doesn't usually get mixed up in any kinda crazy shit like that, but this cracker...Sorry, I hope you don't mind if I call him cracker?"

"No...no, not at all."

"Anyway, this cracker come up in heres like every day for two weeks straight givin' me big tips, like a hundred dollars at a time. I'm like daaaymmnn, cracker you got it goin' on. But, he kept whisperin' in my ear about how he wanted to take me back to his place and all this shit. So I'm like whatever and throwin' shade at him all week until one day he come in here with a big bunch of long stemmed roses and you know how

Miss Gloria loves roses. Anyway, he always dressed nice and wore nice cologne so I'm like, well, maybe Miss Gloria can make an exception. So he takes me out to dinner. We go out to a real nice place and then he takes me back to the Lido. If that ain't bad enough, this cracker started askin' me to do all this crazy shit and had all these crazy toys and shit. I was like, I don't know nothin' about that but he kept insistin', beggin' right and throwin' all this money at me. So I said, OK, I give the guy a little bit of fun and then he just up an dies right then, heart attack."

"Damn," Billy thought to himself. So here again another story deflated before his very eyes. Moncrete's prosaic interpretation had been correct after all.

"Anyway, I got to runnin' and didn't look back. Thought nothin' of it until I see you's in here and I'm like, what? Anyway, that still doesn't explain you not havin' no lifeline. You shouldn't even be alive. But, I tell you what, Miss Gloria's got her cards with her. I'm gonna read about you, mmm mmm."

Billy had never had his fortune read and wasn't fond of the idea, but given there seemed to be no way out of it, he conceded. He said at last in exasperation, "Look I don't really believe in all that stuff."

"What stuff, honey?"

"Voodoo and all that stuff."

"Of course you don't. You don't believe in that stuff 'cuz you's white and you know what the white people did to voodoo?"

"No."

"Of course you don't. I bet you think voodoo is all about evil and stickin' pins in dolls and stuff. But, it ain't nothin' about that at all. See that's what you been taught, because that is what the white man does to put the black man back in chains. I bet you didn't know this, but voodoo used to be very strong here in the South and had a lot of followers. It had a great effect on the people and made them strong. So strong that in Haiti, they even revolted and freed themselves. It was the first time blacks ever had their own independent nation in the new world. Well, the whites didn't like that and they got all the politicians, filmmakers and powerful men together and they destroyed voodoo, they made it evil because they was afraid the black people would rise up and revolt in this country. I bet you didn't know that."

"No. I didn't."

"See here, that's how white people been treatin' blacks here for centuries." As he spoke he spread the cards in front of Billy.

After Billy picked out a few cards, Miss Gloria stared at them intently while he kept shaking his head in silence, repeating over and over "mmm mmm". After a few minutes of this, Billy began to inquire after the grave look on the man's face, asking him what he had read in the cards, but he refused to say. He suddenly became slightly awkward about Billy's very presence.

"Listen, I don't know who you are or what you are, but there somethin' ain't right with you Mister Rubino. I just can't say."

"What is it? Is something bad gonna happen?"

"Somethin' bad done already happened. I'm going to have to ask you to leave, now."

"What? But…"

"You heard me, you gotta get outta here, now."

The black midget came over and spoke to Miss Gloria in an impossibly deep and polished voice, "Is this guy giving you trouble, Miss Gloria? Should I call Charles over here?"

Billy responded by getting up, leaving a wad of cash on the table. "No need for that. I was just on my way."

Within the next few seconds, he had left the bar and quickly descended the stairs. Soon finding himself again in the narrow alleyway, he continued to walk in the direction that would eventually lead him home. His mind was slightly flustered, but it wasn't long before he had the opportunity to reflect on what had just occurred. Although Hokum was a small city, the coincidence was startling. Billy reasoned as such: Hokum, although small, had an even smaller underbelly, thus if one pulled on one of the many cords that had managed with little effort to knot itself into a caricature-like underworld, it wouldn't take a great degree of effort to find where the other end wiggled. Ultimately, all these loose strands formed their tight lump in the very area where he stood and there was certainly no denying that over the last few months, his life had become filled with loose ends that had woven themselves into some kind of frayed fabric that he no longer recognized or comprehended. In the end, however, the incident at the Lido wasn't the coincidence that most troubled his mind. It was mere fact that someone else had mistaken him for the devil. It was the third time in almost as many weeks that he had been referred to as a type of Satan, a moniker he certainly didn't feel he deserved. He pondered the potential motivations for a long time and couldn't come up with a single instance of evil that he had committed. After all, in the last week, he had even taken in a homeless heroin addict and helped an elderly woman with her baggage at the station. Was it the destiny of all coroners to be mistaken for some demonic pollution by the mere happenstance association of their profession with death? It seemed ridiculous, but he was certain that he was no more of a devil than any other public official and even if he were, how could one judge his own particular brand of evil to be an objectifiable wrong? Perhaps his only sin was an overriding ambition, but who didn't have that? Wasn't it ambition that drove his one hero, Larry Campbell to the heights he achieved? Larry Campbell was the most famous of all coroners who had not only achieved the Canadian senate, but managed to have a television show made about him. In Billy's mind, it was merely a force of character that drove him and his hero above the surrounding inanity that would otherwise have consumed them. He saw that the only way for him to rise above the sucking nihilism, the world's drainpipe, he needed to become a noble soul.

However, Billy quickly grew tired of pondering these inanities. It was useless. For Billy, self-reflection was a particularly unsatisfying form of human vanity and ultimately nothing good would come of it. Better to live in the world of people and actions, to live outside oneself and influence the things of this world that will ultimately influence one's life. One had to take control of one's fate otherwise fate would lead one down its own bitter course. It occurred to him that only when one engages actively in a social contract with God or with man, only then does nihilism disappear, only then does evil have a meaning and an essence. Here, he was blessed with the realization of this new irony. He considered further that to engage in this particular form of morality, of public manners, he must recognize also that society cannot always speak for the individual and on these occasions it should rather be silent. Ultimately, one cannot end the conversation by the mere presence of a misspoken word or a badly phrased question like *what is the meaning of life?* One can only judge one's vernacular against the fundamental grammar of his society, provided of course that one is surrounded by well-spoken people, otherwise one must speak the language of the insane, which isn't really a language at all. This all led him to one sickening conclusion: for if life truly isn't a zero sum game and fate is ultimately blind, one is left with little else but to work at improving the lot of the downtrodden and dumb *pluribis*, for the chances of significantly improving one's own cannot be known in advance as society is a vicious and unpredictable animal. However, if one works within the belly of the beast, cowering beneath and occasionally tickling the cockles of its heart in the perhaps futile hope of finally taming it, one can improve the general lot, then (and only then) by improving the overall set of imputations (even for the very least of its members), one can numerically better one's own chance of not being shat out of life's sickened bowels again and again for an eternity.

It was with thoughts of this kind that Billy made his slow way home. His mind's reflex turned back to the rubber fist and the idea of Miss Gloria exercising the instrument while the mysterious "cracker" died of his heart attack. As soon as the image crossed his mind, he laughed a loud, long laugh and his old mood returned. He then thought of the man's wife with the two Hispanic boys he had caught almost *in flagrante* through the door holding lit sparklers. He could only shake his head at the trite unseemliness of human folly. On a sudden, out of the corner of his eye, he imagined he saw a dark presence peeking out of an alleyway to his right. Thinking nothing of it, he continued to walk another few blocks, where he again was prompted by some shadowy reflex to turn and witness what appeared a fleeting darkness move sideways into the blackness of an adjacent building. Instantly, he had the strange sensation that he was being followed, but what for? Walking a few feet more, Billy abruptly swiveled round and charged towards the alley where he had seen the movement. As he ran, he heard the noise of scattering feet, a pair of garbage cans being knocked over. It was clear, someone had been following him and now he was running away. Once he arrived at the alleyway, he saw the outline of a man running toward the opposite end of the short side street. He went on to follow him, turning the corner at almost full stride. He initially lost sight of the mysterious figure, but decided to cut across the adjacent street in the hope of cutting him off. After turning down two more small alleys, he suddenly spotted the same man from the opposite end of the alley. He now ran at full tilt, almost knocking down a young couple, who had just exited a street level bar. He ran as fast as he could for another thirty feet, but to no avail, the other man was simply too fleet-footed for him. He was gone. Billy had unfortunately chased the man in the wrong direction and found himself again in the Lido District, where there were still crowds of people about. Upset with himself and out of breath, he decided to walk straight back home. The night had been too long already. When he returned to his apartment, he found another yellow note attached to his front door:

man is condemned to be free; because once he is thrown into the world, he is responsible for everything he does.
 - sartre

you still owe me money.
 - the warden

7

"A family act goes in to a talent agent…"

Over the course of the next two days, Billy continued the normal routines that constituted his daily existence: surfing the Internet, reading his mysteries, watching old news clips of himself, avoiding as much as possible "deep" conversations with Dawn. At times, he did invite her to critique his collection of television "performances". Given her normally morbid manner of dress, he assumed she might have liked this sort of thing (which she did indeed, proclaiming herself to have once been part of a local 'tribe of Ascians'). In the time since his last memorable dream about Cortez, he had had a number of similar nightmares, all seemingly centered on images of war, massacre, and brutal murder. In this vein, Billy had often felt that his once vigorous ambitions had plateaued for some time and that what his career needed was the publicity attached to hunting and then catching a decent serial killer. It would be the kind of publicity that could ensure his ascension to the upper echelons of his field and perhaps further. However, despite this long held wish, no mass murderer ever seemed to find his merry way to his un-sensational backwater. At times, given its overwhelming dull-wittedness, he thought Hokum was a city just waiting for a serial killer, but perhaps it lacked either the sophistication or the utter remoteness that normally attracted those types. Nevertheless, in his vain desire to prepare himself for the hoped for opportunity, he constantly read a great deal of literature about serial killers, which provided him plenty of grist for his mill and made him see a serial killer's work in even the most humble of accidental deaths. Notwithstanding his voracious reading, these books had never before affected his dreams, especially to the point where at night he felt compelled to leave his apartment and go for long walks in the hopes of arresting his now constant insomnia. He had even started again on Eszoplicone, an old "prescription" he had filled according to the sage advice of the Warden, who as an amateur pharmacologist seemed to have a gift not only for recommending, but acquiring the right drug for any sort of psychological or spiritual disturbance.

It came as some small relief that despite these frequent jaunts, he hadn't caught further sight of the mysterious man. In fact, the erstwhile stranger seemed to have disappeared entirely from his mind for a very brief span of time. However, the reprieve was not to last, for on the third day, without warning, the mysterious man began to reappear again with increasing frequency at odd places and at odd times. In fact, Billy began to see him wherever he went. It got to the point where if Billy hadn't seen the man walking behind him, he began to worry that something untoward was about to occur. For months now, Billy had continued to feel this strange anxiety, perhaps a sense of foreboding as if something was going to happen to him. Conceivably, he concluded, this mysterious entity, his constant presence had something to do with it. Evidently of a darker complexion, the man kept a safe distance, merely regarding Billy with a cold stare, never doing or saying anything. It was as if the man merely wanted Billy to know that he was being watched. In fact, the man didn't in any way attempt to hide the fact that he was blatantly following Billy. Not good with faces, Billy couldn't even determine if it was the same man or perhaps different men. Furthermore, he had no idea what reason someone had to follow him. Given the mysterious figure always wore a hood and the same large jacket, he could never catch a clear look at the man's face. Going through the people who might have reason to follow him, he assumed the man was too big to be Riley and certainly too well built to be Basyli. But who else would want to cause him harm? As his mind began to churn through its unlikeliest scenarios, he began to recall Basyli's ridiculous accounts of the KGB. What if they were in fact accurate? Or perhaps it was the drugs. In fact his diazepam usage had recently gone through the roof and he was taking four times the daily recommended dose. Did this man even exist or was it merely a figment of his imagination? Was he becoming paranoid and as a result having hallucinations? All valid questions, and yet he didn't temper his daily course of diazepam, but if anything increased it. As a result, the previous dreams continued in escalating fervor, to the point where he saw in surprising detail the grisly murders of Jack the Ripper, Joseph Vacher, and Frederic Deeming, celebrated cases of the past which he had been remiss hadn't been repeated in Hokum. However, he now began to fear that a similar evil was chasing him and with this knowledge, he continued to see in his dreams their foul dismemberments, the premeditated horrors they once inflicted on their victims and which he now imagined would be inflicted on him. He soon felt like a prisoner and gaoler all at once, trapped inside himself, he saw his second self running toward endless precipices within something resembling one of Piranesi's nightmarish dungeons. And so, in essence, whether he was dreaming or not, he was harried to distraction. It was obvious even to himself, the former Übermensch, that within his Fortress of Solitude, he was becoming a distracted, nervous wreck. Maybe Dawn was right, he did need 'taking care of'. It was a difficult thing for him to face. Did he in fact need to see a therapist or worse, a psychologist?

One morning as Dawn was preparing his breakfast she spoke to him in an idle chatter that fell in large clumps of muddled words that clattered, spun and ultimately evaporated on the floor just short of his ears. While he read the paper, his phone suddenly rang. Given that he had already adapted his hearing to tune out Dawn's cheerful voice, he didn't catch the ring at first and it was only after Dawn yelled at him several times that the spell of his concentration was broken. Kindly, by the time he realized what had raised the sudden alarm in her voice, Dawn had already brought him the phone. Looking at the number imprinted on the screen, he instantly understood that it was Poundstone. He picked up the call nervously and full of foreboding. However, the now restful tone of Poundstone's voice filled the small receiver, "Hey, it's Poundstone here."

"Hey, how's it going?"

"Listen, I've been simply snowed under with a new case."

"Does it by any change involve a dark complexioned suspect perhaps connected with a series of murders?"

"What?"

"Nothing."

"Anyway, I never got a chance to get back to you on the girl. How's that goin'?"

"It's still going, unfortunately."

"Well I'll be," he laughed. "Anyway, I finally got 'round to the hospital and found that nurse I was mentionin' earlier and the long and short of it is is that I think I got a little information for you."

"OK," Billy said questioningly, while walking into the other room.

"Well, first off, her real name is Dawn."

"Well, you're about a week too late with that information."

"Sorry about that. I thought so. Anyway, you figure out her last name yet?"

"No."

"I couldn't either. The woman at the hospital didn't know much and her English wasn't so good. Anyway, the girl, I mean Dawn, refused to identify or give any information about herself in the hospital, only sayin' her name wuz Dawn. One of them Mexican nurses thinks her father lives outside of town and believes it's his daughter, but this is all second hand information and she wouldn't say much anyway. Only knows her first name and thinks she had heard somethin' bad about the family. Anyhows, she thinks the girl doesn't want to say much because she don't want anyone findin' her in the hospital."

"OK, that's interesting," Billy's voice picked up with obvious interest. "You know why?"

"No, all's I know is that there was a big story about it like twenty or thirty years back. It was all hush hush around here so the local papers didn't go into the details of the story that much. I'd say you could find it in an old paper, but you ain't got a last name. Anyway, I've been tol' there was a big story about it in some local magazine and it has somethin' to do with a kidnappin'. Maybe you can find it at the library. It's called 'A Song about Jeanne and Reggie' or somethin' like that. I got that last bit from the sheriff who remembers workin' the case, but his mind's so full of cobwebs he can't remember any of the names or nothin' else no hows."

Billy's voice began to sound pensive and a definite tone of interest pricked up in his voice, "OK, that's interesting and perhaps helpful. Maybe finding her family will get her out of my house all the quicker." However, just as he said this, an idea instantly popped into his head and he kicked himself for not thinking about it before. He couldn't understand how he had not taken the chance to capitalize on his rescuing the girl. He could certainly have garnered himself some media attention, but after a few days the story would by now have run cold. Furthermore, the girl's real identity was unclear. It was not like him to miss these types of angles. He blamed it on what amounted to a creeping hebetude precipitated by his recent bouts of anxiety. As it stood, without the girl's identity, it was hardly a story, nevertheless, he thought with this new wrinkle, there could be something there he could perhaps salvage.

"Could be, but that's all I got at the moment."

"OK, thanks a lot."

After hanging up, Billy began to consider the state of affairs. He considered whether or not to confront Dawn directly with the information he had so far gathered, but assumed it would be of no use. On the few occasions when Billy had asked her about her past, she adamantly refused to say anything about it, deflecting all attention away from herself. As a rule, Billy didn't like secrets, especially ones being deliberately kept from himself. But, what he hated the most about this particular nondisclosure was the fact that there seemed to be a good story at the bottom of it. Billy thought about the situation for a long while and out of a mix of boredom and desperate curiosity (one of Billy's greater faults), Billy decided to head down to the library, his gross impatience getting the better of him.

Leaving the apartment in a rush, Billy drove to the center of the city where the small public library was located. The library was a curiously quaint, red brick building with russet tinted windows. It was hidden at the corner of a large parking lot that included a massive cineplex, which sat in the shallow depression behind Hokum's largest outdoor strip mall. While the rest of the parking lot was packed to capacity with cars, the library sat in calm desuetude with not a single car parked in front of it.

The library had been built about fifteen years prior and was meant to replace the miniscule library that had existed at the back of a now demolished grocery store. Unfortunately, few people, if any had entered the building that wasn't in any way unpleasant. It was carpeted in blue throughout and had a number of wooden stacks that stood in rows in front of a large checkout desk. Scattered around the main room, there were numerous tables on which to sit and even couches on which to lie. The walls were decorated by colored handprint turkeys and various art projects donated by the primary schools in the area. Having never been in the library and finding himself helpless as to what to do once inside, Billy instantly approached the young librarian, who stood at the front checkout desk quietly reading a large book. The woman was a young, short-haired Asian girl with large glasses, which instantly grabbed Billy's attention. She wore a décolleté blouse with long, translucent sleeves and a knee-length, indigo skirt. She looked up at Billy with a pleasant, full smile that revealed her yellowed, crooked teeth. She couldn't have been more than twenty-one. To Billy's eyes, her smallish face was not unattractive and she seemed to carry herself in the discrete, well-controlled manner that Billy approved of. She soon asked Billy if he needed any help. Billy replied yes and subsequently asked her what her name was to which she replied, "Lin." He then inquired as to what she was reading and she responded with great enthusiasm, "*Dead Souls*". Billy had never heard of it, but it sounded like a particularly morbid title and thus he decided not to pursue it any further. The girl, obviously happy to have a customer, asked Billy if she could help him find anything. He told her that he was in some difficulty in trying to find a particular article that could only be found in an obscure periodical the name of which was 'The Song of Jeanne and Reggie'. The word 'obscure' had evidently piqued the young librarian's interest and she took on the project as a personal challenge. Instantly and with a fulsome energy, she began referencing and cross-referencing various computer systems and electronic databases. Absorbed in her task, she had soon forgotten Billy's presence and went about her work in a quick, meticulous fashion. After twenty minutes, Billy was getting bored and was about to give up the project, but the young librarian wouldn't be daunted. She asked him, "I can't find anything. Do you have any further information?"

"Well, it was published some twenty or thirty years ago and it may mention something about a girl named Dawn."

"OK, that may be helpful," the girl replied perkily without so much as looking up, her fingers tapping various keys with increasing rapidity.

After another fifteen minutes, Billy was certainly tired of the project and after suitably inspecting the contours of her derriere, he began in exasperation, "Listen, it's not that important, maybe..."

"I fount it! I fount it!" The girl jumped up enthusiastically. "It is called 'The Ballad of Jean and Reg' and it is written by

Jean Hewitt and was published in a local periodical called, 'The Whippoorwill's Jamboree' and we have a copy right here in the library. OK, we can go find it." She had clearly become more excited about finding the periodical than he was. She immediately led him to the section where the old periodicals were to be found, but was unable to locate it. Crestfallen, she told Billy the bad news, "It's supposed to be here, but it isn't."

"OK, maybe it's lost then. We can forget it."

"No sir, I'm sure it must be here. We must not give up. We will just have to look through all the periodicals. It could just be misplaced."

Billy looked around the room at the long line of periodicals that wove around the walls and did not relish the idea.

"But that could take forever?"

"Do you have somewhere to go?"

Billy was taken aback by her pointed question.

"This is knowledge at stake that could disappear forever," she continued in a concerned tone of voice.

"No, but…"

"OK, then don't just stand there. I start on this end and you start over there. I show you."

Billy wasn't used to taking orders, especially from small Asian women, but her intentness disarmed him. As she led him toward his assigned place, they both looked over to their left, noticing something strange between a pair of low bookshelves that fronted the microfiche machines. It was a body, lying on the floor and by all appearances it appeared to be dead. The small figure was dressed in an old, shabby suit and wore a pair of battered shoes that had been worn through to the very toes. Billy instantly recognized its deserted frame as Basyli's. Lin put her hands to her hips and began in her usual, heavily accented English, "Here he is again. I tell him several times he cannot sleep on the floor. He comes in here every day. Reading, reading, reading, all the papers in the microfiche and then sleeps on the floor. He is a homeless man and I cannot stop him from coming in. But he smells and spends entire day talking to himself. I need to wake him up."

Billy however cautioned her against the idea. "No, I wouldn't do that. I know the guy and I wouldn't wake him up at least until I leave." Lin, being nonplussed by his suggestion and more interested in finding the periodical anyway chose to follow his advice and began the search in earnest. It took them two straight hours of searching every periodical without success. Billy resorted to sitting on the floor with his legs under him, pulling out one dusty periodical after the next, occasionally laughing at the humorously outdated and provincial magazines. Upon finding a book on the history of demonic possession called *Satan's Hollow*, he began to read through it avidly.

Suddenly, from the other end of the room, Lin screamed and held up the missing magazine. "I found it," she cried in a loud sort of whisper as if she had discovered the Dead Sea Scrolls, themselves. She ran towards him in her flat-heeled librarian shoes, taking small, uncoordinated steps to show him the periodical with glee. The much abused red cover had a primitive drawing of a man that seemed to dance on a mountain top, playing a fiddle to a distant moon that smiled above him. Happy to have the document, she asked him if he wanted to read it there or check it out. When Billy replied he didn't have a library card, she frowned at him, "No library card? Bad. Very bad." She then insisted on registering him for one. Once he filled out the necessary forms and was preparing to leave the library (not before asking Lin for her phone number), Basyli rose from his place of slumber and noticing Billy at the checkout desk, he began to rave in a loud voice,

"The devil. It is the devil. He even comes to prevent me from my studies."

Billy, on his part, tried to urge the woman along so he could leave the premises immediately.

She however turned to Basyli, putting her finger in front of her lips, saying "Shhhhh" and pointing to a sign above her that read, "Silence is Golden". Basyli nevertheless continued on his rant,

"You are devil and you try stop me from finding who you are but I have lots of information. *Twoja dusza śmierdzi gównem.* I show everyone who you are. I make great discovery and I know who you are. You are devil, Mr. Rubino. You are Devil. *Diabeł. Diabeł.*"

As Basyli shouted, Billy took both the book on demonic possession and the magazine under his arm and walked out of the library and towards his car which was parked directly in front. Basyli proceeded to follow him and shouted at him from the front door, "You try to stop my discovery but you no stop me. I will reveal everything. The people will all see who you are. You will then be stopped, *Diabeł. Zjedz moj chuj!*"

Billy quickly closed the door to his car without saying a single word in response to his ever-present *bête noire*. After all, he had no further information to give the man on his case that was quite frankly still languishing somewhere in a pile of paper, helplessly lost within the bureaucratic process. Once Billy arrived at home, he read the article with great interest, but was very disappointed by the end, which literally left him at a cliff's edge. The information the nurse had given Poundstone corroborated his own surmise that Dawn must be the daughter of Jean and Reggie, but he would have to find the second half of the story to determine the ending. After calling to the library again, he quickly discovered to his great disappointment that another edition of The Whippoorwill's Jamboree was never published. Given the quality of the contents he could understand why. The next stage was then to check police records and try to determine if he could find any additional information on either of the parents. Calling into the police office, he quickly determined that Jean Hewitt had died several years prior in prison, but they could find no information on Reggie Hortega. Perhaps he still lived in Hokum, but Hortega was certainly a generic name by all measures. Quickly glancing through the phone directory he noted that calling every Hortega would be an impossibility. He had to decide whether or not to simply present Dawn with the article, force her to tell him the rest of the story and by so doing, arrest the burning itch in his cerebellum or to take the other, more gentle path (but correspondingly more painful for himself) of somehow teasing it out of her with a little bit of gentle persuasion. He decided on the latter course, assuming that confronting her on the subject would merely serve to render her more inexorable. Armed with his new information, he decided that luring Dawn by the prospect of a romantic day spent at the Promenade might be just the thing to loosen her lips. Plying her with alcohol and good cheer would certainly change her attitude and perhaps make her feel more relaxed about sharing her story with him. It would at least soften the blow of his revelation and the logical proposition that followed. He decided that the following day, a Sunday and the last of his vacation, would be the best to pursue his aim.

Unbeknownst to Billy, the following day would present the perfect backdrop to his machinations. The sun was out and the day relatively bright, a nice reprieve from all the bad weather they had been having recently. Billy presented the idea to Dawn and she was of course overjoyed. Besides the occasional trip to a local restaurant for dinner, it was the first time they had spent an entire day outside the apartment with each other. She even conceded to wear something beside her normal black funeral attire, deciding upon jeans and a thick woolen sweater. Billy prepped for the day by taking a couple of pills of diazepam. The Promenade (as it was known by the locals) was a dark, wooden boardwalk that ran along the Onondaga River. Composed of what appeared to be oversized railroad ties or perhaps giant logs, the Promenade was raised from the river by approximately thirty feet. Along its length there were a number of small shops and for the inhabitants of Hokum, it remained very much the place to be seen in one's Sunday's best. The two arrived at the crowded Promenade around eleven. By this point, it was already thronged with people taking advantage of the unseasonal weather. Children were flying kites, while older adolescents skated along the wooden planks of the boardwalk. Many hawkers were outside selling rock candy, fudge, candied apples and cotton candy. It was almost as if spring had arrived early and the entire city had assembled there for a one day engagement. It was exactly the kind of teeming atmosphere Billy detested.

The odd couple began walking down the long boardwalk, which extended almost half a mile in length. Dawn was clearly very happy to be in the sunshine and had even taken his arm in hers as they walked almost like a young, budding couple. With her eyes closed and the wind blowing through her hair, she said to Billy, "Isn't it divine: the wind and sunshine in one's hair. If only every day could be like this." Billy, wearing his dark sunglasses had been looking around, scanning the crowd in an attempt to try and spot the dark man, but surprisingly he was nowhere to be seen. Suddenly, upon catching sight of an interesting storefront, Dawn pulled Billy along with her like a stubborn dog. The store was packed full of bric-a-brac, the kind of store Billy would have never entered on his own, but Dawn was enjoying thoroughly. As the couple walked in, the elderly woman at the checkout desk smiled and winked at them, "Aren't you a cute couple. Are you guys married?"

Dawn merely smiled and answered, "No, he's much too unconventional for that. We are living in sin."

"Oh," the woman gave a knowing smile, "Aren't we all."

Dawn then smiled at Billy and said in her teasing way, "See?" Billy merely grimaced and began to look at all the useless accumulation around him, wondering who in their right mind would buy such tchotchkes: refrigerator magnets, plastic baseball caps, key chains, bumper stickers and the like, all hanging from spinning metal racks. As they progressed through the store, Dawn would pick up a small item, showing it to Billy while shaking her head with a questioning smile. At times, she forced him to try on several funny shaped hats, then a few pairs of glasses and finally, alighting upon a pair of red plastic horns that were attached to a hair beret, she chirped "Oh, perfect." Placing the horns on Billy's head, she turned him around to the mirror and made him look at himself, "They suit you don't they, you big grump?"

Billy, while looking at himself in the mirror asked in a laconic, curious voice, "Do you really think I'm the devil? Everyone else seems to think so. But, I submit as proof that a devil has no reflection, does he?"

"Well, you are a bit mean, you spend most of your time around dead people and you have somehow led me into a strange form of temptation. Not sexual of course, but you do make me somehow want to take care of you."

"That is nonsense."

"You think you could ever fall in love with me?"

"It is biologically impossible."

"Why?"

"For three reasons: one. I simply do not have the constitution for love. It weighs on one's system too much. You need strong intestines for that stuff, which I don't have. Two. My heart has been hardened by what my eyes have seen and finally…"

Dawn then pulled down her cheeks with her fingers and spoke in the pouty voice of a child, "And yet, when I put on my pouty eyes for you that second morning we met and said 'Mr. Rubino, can I please stay in your house?' you melted like a little snowman."

"…and finally you just aren't my type."

"What is your type?"

"Well, I can tell you what it isn't. I don't date junkies or Mexicans."

"Well, that's good because I am neither."

"There is really nothing that offends you, is there?"

"Not much."

"Geez. Otherwise, I thought I'd have you out of my place long ago."

"Why, you're not so bad, compared to many I have seen."

"I take personal pride in my ability to offend and alienate people. I've had a lifetime of practice and women are normally the easiest. You girls are offended by everything."

"We are, are we? Like I said, you ain't so bad."

"Men like myself have been successfully hung or executed in every generation of humankind and here I can thrive amidst people who actually enjoy being offended and abused."

"You are talking to someone who tried to throw themselves over a bridge."

"Well, what is stopping you now?"

"You?"

"Why me? What crime have I committed to deserve this?"

"I figure you were there to save me and someone somehow must have put me here to save you in return."

"Save me from what?"

"Oh, I don't know what. A bus, a falling tree, yourself, maybe."

"Trust me, I don't need saving, especially from myself."

"Well then maybe it's from someone else. I don't know, but for some reason I feel like I've been sent here to save you."

"Find me a squinty eyed girl without a voice box and we'll talk."

"Oh stop it, you're not so heartless. With that waistline, you've gotta have something in there to move all that blood around."

But, how had she known this? That he couldn't be so 'heartless.' Billy thought to himself. Was this a challenge to himself? Did she think he could not mean what he said? Did she actually think she could plumb the depths of his soul with such a flippant comment though she had known him for not more than a week? He was sure a look of anger crossed his eyes, but she seemed not to have noticed and Billy decided to let the matter slide, not wanting to ruin his chances of achieving his ultimate goal. He only let a snide grin cross his face and thought within himself, 'next time'. Without looking at him, Dawn asked if he was hungry. Still smarting from her earlier remark, he answered her with a gruff, "I suppose so." She then replied by making the sound of a duck. Billy looked at her confused, but ignored it.

Walking back out of the store, they decided to have lunch in a large crowded restaurant along the boardwalk. The restaurant, called the "Hog's Noggin" was built almost entirely from large wooden logs, the same color as those that constituted the Promenade and had a family atmosphere to it. There was even a man who stood at the front dressed in the garb of a hillbilly, his face hung with a large artificial beard. He passed out colorful menus while pulling faces for the small children that surrounded him. At the front of the restaurant there was a large open space, which was currently covered by a temporary fabric awning and enclosed by large glass panels. It was Dawn's choice and they had to wait for twenty minutes at the bar where they each drank a large beer. Once seated, they sat down to a hearty meal, which was composed of the following:

> 2x large beers (Billy)
> 1x small beer (Dawn)
> 1x crawfish sandwich with sundried tomato and arugula (Dawn)
> 2x Country Fried Steak sandwich with artichoke hearts and Emmental sauce (Billy)
> 1x fries with saffron essence infusion (Billy)
> 1x coleslaw with Japanese lettuce (Dawn)

After they had finished their pleasant repast and against Billy's wishes, Dawn insisted they play a compatibility game, the object of which was to put their minds together to tell a story. Each added a single word that the other had to follow without repeating any words except for pronouns, articles and the like. Billy was disgusted by the idea, but finally consented. Dawn began the proceedings by announcing, "The Future Story of Dawn and Billy by Dawn and Billy." She then began with the first word, writing the story down and underlining Billy's words in order to analyze them later:

The man and the woman walk and play wonderful tricks on each other. Stupid comments, dumb men play games indeed with suicidal kangaroos. Shit is boring but she helps herself, tries nonsense by kidding herself that love exists inside anyone, truth lies with her however she understands nothing else but beauty fades inside everyone who observes only things not understandable. Hearts break, mend without needing anyone, frightened children look away. Noble minds search never finding what completes them but it sits somehow in-front...

"C'mon, c'mon say it 'in front...'."
"Say what?"
"You know, 'in front...of'. Say it, 'of'."
Billy shook his head in confusion, "Of..."
"Him."
Sensing that she had seized victory after Billy's many efforts to derail the fun, she cheered and stuck her tongue out at Billy's miserable looks. Billy only chided her, reminding her that "in-front" wasn't one but two words and that she had evidently cheated. She merely called him a spoiled sport.

After they left the restaurant, they walked in the opposite direction along the Promenade and soon paused to lean against the railing and look out over the river towards Crowley. Next to them, a number of children were throwing bread and French fries to the amassing sea gulls. The water below them moved in its normal, mindless flow. As Dawn looked down at its brown, unreflective mass she shivered, recalling to herself that the same waters had almost claimed her life only weeks before. She remembered distinctly the experience: she remembered the bitter cold. She remembered the giant tree trunk that she had grasped to keep her tired body above water. She remembered how desperately she held on for a life that only seconds before she had wanted to throw away. She could remember the feeling of her tired arms slipping from the wet wood as gravity wooed her downward, calling her to join the torrid depths. She remembered falling below the dark surface and thinking to herself how the dull green nothingness would be the last thing she ever saw. She remembered herself trying to concentrate on the happiest memory she had ever had when she was a child, running through the woods, catching grasshoppers during the day or fireflies at night. How she cupped one grasshopper in her hand and felt its delicate life twitching between her cupped fingers, aching for release, its ratcheted legs snapping against her tiny palms. How for the first time she felt she could determine the course of another life. She knew now there could be no pain, none at all, but still she didn't want to return there to the darkness, the unconsciousness that gripped her beneath the waters, that caressed her roughly, that put its arms around her waist, through her legs as would an eager lover, waiting to ravage her with the cold kiss of oblivion. Even then, she felt her knees weaken. She felt her legs as they sank and sank, down, down, down into unawareness, into a stained silence. It started with a needle prick, then a cold shiver went through her and she gave out a moan. She looked up, closing her eyes and breathed in deeply. It was a breath she could even cherish; having been on the verge of drowning, the very act of breathing, the luxury of filling her lungs, in fact every breath seemed to her borrowed. She opened her eyes to look up at the sun's yellow disk as it stood impossibly high in the air, then she turned instinctively toward Billy who hadn't noticed a thing and was only looking with disgust at the pigeons as they were being chased in his direction by a small pack of children. They cooed like old rotary phones dialing numbers that no longer existed. As the wind picked up in a sudden gust, she turned her eyes again to the mid distance before her, where she saw sea gulls strain against a building wind. So much effort to stand still, she thought to herself. Billy simultaneously observed her profile, the empty look in her eyes as she gazed out over the river and decided that the time was ripe for his little project to take place. He began by turning to her gently, leaning his elbow over the railing.

"You never talk about your family. Why?"

"Because they're not worth talking about," she snapped back, moodily.

"Well, if we were to be…for instance to be serious, I would have to know about your family, I mean…"

She peered at him suspiciously. It was the first time he had suggested anything remotely akin to a relationship and it was completely out of the blue. She looked at his face with its calm smile and then, pausing for an instant, turned her eyes back towards the river, her hands now gripping the railings that rose to the height of her chest.

"You don't talk about your family either," she suggested.

"All dead."

"Mine too."

"Well that's not exactly true, is it?"

This time she turned her head towards Billy in rapid fashion, her eyes looking a mix between hurt and threatening. "What do you mean?" she asked in a stern tone.

"I mean, Reggie Hortega is still in this town and is in fact still alive."

Incredulous, she came up right next to him, insisting angrily, "How do you know him?"

"Well, it's what I do for a living. I track people down, their identities, their relatives. In this case, I simply did some homework and found a charming little story, the literary merits of which can be debated, but that little tale was called the 'Ballad of Jean and Reg'. That's your mother and father isn't it?"

She instantly turned away from him, slightly unsure of what to do.

"Look, they are nothing to me. I don't want to talk about them. It's them that put the screams in me. So many that I'll never get them all out. You shouldn't have done that."

"Why not, don't you want to speak to your dad? Why are you getting so upset?"

Dawn turned again towards him, with a questioning, almost pleading look on her face. As her implacable eyes trembled and became watery at the rims, it was clear, even to Billy, that she was on the verge of tears, "Listen, is that what you wanted to take me here for? To satisfy your morbid curiosity?" She turned away again so he wouldn't see her cry.

At this point Billy was growing slightly impatient and a look of anger entered his eyes, "Listen, I don't understand what the big deal is. Here is a girl who jokes around about her own suicide attempt and now, when you mention her dear old dad she gets all chocked up."

"I told you, I don't want to talk about it. You are too harsh sometimes. Why won't you give it a rest? Why do you have to go and ruin what was such a nice day?"

"But...but...I just don't understand what the big deal is, I mean..."

She turned ardently upon him again, her hands almost tearing apart the shawl that was in her hands. "You will never understand. You can't understand."

"You'd be surprised. Just try me. Is it a crime to be curious? Maybe if you just give something back after all I've done for you?" Billy stood there taping his foot with impatience, his lips almost trembling. As she stood in front of him, incapable of saying anything, he began to study her face as one would a painting. He began to wonder with some interest at the way each of her features were moving in contrary directions, competing with each other for mastery instead of cooperating. It was as if her lips, eyes, cheeks and eyebrows were struggling independently to decide upon the facial expression that would best represent her state of mind. At that moment, Billy felt a vacuum draw from within himself, the usual evacuation of any sensation whatsoever. He felt it each time he stood in front of a newly widowed mother, an orphaned daughter, any person he had to tell that their loved one had just ceased to exist. It was always like this for him. His head felt like an appendage that had been held aloft too long and he could already discern a tingling, a numbness rising toward the top of his ears. His mind moved to the third person and he wondered what he was doing standing before this woman who was obviously struggling to comprehend a mere triviality. His feet felt like marble and it seemed to him as if his entire being was trapped inside hardened stone. His skin became like a stiff jacket external to himself. He wondered who he was and what he was doing. Had he merely become one potentiality out of the many that coexisted? Why was he inhabiting this body and the person in front of him another? Why couldn't they simply switch roles or perhaps just read a different script? Would any of this make any more sense? He then felt the sudden urge to laugh. He couldn't understand why her body, her face was making such painful contortions on his behalf. After all, he was just a clown. Couldn't she see the whole situation was ridiculous? His lips trembled again and he had to force himself not to laugh in her face.

"You are awful. You won't stop, will you? Fine. Fine, I'll find my own way home." She turned and began to run away, leaving Billy standing there with his arms apart. It was too late. Billy had re-inhabited his body just in time to realize that his entire project had failed.

"Look. I...I just wanted to know how the story ended," he shouted after her. It was no use. She was gone. She began running down the boardwalk. Billy watched her until she had run out of view. He then turned back to look out over the water, recriminating himself for his failure. As he stood there, contemplating the bright reflections on the swells that moved before him, he began to consider his position again. He was now even more intrigued by the mystery. After all, if she were acting the way she was, the second part of the story must indeed be interesting. He would have to keep pressing her, but the strategy would need to be one not of forthrightness, but of gentle coaxing. It would take patience, something Billy didn't normally possess, but he now saw the situation as a challenge. He couldn't let her win. He would wrest the story from her, one way or another.

Once Billy arrived back at the apartment he found Dawn already in the kitchen, making the preparations for dinner. At first, neither said a word to one another and Billy thought it best to leave her alone for the moment. However, once they started eating, Dawn's mood returned to normal and she even apologized for her previous outbursts and told him that she had actually had a wonderful day. In fact, she said, it was the best she had had in a long while. Billy, unconcerned with her apologies or her opinions, spent most of the dinner in deep thought, trying to figure out how he would find this Reggie Hortega. His moodiness continued throughout the rest of the evening and despite Dawn trying to cheer him up, he basically retired himself to his bedroom in order to ruminate over the issues further. At work the following day, Billy found himself in a state of utter desperation and decided to engage upon his last resort, picking up the phone to call a few of the "R. Hortegas" he had discovered in the phone book. As was much to his expectation, he had no luck: a couple were women, two didn't speak any English and the most promising response he had, simply hung up on him flat out. While circling the address he cursed himself again, "Hortega, of all the names. Can't get much more generic than that."

At present, not much was going well in Billy's life. Despite his many trips to Riley's house, it had been almost a week and a half and Riley hadn't shown up at the hospital. Hope was beginning to fade that he would ever show up and the girls were getting tired of sleeping in the hospital even if the bed sheets were clean. Regardless of these concerns, Griffs stubbornly convinced them to continue the project for a few more days. On one of his trips to the hospital, out of a mix of curiosity and boredom, he determined to find the nurse who had spoken to Poundstone. With Poundstone's help and a vague description of her name, he managed to locate the initially unhelpful nurse who gave him a similar story to the one she had given Poundstone. However, once Billy told her the girl's last name the woman agreed to introduce him to yet another nurse who might know the man. The other nurse, who similar to the previous one was a short, pudgy Mexican woman, agreed to call yet another relative who might know the man in question. After a long conversation in Spanish, it turned out that not only did the relative know the man, but knew where he lived. Billy was overjoyed. When one of the nurses gave Billy the address, a very excited Billy kept digging into his pockets to give the nurses each a five dollar bill. Almost unable to contain himself he insisted with what little Spanish he knew,

"Wait, one second. *Mira. Mira. Qui-e-ro pay-gar-lay. Qui-e-ro pay-gar-lay.*"

Unable to find his wallet, he continued digging, almost bending sideways with the effort. With a horrified look on their faces, the two nurses gave him a dirty look and walked away. Not comprehending their strange behavior, Billy assumed they weren't interested in his money and shrugged his shoulders. He then looked at the address in his hand and determined that the mysterious Reggie actually lived in the most northeastern part of Hokum, near the plantations and alfalfa fields. This being the case, it was likely that the man was employed as a day laborer. Billy, not having any pressing cases, popped a couple pills of diazepam, jumped in his car and made the long drive to the outskirts of Hokum.

On the journey toward the fringes of town, Billy began to consider a number of things. The first question he asked himself was why he was going through all these lengths to discover a virtual stranger's story. Was it really an attempt at fame or was it simply his natural, morbid sense of curiosity? Perhaps it was more? Was he somehow beginning to feel something for the woman? Was his unconscious mind participating in the beginnings of a ritual that his rational mind revolted so violently against? Had his feelings welcomed a covert invitation into a world that his intelligence strictly forbade? The thought was preposterous and it was exactly the reason he detested over self-analysis. One was liable to force oneself by the mere act of denying something to actually accept it under the assumption that one's unconscious mind moved naturally in a contrarian fashion to what one had originally reasoned was one's natural desire. Was the human mind really such a renegade, a house divided against itself? Was this evolution or just the inheritance of a hundred years of psychoanalysts patting themselves on the back for out-thinking themselves? The simple fact was that he felt nothing for Dawn and was entirely uninterested by her emotional inner life. He was however interested in tying up loose ends. Though he detested the practicalities of his profession, he did enjoy the element of discovery that came with it. Occasionally, he felt he was somehow privy to everyone else's dirty, little secrets. How many upstanding businessmen had he found who had died of coke-induced heart attacks? How many men of religion had he discovered with venereal disease? How many suicide notes had he read that revealed hidden tales of infidelity, drug addiction and desperate loss and longing? At times it seemed nothing was hidden in death. One only had to spend a day around the Lido to figure out that Hokum had a dirty conscience. The same men who protested against homosexuality, were found out in dirty nooks of the hotel with some paid boy. The same mother who drove her kids to Sunday school could be found buying meth from one of the "vending machines" in the upper rooms. The world was truly a desperate place and it needed a Lido as much as it needed a Promenade. The Lido was not a place to hide from reality, but rather, it was a place to cope with it. Where one could face the reality one usually hid from. Even in these latter days of professed liberality and unctuous *tatemae*, where one subscribed to popular opinions of tolerance, there were still things one couldn't cope with. It seemed that one was allowed an open mind with others, but not with oneself. The Lido allowed the now accepted "homosexuals" to kiss one another, allowed the champions of "legalization" to actually indulge their habits, the abortion supporters and decriers to engage in their horrible little surgeries. One put aside any inner turmoil one might have had at the doors of the Lido. There, it was all about pure action, pure fulfillment and Billy liked that about the place. Billy liked making things happen and it is for this reason that he was on the road to find Dawn's father. He could clearly see that the story hadn't quite ended, but that some small part of it may yet remain to be written. Perhaps Griffs was right, perhaps in his profession, he usually showed up to the story too late. This was finally his chance to become part of a story that had almost ended, but that he had inadvertently immersed himself within. *Diabolus ex machina?* Well, despite his efforts to remain detached from the issues of others (Riley and Basyli, in particular), he was intrigued by his current project. What havoc a few written words can wreck.

After forty minutes of driving through empty stretches of barren farmland that extended outward from each side of the road, he finally came within proximity of his destination. Given that there were very few indications, he was certain to have trouble finding the address. The bleak, two-lane thoroughfare he found himself on was only interrupted by the occasional telephone pole and several unmarked, gravel driveways that appeared to turn off into anonymous nowheres. At one point, he had to stop at a gas station and then a general store to determine if he was even on the correct road. No one seemed to know until he finally found two Mexican men sitting along the pavement on top of large, red Igloo cooler. Beside them lay a green tackle box and some form of fishing net. They both had fishing rods in their hands and were evidently waiting to be taken somewhere. Billy stopped and showed them the name and the address he was looking for. The two men only spoke Spanish but using a series of hand gestures they indicated to him that his destination was only two driveways down. He thanked them, telling them in his very idiosyncratic Spanish,

"*Mira. Mira. Qui-e-ro pay-gar-lay. Qui-e-ro pay-gar-lay.*"

As he handed each a five dollar bill of which they were both appreciative, they smiled and gave him a thumbs up, grabbing his biceps and patting him on the back.

"*Heffe, fuerte. Heffe, fuerte.*"

"No, guys. There must be some kinda misunderstanding here. I'm not that kinda guy. I just wanted to give you…No gay. No gay. Really, no, I'm not interested."

Finally, breaking free of their grasps and ducking back into his car, he drove past two more anonymous gravel roads until he arrived at a third, the address of which was indicated by nothing more than an old, battered postal box. Billy, happy to have found his way, drove down the long, gravel driveway into what seemed nothing more than a large clearing surrounded by weed and brush. From where he had paused the car, no sign of an inhabitance could be seen. After driving along a little further, his vehicle began to yaw violently from one side to another as he navigated the numerous potholes. He then noticed what appeared to be a massive assortment of scrap metal at the end of the driveway. He parked his car next to a number of battered trucks that lacked tires and even engines.

Getting out of his car, he immediately heard the sound of loud banging, which emerged from what appeared like a tin shed. The pied colored hovel of corrugated tin was held up by little more than cut tree branches, which had been buried in the ground to serve as wall posts. As he walked into to the junk-strewn yard it seemed to him that he had found the very place where all the universe of manmade things, its discarded parts and unneeded do-overs had accumulated. In some sense (and perhaps more poetically), it was the final, barren shore where all of Hokum's broken stories had washed up. Scattered throughout the yard in a haphazard way he saw various vehicle parts, a number of old bathroom sinks, a rusted oven range, a welder's mask, an open refrigerator, the motor of a boat, a broken lawn mower, countless wheel rims, a deconstructed motorcycle and a tangle of smashed television sets and VCRs. Turning his head to the right, he then saw a jumble of shattered mirrors that stared blankly upwards, pulling to earth the gray banks of cloud above them. He saw the dismembered plastic pieces of children's dolls, mangled swing sets, vacant car doors, unidentified pieces of circuitry, busted computers, disk drives, all manner of things, all useless it seemed to anyone. All these items lay amongst the patches of crabgrass, between the short slicks of antifreeze and gasoline rainbows that bordered the dusty fields of hardscrabble. To his left, he saw another dilapidated shed, itself also constructed from metal siding and corrugated tin. Rusted through in many places, it appeared like a single, strong wind would have had done with it. The door was ajar and looking inside he saw a glimpse of what seemed to be a sort of living space. The banging had presently stopped and out of the shed from which it had originated emerged a slightly pudgy man with a blue baseball cap and a dusty, blue, sleeveless shirt. His eyes were squinting in suspicion and despite being surrounded by the wreckage of the earth, he seemed rather less than a latter day Utnapishtim. He was of a dark complexion as if suntanned and had a rather sizeable stomach paunch. He held a large, red industrial wrench in his hand and no doubt smelled of gasoline. The sun, which had briefly emerged from the clouds, bounced from one mirror to the next and finally up into the man's face, temporarily blinding him so that when he first spoke to Billy, it was without actually seeing him, "What do you want?"

Billy finally getting a close look at him recognized him instantly as the man who had been following him for the previous week. Taking offence, he spoke to the man, the umbrage clearly ringing in his voice, "Funny, I should be asking you the same thing. You're the asshole who's been chasing me around in the darkness. What's up with that?"

The man also recognizing Billy, tried unsuccessfully to hide the fact though the spring in his eyes said everything, "Listen mister, I don't know what you're talkin' about."

"I think you do."

"Listen, I don't know who you are but you're on my property. I got the right to shoot you if you gonna address me like that. Unless you is the police or the IRS, you ain't got any business here."

At this point, Billy decided to change tact, especially as the man still carried a large, blunt object in his hand. "OK, fine have it your way. If you want to know, I'm here to talk to you about your daughter."

The man again feigned ignorance, but his face clearly betrayed his curiosity as he moved closer, shielding his eyes with the same hand that held the wrench.

"What daughter? Listen, man, you crazy? I don't have no daughter. What you talkin' about?"

Billy held up his hands in exasperation, shaking his head. "It's about Dawn. I want to talk about Dawn, your daughter."

Reggie, realizing that denial was useless, stood uncomfortably close to Billy, looking him straight in the eye, despite his being significantly shorter. "What you want to know about her? Who's askin'? Who are you?"

Billy, bathetic, responded with some awkwardness in his voice, "Well, well…you see. The fact is, she is living with me and…" Billy had to cringe. It required every bit of self-restraint he possessed not to laugh, "and I think…I think we're in love and I want to take care of her, but she obviously has some unresolved parental issues and I just want to find out for her sake what they are. In any case, I think you're the only one who can answer those questions."

Reggie then looked into the russet dust and stood there in deep thought, not moving or saying a word for what must have been two minutes. He finally looked at Billy and asked,

"Did she put you up to this?"

"No, she doesn't know. She won't say anything, but it's clear she needs help. I'm sure you heard that she tried…"

Reggie held up his hand, stopping him before he could say anything else.

"OK, come with me," Reggie replied, inviting Billy into the tin shed that he had correctly surmised was the man's house. The roof of the house was particularly low, not more than six feet, its shallow gradient slanted down towards the back. Billy had to crouch both to enter the door and to avoid hitting his face against the roof's edge that overhung the entryway. When he entered, he saw that the shed was filled with an incredible amount of what he could only describe as junk. Amidst other things there were a large number of plastic shelves upon which rested glass jars filled with various subfusc syrups, an old television set, a transistor radio, a welding torch, several plastic planting pots, an enormous number of keys, some flat, cast iron weights, a scale and various other errata. Amidst them was a dirty mattress and below that sat a tired old mongrel that barely bothered to raise itself from the dirt floor. Evidently the dog had three legs and the only thing that rescued it from being mistaken for last season's roadkill was the occasional movement in its eyes. Reggie sat on an open microwave and reached toward a small refrigerator from which he grabbed a can of beer. He offered it to Billy who refused it with a mere raise of the hand. Billy couldn't accept any foodstuffs from this man as he was extremely put off by his practice of chewing large wads of black tobacco, which he summarily spit at regular intervals into a white plastic bucket to his side. There was nothing left of the romantic notion associated with this man in the 'Ballad'. Billy, sitting on the first thing he could find, which was a discarded car battery and an old plastic milk crate, looked closely into Reggie's face. He noted that time hadn't treated him all that well. Although he bore no signs of wrinkles, his skin was rough and his neck was marred by a large, angry scar. It was obvious the man hadn't shaven in days and his thick, coriaceous hands resembled gorilla's paws, rather than hands. His mouth contained at least two gold teeth and around his neck he wore a small, golden crucifix. The man, without looking at Billy, began laconically, "Well, not sure how much I can really help you. There ain't much I can tell." He then scratched the top of his cap, "You said you guys gettin' married?"

"Well, we're not that far along yet. It's still early stages but," again he had to cringe internally, "I really care about her."

As Reggie continued to look at the dirt floor beneath him his voice betrayed a sense of pain, tinged by a mix of disappointment, "Oh, yeah? Well what is it exactly you want to know?"

"Well, I read the story that your wife, I mean your girlfriend wrote..."

"My girlfriend? Oh, you mean...Jean," he gave away a slight smile and a low, dark laugh.

"Yeah, Jean Hewitt. Anyway it all sort of ends with you in the desert and the second part...well is just plain missing. It's not even on record. I just wanted to hear how it all ends."

"What more d'ya need to see? This is how it all ends," Reggie said, looking Billy in the eye for the first time since he entered the house. He then spread his arm and turned his head side to side to indicate the mess around him. He then spit into the bucket, leaving some of the black substance to trail down its inside rim. Billy's strong sense of disgust and desire to turn around and leave was only barely matched by his impulse to remain and hear the rest of the story.

"But, I want to know who the second part of the story is for, because..." He paused and shifted his weight amongst the uncomfortable protrusions beneath him. He didn't know how much more of this he could take. He hated the thought of saying what he was about to say and felt slightly embarrassed. Forming the words first in his mind, he again fought a powerful urge to laugh as he began to hear what sounded like a disembodied voice in his ears, "...because,

Dawn needs to know. She feels there's been a void left in her life." The last sentence, he said with such plaintiveness in his voice, his eyes softening like that of a Rottweiler who knows it's done wrong to chew off a man's hand. It was as much as he could manage not to keep the corners of his mouth from quivering with the sharp flickers of a devious smile. It was a means to an end, he thought to himself, nothing more. He was extremely glad that Dawn would never manage to hear him say the words he had just spoken. She would have derived too much pleasure from it and held it over his head for the rest of his life. The worst of it done, Billy sat and stared at the grave man who said nothing in response, merely shaking his head as he dropped his head toward the earthen floor. Finally, after another long silence, he dropped his shoulders and ejected his latest wad of grasshopper's gob into the mouth of the awaiting bucket. "OK. OK," he conceded as if it took him his very life to say what he was about to say.

The Ballad of Jean and Reg

Part II

"School's Out"

"Well, how should I start? I guess from the end of what you know. Anyway, that story there, that wuz all written for Dawn (at least the second part), but it never got published 'cuz the magazine she sent it to got shut down. Ran out of money or somethin'. She tol' me she wuz writin' it and she even sent me a copy of the whole thing and the fool I wuz, I even managed to lose it. My head wuz all mixed up and she wuz writin' all this stuff from, well... you see, after the mom went to prison, she had Dawn like six months later. They took the baby straight away from her. After that, she wuz diagnosed and then not long after the cancer took her. She wrote that story as the last thing she did for her daughter. Got it published by some friend of hers who worked at a newspaper or magazine or somethin'. She knew she wuz dyin' and would never see Dawn again."

"But, why was she in prison? After all it was you who abducted her," Billy asked, the deep interest audible in his voice.

"Well, you see, despite the testimony of Inez, Manuel and me, the court ended up belivin' that Jean orchestrated the whole thing. Can you imagine? They used her calls to the husband and the testimony of the border guard and some woman in a liquor store as primary evidence. They said she not only willingly crossed the border into Mexico, but also contributed to the delinquency of minors, buyin' us alcohol, et cetera. If you can believe it, she wuz done for kidnappin' all of us, takin' us all across international borders and even... even statutory rape, in the end. I felt so bad about that, but I couldn't do anythin'. I simply got a few months in juvi for resistin' arrest and shootin' at the cops when they tried to catch me. Her husband had left her, takin' her kids away to somewhere she couldn't find them. I wuz in juvi. She had no one. Not a single person in the world. It wuz so sad. Anyway, I wuz too young to take care of Dawn so her grandmother took care of her in another city not far away and she wanted nothin' to do with me. That woman, she poisoned her.

Poisoned her against me from when she wuz little," Reggie's voice was growing increasingly agitated at this point. "Anyway, when I wuz old enough and got out of juvi, I couldn't deal with it. I left and lost track of her and came back here years ago hopin' to find her but she wusn't here. I had heard she wuz in a mental hospital with troubles...drugs or somethin'... got mixed up in the wrong crowd, but I tried to go find her anyway and she didn't want to see me. Can you believe that? Not wantin' to say the slightest word to her own father, who she never even met. Anyway, I only had one picture of her and didn't know what she looked like all growed up. Then I heard she got out and she came back here a few months ago. I tried to look after her from a distance, knowin' she would never accept me as a parent. When I finally met her, her grandmother had told her such bad things about me that she wanted nothin' to do with me, ever, even when she needed someone the most. A few weeks later, when I heard she had tried to kill herself, it hurt me bad. It hurt me real bad. I wanted to take care of her so much, but I knew she wouldn't let me. Then when I saw you with her, I wanted to make sure who you wuz. I didn't know if you wuz involved with her and her tryin' to kill herself. I had to make sure you wuz gonna take care of her, real good. I've done a lot of dumb things in my life but that girl Dawn never deserved any of this. You know where her name comes from? Dawn?"

"Yes, it from and old song isn't it?"

"Yeah that's right, her mom used to sing it. Beautiful."

The two men sat in silence for a little while and Reggie covered his face as the obvious emotions of pain flashed across it. He breathed in deeply, his entire frame quivering as he did so. His breath sounded as if it had been shattered inside after a deep chill. He was plainly struggling to contain the agony of his remembrance. When he finally managed to look up and stare into the empty distance before him, his eyes were filled with large tears and Billy recognized for the first time the family resemblance. It was in the eyes. They were what she had taken from him. They were the only part of the romantic image that remained. Billy having no idea what to do and satisfied that he had gotten to the bottom of the story got up to leave. Noticing that Billy was on his way, Reggie stopped him, "Listen, I never got your name. What is it?"

"It's Billy, Billy Rubino."

"Hey, can you do me a favor?" Reggie asked, wiping the tears from his eyes.

"Sure, what?"

"Don't tell her we had this meetin'."

"OK, why not?"

"She won't take it well."

"OK." As Billy turned to leave, the man put his course hands on Billy's forearm, "One more question."

"Yes?"

"How is she doin'?"

"OK, I guess."

"Well, you take care of her, you hear. Maybe, one day. One day you can convince her to come see me. You know where I am."

"I'll give it a try."

Billy turned and left the man standing with his head down, silently weeping into the hardscrabble. He had put his hands over his face to prevent Billy from seeing him cry, but Billy didn't care much. He just continued to walk towards his car not bothering to look back. Grief was certainly something he was used to in his line of work. From his perspective, this was a mere trifle compared to the vast sea of cases he normally saw. He wore his emotional detachment as a badge of honor. In fact, Billy considered that his utter detachment was one of the attributes that made him good at what he did. He didn't consider himself anesthetized, but rather he felt incapable of having any attachment to events or to people that didn't concern him. He was merely doing a job, performing a series of rituals much like a priest would at a burial. Death was just another fact of life and like most important facts of life it required someone to do the paperwork. Someone would eventually be stuck with doing his when the time came, but beyond that he didn't think much about death or its significance. People had often romanticized death but for him, who had never recalled actually seeing anyone die, death was merely a lump of flesh and a series of dotted lines. Some in his profession would say that dealing with the families was the hardest part, but for him, he merely found it tedious. He was a communicator, the mouthpiece of the dead, there to give voice to those who couldn't speak for themselves. For him, that meant telling their stories to the widest audience possible and quid pro quo assuring his own ascension through the bureaucratic ranks. His model was again Larry Campbell. Billy made it very clear to himself that his desire was for fame, for glory, not celebrity. He wanted to achieve greatness in the eyes of the world, especially as it seemed the entire planet was attracted by the grit and excitement of his profession. At present, it appeared to him that the only way for him to achieve this desired fame was either to catch a serial killer or become one himself. To him, the present, pervasive culture of decline (one that, for him, had persisted at least since twenty-nine years post the second Defenestration of Prague) seemed death obsessed and increasingly he struggled to find a way out of this nihilistic trap, this ennui that appeared to envelope every facet of his life. He simply had to rise above it: the infinite waste, the endless echo, the spreading plague that engulfed the very finite lives of all of those who danced like fools in the face of endless potential, *das schwerste Gewicht.*

It was occupied with thoughts of this kind that Billy made the long drive home. As he drove through the open country, the sun was setting at the edge of the biggest sky one could find in Hokum. Above him, there was a clear panorama of violet, striated with the lonely contrails of departed airplanes. Everything was in pastels, the depopulated dream world of amateur photographers everywhere, who each carried in their mind's fondest recess a neutron bomb. Suddenly a phrase came to mind, the sound of distant singing. Then, he thought he heard in his ears a German phrase, sung by a mass of children,

'Erhalt uns, Herr, bei deinem Wort,
Und steur' des Papsts und Türken Mord,
Die Jesum Christum, deinen Sohn,
Stürzen wollen von seinem Thron.'

Unfortunately, he couldn't quite place the tune, but he started to hum it with some pleasure. It certainly couldn't have been Grieg, but what was it? He thought he had forgotten what little German he learned a long time ago.

'Es bricht alsdann der letzte Feind herein
Und will den Trost von unsern Herzen'

Bach perhaps, or was it Handel? Billy couldn't decide. Perhaps it was neither, but he was happy within himself that he could remember all the words though they had almost driven him off the road. Thinking deeper into the lyric, he drew for himself a very vivid image of burning spires and engines of war, a medieval city brought to waste, even the smell of smoke and human dread. Once again, he had the vague sensation that despite its impossibility, the vision was something he had in fact experienced before. He'd always kidded himself that he had a gift for insight into murder scenes, but this was something entirely different. Try as he might, he couldn't account for the smell of sulfur in his nose, the dryness of ash in his throat, the tang of gunpowder on his tongue. Suddenly, he felt as if he had been asleep for a thousand years and his present life was just a furious act of dreaming. Had Basyli, that niggling worm, indeed turned him into a Devil? Everything seemed so vague to him now, even his own past, which he now more than ever felt disconnected to. He somewhat remembered reading a book by a renowned hymnologist when he was much younger which had connected the present hymn to the Sacking of Magdeburg. It was the diapason the innocents had sung, while they fell prey to the quenchless sword. As a choirboy, his voice was pointed out as one of great beauty and his instructor, a kindly octogenarian from the Tyrol, moved by the passion with which he had sung Pergolesi's "Eia Mater" had given him the old tome as a gift. He thought it funny that of all times he remembered it now. It made so little sense that Billy began to fear that he could no longer separate his visions from reality as if he were experiencing something akin to schizophrenia. The vision itself kept growing and growing in dark, mucous billows as if emanating from the very heart of hell's unforgiving inferno. The shrill cries, the blood curdling howls, the muffled groans were becoming increasingly vivid until they too inhabited his complete existence and he could think of nothing else but the unremitting maelstrom. He was now completely paralyzed, a forced witness to an atrocity that had occurred almost half a millennium prior. He saw children scream as their throats were being cut, mothers who acted as human shields having their heads bashed in, disemboweled fathers who were granted a final vision - that of their sun-glistened intestines palpitating before their zeroing eyes. He skidded to the side of the road, barely managing to stop the car from entering a deep ditch. For him, it was the final straw. He simply had to stop taking the diazepam, which he was now regularly overdosing on. Immediately, he took the half empty bottle out of his coat pocket and launched it through of the opened car window into the anonymous alfalfa field.

As the tune gradually faded along with the remnants of his dreadful daydream, Billy finally managed to calm his heart and slow his still racing heart. During the painful subsidence, he attempted to focus on something completely different, something that would calm him and arrest his hyperventilation. His first 'happy thought' (a trick a child psychologist had once taught him - to think 'happy thoughts' and 'warm fuzzies' instead of drawing morbid massacres in red and black crayon) was his collection of gloves, then after slow minutes of relative calm, Billy again became preoccupied with what he would do with the information he had just gathered from Dawn's father. Now that his curiosity was satisfied, he had to decide whether or not to present the state of affairs to Dawn or take the father's advice and simply forget the entire thing. Considering what had happened just days before, he knew that a different tack was required. Thinking deeper into the matter, he began to discern the numerous angles more clearly:

this was just the wrinkle in the story he needed to resuscitate his tale of heroism. Furthermore, he concluded that her story, combined with his own heroics, would be the perfect vehicle for his finally being able to achieve some mention in the national press. In fact, he would not only be responsible for rescuing the poor woman, but reuniting her with her father and in so doing, bringing back to life what was thought to be a dead story. It would be yet another of his 'good deeds' and would no doubt put him in good stead with the public to an infinitely greater extent than the countless investigations he was known for launching, but never completing. All he had to do now was to figure out how to go about it. For his part, the father was obviously willing (which was a good start), but he also realized that it would eventually mean putting together two potentially volatile characters in admixture. If all else failed, his natural tendencies as a practical joker would at least ensure his enjoyment in watching the combustion. The previous instant's angst (however improbably) had been completely banished and he was once again captain of his soul. It was finally time to put the atoms in motion.

8

"Better to be known as a sinner than a hypocrite."

Billy's return to the office wasn't as smooth and painless as he had hoped it would be. During his absence, he had discovered that a mountain of work had piled up and instead of someone taking up the slack on his behalf it had all been left there waiting for him. In the previous week alone four mysterious deaths had occurred and would probably all require some degree of investigation. Furthermore, he still had leftover work from the previous weeks and the Riley situation to attend to. Fortunately, for him, he had ceased to hear from Basyli so at least one painful distraction was removed from his purview. However, on the whole, there was simply no avoiding the fact that Billy had to buckle down and bury his nose deep into his paperwork. In order to accomplish this, Billy had closed the door to his office, leaving a 'do not disturb' sign on his doorknob. This particular sign was a souvenir from an early case of his that involved a man who had fallen on the floor after a stroke and who eventually died of dehydration, perfectly cognizant of his final mistake. Much like his apartment, Billy's office was a mess. Paper was piled everywhere, both on the floor and on his desk. Though an old, cream-colored computer sat in front of him, given Hokum's relative slowness in adopting technology, most things had to be done with paperwork. Furthermore, even if some computer work was required, it usually had to be duplicated in hardcopy. Billy had no pictures of family, no statuettes, trophies or any of the normal office ornaments that usually decorate a person's work cubical. Instead, the walls of his office were covered with a number of grey paper clippings and mentions of him in various journals. He referred to it as his "wall of death", the centerpiece of which bore an article by one brave reporter who had been so bold as to profile him for one of the Sunday sections. The vast majority of the clippings dealt with a seemingly random assortment of suspicious and not so suspicious deaths. Above the highlighted sections that carried his name, there was usually a photograph of the deceased in a happier or perhaps more tragic pose depending on the tenor of the accompanying story or the moral position, sexual persuasion or gender of the author. Thus, it was that a number of dead faces stared out at him from the drab stillness of his walls, mute in the utter flatness of their black and white photographs. While the wall of dimly smiling faces and horrid headlines haunted many, they said nothing to Billy. They were stories that he had already told. Besides the numerous paper clippings, his wall contained only three other items: a wall calendar full of topless women, a broken barometer and a framed picture of Larry Campbell, which he looked toward for inspiration. His trashcans were littered with discarded coffee pods from the numerous cups of coffee he would consume in a day. In a forlorn corner, lay some collected paraphernalia from previous cases: the head of a bear suit, a rubber chicken, a pogo stick and the recently added rubber fist. For him they served as morbid reminders of the stupidity of men in life as much as in death.

Unfortunately for him, Billy's industriousness in tackling the mountain of paperwork was quickly interrupted by a flash on his many-buttoned, office telephone. It was Velenet, this time his voice a slight pitch beyond its normal banausic temper, "Hey, Billy, we got a situation here." 'Situation' was one of the words he began to dread the most.

"What is it?"

"It's that old crazy guy."

"Who?"

"You know, the dead guy."

"What do you mean? They're all dead by the time you call me."

"You know what I mean, the Russian."

Billy winced, realizing he was talking about Basyli. "Oh Lord, will I ever be set free? Now what?"

"Well he's makin' a scene in the square and passin' out a bunch of fliers sayin' all crazy kind of things about you."

"Well what do you want me to do about it?"

"Well, Griffs wants you to take care of it."

"Me? Why me? What can I do? You are the police. Can't you guys take care of it?"

"Well, we can't arrest him for causin' a public disturbance yet 'cuz he ain't done nothin', but Griffs wants you to settle it all quietly. Especially 'cuz he says you the one seems to be gettin' these crazies all riled up out here so you should deal with it. Also, he don't want any more bad press for the officers after the Riley incident. People still think the morgue was a powerful and artful piece of protest."

Billy silently cursed himself again. "Bad press for the officers, what about me? Does anyone ever care or think about me? I'm never going to get any work done with all these distractions and I'm certainly not going to garner any good press."

"Sorry, sir."

Realizing as with so much that was happening in this life, that ultimately, there was no way out of it, he conceded defeat yet again.

"All, right, I'm on my way."

Billy, profoundly upset, left the darkness of his office and walked down the empty corridors toward the front door. The passages of the building were all unlit and most of the rooms that lined the main hallway were unoccupied. Besides himself, there were only three others in the office that day. He wondered how they coped. Rarely did Billy take the time to speak to his coworkers except for on a strictly professional basis. Not that he disliked them, but he felt there was little he had in common with them. Occasionally, he had to suffer through the odd birthday party or the team Christmas get-together at a local bar, but otherwise he was fairly cynical about all his employees except for the eager Asian intern Moncrete had hired as an assistant. She was what was known in technical terms as a 'F.O.B.', a characteristic he particularly enjoyed. Though the 'process' could be a little painful at first, it usually meant that most of the conversation was one sided and would ultimately favour himself. As he approached the end of the entryway, he looked to the left and saw that someone had already put up pictures of the recent Christmas party on the pushpin board. In each one, the group of middle-aged women and Moncrete posed around him as he glared with increasingly bleary eyes at the camera. In one picture, he wore a yellow coned hat and held in his hand the multicolored party blower that had been foisted on him. The moue on his face was in stark contrast to the ecstatic smiles of his coworkers. The other women, mostly administrative workers, always made fun of his grumpiness and treated him like some kind of overgrown teddy bear. No matter what he seemed to say to them they assumed he was joking and that it was just his way of showing affection. He thought it ridiculous, but as long as they largely left him alone, he didn't mind (though they always had a bad habit of trying to set him up with older Caucasian women he in no way liked).

As he exited the front door of the office, he looked upward to determine if the weather reports had in fact been correct. A small amount of sleet had begun to come down and the weathermen predicted that an inch of snow was to be expected. Billy's primary concern was the icy roads as they would probably deliver a couple more cases by the end of the day that he would no doubt have to attend to. In Hokum, any time the city had more than an inch of snow, the city shut down and schools were closed. Hokum had no provision to deal with any amount of snow and even the slightest of snowstorms would evoke a local state of emergency. Billy himself didn't mind the snow, but professionally, it meant no chance of a quiet afternoon if the roads froze over with black ice. With this in mind, Billy jumped into his much-abused vehicle and made the drive back to the center of town, full of foreboding. When he arrived to the city's main square, called creatively enough, Hokum Square, he parked his car in one of the spaces reserved for the city officials. He made the short walk toward the center where Basyli purportedly stood, causing some damage as he cut through the landscaper's omnipresent, pine islanded streams stuffed as they were with hydrangeas, rhododendrons and small dogwoods, perhaps trampling a few of the low-lying shrubs as he made his deliberate way forward. Billy was in no mood for interruptions and this little odyssey would cost him at least two hours of work. From a distance, he could already see

Basyli moving hither and thither, fulminating as he tried to hand his large stack of fliers to passersby who did their best to avoid him and in some cases even pushed him away. Given it was the lunch hour there were a number of people about as they walked from their offices to the various eateries, fast food restaurants and cafes that dotted central Hokum.

As Billy would later discover, Basyli had spent the last couple of weeks industriously, consuming entire days in deep study, scouring the library, the Internet and the county's public archives, hoping to find information that would further his series of arcane researches. In the last week, Basyli had resorted to begging on the streets to raise the money he needed for food and other necessities, his previous funds having run dry. Furthermore, given his dreadful sciamachy had reached new heights, he had used the little that remained of his earthy wealth to fund his current project. Over the previous few weeks, he barely had time to sleep or eat and he was in an even greater state of dishabille than he had previously been before. However, at present, it wasn't only his physical appearance that showed the signs of complete upheaval, but now his wild, unfocused eyes also betrayed a mind in some state of trauma. What remained of his once great intelligence, he now devoted to what he thought would be his life's work: the ontological proof of evil incarnated in a single man. The abstruse workings of his mind had led him to conduct research not only on Billy's personal history, but also on the cases where he had served as coroner. Furthermore, he did a great deal of research into Hokum's crime statistics over the last one hundred years, which had never before been tabulated in a consistent manner. Though he could find very little on Billy's personal history, there was plenty of grist for his mill regarding the various crimes in Hokum and Billy's seemingly arbitrary manner of handling investigations. It was no surprise that many of the investigations that Billy had ordered resulted in few firm prosecutions. Furthermore, many of the scenarios that Billy painted approached pure invention. Most interestingly, from a strictly numerical point of view, he had deduced that the number of crimes treated as suspicious had quadrupled since Billy becoming coroner. The coincidence was startling and though correlation doesn't presuppose causality, he based his conclusions on the simple premise that Billy's evil aura was enough to satisfy causality. And if one needed any more proof of his position, Basyli could point to the numerous death certificates signed by Billy and to the fact that many of them suggested fantastical causes of death that not only failed to corroborate the available evidence, but appeared to contradict the opinion of the medical examiner. Although Billy had certainly been industrious in opening a number inquiries, rarely did they amount to anything. Finally, in his *coup de grâce*, he noted that the number of disappearances in Hokum had increased threefold, considerably higher than the averages for the state and that many of these disappearances were located in the Lido District not far from where Billy lived. There was certainly an evident statistical pull in the location and frequency of crime toward his apartment. It was as if Billy were one great magnet for crime. In some of his closing postulates, left as a project for others to investigate, he sketched an incunabula of what would no doubt be a great work linking the increased incidence in storms, sunspots, the birth of womb-less cows and a whole host of malign natural phenomena that could naturally be attributed to Billy's evil presence.

It was about these and a number of other strange notions that Basyli was raving in the streets though his efforts were largely needless as most people simply ignored him given his state of dishabille and the inanities he was shouting, which included such words as "leptokurtic", "hidden Markov processes", "Kalman filters", "Baysian networks" and "Baal". Despite his energy and his sincerity, he struggled to get a single person to listen to him and he had to resort to following people a ways down the street holding his pamphlets in their faces as he shouted, "The devil always come in sheep's clothing. He will always look like one of you. But, he will destroy you and the entire city. You cannot see but I see everything. *Zobaczysz, jak swinia niebo.*" People merely shook their heads as he pleaded before them. Two police officers now stood off to one side, powerless to do anything. Almost arriving at the spot where Basyli was shouting, Billy picked one of the discarded pamphlets from off the ground. He looked at its contents. The first page was scrawled with the following text:

The 153 proofs that Billy Rubino is the Devil

By Basyli Jach

Definition 1: X is a Satan-like if and only if X "incorporates" as properties those and only those properties which are negative.

Definition 2: A is an essence of X if and only if for every property B, X has B necessarily if and only if A entails B.

Definition 3: X exists if and only if some particular essence of X is exemplified.

Axiom 1: Any property entailed by – i.e. strictly implied by – a negative property is negative.

Axiom 2: If a property is negative, then its negation is not negative.

Axiom 3: The property of being Satan-like is negative.

Axiom 4: If a property is negative, then it is necessarily negative.

Axiom 5: Necessary existence in and of itself is a positive property, however an unnecessary existence is a negative property.

Axiom 7: Unnecessary qualities exist and are therefore negative.

Axiom 8: Unnecessary qualities can only exist alongside and as a negation of necessary existence.

Axiom 9: Free will is a positive property and only exists with the possible negation of the positive.

Theorem 1: If a property is negative as absolute negation of the positive, then it is consistent, i.e. possibly exemplified.

Corollary 1: The property of being Satan-like is consistent.

Theorem 2: If something is Satan-like, then the property of being Satan-like is an essence of that thing.

Theorem 3: Unnecessary in all possible worlds, nonetheless, the property of being Satan-like is
exemplified in some.

Theorem 4: The property of being Satan-like has its
opposite which is positive and consistent.

Theorem 5: Billy Rubino negates necessary existence
and thus exemplifies Satan-like qualities.

Theorem 6: In negating all positive qualities of existence
Billy Rubino exemplifies all qualities in
negation of a God-like presence.

Flipping quickly through the document, Billy could tell that
the rest of the pages were covered with heavy mathematical
symbols, complicated charts, a number of quotations, both
from the Bible and diverse philosophical texts. Furthermore,
there were several annotated maps and a host of statistical
distributions that described stages in the progression of crime
throughout Hokum. If it weren't the product of a fevered brain,
one could almost believe that this great body of work would
serve as a profound addition to the study of criminology and
at the very least to Hokum's crime prevention efforts. Finally,
included on the very last pages were a short biography, a list
of references and his own version of the events that had led to
his present status. Basyli did not even notice Billy approach
until the equally angry coroner touched him on the shoulder,
at which point he immediately became wild and vociferous
to the point of foaming at the mouth. Pulling himself out of
Billy's grasp, he held one of the pamphlets up to Billy's face,

"O wilku mowa, a wilk tu. Diabeł. Diabeł. I told you I
would show everyone. I told you."

Without a single word from Billy in response, Basyli
lunged at Billy, which quickly prompted the police to attempt

to restrain him. Predictably, this led to Basyli trying to strike back at one of the officers to counter their heavy-handed force, which ultimately induced the other policeman to Taser the exiguously limbed Basyli. The effect was instantaneous and Basyli fell to the ground like a sack of dried potatoes. The officers then took him by the arms and dragged him quickly to a nearby police car. They then drove him to the police station, leaving Billy to pick up the remaining copies of Basyli's pamphlets off of the damp pavement. Billy then returned to the office to resume his work, shaking his head upon reflection of the incident.

When Billy finally arrived at home it was very late and the snow had begun to stick on the roads. Fortunately for him, there had been no reports of accidents or road fatalities in Hokum. He found yet another yellow note taped to his door, it simply read:

> as if the blind rage had washed me clean, rid me of hope; for the first time, in that night alive with signs and stars, i opened myself to the gentle indifference of the world.
>   - camus

> pay me or don't. nothing matters.
>   - the warden.

The next day, the entire city was closed down and Billy was left to spend the remains of the evening with Dawn. Ever since his meeting with Dawn's father, he had been considering how best to approach Dawn with the news of his clandestine rendezvous and furthermore, how to convince her to meet with the man (preferably with a news crew or two in tow). He agreed with Dawn's father that the impunity of his actions would not be well received, but he reasoned that with further coddling and perhaps by spinning his meeting with her father into an instance of complete happenstance he could ultimately convince her. It would take some work, but he thought himself up to the task. He was hopeful, perhaps overly so and blind to his limitations in anticipating the swervings of the human heart. Thus, Billy once again laid the foundation by being uncommonly nice to her, even engaging her in conversation and going so far as to propose that the two of them go on a small trip with one other. Dawn was made extremely happy by these overt attentions, suspecting nothing and even concluding that love was taking its natural course. Furthermore, she took the opportunity to break to him the bulletin that she might have landed a job somewhere in the vicinity of his own office. Billy feigned contentment, but in reality, he just wanted to get the whole matter over with. He began drafting a proposal for the local news station's editor and had gone so far as to promulgate a list of friendly journalists who he imagined might be interested in a heartwarming story of tragedy and heroism just in time for the Christmas season. Billy could already imagine the many accolades he would receive, the mass publicity that might very well culminate in a talk show appearance or better still a daytime special. At the very least, he thought he deserved a place on one of those ghastly late night shows that recount the stories of missing people using dreadful actors and improbable sets to convey the action of these horrible, little stories.

Accompanied by these thoughts, he spent the entire next day daydreaming and plotting until these dulcet preoccupations were interrupted by yet another call from the police station. It turned out that Basyli had not been the best of guests and that Billy's services were once again required. Not only had Basyli continued to rave at all hours of the night, but he also refused to eat and was growing weak. Fearing for his safety (especially given that the other inmates had already grown antagonistic both to his putrid smell and his non-stop frenzies), the officers had taken the decision to separate him from the rest of the population, removing him from a communal holding cell and instead putting him on his own in another small cell at the end of the block. Ultimately, the police wanted nothing more than to cast him out on the street having already assumed that it wasn't worth their while to bring assault charges against him. Nevertheless, protocol dictated that because he was in custody and had acted in ways bordering on insane, they needed Billy in his capacity as coroner to establish his sanity and potentially have him committed based on the result of his investigations. This was particularly important given that none other than the mayor had stated several times that he did not like "crazies" wandering about town as it was a clear detriment to Hokum's already wounded image.

Thus, Billy was forced again against his will to deal with the diminutive Pole. Over the last two days, the snows had made their way from Hokum and the roads and public facilities had returned to normal. As a result, it didn't take him long to arrive at the police station, which was not a great distance from the courthouse. The outside of the police office was fairly plain: a reasonably sized, one story building formed from repetitive trapezoidal blocks of red brick and sandy colored cement. The building was built at some point in the late sixties and contained very few windows, those which it did endure were brown and rectangular, each shielded internally by drawn blinds which hadn't allowed light in for decades. When Billy arrived at the station, the officers were all waiting for him and escorted him quickly to the small row of jail cells. The blistered, vinyl floors of the quaint cellblock were colored a sickly green and remained glossy from the recent passage of a filthy mop. The left side of the corridor was lined with off-white prison bars, while the right side wall was hung with posters that included such subjects as far away beaches, resorts full of bikini clad women, portraits of gay couples and monkeys caged at the zoo. They were the product of the Hokum police force's strange brand of humor. For the benefit of the other inmates, they placed Basyli in a cell at the very end of the passageway.

The entire cellblock contained merely seven or eight cells, but as he walked by, each of the men who filled them tried to catch his attention, thinking he was some kind of warden or official. When he finally arrived at Basyli's cell, which accommodated only a single pull-down bed, a small toilet and a corner sink, he saw Basyli, lying on the floor sideways, next to the bed that hung open from the wall at his right. The folded blankets and pillow remained on the bedframe undisturbed, while Basyli sat in a near fetal position, with his hands covering his head, his face toward the wall. Billy observed him closely and noticed the peculiar, dark streak of hair that arched the area near the center of his rather large head, front to back. It appeared to stand in even greater contrast to the rest of his hair, which seemed to Billy to have whitened even further than when he had last seen him. His esurient figure was dressed in the dun prison garb usually reserved for permanent inmates. As he looked at Basyli's small, emaciated body, he wondered if he was even alive. Billy bent down on his knees and tried to address Basyli several times, but Basyli was completely unresponsive. After the third time that Billy said his name, Basyli, finally roused from his torpor, lifted his head out of his arms, not even turning to look from whence the voice was coming. Billy spoke in a gentle, almost reassuring voice,

"I told you already, there is no use going on like this. If you want to know, I have heard very positive noises and it seems the inquiry into your case may begin as early as next year provided a series of things happen and that there are no further delays. Don't you want to make it to see your trial?"

Basyli, after some time, responded in a morose voice, "Next year too long. I no trouble anymore. *Żaden w swej sprawie sędzia być nie może.* No one listen to me. You just tell me many lies."

"Look, I'm trying the best I can for you. But, you're not giving me a whole lot to go with."

Basyli just sat there, continuing to stare blankly at the wall. "I no eat. I just die here. Leave me alone."

Billy replied, "What kind of attitude is that? How are you ever going to get anywhere in life with that attitude?"

"I no care. I no have life. *Kogo Bóg chce skarać…*"

Billy's contrarian side had begun to take over and for the first time since he had met Basyli he began to seriously contemplate taking on the man's case, not out of any great abundance in his heart, but merely because he wanted to prove this man wrong. He wanted to show him that he was worthy of faith. Although Billy had become impressed by the lengths to which Basyli had gone, his ego simply wouldn't tolerate anyone ignoring his advice or power, not on issues over which he had some degree of control. Indeed, Billy felt a deep need to make this man see that he was becoming a disgrace to himself, not for his recent actions, but for his desire to become a social parasite. Billy hated vagrants, reprobates, social security freeloaders, even hippies, in fact, anyone who he thought simply didn't contribute. In this, he believed he shared much with his other great hero, Ronald Reagan. Billy could be exceedingly stubborn once he got a notion in his head. Thus, he decided to take a hard line with Basyli, speaking to him almost like a father would speak to his offending son,

"You realize that as a coroner I am granted in certain cases the power to determine the sanity of individuals. That means I have the ability to commit you to a mental institution where they will force you to eat and take meds. You will lose your liberty, Basyli." Basyli? Had he really done it? He had actually called Basyli by his name for the first time? Billy even surprised himself by this allowance. Did he really believe this man or was it just a simple slip of the tongue? Perhaps he was just trying to give the man hope. Either way, Billy wanted nothing more than to wake the man out of his inexplicable insouciance, to cure him of his perverse nihilism (something he could no more accomplish for himself). For Basyli, it made no difference. Taking exception to Billy's threats and tone of voice, the edge started to return to the poor Pole's voice, "I no crazy, you crazy. You understand nothing about how the world is. Now you listen to me. I will tell you story. Listen. A great physicist once ask question, 'You are standing in a field, any field...an empty field. Your arms are resting free at your side and now for some reason you look up. You look up and see the normal thing, the stars and more importantly, that these distant bodies are not moving. Now, for some reason, you don't know why, maybe curiosity, maybe you are for a moment crazy, you start to spin. Now, the stars are moving all around you and your arms are pulled from your body. But then you stop and think. Why should your arms be pulled away when the stars are whirling? Why should they be dangling freely when the stars don't move?' The answer: this is how the universe is. This question is not about physics or science, it is about life and the way the world is made. The Greeks, you see? We are guided by stars, our destiny is written in them and our lives are set to their dancing. No matter how you see it, it is same. You see? Truth is never relative, it only is. With freedom too, we can sometimes lose ourselves, in fate, we always find we are nothing. It is this that has given you power over me. You already take my liberty. You take my life. You take my identity. You erase me."

Billy considered the situation a minute more before responding. Though he wasn't quite sure what the Pole meant, he was intrigued by its philosophical import. In Billy's mind, there weren't many intelligent people in the world who weren't locked up or somehow silenced, essentially treated as insane. Thus, he suddenly felt compelled to keep this one outside of a cell. He then wondered how he could make his becoming involved in this case worth his while. Even if Basyli wasn't who he said he was, what was the point in a man's possessions going to the state? It seemed a bad way to end a poor story. He thought to himself that there must be a way to turn the situation into a positive for both of them. Thus, he began to think of ways in which to build a plot around it, to somehow turn himself into the hero of the situation. The more Billy reasoned, the more he became intrigued. Perhaps he could redeem the state of affairs for both of them. In a moment of divine afflatus, he saw the entire story in a flash: how he alone, against his own professional intuition and the advice of his superiors, decided to open this man's case and restore the life that was taken away from him due to a petty clerical mistake. Billy would be the man to take on the entire system. Even if the local papers wouldn't be interested in Basyli, he hoped they would be interested in his own heroism. Billy was skeptical of the idea, but he thought there was a small chance it could work. However, the pitch would have to be exactly right to avoid turning any undue embarrassment or suspicion on himself. Furthermore, he would have to assure Basyli's strict cooperation. If the story didn't work out with Dawn, this could be his potential backup. Having established the kernel of an idea, Billy pursued a different tack with Basyli, softening his voice accordingly,

"Look, Basyli, stop being such a fatalist. You sound like some kinda French lackey. I'm not trying to erase you, I'm trying to give you your life back, but I need to find your story."

"Evil wakes while the people sleep. You are liar. You are Devil. *Czochraj bobra.*"

"Listen Basyli," he said, putting some amount of feeling into his voice, "Give me a try. I am going to do my best for you."

Basyli adjusted his body and inclined his head so that he could finally look Billy straight in the eye. "When I was little boy, I grow up near Lwów. You know this place?"

"No."

Basyli sounded surprised, "How you not know? You were there."

"I don't understand."

Basyli could barely speak at this point. His voice was very weak and faint. It trembled with exertion. Lifting his right hand with effort, he signaled for Billy to come closer. At this point, Billy had to virtually lie down and put his face right up against the bars of the cell to hear him.

"As a boy, I saw thousands of my countrymen. Even my brother, a writer carried to Katyn forest and killed. My uncle, professor, killed in street. They killed many men. Many starve. My family nearly lose everything. The Russians they treat us very bad. First the Germans treat us bad. Then the Russians. And then I see the Polish people even kill more Polish. Then they keep killing the Jews after war. Then the Soviets try to erase everything. They bury it under ground and no one can talk. They even try to burn all documents. They want to erase thousands of lives. How you explain such evil? But no one ever do to me what you do. Nobody take my entire life from me. No one erase my identity while I still live. No one but you, Devil."

Billy jerked his head away from the cell, his previous nightmares of the Magdeburg still ringing faintly in his head, this last statement drove too close to home,

"You are really starting to upset me. Do you have any idea what I have done for you? Do you have any idea what I am willing to do for you? Do you? No, you don't do you? Go ahead and turn your head away. Have it your way, but don't think we are done with this."

Billy was practically shouting and his voice echoed through the halls so that he drew the attention of the officer who had originally escorted him over. The young policeman sensing something was awry, returned to check on Billy, "Everything OK? Is he givin' you trouble?" The officer looked down at Basyli with a harsh stare. "We already had to hose him down earlier. That quieted him down some, but if we have to put him in restraints…"

"No. No, it's fine."

Billy stood up as Basyli had by this point put his head back between his arms and ceased to listen to him. Billy slowly turned to the young officer, continuing with some degree of resentment in his voice,

"I don't know what it is, but here I am forced to deal with another *Looney Tunes* character. I got Riley after me, threatening to kill me because he sees ghosts and then this fool here who won't leave me alone because he wants to prove to me that he isn't a ghost and then when I finally agree to help him prove that he is actually alive, he simply wants to sit there and become a ghost again."

The officer merely scratched his head and gave Billy a quizzical stare. "Want to run that by me again?"

"Oh, no. Just forget it. It's ridiculous anyway."

"Yeah, well I hurd 'bout that Riley situation…too bad. How is that goin' anyhows?"

"Ridiculous, they treat me like shit. I still have to drive up to his place every night at seven and pick up his family and take them to the hospital because the sheriff thinks that it might lure Riley over there. Then, every morning at seven, I take them back home. Kids think it's more fun than they ever had watching cable and the mother gets free meals at the cafeteria, which she thinks is some kinda fancy restaurant. Anyway, it's all a joke and I simply stopped caring long ago. Today's supposedly the last day after the sheriff extended my duty twice."

"Aw, man. That is the shits. Say, you still datin' that Dawn chick?"

"Oh her, well we're not really…I mean…"

"Ca'mon, don't lie. Me and the boys saw you with her jus' the other night. That girl sure is a looker. How did ya pick her up anyway? Poundstone told me to ask you."

"Well, it's a long story."

"Right. Always keepin' secrets. Anyhow, what is it you want us to do with this guy?" The officer looked over at Basyli's motionless frame. Billy turned it over in his mind and even considered committing him given the precarious nature of his health. However, he soon concluded that although it might prevent Basyli from having further episodes and it would certainly allow him to keep closer tabs on the crazed Pole, it would not further the story he had just concocted to have a drugged, dribbling zombie whom he purported to have saved, committed to a mental institution. No, it wouldn't look good at all. Instead, Billy reached into his wallet and pulled out all the money he had, $44.38 and he handed it to the officer, whispering in his ear, "Give this to the guy and then let him go. There is nothing else we can do for him. Don't tell him I gave it to you. Just stick it in his pocket."

The officer looked back surprised. "Well, that's awful nice of you. Will do."

With that, Billy took his leave of the young officer and exited the station. As he drove home in his car, he decided that the time was well past to put his plans for Dawn into motion. It was clear, he needed to act soon, before the entire story lost its immediacy and the season of heartwarming Christmas stories was over. Billy was fortunate. Since he had mentioned to Dawn the possibility of their going away on a short trip, she wouldn't let him hear the end of it. Thus, upon his return home, he announced on the spot that the coming weekend would be the very weekend for them to depart. Dawn, who was sitting on the couch surfing the web at the time, had already located a suitably scenic area whose postcard quality would no doubt induce the wonted atmosphere of romance. They could rent a cabin and take long walks, chattering about sex, relationships, whatever it was they weren't doing or didn't have, much like any other couple in suburban America. By this point, Billy began to fear that whatever association they did have was beginning to resemble some sort of inadvertent relationship. Had he already committed himself? The warning signs were all there: she had long ago begun to colonize his bathroom with her personal effects, his closets were populated with the small amount of black apparel she had retained with her, she had her own key to his apartment and was even helping him in his search to find a new place, suggesting they should go on viewings together. Billy didn't have time to consider these minutiae, but he did require her help in completing his *beau* stratagem. So it was decided, they would leave that day and spend the entire weekend at Lake Wakanda, below the Onida Falls. Dawn was as excited as could be and Billy had some small degree of interest, not having left Hokum or its environs for well over two years. Realizing the mental strain it would put on him, Billy with some degree of recalcitrance, fell back on his previous habits and took a healthy dose from his emergency stash of diazepam, which he would use throughout the days in order to suffer through the boredom and feigned intimacy he would not doubt have to endure.

The drive up to Lake Wakanda was fairly uneventful. The terrain was relatively drab, mostly pine trees, desolate towns and the odd piece of scenery. When they arrived at the lake it was already late and they had some trouble locating the hotel. Once they had found it and had secured the keys from the gentle, old lady at the front desk, they drove to their secluded cabin from which they could hear the thundering of the Onida

Falls in the distance. They had asked for separate beds, but despite their pre-booking, only cabins with single beds were now available so it became clear they would have to share one king size bed. This blatant inconvenience didn't bother Dawn, but Billy fretted over his ability to sleep. Given the drive had been one of constant ascent, they found that although the weather was surprisingly temperate considering the previous days of snow, the mountain air was considerably more frigid than that in Hokum. Billy, feigning tiredness, suggested that they go to bed immediately so that they could make an early start of it. Evidently, she interpreted his revulsion as his being a pure gentleman.

In the middle of the night, Billy was woken suddenly by a violent dream, his worst yet. Evidently it had troubled him to such a degree that he woke up shouting, his body pale and damp with sweat. Dawn, shocked into a similar state of alertness, tried to comfort him, but Billy resisted her efforts, simply stating that he had had a bad dream without revealing its still mysterious contents. Yet, it was exactly these contents that kept him awake in puzzlement for another hour or two. As expected, his present dream seemed to follow the pattern of the others, being overtly bereft of recognizable surroundings, yet somehow approximating something not altogether strange or unfamiliar. In this latest installment, he appeared to be standing before a large crowd, though separated from their inaudible voices by a spluttering wall of flame. He was bound, unable to move. Evidently he imagined himself some kind of martyr being burned at the stake in a sort of *auto-da-fé*, though he was noticeably spared of the *Sambenito* employed in the Spanish flavor of such entertainments. Before him in the crowd, there was a group of women, resembling strangely enough, nuns, who bore their D-sized breasts toward him, beating and scratching them with an uncontrollable passion to the point of bleeding. They called forth with an entire host of peculiar names such as *Asmodeus, Zabulon* and *Isacarron.* Though he couldn't hear their voices, he could see that their eyes were clearly filled with tears. They seemed to be professing their love for him as he burned. The irony was not lost on him that it was they who wanted to possess him, yet it was he who burned, uncontrollably. As he looked into their faces, he thought he saw one he recognized. Indeed, it was unmistakable. Right before his broken shell of a body stood a face distinctly resembling that of Dawn, dressed in the habiliment of an Ursuline nun. Like the others surrounding her, she stretched her arms toward him, pleading with the dour face of one of the Elder Lippi's Madonnas, while he was subsumed by a more than mortal flame. Indeed, he had long begun to wonder if he was the one who was being duped. That he had somehow become a martyr torched on the pyre of her passion, instead of his own.

When Billy awoke again the next morning, he saw Dawn standing at the window, staring out through the alpenglow with a pair of complimentary binoculars. She was dressed in nothing more than a pair of turquoise panties and a black T-shirt. Her silhouette was sublime, but unfortunately for Billy, her charms were still lost on him. When she noticed that he had woken, she signaled him to the window, forcing him to look out at the placid lake in which was preserved a perfect negative of the surrounding landscape. The day was indeed beautiful, but cold. Billy wondered why he had decided to travel to the mountains where there was little to do besides hiking, given that in the offseason it was impossible even to fish. The fact was, there was little else in the area as far as entertainments and Billy had practically exhausted his vacation time. He was surprised that the cabins were completely booked, but the irenic, old lady at the desk had explained that there was an avid group of hikers who had all booked in over the previous week. Furthermore, there may have been a small mistake in booking their original reservation.

After going through the normal course of getting dressed and eating a hearty breakfast, they decided to take a boat trip out to the middle of the lake. After initially taking the oars, Billy left the majority of the task to Dawn as he fretted over his new, engagingly chartreuse gloves. She was completely captivated by her surroundings, being excited by every small bird, the bark of each tree, the smells of the world that surrounded them. As they took the small hike up to the famous cataract, she gasped at the beauty and the power of the falls, amidst whose thundering presence a caliginous rainbow fell in and out of existence. As he looked at her sparking eyes, he saw in them a childishness, a sheer wonderment about everything. He couldn't understand it, but he realized she was truly happy. As they stood at the foot of the falls, overcome, she turned to Billy, closed her eyes and kissed him on the lips for the second time since they had met. What was he to do in his present state of zugzwang? It seemed his fate was sealed. He felt embarrassed by her maudlin conduct. Humanely, Dawn didn't make a great deal of the kiss, but simply turned back toward the falls as if nothing had happened. For the rest of the day, she could be seen leaning against his arm, putting her head against his shoulder. Billy for his part didn't know what to do and was completely conflicted. Robbed of his ability to insult her, he would now have to play his part in a scenario that appeared to be developing much too quickly for his own tastes. She took an eyelash out of his blinking eye and asked him to close his lids and make a wish and what did Billy wish for, but that after all his efforts she would consent to his plan. As the day wore on, Billy became increasingly confident that his stratagem would succeed and was at times even beginning to enjoy her caresses, feeling that they were somehow collaborators, or perhaps equal conspirators in what would be the first step in his apotheosis. As they sat down to a romantic dinner in the lodge, Dawn reached for his hands and he stared into her eyes, imagining them filling with tears before a talk show presenter as she described Billy's unflinching heroism. That night, when they had settled down for bed, Dawn put her arms around Billy and gave him a quick kiss on the neck. She whispered in his ears, "Don't take it too seriously if I say I love you. It's only the altitude." Billy laughed and they spent the night like that: she with her arms draped around him for warmth, he thinking his plan was assured of success.

The next morning they woke up together. They had forgotten to close the curtains so the blinding, matutinal light of a waxy sun aroused them at daybreak. Dawn suggested that they take one last walk around the lake, which they did. The lake was far too large for them to trespass its entire circumference, but they managed to walk a good portion. On the other side of its limpid surface, they found a large, rustic restaurant where they could enjoy a simple lunch. They were sat in large, russet couches next to a set of thirty-foot high windows where numerous nature lovers were using binoculars and various other types of vision enhancing equipment to stare out of the glass at the nearby lake. They talked about this and that in casual conversation, while Billy waited until their eyes met again in a wordless stare: she perhaps looking at some form of future husband and he thinking the time was ripe to hatch his *arrière-pensée*. However, she usurped his opportunity asking him the question she had patiently waited two days to ask,

"Listen, you were having some pretty rough dreams that first night. What was that all about?"

"Nothing, just dreams. Just some stupid little dreams. I have them sometimes."

At this point she grabbed his hand and caught his eye with a look of deep concern,

"They didn't sound stupid or little. C'mon. Listen, you can trust me. You don't have to be afraid. I am here for you. I mean, if we are going to be in a relationship..."

"A relationship?" Billy started almost too eagerly, having to restrain at the last minute his temptation to laugh so as not to spoil all the work he had put in so far.

Dawn, undeterred, continued on, "I know it's early stages, but I want to help you get through this. We can get through this together. I didn't want to say anything, but I've noticed you've been hitting those Valium pills pretty hard. Is there something wrong? Something going on?"

"You will never understand," Billy responded, almost under his breath as he felt Dawn was always putting him in the position of reading his lines from a bad soap opera script. He hadn't taken any diazepam that morning or for most of the previous day and he was feeling a bit out of sorts. Dawn could sense his discomfort and wasn't unaware that a slight edge had entered his demeanor.

"Why don't you try me? I've seen all sorts. Believe me. What did you see in your dream that caused you to scream like that? You can take it from me, you shouldn't ignore these things, especially when you're self-dosing like that..."

"Well, if you really must know, it was you."

"Me?"

"And not just you, but Jeanne des Agnes and Doctor Fourneau."

"Who?"

"The Loudun possessions. Haven't you read Huxley?"

"OK, now you've lost me. What are we talking about here, a book?"

"And it's not just them. I see visions all the time. Horrible visions. And all kinds of terrible people, people like Fredrick Deeming, Cortez, mass murders, wars, executions…"

"Who…what? Murderers? I don't…Well, I guess maybe it's because of your job. I mean being a coroner and all that would be the obvious…especially given those books you're always reading about mass murderers and demonic possession…"

"No, that's not it. Not it at all. Every night it's the same and they all seem so real, to the point they are almost like memories. There is a condition, you know. It's called False Memory Syndrome. It's when your mind cannot differentiate between memories and dreams. Or maybe it's paranoid schizophrenia, I don't know. I'm beginning to think that maybe there is something wrong with me. Like, I think maybe I'm…"

"You're what?"

"I'm the Devil."

Dawn jumped back in her chair and laughed, only containing herself, when she noted the completely serious look on Billy's face.

"But…but that's ridiculous. You're a bit grumpy, but believe me, you are no devil. I've hung out with some cult kinda guys who thought they were Satan, but unless you've invited me up here to this remote lake so you can paint the forest with me…"

"No you don't understand. Listen. You ever felt like maybe you've done something in a different life and that you are paying the price for it in the present? Believe me, I know it sounds ridiculous..."

"No, believe me, I know everything about inheriting the crimes of others..."

"Well, I don't. But, I know one thing is for sure, that this is on a massive scale, almost cosmical. I know it all sounds crazy to someone who can't see these things like I do, but I don't know how else to explain all this crazy shit that's been happening to me. Sometimes I feel I'm being punished for being intelligent and that this entire earth should go to hell and I want to be the one to send it there. I am surrounded by idiots, real idiots, yet everyone seems to think I'm the Devil and I don't know why. I can't stand idiots. I hate them. They should be chemically sterilized. You know what it's like to be surrounded by idiots all your life? The South is full of them. Can you imagine if Galileo had been born in Mississippi? I shouldn't be here. My heart is broken and not for the reason you think, but it doesn't always work and it's caused me these problems. Then there's the drugs and all these lunatics I keep running into over and over who think I'm crazy, that I'm Satan. Maybe I am."

"But, Billy, maybe you should slow down on the Valium. Maybe it's becoming a problem. You know it can cause you to hallucinate, even Valium. Trust me, I've had problems with much heavier drugs before and I know just coming to terms with it can be a difficult thing. But, maybe these dreams, the screaming are a sign, a wakeup call."

Billy's eyes began to widen and a certain wildness began to enter his demeanor.

"Yes it is. Indeed, you are correct. These visions must be a sign. And it seems you're part of it, part of all this stuff that's leading me to something, something bigger. As Neitzche would say, this is my *High Noon*. I mean, have you ever heard of his concept of eternal return?'

"It doesn't ring a bell, but…"

"Well, basically, he says that we are all locked into this loop of existence that plays out again and again like reruns of *Bonanza*. Anyway, he says we can only find redemption by claiming and recognizing our fate as our own. We as individuals and we as an entire society must find our *High Noon* or our history will force us to awake to the same nightmare again and again, the nightmare that is history."

"Well, all this sounds a bit high minded, but your heart is in the right place. When I was in rehab they always told us that we needed to break the cycle. To accept ourselves for who we are and embrace our past no matter how bad it is. I know this all sounds like a bunch of garbage, but it's true and I have just begun to be learn to accept myself and my past."

"No, one must rise above history, one must move beyond good and evil, right and wrong, break from it completely in order to tell an entirely new story, a new history of humankind. One must be a noble soul and achieve ultimate power over oneself and over one's history. Indeed, there are some of us who still scream for release, to break this neurotic cycle of history. These visions I have, I think must be something from my past, something I must escape. Maybe I'm not making any sense, but I've been thinking…random, but have you ever heard of the myth of the Wandering Jew? Well maybe that's me? I'm like the Wandering Jew with Alzheimer's"

"Wait, what? Now you are telling me you're Jewish?"

"No you don't get it. I mean…"

Dawn began laughing again in an attempt to lighten the mood, "I may have risen from the dead, but it sounds like you are the one who has a real Messiah complex."

Billy paused for a moment, feeling somewhat estranged from everything he had just said. He then lowered his head and began to stare intently into the table. He wasn't exactly sure what had come over him and why he felt the sudden need to unpack his soul, but he thought he'd better change the subject quite quickly, swerving the conversation into the direction of Dawn's father.

"Listen, there is something I wanted to say to you."

"Yes, something else? Can there be more?" Dawn responded hopefully, if perhaps a little incredulously.

Watching indirectly the workings of his mind, she could read in his eyes that he wanted to say something important so she touched his hand lightly, thinking he might say something as foolish as that he loved her. As Billy's eyes softened, she giggled at the pleasant notion, her face betraying an open smile. "What? What is it? What is it you want to tell me?" She pulled her hair back from her left ear, her voice full of expectation, her head tilted in a questioning posture. Billy looked her directly in the eye, but spoke with a clinical coldness.

"Anyway, forget it. This stuff is all ridiculous. Let's change the subject."

"No, go ahead, you wanted to say something. Don't be afraid."

"Well, you said something about confronting the past and you will never guess, but a couple of days ago, you will never believe who I ran into."

"No, who?"

"Well, I was out looking at a homicide and one of the key witnesses was…"

"Who?"

"Well, you will never believe, but it was actually Reggie Hortega, your father."

He paused, while Dawn's jaw dropped instantly.

"And well, given that you never liked to speak about it I decided to satisfy my own curiosity and asked him about all the stuff I had read. We spoke for a long time and he told me what had happened. Anyway, he wanted to give you this. It's his phone number. He said you would never want to talk to him. I would have just thrown it away but…"

She sat stark still in mute disbelief as she looked down at the paper, the thoughts flocking in and out of her head like a swarm of starlings. Her hands began to tremble while her opened mouth turned from an O of surprise into an O of sheer horror. Then she slowly raised her face toward Billy giving him the fiercest of stares.

"I am a little confused. You lay all this crazy shit on me one minute and then the next minute you come up with some bullshit like this. Maybe you are going crazy. You really expect me to believe that?"

"Believe what?"

"That you just ran into my biological a week or so after you found the story about him?"

"Well, coincidences happen all the time."

"Billy, give me some credit that I'm smarter than that."

"Smarter than what? I am telling you the truth."

"Billy, stop it. Why do you have to lie? I thought we were being honest with one another. I know you a little better than that."

"I'm not lying."

By this point, Dawn's rage had begun to gather the momentum of a large boulder and her voice was rising to the point where the diners behind them started to turn around, "I can't believe you…you went behind my back and went to see…that…that man even after I told you I wanted nothing to do with him. Why did you do this? Why, Billy?"

Not prepared for the ferocity of the reaction, Billy started stuttering, "Well…I just thought…look, I never got the rest of the story and I thought for your sake, in case you didn't know…well…"

"So this is what this is all about? Well, well, well. Finally the truth comes out. I should have known. So you just wanted to hear the rest of the story about the junkie girl whose parents abandoned her and left her to live in a household where she was abused, is that what you wanted to hear? You want to just help a little junkie Mexican girl out so you can go on about it on TV like with all your other investigations. Is that it? Is that what all this stuff is about, these dreams, these visions of grandeur? It's about you, right? Fulfilling your destiny or something? You want to go arrange a press conference right now?"

"Well, I guess…look the guy had been following me around the streets for friggin' sake, because he was worried about you."

"What? What are you talking about? You never told me any of this!"

"Well, I wasn't sure at the time and anyway, I was left with this story and I didn't know the end. I just wanted to know what happened." Unlike his last fight with Dawn, Billy didn't feel the vacuum below his abdomen grip his soul. No quite the contrary, he could feel the heat rising up his neck and towards his ear lobes. He simply couldn't understand why she was behaving this way. His inability to communicate with her in a sensible manner was starting to frustrate him. He gripped the metal fork in his hand so tightly that the tines began to bend into the table. He couldn't control her emotions and it made him feel incapable, especially as he was beginning to loose mastery over his own. He felt as if he were turning the wheel of a rudderless ship that was quickly headed over another scenic waterfall. No warmth from these feckless creatures had ever pervaded the cold labyrinth of his heart (with the probable exception of his mother). Thus, he wondered why he could never understand these odd life forms that stood before him. Why they always resorted to these displays of emotion that had nothing to do with him or anything he had done. He was simply trying to give to her a piece of information that she chose to feed back to him in a garbled mess. How could she not see the beauty in his communication? In the gift he wanted to bestow on both of them? He raised his voice against her own, "Can you really blame me for that? You live in my house, you eat my food, can you really blame me for being a bit curious about who you are?"

"We'll I'm glad you've now satisfied your only curiosity about me and I'm sorry I've been such a burden on you. But, that will change. I really don't get it. I asked you one thing Billy. One thing."

"Listen, I thought we were in a relationship. I thought I could put you back in touch with your father. Complete the story. What about all this group session shit you just threw at me? About learning to confront your past? I mean, isn't this it?" Billy had honestly been caught off guard by Dawn's reaction and began to flail hopelessly. "Isn't this part of the process? I mean, shouldn't we tell everyone the real story that your mother tried to tell?"

"You have the nerve. My mother's story was for one person and that was for me. It has nothing to do with you or anyone else. I never knew my mother. I never knew my dad and I never wanted to. I mean, who would after being the product of some sick, fucked up story like that? Huh? And having everyone know about it."

"Well, in my line of work I see all kinds of fucked up stories and believe me…"

"Fuck your work. This is about me and you. I'm not just another one of your investigations, Billy. This is about the trust between two people. Why can't you ever understand that? I asked you not to bring this up again yet you let your curiosity get the better of you because your curiosity is more important to you than me."

"Well, maybe it was my subconscious talking to me. Ever thought of that? Maybe it was the part of me that wanted to get to know you better. To do what was right to get closer to who you are."

For a minute, he thought he was being honest, but the words sounded ridiculous. However, he really wanted to feel something. He not only wanted to feel something, he wanted very much to feel the appropriate thing. He was desperate, but he couldn't possibly make her understand his honest desire to experiment with the drug she was obviously under.

"You are incredible. Don't give me that bullshit because I know you don't believe in any of it. You are the most shameless person I've ever met."

On his part, he felt she had grossly underestimated him yet again and had forced him into an unforgiving corner. His only defense was to return to his normal course of insults and sarcasm, "C'mon, haven't you seen what's on television lately? You sit and watch it all day."

"Pitiful. You know, you were always right. You are incapable of love. You're just another selfish asshole out of the millions of selfish assholes out there that I seem constantly to be getting involved with. Well, this is it. I never, ever want anything else to do with you. And to think I even thought I could love you. To think I trusted you. You know, I wish you would have never found me lying out there by the river then I would have just died right there and I would have been just another case for you, another investigation which is all you wanted anyway."

Billy paused for a minute, not knowing what else to do. He had become bored by the situation and even he recognized all was lost. Looking at the quizzical faces at the next table, he tried to save face. "Aren't you overacting a bit?" he let out feebly.

"Just shut up. I fucking hate you. If you want to know, Billy, you are the Devil. A real Devil, I hope you know that."

By this point, several people in the restaurant had begun to turn around. The waitress, unsure of what to do, stood there in shock with a hot pot of coffee in her hand. She merely shook her head in disapproval at Billy. Dawn grabbed her coat and stormed out of the restaurant. Billy sat there by himself, trying to figure out what had gone wrong. Not hungry anymore, he decided to find his way back to the hotel where he had already checked out. When he finally arrived, he was surprised to find that Dawn's bags were gone. According to the young woman at the desk, Dawn had come by for her luggage and asked for directions to the nearest bus stop. For all the red-haired receptionist knew, Dawn had hitchhiked her way to the not too distant town in order to take a bus.

When he asked her how long ago she had left, the woman made the baaing sound of a sheep. When Billy raised his finger to question her about her strange response, he thought better of it and simply walked away. Billy had little else to do. He didn't have Dawn's phone number and she wasn't to be found on the premises. He then drove toward the town indicated by the receptionist and tried to find her at the bus stop but to no avail. Furthermore, no one he asked had even seen someone who remotely fitted Dawn's description. With nothing else to do, he made the long drive back to Hokum by himself, realizing that both of his plans to court some small modicum of fame were on the verge of failing.

After feeling sorry for himself for an hour, a smile quickly returned to his unshaven face. He didn't actually need any of these people, he concluded. He would finally be able to spend the night by himself and tomorrow was a new day. In this life, he had long ago realized that there was always something to be doing. Indeed, he would just have to drive a new course. He would in the end have to find his own story and not rely on others to provide him with theirs.

9

"Vae, puto deus fio."

The news stations where all obsessed with it. It was to be Hokum's largest hurricane since the big storm of '57. A level five hurricane, Hurricane Cassandra was to touch ground in the next twenty-four hours. The hurricane was still building strength despite having reached the Gulf coast. Though it was expected to diminish considerably once it hit landfall, it had gathered enough momentum over the ocean to wreak extensive havoc on land, especially given its projected path. Gale force winds were expected in the region of one hundred and fifty miles an hour and the coastal cities had already been evacuated long ago. Though the hurricane's original path was expected to hit the usual, more populated areas, these zones were preserved at the last minute as the steering winds changed their course, driving the storm like a bucking horse toward the less populated, but more direct paths that led straight towards Hokum. Given the warmer than normal temperatures and increased humidity, the hurricane was expected to diminish at a slower rate and would probably cause extensive damage if it managed to slam into the barrier wall of the Maralah Mountains. It was exactly the case as in '57, when Hokum not only experienced floods from the river, but also from the mountains as the subsequent mudslides meant the city was almost subsumed by a torrent of earth. The Channel 7 weatherman spoke of tropical depressions and areas of pressure as he would have about turnips or cauliflower. In this region of the country, hurricanes were cultural phenomena. People even had hurricane parties. The local AA baseball team was called the Hokum Hurricanes. The city's most popular restaurant: Hurricane Joe's. It's not that people took them lightly, quite the contrary, they did not. A state of emergency had been declared in Hokum and the surrounding towns. Already, people were plundering the grocery stores, stocking up on everything from batteries and kerosene to marshmallows and milk. It had been raining almost constantly for three days and already extreme measures were being considered: forced evacuations, hurricane shelters, a call for the military to sandbag the entire waterfront. The state of affairs was one of chaos and numbers of people had already begun to evacuate their homes. But there was a small minority of "sane" heads. The always present "greater minority". As in every catastrophe, there are those recusant skeptics who merely take things in their stride, recognizing the media's constant need to whip-up hysteria to the point where they assumed that the entire hurricane was a mere invention of some remote authority, only meant to drive up advertising fees and gasoline prices. This was the crowd of the Red Queen, the brave doubters, the consummate cynics who viewed such rabble-rousing not only with arch circumscription, but with a corresponding sense of high dudgeon. Though everyone at the Red Queen was tuned into the news, watching it on one of the many large screen televisions, some viewed it with the same relish as they would a sporting event, even laughing at the foolishness of the suited commentators. The mood was one of great levity, almost festive. Everyone in the bar was enjoying himself except for Billy, who was finishing his third beer.

It had been two weeks since he had heard from Dawn. At first, he was glad to have had his space to himself again, but lately, he had to admit that a sort of emptiness had entered his life. Not only had his plans for fame and glory been all but destroyed, but he was suddenly left again to adjust to a new regime. Despite his professional life being anything but routine, Billy was naturally an incorrigible creature of habit and to the extent he could, he liked to attach himself to certain domestic habits, which gave his life some semblance of order. However, the unforeseen loss of her presence meant that the previously normative routines, which he had taken such pains to adjust to, would now have to change again. Beyond the cooking, the cleaning, the grocery shopping, could it have been that he actually missed her? When she had left, she too had called him the devil: a name, which he had grown accustomed to. "Well," he asked himself, "if the devil had a subconscious, what would it say?" He then posed the question to himself of whether he was merely in denial about his desire to do good by the girl? Unlikely, but he did have to admit that she made his life easier in certain ways and she, unlike many others, truly cared about him. He had gotten used to her cooking, her attention to his clothes and general maintenance of his apartment. Even the women at the office commented on his better sense of dress, his being more genial at work and his general collectedness. However, bereft of her beneficent pollution, both his apartment and his person had quickly returned to their former shabby state. So, there was no doubt that she had an effect on him, though the extent and quality of which might be debated. He had no idea where she had gone and hadn't even received as much as a phone call from her. Though he had checked his messages several times, it seemed she had disappeared from his life for good. Given that she had taken a good amount of her earthly possessions along with her on the trip, there was little reason for her to return to his apartment.

At first the loss hadn't affected him at all, but after a week, the prodromes became increasingly worse, almost chronic. At times his heart would pitter-patter, a sensation he couldn't ever recall feeling, except perhaps once, a long, long time ago. Dear Lord, he thought, could I be having a stroke? At times he broke out into inexplicable sweats and was left leaning against a wall, spending long minutes, counting the receding seconds between the brief intervals in which his heart raced. He imagined he must be dying and at these points, a more deceitful apprehension occurred to him, one which gripped him with a mortal fear, only equivalent to that experienced during his bouts of delirium. He began to wonder whether the explanation was more complex, that the sole rationale for the dreaded sensation of longing that he felt, of loss, yes, the only possible explanation for this new found ability not only to notice, but to "feel" another person's absence, his jarring inability to take joy in anything or to "feel" complete at any time, was that he was experiencing something otherwise known as…Yes, though he couldn't conscience the word in his mind, he felt a faint glimmering of what he had read that most banal of words – love – was supposed to "feel" like. The signs were all there: the sweats, the loss of appetite, the staring into aimless space, the shortness of breath and resultant emptiness in one's chest. Then again, he thought, this could just be angst. But, even there he had to admit to himself that what he felt was clearly different than any angst, because the present sensation had a specific magnetism, a definitive pull toward something outside of himself, a wanting to be whole. Perhaps his nihilism was just that, a fear of being left alone

within the boundlessness of an infinitely cold and forbidding night, left naked, afraid and truly unloved. It was therefore, nothing else but a longing for love whose abdication left one to face the corresponding dread of utter absence, the lack of a singular divinity, an all-encompassing divinity that was the source and object of all love. It hit him all at once like a punch in the stomach with the resultant nausea left in its wake. The mere thought revolted him. He decided conclusively that it had to be his heart, for even assuming some psychosomatic relationship between Dawn's absence and the strange contortions of his ailing muscle, the more probable and scientific explanation was his recent and sudden withdrawal from the drugs. He was now resolutely sure he had to see a doctor about his symptoms, otherwise he risked another stroke. Undoubtedly, his most likely immediate remedy was a heavy dose of Pepto-Bismol.

But, here amongst the revelers and hard drinkers at the Red Queen, who spent their time engaging in end of the world drinking games, Billy was partially sullen for an entirely different and more pressing reason. As Billy listened to the many disaster scenarios being portrayed on the television screen, he began to fret over the immediate consequences of the storm. He considered carefully the potential numbers of casualties that would doubtless occur, tabulating the probable number in his mind and then equating to each casualty a thickness of paperwork. He looked at the fools around him and counted them in this number: probable cause of death, alcohol poisoning followed by drowning. The papers and television networks had already run through the numbers of casualties from previous storms, in '57 forty-three people had been killed and in '34, a whopping one hundred and eighty seven. One hundred and eighty seven in the course of twenty-four hours! Would it have been possible? Forty-three would have been bad enough, but one hundred and eighty seven! If that many people had died, he would have been stuck doing paperwork for the next year! It seemed a particularly bad case of Schadenfreude on the part of the newscasters. As he began to sum up the sheer stacks of paper that the effort would require, his mind grew weary. He estimated that each soul would be worth a pound or two in paperweight. Not only would there be the death certificates, but there would be the notifications, the orders for burial, the removal notices, the certificates, the orders for medical examination and if god forbid, there was an inquest, the sheer paperweight would multiply (all told enough to weight his own soul to hell). He thought maybe the best course of action would be to resign ahead of time or even fake his own death. He had already been placed on standby, but given the chaotic state of affairs it appeared to be every man for himself. His contributions wouldn't be needed until after the event, anyway. It was while ruminating on these very important personal considerations that Billy's phone rang. When he picked up the line, the voice on the other end was unrecognizable. It sounded desperate. The mix of a bad line and the quick jumble of words was indecipherable. It wasn't until Billy had asked the other party to repeat themselves that he identified the voice as Poundstone's. Catching his breath, Poundstone simply said,

"It's Griffs. He's had a major stroke. Doesn't look good."

"Oh, shit," Billy replied, thinking to himself, so it has already begun, number one already notched on the list before a single tree branch had fallen. Could it be that they were already asking him to go into action prior to the man even being dead? It all seemed irregular. "And?" Billy inquired questioningly.

"Well, the mayor's already done called a state of emergency and there is a big meeting at the city hall. You need to get your ass over here as quickly as possible and I mean ASAP."

"Sure thing," Billy responded, the immediacy in Poundstone's voice was a barometer that said it all. Without allowing another word, he hung up the phone, paid his bill and went outside to find his way back home. As he instinctively looked up at the sky, the air quavered beneath the sheer weight of the blackish thunderheads. The clouds moiled as if the gods, twisting them in knots, wrung out the last bit of water onto the pallid asphalt. Only a little rain fell and despite the many warnings, the present conditions certainly didn't appear to portend the horror scenarios that were portrayed on television. When he began to drive as if to contradict his hope, the rain came down with increasing intensity to the point where it became almost impossible for the windshield wipers to clear away enough water for him to see the road in front of him. The gutters were already overflowing and what few cars there were on the street drove incredibly slowly, their ghostly figures seeming to sail across the submerged streets like motorized boats. The rain sounded like a million fingers drumming nervously on his windshield and roof. Billy remembered when he had originally made the drive down to Hokum so many years back. He drove through a snowstorm and given the lack of visibility, he imagined it wise to drive immediately behind an eighteen-wheeled truck as it was otherwise impossible to see the road before him. He drove behind the juggernaut for a great length of time and would have probably followed that truck over the brink of hell if it were headed in that direction. As he looked to the side of the highway, he saw a number of jackknifed hulks, turned over on their sides like dead carcasses. He drove like this for hours to the point where he began having trouble making out the truck's taillights even if they still glowed like dim coals a mere ten feet away from the windshield. Given the danger of the roads, he feared the truck would run off the road and he would then crash helplessly into its rear. He drove alone the entire night through what he envisioned as a great, impenetrable blizzard. However, he would later discover, that the truck's back wheels had thrown up so much snow that his headlights were completely caked and thus rendered powerless in the darkness. Additionally, these same tires acted like snow cannons, creating Billy's fictionalized blizzard. On pins and needles, unable to stop, he felt he had driven over a dark, frozen lake, whose ice could have given way at any time. When finally, out of necessity, he stopped at a gas station and discovered the reality, he saw that his only real danger was his own complete ignorance. He now felt himself to be in a similar situation. The news stations spoke as if Hokum and the surrounding cities would be wiped from the very face of the earth and all night prayer sessions had already been arranged amongst the local churches as some parochial zealot had proclaimed that the final days of earth had truly arrived. According to some local historians, many of the people who died in the previous hurricanes were people who perished because they refused to leave the city, either for religious reasons or because they were uninformed, infirm or all three. It was likely that the mayor would take no such chances this time and though people had already barricaded themselves inside a few of the churches, they would be forcefully removed.

When Billy finally arrived at the door to the city hall, they were all waiting for him. In the heavy rain, he had no time to look up at the words written atop the mantle of the great edifice that said "In God We Trust" in large gilded letters. The city hall was directly next to the building that Riley had used as a stage only weeks before. It was another large, antiqued monstrosity, made in red brick The original city hall had burned down in the last century and successive ones had either been blighted by hurricanes or irreparably flooded. It seemed Hokum didn't have much luck with city halls. The only structures in central Hokum that were bigger than the city hall and the sheriff's offices, were the cineplex and the city's numerous churches, which grew like mushrooms after each proverbial storm, each one progressively bigger than the last as if fortifying the center from the great wave of evil that emanated from the Lido. When he arrived at the steps of the great building, he already suspected something was amiss when several complete strangers in business suits quickly ushered him into the large auditorium, full of a number of law enforcement officers, city and county officials, news reporters, interested citizens and hordes of faces he had never seen before. At the front of the auditorium, standing on the large stage was the mayor. Billy was helped to his seat by no less than four people and placed on the fifth row next to Poundstone. The mayor was dressed in his normal habiliments, jeans and a brown corduroy jacket, but instead of his usual florid expression, his pallor was that of a carp's tum, his features drawn and his voice grave.

"...And so we find ourselves in this unfortunate position. As you know, Griffs had previously begun preparin' evacuation procedures and a number of forward thinkin' citizens have already taken it upon themselves to evacuate the city. I can't stress how grave the situation is. I don't want to cause a panic, but as I'm sure you've all seen and heard, the news stations are already estimatin' the potential casualties to be in the tens, even the hundreds. I don't want to stir up any bad memories, but some of us can probably still remember what happened to Hokum in 1957."

As Billy sat in his uncomfortable plastic seat, he heard the words and the numbers he least wanted to hear. Oh, that infernal year. Only to be outdone by 1934. He surrendered his face into the palms of his hands.

"I can't stress how important it is that we be prepared for this. We are going to have the whole world lookin' at us. Water levels are already risin' and there are reports of severe floodin' in several districts of Concrain and we are just beginnin' to hear reports of severe floodin' in Hokum. Extensive lootin' and lawlessness has been reported in a few of the coastal cities and it is expected the same trend will continue here as people begin to leave their homes in mass. Firefighters and police have already begun to put barricades on the river, but this has taken them away from their normal patrollin' duties. As a result, given the general level of panic, police here have already reported three cases of break-ins and one grocery store has already been ransacked. Things are startin' to turn down right disorderly and panic is beginnin' to set in. I can't stress enough to you people and I will say it till I'm blue in the face, please just remain calm. We will have this situation under control. We cannot give ourselves over to pandemonium. Hurricane Cassandra…"

For some reason, the thought of Dawn again entered Billy's mind. In an attempt to rid himself of it, he remembered, but still couldn't laugh at the familiar joke: "Women are like hurricanes, when they come they're wet and wild and when they leave they take the house and the car…" It was true, he considered. Very true. Returning his attention to the stage, the mayor's hurdy-gurdy-like droning welled up in his ears as so much water bubbling forth from the mouth of a flooded sewer.

"…Due to its rapid progress. Many cities were unprepared and we have precious little time to prepare ourselves. On top of this, we have the sad news just reported to me this mornin' that Sheriff Griffs, our dear friend and I'm sure you all know him well, who had been placed in charge of our preparations, has had a massive stroke. His present condition is unclear and our prayers go out to him and his family. However, in our present circumstances given our level of unpreparedness, it is important that we all go into action and take over the great work that Griffs began. I have already spoken to the Governor who is gravely concerned about the situation and we both agreed that we need to do everythin' possible to ensure the continued safety of our citizens. Therefore a forced evacuation will be held. I repeat, a forced evacuation will be held. But, we will get to those details in a minute. However, before any of this happens, the immediate need is to replace Sheriff Griffs. Normally, in this situation, his successor (cough) and though I'm sure you will understand that there is a great deal in flux and I am sorry and embarrassed to say that we've only gotten to figurin' it all out just before I came up here to speak to you on stage (cough)"

At this point, Tommy, the tall, well-built officer who had long been Griffs' unofficial deputy, stood up from his seat in the first row and walked toward the stage with his confident stride, his large jaw tilted upwards, brimming with all the self-importance still left in Hokum's imperiled world. The entire convocation turned towards him as he began to ascend the staircase that led to the stage. His every feature was imbued with consummate gravitas, his stern features unwavering before the dread prospect that awaited him, the assumption of the very mantle of power that he had always coveted as his own. The camera flashes began to flicker as he opened his mouth in an almost ceremonial fashion, "Hello, Mayor, I'm here and ready to do my duty. I am proud to assume Sheriff Griffs' duties as his appointed deputy."

As Tommy, the tall, would-be imperator approached with all the grandeur of destiny, the small statured mayor pulled down his reading glasses and arrested with a single glance his approach, "Not so fast, Tommy. Though that's what we may all have liked, legally that is not the way it's gonna be. I've consulted with the Governor and we've gone through the normal laws and procedures together (cough). Sheriff Griffs has been the sheriff so long that we've never even had to consider an instance like this. Well, as it turns out, by law, in the instance that the sheriff is unwillin' or incapable of performin' his duties (cough) in this event, his powers would normally devolve to the coroner's office."

Billy couldn't believe what he was hearing and neither could Poundstone who breathed in disbelief, "Dear God, so that's what all the fuss was about." He shook his head and buried his face in his hands. As a murmur of confusion began to spread throughout the audience, the mayor continued, "Quiet please. Can we have quiet please? What this means… what this means in simple terms is that Billy Rubino will be the city's sheriff until another can be elected. Therefore he will be placed in charge of the entire police force and the evacuation procedures." It was as if the entire room suddenly gave out one simultaneous gasp. In the split second it took most people to even remember who Billy Rubino was the auditorium was for an instant silent as one by one a number of faces flickered; soon, the transmission of discernable horror moved across the room as each person realized in turn who the name legally belonged to.

"You mean that buffoon who likes being on TV?" one angry citizen yelled out from the back of the auditorium in a shrill and angry voice. Billy didn't immediately recognize the woman, but he thought it might have been the very same woman whose husband he had mistaken as having died from an Ecstasy overdose. The murmurs of confusion continued to spread throughout the room as the congregation was overtaken by a transport of utter bewilderment.

Poundstone leaned over Billy's shoulder and said under his breath, "God help us all, but better the devil you know than the one you don't, I suppose. You finally done got what you wanted didn't ya?"

Billy, unable to respond, merely looked up at the stage as a number of worried looks turned in his direction. As the discontent evidently spread, mostly among the now obstreperous members of the police force, several people started to stand up including a number of people associated with the sheriff's office. They began shouting and seemed ready to mutiny. The mayor, for his part sensing things were getting out of control, pushed his hands downward in an attempt to calm the crowd. "Quiet please. Can we have some quiet please? Everythin' is under control. If you would just sit down and be quiet, we can go through all the details." When the mayor had finally managed to quell the audience and everyone was once again seated, he resumed his speech, "Billy, can you please come up here on stage?" Billy, unprepared and unsure of what to do, made the long walk up to the stage. As he walked up the staircase, trying as best he could not to trip on any single stair, he passed Tommy who gave him the evilest of eyes, despite his remaining frozen in shock. Furthermore, he could feel that every eye in the room was trained on him and as he looked out over the audience, he began to see amidst the blur of faces a number of flash bulbs twinkling in the background. The stairs squealed under his weight with a sound loader than thunder.

When he finally reached the stage and stood by the mayor, the city's top official whispered in this ear, "I hope you're ready for this you sonofabitch. I'll have you know that up to the very last minute I tried every damn thing short of an official declaration of secession to avoid this." Without missing a beat, the mayor turned and smiled at the audience. "This is truly an unprecedented event in Hokum's history and I can't stress how important it is that we have strong leadership at this crucial juncture. Although we might all wish Sheriff Griffs were here to lead us through this time of tribulation and turmoil, I can honestly say (havin' worked with him several times in the past) I have every confidence in Billy's ability to do the job and save our little city on a hill. And I can assure you that Billy will ONLY be actin' under my constant supervision, of course. Now, there are a number of challenges to be met and we have to make sure the city doesn't descend into utter chaos. Thus, by the power vested in me by the governor of this state, I proclaim Billy Rubino the new sheriff with full powers over law enforcement, effective immediately." He then looked Billy straight in the eyes, continuing to speak into the microphone, "A lot of power and responsibility comes with this position, especially at a time like this and the lives of an entire city are at stake. We will not let chaos and lawlessness continue to descend upon Hokum at this most unexpected crossroads. Law and order needs to be established. Billy Rubino, the city of Hokum is in your hands. Anythin' you'd like to say?"

The mayor moved to one side giving Billy the podium. As he turned toward the sea of blank faces, the television reporters had already begun to move in for their close-ups and he could hear the mechanical winding of their lenses as several microphones and television cameras were pointed at his astonished visage. Billy could think of nothing else to do than to tap gently on the microphone, "Ahhh...can you hear me?" A sudden hiss, then the loud, ringing of reverb twisted everyone's features. A smile crossed Billy's face. His moment had finally arrived and he wasn't going to let it pass. When Billy began to speak, he began with a shout. He sounded like a great Baptist minister, rousing his flock with a hoarse voice drawn through the very coals of hell,

"We're all gonna die." The entire audience looked at him in disbelief, their mouths dropping open. As he continued, he spoke with vehemence and a terrible aspect. His eyes flashed with mortal anger as he seemed to draw thunder from his very lungs, "Yes, indeed, we're all gonna die." The mayor turned to look at Billy with a mix of shock and sheer anger on his face, his visage again returning to its normal reddish pallor. At that moment, he appeared ready right then and there to grab the microphone from Billy's mouth. Undeterred, Billy continued, "But, we are not going to die today. No, sir, today isn't a day for anyone to die. Because I, Billy Rubino, am going to fight with my life to protect every last citizen of Hokum. Yes, I am going to fight against that great silent shadow of death, just as I have always done. Before today, I have been the voice of the dead, the voice of those who could not speak for themselves. But today, I am going to fight for those still living even if it means that I must make the ultimate sacrifice. Because, what Hokum needs now is a hero. No, in fact it needs several heroes. What is a hero, but someone who can look deep within himself? Can look into his deepest heart and cast aside every quality in himself that is human, frail and weak and become more than human, more than the sum of his parts. Only then can he embody an ideal and lead others to embody that very same ideal. And what ideal are we fighting for this afternoon? All the ideals that make Hokum a great city, a city to aspire to. We are here to do more than save the buildings, the monuments, the houses, we are here to save the city that is embodied by each and every one of its citizens. We are here to preserve the life of the city, not to see its demise. We are here to preserve the inheritance that is in all of us. We cannot be afraid. Hokum has survived storms before and come through stronger and better than ever. We are here this afternoon to save Hokum yet again and we all need to rise as one. We all need to get up, my brothers and sisters and stand up to the occasion. And I, more than anyone else, feel privileged to be able to have the opportunity to be a leader amongst many leaders here today and I hope you do too. Now, while some here thought it best to lead me up to this great stage with little if no preparation, probably because they might have assumed I would embarrass myself, I am here to tell you all that I do not plan to back down. I do not plan to be swayed. I do not intend to let Hokum fall into the hands of distress and disorder. But I cannot do it myself. I will need each and every one of you to be by my side so that we can save every last citizen of Hokum. I promise you, we shall overcome! We shall overcome! So with that, I beg all of you to let me, let us all, get to work on this great task." Billy's peroration had not only roused the entire crowd to its feet, but induced a spontaneous and sudden enthusiasm, manifesting itself in a wild round of thunderous applause among shouts of approbation. Even the sheriff's officers had to rise and clap at this point. "Yes, let us rise together as one." Billy waited for the crowd to settle down a little from their fervent clapping and whistling. "And one final thing. Before you go, I want to let you know that I will of course be happy to speak at any time to the press to make sure that every last person is aware of the latest details. I am at your service. Thank you very much." The entire audience continued their standing ovation. For several seconds, Billy stood in glory, receiving each new round of applause as the mayor, not to be outdone, tried to regain the podium in an attempt to have the last word, but it was too late. Billy had already begun to descend the stairs where he was immediately engulfed by a crush of television reporters and well-wishers.

For the next five hours, Billy was locked in continual meetings with the sheriff's office, the fire department, the mayor and even had a chance to speak to the state's Governor. Many were surprised to find that Billy actually managed to take over his role with great facility and a seemingly unflappable energy. In meetings he was attentive, assured and was surprisingly prompt in making critical decisions after hearing opinions from a number of disparate parties. He delegated tasks and stood up firmly to anyone who questioned his authority. Many couldn't believe that it was the same foolish Billy they had always known and wondered whether he had indeed been possessed by an alien spirit. When the time for action came, he was brisk in overseeing the various police activities that were required: setting up several evacuation points, organizing the clearing of roads, assisting in the placing of sandbags to barricade against the river. He of course never missed a chance to provide the local and national news stations with minute by minute updates on the situation, explaining in great detail the diverse difficulties he had to face and would no doubt overcome. The

news stations appreciated his dramatic flair and were keen
to note his bravery and his overwhelming humanity. He had
already been approached for several television appearances
and even a book deal, provided everything worked out. Billy
hadn't stopped for fourteen hours straight and without many
noticing it, one day passed quickly into the early hours of
another. All the time, he could be heard humming to himself
and in front of the cameras the tune he now recognized as one
of Bach's Cantatas,

> 'Es bricht alsdann der letzte Feind herein
> Und will den Trost von unsern Herzen'

In the early morning hours, over the black ridge of the Maralah
Mountains, a strange zodiacal light arose. The hurricane which
was meant to touch ground in Hokum within the next eight
to ten hours, loomed like a lord's shadow across the threshold
of his lowliest servant. Billy, having set a number of the main
initiatives into action, had time to briefly collect himself in
one of the tents of the main evacuation point. He considered
making a clandestine trip to the Red Queen for a drink or
perhaps to his house for a snort of cocaine, but decided that
with all the press around, it would be impossible. Outside of
the tent, three national news vans were parked, each sending
minute by minute updates up toward the stratosphere. He
was surprised to find to what extent he had lost track of time,
it was only nine in the morning and the Red Queen wouldn't
open in theory for another three hours. Suddenly, Billy's
phone rang, something that had previously made him anxious
given that it always seemed to portend bad news. When he
picked up the phone, he heard a faint, indistinguishable voice
on the other end. The voice was extremely muffled. It almost

sounded as if somebody was speaking through a heavy piece of fabric. On the other end, he heard a slow, deliberate voice, "Billy, this is Riley. I have Dawn."

Between the loud rush of air and the edges of tarpaulins that snapped in the wind, Billy couldn't discern what the mysterious voice was trying to say despite his putting his fingers over his free ear in a vain effort to foil the phone's dark crepitations. Desperately tired and unable to understand, he replied with some annoyance in his voice, "What? What did you say?"

"This is Riley. I have Dawn in my house. I will kill her."

Billy, still uncertain of what was said, not trusting his own ears, asked once more, "What? Riley, you say? Who do you have?"

"Dawn in my house. I will kill her. Come now."

"What? Why? Why would you do that? She has nothing..."

The voice on the other end simply hung up. Billy, despite his exhaustion suddenly found himself in a profound quandary. For the first time in several hours, he wasn't sure of what to do. He couldn't abandon his duties, yet he couldn't simply let Riley kill the poor girl. He wondered how Riley had even managed to find Dawn when he wasn't able to do so himself. Regardless, why would Riley do a thing like that, now? As crazy as he was, even he had to recognize there wasn't much time until the hurricane would strike them down. Fortunately, the main evacuation points were to the north of town, furthest away from the river, which had already begun to overflow. Incidentally, the northern part of town, which stood at the foot of the Natahawa Hills were also the highest in elevation so they could continue to evacuate people until the very last minute as the river was unlikely to reach that point. He knew it would take twenty minutes from where he was to reach Riley's house if he drove quickly. The evacuation routes had avoided the mountains so there would be little traffic. Billy had no time to spare. He ran out of the tent and quickly located Poundstone who had stood by his side from the beginning.

"Listen, Poundstone, can you get someone to take over from here?"

"What? Why? What's goin' on?" Poundstone looked at him with a concerned voice.

"Riley just called me and told me he has Dawn up at his house. He said he's gonna kill her unless I go up there. I need to go up there now."

"For Lord's sake, Riley? Well if that crazy ol' fool doesn't choose the best times…You sure he ain't jus' pullin' your leg after seein' yous on TV?"

"Maybe so, but I can't take the chance. I have to make sure."

Poundstone patted him on the shoulder, "Yep, that's probably right. No problem, we can take over from here."

As Billy turned to leave, Poundstone grabbed him by the shoulder. "Listen, you really impressed me here today. I would have never have thought. A lot of people are goin' to owe their lives to you today."

Billy turned and looked him in the eye, "Yeah, well, I'm just trying to save myself the paperwork."

Billy made his way to his car and began to make his furious way up to the house. Under normal conditions, he would have been reluctant to leave the television crews behind, but this time he sprang into action without thinking. Was it true that Dawn had had some truly powerful effect over him? At the mere mention of her name, he felt a flutter in his chest. It couldn't be, he again decided. It had to be something else. After all, here was his opportunity to once again be a crusading hero. As he started driving, he regretted not bringing at least one of the news stations with him. He thought about Larry Campbell and what he would have done in a similar situation. His visions of general fame were finally coming true. This was the first step. Riley was an old drunk and certainly could be of no danger to him: half crazy, all he needed to do was talk him down. Furthermore, it was unlikely that Riley even had Dawn as she had left town long ago. As Billy drove up the side of the mountain he peered down at Hokum as Breugel might and for the first time saw his true nemesis first hand, the giant storm cloud that now took over the entire sky. He watched as that great dumb thing made its imperceptible approach toward Hokum, threatening to consume it within its still undefined blankness. In its vastness it resembled some elemental destroyer, a primordial creature, the serial wrecker of civilization. He regarded it as it simply hung there, hung stupidly there, suspended from a dark sky, giving out on occasion monosyllabic grunts; it hung in the deep distance like a great lion's mane jellyfish, its procellous tentacles falling down over the ground as it slowly rotated, a heedless, unfeeling, unstoppable force. It looked like the very image of doom itself. It was the physical manifestation of his secret nihilism. It knew nothing, it could say nothing, yet he had to respect it and run before it towards the light. He then thought of the image of Dawn as she stood there staring out of their room, how she had kissed him near the waterfall (hadn't the birds tweeted, the maidens sang in their gossamer threads?). He then imagined the terror in her eyes in front of a creature so low as Riley. He felt like an actor, a puppet impelled by the slender cords of his own sense of the dramatic. His heart began to flutter. Dear Lord, he thought, let me not have a stroke at the very moment of my ascension. All at once came the cymbal clash of Sigurd Jorsalfar's, *Norronafoket*, the impetuous *thrum-thrum* of his heartbeat…Grieg never failed to find the right moment. A sudden erethism rose in him and he felt like his entire being had become focused in a single, tiny point as if at the nib of a pen, as if with that instrument, he was to draw his destiny in large letters with naught but a slender facility. Before him, he saw painted in sheer light across the darkening sky a scene, one that had played out before him a hundred different times through a hundred different lives all passed through in the same high fidelity. For him, it was Prime Time. He pressed the pedal of the accelerator to drive further thought out of his head. He had to preserve his future and his legacy. The car couldn't go fast enough.

When he arrived at Riley's house it looked to be deserted. The rain was falling over the roof like a waterfall, though it was still less intense than in the city below. He was afraid his car would get stuck in the mud so he parked it along the road and ran a good distance toward the house. By the time he arrived to the door, he was absolutely soaked. He called several times from the outside but there was no reply. Thus, he decided he would knock down the door if need be. However, he found it unlocked and pushed it open with ease. As he took a step inside he suddenly felt a sharp pain in the back of his head. Before he could turn around, he felt another hard blow in the same spot. Instinctively, he fell to the ground as an intense pain and a dull ringing began to ramify throughout the back of his head. As he writhed on the ground, he tried to turn to look at his assailant, but before he was able, he felt a hand cover his face with a dirty cloth that stank with a heavy, chemical odor. Soon his eyes went black and Billy lost consciousness. Over his now listless body stood Basyli in triumph, wearing a small, woolen sack over his head, holding a baseball bat and a rag soaked in homemade chloroform.

When Basyli had finally left the jailhouse just over two weeks ago, he had spent the time meticulously planning Billy's downfall. Not able to convince anybody of the truth behind Billy's existence, he had been forced to take matters into his own hand. While still in the jail cell, he had overheard the conversation between Billy and the policeman concerning the mysterious Riley character and what he thought to be the object of Billy's affections, Dawn. After days of careful consideration and a fortunate hurricane to clear the way, he put two and two together and came up with a plan. Right when the news stations began reporting the hurricane, Basyli went into action. First, with the $44.38 Billy had given him, he had bought exactly four items: bleach, acetone, ice and a glass container. He used these to make chloroform. He had considered sending Billy a letter laced with ricin and had even gone so far as to locate the ingredients, but decided the chances of the plan actually working were probably slim to none. Thus, once settling on chloroform, he soaked a rag in the deadly liquid and stored the combination in a small thermos he had found in the garbage. He then made the long walk up to Riley's house and waiting, watched the family as they went about their business. When the mandatory evacuations occurred as he knew they would, he watched as the hurried family of four left their house and were picked up by a police van. He then used the family's phone to call Billy, trying his best to hide his accent and saying as little as he could in order to impersonate a man he had never met.

As he stood there, staring down at Billy, he now needed to decide how he would finish him off. Mumbling to himself various things about Moloch, Beelzebub and the devil, he looked around the messy, dilapidated house for the closest instrument he could find to kill him. The house was extremely dusty and filled with an amazing variety of things, clearly the product of a hoarder. The first object he found with potential was a corkscrew, which he instantly discarded as useless. He then found a pair of scissors, which also seemed inappropriate for his purpose. After which he discovered a small hammer. As he gripped its weight in his hand he considered that the task would take several blows to the head and produce a great degree of blood. No, it simply wouldn't do. In a second he found a small kitchen knife, just as bad, he thought to himself. He searched around again and found a bigger knife. No, it wouldn't do either. Too much stabbing and cutting he concluded. After five minutes searching around the back of the house, he came back with an axe. He again decided it would also be far too messy. Finally, under one of the beds in the main bedroom, he found a loaded gun. It would have to do.

Again he found himself standing over Billy with the loaded gun trembling in his hands. Above him, the tin roof rang like thunder in his head as the rain crashed upon it with increasing intensity. At several points, large drops of water fell through the ceiling into small, preplaced buckets all nearing their brim in fullness. He just couldn't do it. He dropped the gun on the floor. He mumbled over and over to himself, "I am weak. *Kruk krukowi oka nie...kruk krukowi...*I cannot do. I cannot." There was no other way, he simply had to find a way to kill Billy in a manner that wouldn't involve him either using his own hands or witnessing the act all together. Since his youth and due largely to the atrocities he had experienced with his then unprepared eyes, he couldn't bear the sight of blood. It made him sick as he remembered the ashen bodies that lay strewn around a spring wood full of young yew trees, the carcasses of horses, men and women, even children as they rotted amongst the mulch of dead leaves, the horrible smells of creosote, turpentine and rot, the wailing, the flies, the maggots, the prayers that rose into the acrid, smoked filled air, the vacuous eyes that stared into the emptiest of spaces, the red, red blood that was everywhere and covered everything, the death, the death and the lack, the utter lack of any perceivable God. It was all too much. Basyli had to find another way. He began looking around the house one last time and finally, after great effort, managed to find what he was looking for: a large can of kerosene. He took the can and poured out its contents at various points throughout a number of the rooms. He then put the chloroformed rag once more to Billy's face as his unconscious body had started again to groan. Finally, Basyli lit the match in the farthest away room and didn't wait to watch as the house began to go up in flames. Avoiding at all costs looking toward the house, he immediately jumped into Billy's car and drove away down the side of the hill.

Dawn had finally arrived to the evacuation point and began looking desperately for Billy. She had been staying with a distant family friend and had barely left the house in the last two weeks, trying fiercely, but ultimately unsuccessfully to rid her mind of Billy. When she saw him on the news, her heart began to quaver and she again pined for him, ready to forgive him everything. She hated herself for it, but she was a hopeless case and could do nothing else. It took everything she had in her soul not to immediately run to the center of town and fall into his arms. The only thing that stopped her was the realization that he was now in a position of great importance and would have no time for her pitiful apologies. She couldn't bear the thought of him rejecting her, of him looking at her with those pitiless eyes as she tried her best to make him understand how she felt. The previous two weeks she'd spent recriminating herself for her actions, thinking that perhaps she had been unfair with Billy, that perhaps he was actually attempting to do right by her in his clumsy attempts to reunite her with her father. After all, how could he be expected to understand the pain, the regret, the depth of resentment she bore toward her parents? Perhaps her ability to hate them, people she hadn't even met, was also showing signs of fade. What right did she have to loathe people who had made mistakes just like herself, mistakes of the blood and bone, which she also carried inside herself like some hidden piece of malware, some little subroutine of inevitability? After all, a family in whatever variety of its heterodox manifestations is nothing more than the deliberate recurrence of history. It was now evident even to her that by blaming her parents for her own mistakes, that by using the excuse of their tarred past, blackened by an even darker absence she had granted herself some temporary relief, some ability to accept herself amidst the emptiness left by their intangibility. However, she had lately begun to realize that ultimately she was the only one who could answer for her actions and thus her more recent circumstances. Though they were not there to stop her, to stay her hand in anything, she could also have done better by them. In this culture of blame, where parents are in many cases a novelty, their story if nothing else should have been a warning, a lesson not an invitation. Though she may not have liked to admit it to herself, she was part of them and they of her: history is carried in one's blood, forward and backward, its tiny signals pulsing through us as through that crude red ribbon by which mythical Chinese doctors can read a royal concubine's failing heartbeat like a cardiogram: blood measuring blood, and so she now felt that in similar circumstances, she may have done exactly what her parents had done. She was as flawed as they were and just as confused. Only by freeing herself of this hatred of them, could she even begin to love herself again. In any regard, she no longer cared who was right or wrong, she simply wanted him back. She avoided as long as possible the inevitability of making her way to the evacuation point, fearing that she would run into him. Now that she had arrived and felt his rather anodyne halo, she couldn't resist and looked everywhere for him. However, no one knew where he was, a few were only able to say that he had been there just minutes before. Suddenly, she saw a familiar face and recognized it as the man who had questioned her in the hospital, Poundstone. She immediately ran up to him and tapped him on his shoulder. When he turned around she was shocked as he was. He shouted in disbelief as he grabbed her around both arms, "What the blast are you doin' here?"

Not comprehending, she replied in confusion, "What do you mean? I'm looking for Billy."

"Well he's been lookin' for you! He literally just left five minutes ago. Riley called and said he had you up at his place."

"What? Who is Riley?"

"Riley lives up in the hills over up the road there. Aw, shit, that must mean Riley was pullin' his leg after all. Don't worry, I'll try and call him." After several attempts and not getting through, Poundstone gave up.

"Well, I can't get through. I guess Billy will just have to sort it out himself."

Dawn, already anxious, was beginning to get frantic, a bad feeling aroused in her stomach. "Don't you think he might be in danger?"

"I wouldn't worry. Riley's just crazy. He won't do Billy any harm."

"Are you sure?" Dawn said on the verge of tears.

Poundstone took her again by both arms. "Listen, Billy is a big boy, he can handle himself."

"But, can't you take me up there? Just help me to make sure?"

"Listen, little lady. As much as I'd like to, I can't leave here. We gotta get these people evacuated. That storm's a comin' through."

"But we can't just leave him…"

"Sorry mam, we can't do much. Like I said, Billy's a big boy, he can handle himself."

Dawn was at her wits end as to what to do. As Poundstone turned again to the two officers who were awaiting his instructions, she could feel herself sinking once again in the torrent. Her knees grew weak. As she closed her eyes, she recalled the prick of the needle, the gentle oblivion, the green void that swirled around her, embracing her in a final kiss. She had to pull herself back to the surface. She opened her eyes and saw the wide sky above as it poured rain through her already damp hair. Once more, she breathed in the thick, humid atmosphere and instantly the spell of paralysis was broken. She finally knew what she had to do. She picked out a torn piece of paper from her purse. She dialed the scrawled numbers on the surface and when someone picked up from the other end, she spoke softly, her voice choked with tears, "Dad…"

As Dawn spoke on the phone to her father, the last lines of people hovered around the evacuation point. The ragged crowd was composed of the elderly, the poor, the infirm – all huddled under blankets and parkas that the volunteers handed out. There were people wearing florescent orange vests and shouting in megaphones in an attempt to corral the sick, worried and frightened citizens of Hokum into makeshift lines. The winds had picked up considerably and several of the temporary tents had already blown away. The dreaded hurricane would arrive on the shores of Hokum in a matter of hours. The long, morose line of cars made their way up toward the highway that ran west under the shadow of the mountains. As crowds entered the buses, one by one, they shivered, not daring to look back at the surroundings they weren't quite sure they would ever see again. The volunteers were passing out cups of coffee, blankets, trying as best they could to attend to the needs of the remaining townsfolk. Suddenly, the group of evacuees' attention was diverted by a truly singular sight: it started out in a low moan, a haunting dirge that came from far away. Then finally, as they looked down one of the streets adjacent to the square, they saw the great mass of singers, a group of black churchgoers who had been crooning in low tones as they swayed gently from side to side as if they were possessed by some trance. The low moans that comprised the song built and built until the words became distinguishable,
"Way down in Egypt Land
Tell all Pharaohs to
Let My People Go!
When Israel was in Egypt land...
Let My People Go!
Oppressed so hard they could not stand..."

They marched in two long rows, wearing white robes and holding large black umbrellas as they walked. As they made their way slowly toward the evacuation point, the intrepid runner, dressed in his usual spandex attire, ran by them, off into the distance, seemingly heedless of anything that was going on.

When Dawn's father picked up the phone, he couldn't believe it. He had only heard his daughter's voice once in his entire life and on that occasion she had barely spoken to him. Now, when he heard her voice again, it froze him and he almost fell to the floor as if he had been hit in the chest. When his phone had rung, he was waist-deep in water, wading through the hallways of a flooded house, salvaging various appliances and minor valuables out the rainwater, being careful to leave anything behind of considerable worth or sentimental value. Early that morning, he had driven from his far away home, toward Hokum's center, targeting an area he heard had been flooded early on. From the news stations, he had gathered that one of the river's many tributaries had overrun the levee and flooded a large number of houses, which had been left abandoned for two full days. Seeing opportunity where others saw fear, he used the storm's cover not only to loot the riverfront buildings, but also some of the houses closer to the center of town. Though it had become far too dangerous to continue his work at the houses nearer the riverside, the forced evacuations had given him plenty of opportunity in various places all around the city. All he had to do was to avoid the police, who seemed to have enough on their hands not to worry about him. He would return once again after the storm had passed over, but the best and safest time to raid the houses was before people had gotten a chance to return. His truck was already full of a number of items and he was going to make his last trip before the storm hit the town's center. He reasoned that people would never need most of the stuff anyway, especially once the storm had time to ruin them. When Dawn spoke to him on the phone, she simply told him she needed him and asked him to drive to the center of town as quickly as possible where he could find her near the evacuation point. Without thinking, Reggie ran out of the house and into his truck. He drove at a furious pace putting himself in a great deal of danger. It took him fifteen minutes to arrive through the deserted streets and find where she was. He realized he risked a great deal driving his truckload of stolen property right into the center of police operations, but he didn't care. They had prearranged a place to meet, which was a little ways away from the chaos of the evacuation point. The rain was so intense that he could barely see out of his windows. Finally finding her, she jumped into the truck and told him to drive into the mountains. She was soaking wet and didn't even give her father the slightest chance to look her over. She had a map in her hands given to her by one of the officers and was already aware of where Riley's house was. She told her father to drive as fast as he could, that her life depended upon it.

Fortunately for Dawn, the great cavalcade of cars was attempting to avoid the mountain passes completely so they circumvented traffic quite easily, taking the very same path Billy had previously taken up the mountain. It took them not more than twenty minutes to drive up through the hills and they soon found the indicated road, given that it that was one of the few in the area. As before, the rain in the hills wasn't nearly as intense as that carried in large perpendicular sheets throughout the heart of Hokum. As they drove up the mountain, they saw what looked to be Billy's car coming in the opposite direction at great velocity. It sped by so quickly and drove so violently, it almost knocked them off the road and they could feel the wheels beneath them begin to hydroplane. In the heavy rains, Dawn couldn't be sure it was actually his car so they drove on. As soon as they skidded into a muddy driveway still some distance from Riley's house, Dawn could see the black smoke billowing forth from one of the house's back windows. Instantly, she knew something was wrong. For some reason she couldn't explain to herself, she knew for certain that Billy was trapped inside the house. Dawn yelled for her father to stop the car. Once he had come to a sudden stop, she immediately jumped out of the passenger seat and began to sprint as fast as she could toward the house. Her father went on to park his truck, but once he saw the direction to which she was running he soon stopped again, yelling after her, trying to get her to stop. Suddenly Dawn heard another shout to her right as a haggard, muddy figure emerged from the woods, holding what appeared to be a double gauge Winchester rifle. It was none other than Riley and he looked as if he was drunk, barely able to walk in a straight line. He was howling in the rain that had begun to come down at a furious pace. The loud peels of thunder echoed against the sides of the mountains, through the ravines and down into the deepest depths of the caves. The rain pelted everything so hard that its large drops stung the skin of the two strangers like hornets. The weather was unseasonably warm and Riley, who wore a pair of jeans and a torn white shirt was completely soaked through to the point where she could see the color and the contour of his pinkish body which was pasted to his ragged fabric. He shouted at her as he dragged the gun behind him, walking in a hunched over fashion,

"Hey, what you doin' here? You done set my house on fire. Is that what yous done did?"

Dawn, not knowing who this man was, but seeing the man's wild eyes and the gun upon which he now leaned, assumed it must be Riley. "No, I had nothing to do with it. Are...are you Riley? Did you put Billy in there?"

"Billy? How do ya know Billy?"

"I'm...I'm his girlfriend."

"What?" Riley shouted, trying to straighten himself. His red hair was completely matted against his skull, his long red beard hung low as small rivulets of water poured through its ragged curls. "Did Billy send you here to burn down my house? That bastard. I'm gonna kill him and I'm gonna kill you."

"But...but why? What has he done?"

His eyes were livid with rage and it took him a great amount of effort to straighten himself and point the gun in her general direction. Without warning, he then inclined his head toward the sky and spoke to an invisible presence, "What? What is that you say? Shut up you. Shut up, I'm not listenin' now." He then turned back to Dawn. "Well girlfriend, you finnin' to die 'cause he done took somethin' from me and I'm fixin' to take somethin' from him."

"But...but...I don't understand," Dawn screamed, doubling over in her anguish to be heard through the thundering deluge. Her eyes stung with tears, she didn't attempt to move out of the way even as Riley steadied the gun towards her head. Just as he pulled the trigger, Reggie who had been running after Dawn, pushed his pleading daughter out of the way. Riley, falling over as he shot, managed to hit Reggie square in shoulder. Reggie subsequently fell into the mud and Dawn, looking into her father's pain-stricken face, screamed, "Oh my, gosh." As she bent over him, he looked her straight in the eyes for the second time in his life and told her in a strained voice to run. She instinctively stood up, turned toward the house and ran as best she could toward the front door. Riley, slowly getting himself off of the ground, began to run after her holding the shotgun in her general direction. While he ran, he tried to shoot her again, but missed, hitting one of the posts of the front porch. He would need to reload. Dawn made the stairway and ran into the burning house, whose inferno was fighting mightily against the rain. As she entered, she saw great billows of red and black flame coming from the ceiling and Billy lying on the floor motionless with a gun next to him. She picked it up.

Suddenly, having reloaded his gun, Riley came through the door. She closed her eyes and fired. Riley toppled to the floor. A bullet had pierced his throat. Splayed on the floor, his arms moved in spasms as he tried to clutch his neck, desperately attempting to breathe. The blood spurted from his throat as his windpipe gave out a horrible wheezing sound. Finally, his mouth filled with dark blood as he began to drown, gurgling up thick clots of gore. When the panic faded and a profound slowness overtook him, his pupils turned backward into his head. In a matter of seconds it would be over. It was clear he was going to die. Reggie came in seconds after Riley and stopped in the entryway, gripping his shoulder, which was now hemorrhaging considerably. He stared in shock, first at Dawn who sat on her knees still gripping the gun as she cried, then he looked down to see Riley's last gasps as he died there before his feet. Dawn soon dropped the gun. She then crawled toward Billy's motionless body. The smoke had begun to get to her and she coughed profusely as she turned over his body, trying to search his face for signs of life. She held his face between her hands as her eyes burned with a combination of smoke and tears. She couldn't believe it. It seemed as if they had arrived too late.

Meanwhile, Basyli arrived to the evacuation point in a tumult of noise. His car skidded as it jumped the curb into a grass island in the middle of the road. As the final group of evacuees were entering the large bus, they turned in shock toward the source of the noise. Basyli emerged from the car, unscathed and shouted, waving his hands triumphantly, "I have killed him. I have killed the devil. I have saved city and all people." Due to the strong winds and the heavy rain, the people in the bus couldn't hear at all what he said. They only saw this poor man wildly gesticulating amidst the whistling winds, the thunder crashing down upon their ears, the sound of the broken tents popping in the air like fireworks. They signaled him to come over but he just kept shouting while fighting the gales as they pitched him to and fro. After several minutes, they gave him up as crazy and left him there by himself to find his destiny at the fatefate of the winds. As the bus slowly drove off, Basyli kept shouting, "Why you won't listen? Why you won't listen? I have killed him. I have saved you. I have saved the city. *Uwaga. Stary pies szczeka.* I am still alive. I am still alive."

10

"There will always be a Meersman."

After several hours, when Billy finally came to, he was disoriented and had no idea where he was. At first his vision was a blur and his eyes stung. He saw a number of bleary colors, daubs of hazy light that resembled flowers, perhaps balloons. He couldn't be sure and had to look toward the ceiling to regain his orientation. Then, finally able to focus on a point in the ceiling, he looked around him and saw all the equipment one would normally see in a hospital. Everything was shimmering with a hazy patina. He felt a dull pain in the back of his head and when he touched what he thought was going to be his hair, he felt the soft gauze that bandaged his skull. There was a muffled ringing in his ears as if the tinniest of pitchforks had been struck, the tinny sound was like something one might hear upon lying at the bottom of a swimming pool. He soon realized that he was in a hospital bed. To his right, sitting in a chair before a large window, he saw the hunched image of Dawn quietly reading a magazine. When she noticed him moving, she instantly came over to him, a big smile on her face. She said in a soft, reassuring voice, putting her face right up to his,

"Hey, hey. You are finally awake."

"What? Where am I?"

"You are in the hospital."

"What am I doing here?"

"Oh, it must have been the sedation they put you under."

"The last thing I remember was being in Riley's house and then I can't remember much after that." Billy felt slightly groggy, but as he shook his head, his awareness quickly returned and the sounds around him were restored to their proper volume and fidelity.

"Yep, you almost died there too. Riley tried to kill you. Burned down his own house. Why don't you try to relax and I can tell you all about it later."

"What? Burned down his house?"

"Yep, shot my dad too, but don't worry, I killed him."

Billy looked at her questioningly.

Dawn smiled and cocked her head to one side, "Yep, I'm the product of violence I guess."

"Indeed, so it seems."

"Well, it meant that we managed to pull you outta the house just before the ceiling came in. A minute later and you would have been ashes like that lunatic who tried to kill you. See, didn't I tell you I was here to save you?"

Billy, now recalling what had happened at the lake, asked in a confused voice, "But you left. I thought you were gone for good."

Dawn laughed and kissed him on the lips. Then she sat back in her seat.

"Well, I thought I was too, but then I got to thinking. Maybe, just maybe, you ain't the devil. And maybe – and I'm not completely convinced yet – there was something to what you said after all. Maybe you did find my father because you cared for me. I guess it sorta was a romantic thing to do."

"And maybe, just maybe you are a crack junkie after all."

Dawn laughed innocently. "That may be true, but given all the stuff they've been giving you. You might also qualify."

Billy suddenly felt a wave of horror swell up within him. His eyes opened in panic, "And the hurricane? How about that?"

"It's all over with, passed over last night and yesterday."

"How many casualties?"

"A lot. Early numbers, but they think it could be as many as twenty or thirty."

Billy's head fell back into the pillow and he covered his face. He could feel the paperweight weighing against his soul, compressing his chest so he couldn't breathe.

"Hey, don't take it so hard. I know it's a lot and it's awful for the families, but..."

Billy could no longer hear and could only think of the mountains of paperwork that would be left for him. It certainly could have been a lot worse, but thirty was still a large number. "Shit," Billy said rather involuntarily, only meaning to say it to himself.

"Hey, don't get so down on yourself. I mean everyone recognized the great work you did and loads of people have said the number would have been a lot higher if it wasn't for you. People are already calling you a hero. Saying you should be the next sheriff if not the mayor."

At this point Billy perked up, sitting straight up in his bed. He couldn't believe his ears. "Really?"

"Yes, indeed. Even now you'd be happy to know there are a number of television networks outside waiting for you. Some of them even international."

"Really?" Billy's voice picked up into an even higher register, thinking it impossible that he could be so flattered by reality. Billy looked over to the end of his bed and saw a dark figure who he immediately recognized as Dawn's father. Dawn instantly understood his questioning look as he looked between them both in repeated succession.

She laughed softly. "Oh yes and my dad's here."

The father, surrounded by a large number of balloons and flowers, stood up slightly from his seat and waved with his good arm, nodding his head with a sheepish smile.

"And don't worry, I plan to tell them all about how you brought us two together again."

Billy smiled and put his head back in the pillow. He tried to get out of bed, but they wouldn't allow him for at least another twenty-four hours. Due to smoke inhalation, his throat and lungs felt as if he had spent the night swallowing sandpaper. He indulged the following days reading through a number of cards left by well-wishers. One particular envelope had nothing written on the outside. When he opened it, he found a yellow note on which was written:

> we can regard our life as a uselessly disturbing episode in the blissful repose of nothingness.
> – schopenhauer.
>
> get well soon.
> – the warden.

The hospital hadn't allowed in any press and he was eager to address his public. When he was finally permitted, it couldn't have been too soon. He quickly dressed himself with the help of Dawn, wearing his nicest suit and even putting on a tie. He opened the front door of the hospital to a melee of light. The air was cold, but the sky was a perfect azure, showing no sign of what had transpired just forty-eight hours before.

Amid its apricity, the sun dropped in trinkets verses from Olav Trygvason's '*Giv Alle Guder Gammens*', orisons of praise filled his heart and his ears. Prior to engaging his eyes, he heard a confusion of voices beneath him and he was shocked to see the sheer mass of news people who had crowded the hospital's front stairs. There must have been fifty people (a hundred even) with their cameras, their microphones and their confused fray of questions. They had selected their hero of the day and for Billy, it meant he was living out his fantasy.

For the next twenty minutes, he addressed the barrage of queries, some serious, some ridiculous, some flippant. He spoke in serious tones, telling the media over and over again that his present condition was of no concern, that what was most important was the citizens of Hokum and that he wanted nothing more than to survey the wreckage and begin the cleanup process at once. The news stations couldn't get enough and they followed him through the city from which the floodwaters had just begun to recede. In many places, the city was still underwater and one could see rivers were there once were streets. Mud covered almost everything and the wind had pulled down trees, roofs and toppled cars. At points, the waterlogged city was almost unrecognizable. No matter to what degree the people wanted to will the water away, it simply sat there in mute silence, unwilling to move, knowing full well it shouldn't be there, but not caring much what people thought or did. Its presence filled the houses, the eyes, the lungs and even the dreams of many. For a time, it seemed there was nothing that the water didn't inhabit. Despite its gloomy pollution being carried away by the bucket and tissue-full, its existence was seemingly inexhaustible. Armies of men waded through the wreckage, in boats, wearing rubber overalls, yelling into empty houses after potential survivors. All the while, Billy pointed out particular places of interest, grimacing with pain, bowing his head in solemnity as he walked amongst the emergency crews. With these and many other *beaux gestes* he entertained and enthralled. Enjoying the attention, he shook hands with a number of affected families and cleanup workers. Even the mayor had to thrust himself through the melee of cameras to shake Billy's now very public hand, telling him that he could expect glorious things ahead. At long last, the great Rubino had made his apotheosis into the realm of pure Symbol. The complete evacuation of his former, anxious self had been a profound success. He had become a living monument and as such he realized he could now speak in a new language, spewing forth spiritual bromides that would no doubt be interpreted as profundities. His thoughts had already begun to assemble themselves into a refined type of Haiku.

As a Symbol, he felt it easier to understand how one should act toward others, to put himself in their grammar. In fact, it became natural for him to adopt the gestures of great men and in so doing achieve an inscrutable beauty, a weighty vacuity, an utter simplicity of universal communication. Presidents, gurus and tyrants did it all the time. In a way, he felt relieved. It was the very analgesic he needed, the wondrous mithridate. The weight of the human was sloughed off him. He felt giddy in the rarified air, assuming that he needn't indulge other's feelings or even his own and nonetheless, he wouldn't feel pained at the strange lack of sensation at 30,000 feet for he had become nothing short of a mouthpiece, a veritable echo chamber, a form of living word. With a most august abandon, he carried on with the easiest of *noblesse oblige*. As he walked toward the final evacuation point, which he had left days ago to find Dawn, out of the corner of his eye, he spotted a lone figure lying on a cot next to a medical tent. The person was clearly in bad shape and had an oxygen mask covering his mouth. As he came closer, he instantly recognized it as Basyli. He went over to the man, who lay amongst the casualties. He wore a triage tag. It was clear he couldn't talk and his eyes moved slowly with all the torpor of stones. The frail man seemed utterly paralyzed. Dawn, who had been holding Billy's hand as the news stations followed him, asked Billy quietly, "Who is he? Poor man, he looks almost dead."

Billy responded with a smile on his face, "Oh, not to worry, he's just an old client of mine." As the news crews waited for a photo opportunity, Billy bent down towards Basyli, speaking in a quiet voice so that no one could hear, "Hello Basyli, I'm glad to see you made it. Unfortunately, it seems your case will now be put back even further after this grave incident, but as I told you in the police station, please don't give up hope. I still have your best interest in mind and I want to see you set free." As he spoke, Billy leaned even closer so that his dark, ballooning face was all that the frightened Pole could see. "And you should know that after the experience I've just had, I have thought deeply about your assessment of me and my moral character." Basyli's pupils stared almost uncomprehendingly into Billy's face. Unable to speak, his eyes were a mix of anxiety and utter dread. As Billy stood there, smiling his demonic smile, Basyli was sure he had seen again the green flame alight in Billy's sockets, this time for a much longer duration. He began to tremble with trepidation and a cold frisson gripped his body. He had no idea what Billy might do to him and he was utterly powerless to stop it. Billy was now so close to him that no one else could have seen the sustained glare that inhabited his eyes. Billy leaned down further into his face, so close that Basyli could feel Billy's hot breath on his cheek. He wasn't sure at this point if Billy was going to steal the very breath away from him. But, he stopped short, whispering into his ear,

"Well, after all, if I am indeed the Devil, then I've found myself to be a mere irrelevance. It is my existence that has been nullified. Any certainties in this world went out with pantaloons and horse-drawn carriages. Thus, we are finally free to sort things amongst ourselves and in this you are and will always be your own worst enemy. You may think that I am content to let sleeping dogs lie, but I will still do what I always intended and will not forget how things are between us. If I have any advice to you, it is to learn to love what is yours, because it will only and always be yours over and over again. *Amor fati.* I truly hope you will find some way to get your affairs back in order and if you continue to listen to me, you will. I'm sure by working together, we will find it. Let us then bid all our farewells their fond farewell. After all, we have an eternity. Goodbye to you, poor Basyli. Goodbye."

The End

QUENTIN CANTEREL

For Ilaria
Emergence

You and I had something between us
before we met, that worked
with a guile uncomfortably like magic.
When I found your face where you had lost it
I felt as if a seed had finally been sown,
left on this jilted earth,
for some casual downward power
to exert itself amongst the still reeling elements.
For shrill weeks this capsule of a "new life"
was blown amidst the joyous knock and tow
of a new found freedom.
It sailed through spells across emerald acres
before it met its resting place,
here under a swash of branch
that fanned the ignominious head
of a now faceless cherub.
Waist deep in waves of wheat
through springs and neaps,
we waded the silvery sea,
aimless as a glance across
the ocean's wide empty water.
We tumbled down like Jack and Jill
seemingly sprung from the folding grasp
of a wrecked bicycle
and found our own gravity under a craggy tree,
bent over us with a prying look.
It was as if the entire earth had glazed over
and from your newly hewn manger,
culled from broken shafts of willowy wheat,

you spread your arms like you wanted
to embrace the entire sky,
leaving me here to wonder,
'What is this effulgence that isn't light
that gives such opulence to the whole affair?
What is this warmth that praises
the snug grace of a smile
with a grandeur beyond the reckoning
of any simple measure of Fahrenheit?
What is this sweetness that isn't recorded
by the wagging tongues of poets,
who drip the morsels of half-digested thoughts?'
'What? What,' I ask, again and again...
'What is this smell of carnations,
suffusing your skin as if you'd become
a sacrament for my all too willing hands?
What is this silent song
to which the whole world dances
in coordinated movements,
understood by none of those who dance.'
I ask once more as the wind rushes
giddily through the jigsaw branches,
'Is all this too much for our dull heads to deduce?'
We, who are but children caught in the wilds –
'Is this life that has been crafted for us
a simple assortment of odd moments,
coy seductions come a cropper,
pared faults that in each of us reflect something
that the other needed to redeem?'
Somewhere a pair of bicycles giggle
across a ridge of dusty cobblestones.
somewhere an ambulance trails

down a hill in swift acceleration.
Somewhere the smell of a small bit of life
is spilt on a patch of pregnant earth.
Out of how many accidents emerges
this eternal pattern of beauty?